CREDIT WARNING

BOOK ONE

By Brian Christopher

KALAMAZOO PUBLIC LIBRARY

This story is for everyone who knows something is wrong, but doesn't quite know what, or what to do about it.

Sold on Amazon.com. <u>FREE</u> to Kindle Unlimited subscribers. Kindle (non-subscriber) edition, $3.99. Hardcopy edition, $9.99.

Acknowledgements and Copyright

Thanks to my wife Lorraine, without whom I would not be alive.

Thanks also to Allison for her generosity and wise counsel.

I am also grateful to those who provided advice and encouragement along the way including Lorraine, Megan, Eric, Brandon, Todd, Corlice, CPT Jenson, and Gary.

I am especially grateful to the artist, Virginia, for the captivating cover art.

Copyright © 2015 by Brian Christopher

All rights reserved. No part of this publication may be reproduced, stored in a retrieval system, or transmitted in any form or by any means, electronic, mechanical, photocopying, microfilming, recording, or otherwise without the written permission of the author, except where permitted by law.

This is a work of fiction. Names, characters, businesses, places, events and incidents are either the products of the author's imagination or are used in a fictitious manner. Any resemblance to actual persons, living or dead, or actual events that have happened, are happening, or are about to happen, is purely coincidental.

ISBN-10: 1515113809
ISBN-13: 978-1515113805

[V5 1215]

CONTENTS

Prologue

Ninety-three million miles away from Earth, the distance of one astronomical unit, a flare appeared on the surface of the sun. On Earth, the flare was not visible to the naked eye, but satellites dutifully recorded the event and relayed the data. Within an hour, a very small number of astronomers working for organizations like NASA and Roscosmos, the common name for the Russian Federal Space Agency, were reviewing the information.

The rest of Earth's seven billion people had no knowledge of the flare. Well, not at the moment it happened anyway. When the information belatedly went public, a computer-enhanced video of the flare was broadcast thousands of times in special news bulletins – until many of the world's television screens went dark. The flare had given birth to an electromagnetic shock wave. In the next thirty days, it would be a death sentence for twelve million people in North America. After that, the death toll would get exponentially worse.

"This country, indeed the world, is not prepared for a Coronal Mass Ejection. Our electrical grids are not hardened, and our transformers are not protected. For Americans, electrical power is not a convenience, but a necessity to sustain life. If North America were to take a direct hit from a large CME – like the one that hit the United States in October of 1859 in what was called the Carrington event – it would cripple our grid and plunge us into darkness for months, maybe years. Our modern civilization would be obliterated. Many Americans would die. The survivors would be thrown back to the eighteen hundreds."

Franklin Z. Maddow, NASA Scientist

Chapter 1:   Escape from New York City.

Tuesday, 11:50 AM, Day Zero

New York City Police Officer Pablo Jose Jenkins got the call at 11:50 AM. His lunch break was supposed to start in ten minutes. The dispatcher said there was a disturbance at the federal courthouse at Foley Square. PJ Jenkins didn't know what to make of it. Some guy had driven his motorcycle over the curb, up the stairs and parked near the front door.

Dispatch said that the guy had a backpack, but didn't appear to be a deliveryman, because he hadn't gotten off the bike. Jenkins was less than five minutes away from the scene, but he figured the bike and driver would be gone by the time he got there. Jenkins drove slowly just to be sure. To Jenkins, the day seemed calmer than usual, even for a Tuesday. His duty shift had started almost four hours ago, and this was his first substantive call from dispatch. Jenkins made a U-turn on Centre Street and headed south toward Foley Square. The day was warm, clear, and sunny. It was unusually good weather for mid September. Perhaps the usual troublemakers were enjoying the weather, and the guy on the bike was just having fun.

Five minutes later, Jenkins made another U-turn and parked his cruiser at the curb in front of the federal courthouse. The building housed both the United States Court of Appeals for the Second Circuit and the United States District Court for the Southern District of New York. Jenkins had not driven slowly enough. The bike and driver were still just a few yards from the door to the building. The bike was not obstructing the entrance, which confirmed Jenkins' earlier thought that the call would not escalate to a felony arrest. However, parking a motorcycle on the steps of a federal courthouse wasn't a common occurrence, and the U.S. Marshal Service wouldn't take it lightly. Jenkins was more curious than concerned.

The Thurgood Marshall United States Courthouse is in lower Manhattan. The World Trade Center is less than a mile away to the southwest. Directly behind the court building, on the other side of Park Row, is the headquarters building for the New York City Police Department at One Police Plaza. The Department could have had a faster response time by simply directing a police officer to walk from the headquarters building to the federal building.

As he got out of the cruiser, Jenkins carefully adjusted his cap and checked his uniform. Who knew? Perhaps a supervisor would make the brief walk from headquarters to see how Jenkins handled the call.

Jenkins glanced up the staircase toward the front entrance of the courthouse, and took a closer look at the man sitting astride the motorcycle. The rider was talking to a blonde haired woman. Even from thirty yards away, Jenkins could tell the woman was a white-collar professional, and she was beautiful. She wore a dark jacket and skirt with a low-cut bright pink blouse that further highlighted her stunning attributes. Jenkins was already glad he had gotten the call.

Jenkins' law enforcement instincts, however, were in high gear. He never let eye candy distract him from his number one goal, which was to be alive at the end of his shift. Too many unwary cops had been killed at simple traffic stops and other situations where there appeared to be no threat. Jenkins' instincts told him that the biker presented no threat to Jenkins' life, but Jenkins always double-checked the data to see if his instincts were correct. He carefully surveyed the scene as he slowly walked through the lunchtime crowd on the sidewalk at the bottom of the stairs. He even did a 360-degree scan to "check his six" and the police cruiser he had just exited.

Still nothing. Jenkins again looked to his front. In addition to the man on the bike, and woman who appeared to be talking with the man, two marshals from the federal building were near the bike. One man was in his late fifties. He was one of the marshals who checked photo identifications, and put bags through the x-ray scanner. He'd been on the job at the courthouse for longer than Jenkins had been a cop. He was four inches shy of six feet and a little pudgy. Jenkins had been to the building enough times to recognize the man, even though he had never spoken to him.

The other man was much younger, perhaps in his early thirties. He was about six and a half feet tall, and appeared to be in excellent physical condition. He also worked for the US Marshals Service, but he wasn't a bag checker. His sole function was to ensure that any clear and present danger ceased to exist before it got within shooting distance of a federal judge. The man carried a Smith and Wesson .40 caliber pistol on his left hip, and a taser on his right. His hands were not near either weapon. Jenkins guessed, correctly, that the older man had seen or heard the motorcycle outside, and called the younger marshal for backup. The marshals who guarded the federal building liked to do as little police work as possible, particularly if an arrest and overnight detention were likely. When a member of the public created a problem, the marshals were anxious to let the New York Police Department handle the situation, particularly when the problem was still outside the building. Jenkins knew if the man on the bike needed to be arrested, then he would be the arresting officer.

As he started to climb the sixteen steps to the entrance of the building, Jenkins gathered clues from the body language of the two courthouse marshals. The clues indicated nothing much was going on. Both marshals appeared relaxed, and the shorter one seemed a little bit embarrassed. It appeared to Jenkins that both men had recently determined the man on the bike was more of a nuisance than a threat. From the way they were looking at the woman in the pink blouse, it was clear they knew her. Perhaps she worked inside the building, or was a frequent visitor. The low cut pink blouse and short skirt looked too flashy for something a lawyer would wear to court.

Jenkins' read of the bike rider was different. The rider was clearly the most agitated of the four people on the scene. The front of the bike was pointed toward Jenkins and the street, but the bike rider was looking to his right at the woman in the pink blouse. He wore a full-face helmet, and the visor was up. The bike's engine was idling, and the driver was poised for a hasty departure. It occurred to Jenkins that the driver might do something stupid or violent and then split. Perhaps the man was a wife beater and he was now verbally abusing his wife or girlfriend at her place of work.

Jenkins could see both of the man's gloved hands on the handle bar grips of the bike. Neither hand held a weapon, but it would take only seconds for the man to pull a weapon from his jacket, or from somewhere on the bike. Without looking down, Jenkins checked his taser and his pistol. They were both ready for rapid deployment. He continued to climb the stairs slowly. Jenkins couldn't quite make out the words, but it seemed the man on the bike was arguing with the woman. The argument seemed to escalate when the bike rider reached out, took a hold of the woman's left hand and pulled her closer to the bike. One of the marshals stepped forward. The woman pulled away from the biker and exchanged words with the marshal for a few moments. Then the woman took a call on her cell phone. The call ended quickly, and the woman began speaking to the man on the bike.

Jenkins' slow climb transitioned to a full stop as he heard an approaching helicopter flying north over the Hudson River. He looked up. The helicopter was a passenger aircraft that typically moved the most successful lawyers and Wall Street executives around the city. This one had drawn Jenkins' attention because it was flying lower and faster than usual. Jenkins glanced around and spotted three other nearby helicopters all flying into the city. Jenkins was sure all of them were exceeding the Hudson River speed limit established by the Federal Aviation Administration.

Corporate helicopters were common. About one hundred such aircraft made regular flights in and out of the city, making more than seventy thousand landings a year. Still, the volume of air traffic seemed unusually high right now, and Jenkins briefly wondered why. When Jenkins glanced to his front again, the scene had changed. Like Jenkins, the woman had looked up at the helicopters. She was still talking to the biker, but her demeanor was different. The conversation no longer looked like an argument.

Jenkins had a vague uneasy feeling, but he couldn't identify the source. He was certain the woman and the biker were not a threat, but maybe someone or something else was. Jenkins was standing halfway up the staircase where he had paused to look at the first helicopter. He stayed there as he did another long slow 360-degree scan. He saw nothing to explain his uneasiness. When Jenkins looked back at the biker, he was pulling leather clothing from a pannier. He held the clothing in one hand as the woman in the pink blouse placed her cell phone in his other hand. She put her purse and a shoulder bag into the bike's pannier, which was still open. Then she did the very last thing Jenkins expected. She took off her clothes.

Jenkins continued to stand still, while he stared for a moment. This woman looked like a respected professional, but her sudden behavior contradicted everything Jenkins had observed and surmised. She was drop dead gorgeous, and within a few seconds, she had stripped out of her skirt and jacket. There was a brief moment when the woman stood there wearing nothing but her low-cut pink blouse and a red lace thong. Then the man on the bike handed the woman a pair of black leather pants that he had pulled from a compartment on the motorcycle. The woman began climbing into the pants. They were much too big for her.

Jenkins looked at the two uniformed courthouse employees. They were as shocked as he was, and stood there with their eyes and mouths wide open. It occurred to Jenkins that none of the men, including Jenkins, and several passers-by, had the decency to turn away. The rare and beautiful spectacle lasted mere seconds as the woman quickly slipped into the leather pants and a leather jacket. The biker stuffed her discarded outfit into the same pannier from which he had taken the leather pants and jacket. The woman crammed a helmet on her head, fastened the snap, picked up her designer shoes from the pavement, retrieved her phone from the bike driver, and climbed on the back of the bike with nothing on her feet.

Jenkins' previous concern, that he was watching a transplanted domestic dispute, dissipated. The man on the bike had not threatened or coerced the woman. The moment after she had observed the helicopters, she hung up her phone and changed her demeanor. She had willingly taken off her clothes, and put on leathers. Now, she appeared as anxious as the driver to leave the building as fast as possible. Jenkins realized he had been standing still for more than two full minutes, and started climbing the stairs again. Jenkins was deliberately moving slowly enough so he wouldn't get to the bike before the bike left the scene. In his younger days, he would have run toward the bike and tried to prevent its departure, but no experienced NYPD officer would do that.

The task he'd been given by the dispatcher was to prevent or reduce a public disturbance, and get the bike off the steps and back onto the street. All of that was about to happen without any action by Jenkins. Jumping in front of the bike would just slow the completion of his assigned task, and might even force Jenkins to issue a ticket, or worse, make an arrest. Both of those events required paperwork. Like most cops, Jenkins hated paperwork. Just to be certain the problem would take care of itself, Jenkins slowed his pace even further. Sure enough, as soon as the woman's feet hit the foot pegs, the bike started moving. The driver glanced to his front, and for the first time saw a police officer approaching. The driver had just flipped down the tinted helmet visor. Jenkins couldn't see the surprise on the driver's face, but he knew it was there.

The bike swerved awkwardly to avoid Jenkins, and the driver almost lost control. Jenkins tried to step away from the bike's path, but he underestimated the bike's speed. The very last thing he wanted was for the bike to crash on the steps. Paperwork would be unavoidable at that point. The driver quickly turned left, then corrected right, and gave a muffled yell to his passenger as his knee almost touched the pavement. The bike straightened just before the front wheel cleared the top step of the long staircase. Jenkins saw that the passenger dropped her high-heeled shoes to the ground as the bike continued to move. She wrapped both her hands around the driver's midsection, and turned her head sideways so she could squeeze her body more closely to the driver. Obviously, this was not her first motorcycle ride.

The bike almost literally flew down the stairs, and Jenkins even heard the bike accelerate and change gears before it reached the street. The driver was clearly an expert. The initial steering error had probably been caused by a combination of Jenkins' unexpected presence, and the woman not moving in synch with the driver as he made the unexpected turn to avoid Jenkins. The driver timed his entry to the street perfectly to enter a narrow gap between two cars as he turned right and went north on Centre street. The biker briefly stayed with traffic, but then the bike's front tire rose off the ground slightly as the bike again shifted gears and rapidly accelerated. Jenkins continued to watch as the bike weaved through heavy traffic, ran a red light, and drove several yards on a sidewalk to maintain its speed. It was probably a good thing that the passenger couldn't see what was going on in front of her. Jenkins imagined her eyes were tightly shut.

It was a testament to Jenkins' professionalism that he didn't even think about giving chase, or calling dispatch to have another officer posted somewhere along the bike's route of travel, to attempt to stop the bike. No police cruiser would be able to stop a rider who drove like that. It would take half a dozen cars, and lots of time and effort. Besides, somebody, perhaps the beautiful blonde, might get hurt. Jenkins turned back toward the U.S. Marshals. Like him, they had watched the bike's frenzied departure. Jenkins was only a few yards away, and as he closed the distance, both men turned toward him. The bike was now out of sight. Jenkins glanced at the blonde woman's abandoned shoes as he walked the last few steps toward the marshals. They looked too new and expensive to throw away. If the marshals hadn't been watching him, he might have picked them up.

The taller marshal said, "Hello Officer," without adding, "what took you so long to climb the stairs?"

"Good morning. I assume you both work in the building. Do either of you know the woman on the bike?"

The short marshal nodded, but said nothing. Both marshals were clearly not interested in volunteering any information about the woman.

"Is she some kind of trouble maker?

The shorter older marshal now seemed anxious to answer. "No, no Officer, she's never been any trouble at all. Nothing like this has ever happened before." The tall young marshal stood there looking like he needed to attend important business elsewhere.

"So there's no problem here, and you don't need my services for anything?" It was a leading question. Jenkins was openly asking to be dismissed from the scene.

This time, the tall marshal spoke first as he silenced the older marshal with a wave of his hand. The guard took a step forward and extended his right hand to shake with Jenkins. "That's correct Officer, we've got no problems here. I am Marshal Matthew Madison." Madison gestured toward the shorter marshal as he said, "And this is Marshal Tony Stevens."

Madison let go of Jenkins' hand as he continued to speak. "Tony here told me about the motorcycle, and I called the police department. We are very grateful for your fast response. When I got the call about the bike, I was still inside the building and had no idea that the driver was here to see one of our most respected litigators. I apologize for wasting your time."

The marshal was brief, smooth, and professional, but Jenkins could tell the man hadn't been hired by the Marshal Service for his public relations skills. Having just felt the tall man's powerful grip, Jenkins had no doubt that if the biker had tried to do something stupid, Marshal Madison would have rendered the biker unconscious without any help from Jenkins.

Jenkins responded, "I'm Officer Jenkins. You didn't waste my time, Marshal. I know you're required to follow protocol and call us. I'm just glad it all worked out." Madison gave Jenkins a small nod and brief smile. One true professional had just spoken to another, and there was a lot that didn't need to be said.

Jenkins did not ask for the woman's name, or the name of her employer. He also did not ask why the woman had taken off her clothes and left in a hurry. Some of that information would have satisfied Jenkins' personal curiosity, but none of it was relevant to Jenkins' professional duties – particularly since he wasn't going to fill out any paperwork. He would tell dispatch the bike and rider had cleared the scene before he got there; which was true because Jenkins had made certain of it by deliberately slowing his arrival. The "scene" was where the bike had been parked by the door, and Jenkins had not gotten to the "scene" until the motorcycle was literally out of sight.

"Well gentlemen, enjoy the warm, wonderful day, and the beautiful view." The other two men smiled. All three men had very much enjoyed the view.

The two marshals simultaneously said, "You too, Officer," but they said it to Jenkins' back. He was already walking toward the cruiser. Jenkins noticed that the abandoned shoes were gone. They had apparently been picked up by some lucky pedestrian. On his portable radio, Jenkins told dispatch the scene was clear, and he was again available. As he walked down the steps, Jenkins looked to his right at the departure path the bike had taken. Now that his task was done, Jenkins let his mind wander. *Why had the driver of the bike left in such a hurry? Did the helicopters have something to do with it? What kind of emergency makes a beautiful professional leave work in the middle of the day, strip to her panties in public, and jump on a motorcycle with a seemingly deranged man?*

There were no obvious answers, and Jenkins had no illusions about his ability to make sense of all the weird stuff a beat cop saw on a typical day in New York City. Jenkins arrived at his car, unlocked the door, and opened it. He looked at his watch, it was 12:08 PM. Jenkins was eight minutes late for his lunch break. He'd be sure to add the missed time to the back end of his break. Ignorance is not bliss. It is sometimes a death sentence. If Officer Jenkins had known how his involuntarily extended shift was going to end, he would have jumped into the cruiser and gotten out of the city at the same speed as the motorcycle. He would have taken a different path; one that went west, not east. But Jenkins was not clairvoyant, and the man on the bike – who did know what was coming – hadn't bothered to tell Jenkins why he left in a hurry.

Less than twenty-four hours later, Officer Pablo Jose Jenkins, loving husband, devoted father of three, lifelong member of the First Baptist Church of Queens, and an eighteen-year veteran of the NYPD with two awards for valor, died in the line of duty. Like that fateful day on September 11th, more than a dozen years before, many other public servants would also die. Unlike the September 11th attacks, there were no memorial services for any of them.

Chapter 2: Five hours earlier, Mae goes to work.

Mae, short for Mabel, was poised and confident as she walked purposefully into the office building on Madison Avenue. She spent every weekday and most Saturdays here. Jordan, the doorman, held the door for her as he did every weekday and most Saturdays. It was a highlight of his day. For anyone who entered right after Mae, the door would be open, but Jordan wouldn't see them. He'd be looking the other way, into the building. Mabel Abigail Seymour had a beautiful face and a perfect posterior. Jordan always took a long, and what he thought was a discreet, look at both.

That warm September morning, Mae wore a low cut, hot pink Amanda Uprichard silk blouse from Neiman Marcus. She preferred Amanda Uprichard to the more well-known designers because of the bright colors and low necklines. She had purchased her black Armani Collezioni skirt and jacket at Saks Fifth Avenue. She wore mercury suede paneled patent leather pumps by B. Brian Atwood, and had a Gucci bag on her left shoulder. She wore a twenty-four carat gold necklace with a small diamond pendant and matching diamond stud earrings from Saks. Her clothes cost more than three thousand dollars and the jewelry and accessories were another three thousand. Her skirt ended three inches above her knees. She was desired by most of the men who met her, and her services cost almost one thousand dollars an hour. She was of course, a New York lawyer.

Jordan said, "Good morning, Miss Seymour" because he knew she didn't want him to call her Mae, Mabel, or Missus. Mae said hello and gave him one of her most sincere fake smiles because she always tried to appear kind to the little people. Her daddy used to say, "Mae, be nice to the little people because you never know when you'll need a favor from someone who does the dirty work." Maybe Jordan would throw himself on a grenade for her one day. Thoughts like that always made Mae smile as she said hello to the little people.

Mae had a nice bay-front colonial home with hedges and a wrought iron fence on Long Island in Islip, New York. She would have preferred to live in or closer to the city, as she worked her way up to full partner in the firm. The location had been a compromise with her husband, who wanted to raise their children in a suburban neighborhood with a big yard. The commute by train took almost two hours. By splitting the commute time among three clients, Mae always billed at least two full hours during the ride. Each way, of course.

Mae had structured her life to gain the maximum distribution from a multi-million dollar trust created by her father. Her father had died when Mae was in her fifth year of practice, but he had explained the terms of the trust to her while she was still in high school. The trust was large, but Mae would only receive a portion of it. On her fortieth birthday, the remaining portion would be paid to her father's favorite charity. The size of Mae's payout depended on how she lived her life before she turned forty. Her father, Ellis Anderson Seymour, wanted to leave a legacy. His legacy would be Mae's accomplishments, which included her offspring. Mae got a nice annual stipend, but the size of the stipend, like the final distribution, was determined by Mae. If she hadn't gone to law school, worked as an attorney, and had kids, her annual and final trust receipts would have been smaller. The higher her income, the higher her trust receipts. Daddy wanted her to be a lawyer and a mother, and be highly successful at both.

The kids would get trusts of their own, but their money would come from the portion of the trust that would otherwise go to charity. Mae would get more money if she had more children, but two was enough. She intended to be still fabulous at forty. Having maxed out almost all the incentives, Mae was on track to receive a multi-million dollar final distribution. She had some say in how the trust fund money was invested, but her distributions were strictly tied to the incentives created by her father. Shortly after her fortieth birthday, Mae intended to pay cash for a house in the Hamptons on Long Island. If she chose to commute to the city from her new home, she would travel by chauffeured limousine or helicopter. If her husband and kids wanted to stay in Islip, that would be fine with her. Maybe she would visit them on weekends.

That morning was the last time Mae walked into the building. It was also the last day that Jordan ever held a door for anyone, or had a glimpse of the perfection that was Mae Seymour. But Mae didn't know that, so her mind was focused on her schedule, which included a deposition from nine until eleven, an overlapping telephonic mediation session from ten thirty until noon, and then one hour to prepare for a meeting with a big potential client. If that meeting went well, it would take a few hours to hammer out the details of a representation agreement. After the meeting, Mae would use the rest of the day to make phone calls, and review documents which had been drafted by less experienced attorneys. She would sign the documents, and bill the preparation time at her rate, rather than the associates' rate. If the firm landed the new client, there would be a celebratory dinner tonight. The firm would pick up the large tab.

With the half-hour overlap between the deposition and the mediation session, Mae would have to be in two places at once. Her daily schedule often contained such a challenge. Mae would take a break from the deposition to start the telephonic negotiation, and then go back to the deposition. Once the mediation started, her co-counsel, a second-year associate, would stay on the phone and say stuff like "that offer is too low" or "my client is happy to go to court," until Mae returned.

Mae would bill the overlapping half hour to both clients. That's why Mae, and other New York attorneys, still preferred telephone conferences to video conferences. It enabled them to be in two places at once, and bill for both. How else could they bill 2,600 hours a year, get Sundays off, take a four-week vacation, and eventually buy a house in the Hamptons?

Mae walked through the lobby and gave a fake smile to the guards at the desk. She didn't recognize the Hispanic guard, but the former football player on the right, had been there for years. She said, "Good morning, Victor," to the guard on the right.

"Good morning, Miss Seymour." He too knew better than to call her "Missus." "Is there anything I can do for you this morning?"

He offered his assistance every morning. Mae sometimes had a menial task for him. Mae always tipped the little people, and gave them small cash gifts at Christmas; well, small to her. The minions seemed to think one hundred dollars was a big deal. So the little people, even the ones who were over six feet tall, were anxious to help all year long.

"No Victor, not today, but thanks for the offer." She flashed another fake smile and continued toward the elevator without breaking stride.

Unlike Jordan, Victor did not follow Mae with his eyes after she passed by. He was more of a breast man, and had already taken a look at Mae's low-cut blouse. The new guard, however, stole a quick glance at Mae's retreating form. Mae waited for the express elevator that by-passed the first ten floors. After the doors opened, Mae inserted her access card, punched in a four-digit code, and hit the button for the twenty-first floor. The building had no elevator attendants, which meant Mae didn't have to part with another fake smile. The law firm occupied the top three floors of the building, floors twenty through twenty-two. Clients and other visitors were given access to only the top floor, which required assistance from a guard who issued a limited-access elevator card.

The top floor had a receptionist who sat facing the elevator doors, and greeted all visitors. The doors to leave the reception area were electronically locked, so no guest could leave the area without assistance from someone in the firm. The top floor had several conference and meeting rooms, a kitchen, a dining room, a gym, and offices for the firm's advertising and public relations departments. The conference rooms were named for the firm's oldest and most senior attorneys, some of whom had passed on. This morning, Mae intended to use two of the smaller conference rooms simultaneously. One was named Harvey B. Middleman, the other Olaf A. Wrightlinger; two dead white men Mae had never met.

Mae's card accessed three floors leased by the firm. Mae gave two more fake smiles as she went to her office, one for a new paralegal whose name she didn't know, and one for the cleaning lady who just finished her shift. Mae gave a real smile to her assistant, Amanda

Perkins. Everybody called her "Perky" because she was. To Mae, Perky wasn't one of the little people. Well she was, but Perky wasn't going to stay that way. Perky had gotten her bachelor's degree by going to school at night and on weekends. She was in the process of getting her law degree the same way.

To Mae, Perky was a project. Perky's drive, determination and relatively low station in life made Mae think of what her father's early adult life must have been like. With a little help from Mae, perhaps Perky could travel a similar path from humble beginnings to wealth and success as an attorney. Mae treated Perky as something more than a paralegal, but less than a friend. Mae didn't have any real friends. After Perky graduated and passed the bar, Mae would ensure that Perky got a position at the firm. Once in a while, when Mae was in a good mood, she would tell Perky that the two of them would one day be co-counsel on the same case.

Mae kept walking as she passed Perky's desk, but said "Good morning," and got a return greeting before she said, "Coffee please."

Perky knew Mae wanted what she always did when she arrived at work; a Caramel Skinny Macchiato Venti from Starbucks. Perky was not allowed to have the coffee waiting for Mae upon her arrival. Mae's Macchiato had to be hot and fresh. Perky called Starbucks, placed the order, and started walking toward the elevators. The coffee would be ready at the same time Perky got to Starbucks, and it would be on Mae's desk less than three minutes after that. The firm had an excellent coffee service that provided a variety of free hot beverages to all its partners, employees, and clients, but Mae still made Perky do the Starbucks run every morning.

Mae walked into her office six minutes before eight o'clock. She had an hour to catch up on overnight e-mails and phone calls before her nine o'clock deposition. She might also have time to review her notes for the new client meeting. She had only a secondary role, but it was one of the biggest deals the firm had ever done, so her performance needed to be perfect. Nobody could tell by looking, but Mae was a bit nervous about the meeting. She went to her desk and pulled out her chair, but didn't sit down because a small, beautifully wrapped gift box was in the chair. Mae knew the gift-giver hadn't wrapped it himself. She read the tiny gift card that was taped to the lid, "Put this on and be quick on your feet today." The note was not signed, but she knew it was from Johnny Davis, a peer who had joined the firm one year before she did.

His given name was John, but everybody called him Johnny. Even in his mid-thirties, he was still the best male eye-candy in the firm. Among the women, Mae held the eye-candy title. Mae opened the box and gasped. She thought about it for a second, then smiled. *What the hell, why not?* She ducked into the private bathroom she shared with just one other office, and followed the note's instructions. Mae went back to her desk and turned on the computer. She didn't look up again until eight forty. She had ten minutes to collect her things, and ten minutes to get to the conference room. The trip would take only five minutes, but Mabel Abigail Seymour was *never* late. Five minutes early was the minimum cushion. The cushion didn't cost her anything, because she would bill it to a client; maybe two.

Mae traveled to the top floor using the elevator. Members of the firm could travel between the firm's three floors using two access-controlled private staircases. With her form fitting skirts, Mae rarely took the stairs, even though the stairs were faster. She pressed the up arrow for the elevator. As was often the case, Johnny showed up while Mae was waiting for the elevator. When she didn't want to deal with his flirtation and innuendo, she would take a longer route to the elevator which did not require her to pass by his office.

Johnny glanced around to ensure nobody was within earshot. "So, um . . . did you get the gift I left in your office?"

Mae knew Johnny was nervous. He had never before given her anything but flowers from a "Secret Admirer." He was careful not to make his advances obvious to the senior partners. Of course, all the secretaries and paralegals knew. It was impossible to keep any office romance or rumor from them. They were jealous that Johnny focused his flirtations on Mae, but they shared their secrets and gossip only amongst themselves. It was the same in all the big firms. Two radically different socio-economic classes spent their entire careers working side-by-side, with almost no truly personal interactions taking place.

"Yes. I got your gift."

The elevator arrival light flashed on just as she said yes. There was a loud ding as the doors opened. The two of them stepped into the empty compartment. Mae pressed the button for the twenty-second floor and the doors closed. When she stepped back from the panel, she and Johnny were standing side-by-side with their backs to the wall. Johnny had no reason to go to the next floor. He was making the trip to get a private moment with her. When he got off the elevator on occasions like this, he would usually cover his tracks by talking to the receptionist about a conference-room scheduling issue. Then he would take the private staircase back to his office.

"And?"

"And what?"

"What did you think of it?" The elevator bumped to a halt. The doors would be fully opened in less than two seconds. Mae placed her left hand on the left cheek of Johnny's buttocks, and gave it a good squeeze.

"I'm wearing it."

As the elevator doors opened at 8:53 AM, Mae quickly removed her hand, the one with her wedding band on it, from Johnny's butt so nobody outside the elevator could see what she had done. She left briskly without saying another word. Johnny was pleasantly surprised.

The relationship was progressing nicely. Like Jordan had done earlier, Johnny admired the view as Mae glided away on her three-inch heels. The doors started closing before Johnny realized that he had been openly staring at Mae's ass. He quickly pushed the button for the floor below, and let the doors close. He wouldn't be taking the stairs today. Through the shrinking gap of the closing doors, he saw the receptionist looking at him with an amused smile. She had caught him staring at Mae's rear. Another tidbit of gossip would reach Johnny's assistant before Johnny reached his office.

Johnny went back to his office, sat down at his desk, and tried to stop thinking about Mae. He billed the next two tenths of an hour without reading, writing, or speaking a single word.

Chapter 3:   Mr. Mom.

Gary Adams looked at the clock on the kitchen wall of the comfortable bay-front home in Islip. It was 7:50 AM. He was running late as usual. His wife Mae had left for work two hours earlier. He opened the Keurig machine to put in a cup of Folgers classic roast. Mae hadn't removed the used cup of Starbucks Verano after she had made her coffee earlier that morning. Gary wasn't surprised. She routinely expected Gary and the hired help to clean up after her. Mae only drank the Keurig coffee because there wasn't a Starbucks on the front lawn of the house. Gary knew Mae would have a cup of Caramel Macchiato delivered to her office. She drank at least three cups a day. Gary consumed about the same amount, but his costs were considerably less. He drank coffee for the caffeine and wasn't finicky about the taste.

Mae's commute required her to drive to the Bay Shore station of the Long Island Railroad. She took the train to Penn Station in Manhattan, and the subway to her office on Madison Avenue. When the weather was bad, Gary traveled to the New York University (NYU) Polytechnic School of Engineering in Brooklyn by train from Bay Shore to Jamaica, and by subway to Metro Tech Center. When the weather was good, like today, Gary rode his motorcycle. Ana, the nanny, or "Ana the Nana" as Gary's two daughters called her, had arrived half an hour ago. Gary could only blame himself for being behind schedule. *No problem,* he thought, *I'll make up the lost time going a little faster on the bike.* Without speeding excessively, Gary could make the trip in just over an hour.

Ana was a sixty-something year old widow who had been working for Gary and Mae since Jane was born five and a half years ago. Josephine, or "Josie" was born three years later. Now that Jane was in kindergarten, Ana had only Josie to watch. Ana had one daughter of her own, Isabella. Isabella was a dysfunctional thirty-year-old former heroin addict who never had kids. She lived in Ana's apartment in West Babylon. Ana treated Jane and Josie like the grandchildren she didn't have.

As an Associate Professor of Civil Engineering, Gary was "Mr. Mom" of the household. He had two days a week with no on-campus classes, and every weekend off. Like the students, he also had fall, winter, spring and summer breaks. Gary labored under a professor's "publish or perish" pressure but research, writing, and grading student work could be done at home, while the kids were sleeping. When they were awake, and the workload was light, Gary did what he loved most and spent time with his kids; which was a lot more time than Mae spent with them.

Gary enjoyed being "Mr. Mom," and even enjoyed some of the housekeeping chores. With their two professional incomes, Gary and Mae earned a lot of money, but they had no trouble spending most of it on automobiles, property taxes, commuting, dry cleaning, a nanny, and a housekeeper. Gary didn't want to be obligated to do all the chores, all the time. Gary knew his wife was rich, but he didn't know how rich and it was something they didn't discuss. Gary hadn't married her for her money. When he was at home and not buried in paperwork, Gary often gave Ana time off without reducing her pay, and without telling Mae.

While pursuing his doctoral studies, Gary had been a teaching assistant at NYU. After his thesis was published, he landed a paid, full-time teaching-assistant position, which eventually translated into an Assistant Professorship. In his first year as a full time instructor, Gary met Mae while she was in her third year of law school. He was a couple of years older than she was, and he was employed. He wasn't as intimidated as most men were by her rich bitch veneer.

At their first meeting, Gary, unlike most other men, did not respond to her stunning beauty by drooling on himself and groveling at her feet. Instead, he deliberately responded to her expectations of drool and grovel with an almost disinterested attitude. It was a new experience for Mae and it piqued her curiosity just enough for her to grant him a second meeting. That's all Gary needed. In that first wonderful year, while the brilliant Mae cruised through her legal studies, Gary routinely did for Mae what no other man had done. He made her laugh loud and often. As they walked across campus to one of her classes, the woman who was cold to every other man, was warm, fun, and happy. Other men glared at Gary as he and Mae went by. Their eyes were daggers of hate and envy; which made Gary enjoy Mae's laughter even more.

Their initial relationship had been built upon words. Words rapidly exchanged during fast-paced conversations that jumped from topic to topic with no apparent connection to an average listener. Mae was an extraordinarily quick thinker. As the litigators say, she was fast on her feet. Gary kept pace. Barely. As he struggled to keep up, he'd throw out a bit of sarcasm, or counterintuitive humor that forced Mae to come to a halt mentally and sometimes physically, as she adjusted and often laughed at the unexpected turn of the conversation. That was Gary's gift. As quick as she was, he could sometimes surprise her intellectually, and unexpectedly take her mind to places it hadn't anticipated.

The intellectual jousting was enormous fun, but Gary had to work to keep up with Mae. Gary deliberately inserted the humor to create a conversational pause while Mae was laughing. During the pauses, Gary's mind was often racing to catch up to hers, and then try to get ahead by an inch. The verbal relationship eventually grew to include physical intimacy. It was, however, the mutual intellectual satisfaction, that led to a wedding after Mae graduated. Observers correctly concluded that Mae "wore the pants" and dominated the relationship. Gary could keep up with her, but he never felt the need or desire to lead or control the relationship. He rolled with, rather than resented her high stress levels and sometimes-unpredictable moods.

As the years went by and her responsibilities and reputation at the firm increased, all aspects of Mae's personal life, for which she had very little time, cooled down and eventually went cold. She gave birth to the two kids that Gary and her father's trust fund wanted, but motherhood was something to which she gave little time, and from which she received little joy. For the birth of each daughter, she took just four weeks of maternity leave. Then she went back to work fulltime at the firm. She delegated the parental and household responsibilities to Gary, the nanny, and the housekeeper. She paid the bills and could keep the entire operation running even if Gary was unemployed. Wasn't that enough?

Gary gave his daughter Josie, a quick hug and a kiss and shouted the usual instructions to Ana as he went through the kitchen toward the garage. The two-car garage contained a Volvo station wagon, a five-by-eight utility trailer, and Gary's BMW F650 motorcycle. He had been able to buy the exact bike he wanted because an insurance settlement covered the purchase price. Gary had been making the commute to NYU for several years, and had figured out long ago that the way to beat the traffic was a motorcycle. Gary had ridden dirt bikes as a teenager, and was thrilled to have an excuse to ride a street bike as an adult.

The yellow 2012 F650 BMW motorcycle had a two-cylinder, parallel-twin engine and a chain drive. Gary had added two aluminum Touratech Zega panniers. The silver aluminum didn't match the bike's black and yellow color scheme as well as the black Vario panniers would have, but Gary preferred the rugged top-loading aluminum cases to the side loading plastic expandable Vario cases. The panniers allowed Gary to take his laptop, lecture notes, and student papers to and from NYU. The bike had locking brackets for two helmets. Even when he didn't have a passenger, Gary kept the spare helmet locked onto the bike. He figured it was better to have it and not need it, then to need it and not have it.

Given the warm cloudless day, Gary was glad he hadn't taken the bike off the road for the winter, but that event was probably only a few weeks away. When they were dating and for a few years after they had been married, Mae would occasionally take summer rides with Gary out to Montauk. Mae was a good rider, and she could drive the bike solo if she wanted, but she had never bothered to get a motorcycle license. When they rode together, they would chat or listen to music on the helmet intercom system.

Gary understood the dangers of riding a motorcycle, and the damage caused to human flesh when the rider's body separated from the bike and slid along the pavement. He had been violently separated from a moving street bike on two occasions. The first time had been his fault. He took a turn too quickly and unexpectedly encountered loose gravel in the roadway. Several years later, just three years ago, Gary had been driving inattentively when a tractor trailer truck ran a red light and abruptly cut in front of Gary's motorcycle. Gary's three choices had been to steer into two lanes of oncoming traffic, hit the truck broadside at fifty miles an hour, or lay the bike down and attempt to slide under the truck. Gary chose the third option. It was the only option that offered a possibility of survival.

Neither accident had resulted in serious physical injury. In the first accident, he had been wearing street clothes, and suffered road rash over a significant portion of his body. It was very painful to move for a few weeks as scrapes turned into inflexible scabs, and the scabs cracked and oozed. But he had been wearing a helmet, and had broken no bones, so he counted himself lucky. After that first accident, Gary wore full leathers, jacket and pants, whenever he rode; even in the summer time. The lesson from the first accident enabled him to emerge almost injury free from the second accident. As he laid the bike down to slide under the truck, he held his thumb on the bike's horn. The shocked rig driver look to his left, saw Gary's bike approaching at high speed, and locked up his brakes.

After Gary dropped the bike on its left side, it slid for several yards. The front tire of the bike clipped the rear wheel of the truck's cab, and the bike spun counter clockwise as it slid under the trailer. Had the driver not locked his brakes, Gary might have been crushed by the rear wheels of the trailer. Instead, the bike continued to slide and spin for several dozen yards. Before the bike completed its first rotation, Gary kicked himself free of it and began rolling. He continued rolling all the way to grassy shoulder of the road as his momentum dissipated. His bike skidded into the lanes of opposing traffic where it was tossed, shattered, and crushed by five different vehicles.

Gary's quick reflexes saved his life, and his leathers saved his skin. His left leg had been the first part of his body to encounter the pavement, and the leather pant leg was shredded all the way through. The side of his left knee had been scraped just enough to draw blood over an area of about two square inches. But that was it. That and a few sore spots had been his only injuries. Seconds after Gary finished his violent journey to the shoulder of the road, he had stood up. The truck driver ran toward Gary yelling at the top of lungs, "Are you okay?! Are you okay?!" When Gary nodded yes, the burly truck driver gave Gary a bear hug, lifted him off the ground and spun him around a couple of times. The man had tears in his eyes, as he laughed and cried at the same time. *The rider had survived! It was a miracle!*

Of course, the driver had been at fault so he lost his job. But he didn't go to jail for manslaughter. The huge company that employed the driver and owned the rig soon offered a settlement that was almost as generous as any lawyer could have gotten after a year or two of litigation. Gary had mentioned his wife was an attorney, and the trucking company had apparently done some research on her. Gary accepted the settlement, knowing he would have gotten less money if he took the case to court and gave a lawyer a big chunk of the payoff.

The accident didn't make Gary stop riding motorcycles. He never said it out loud even to his wife, but the accident had only made Gary more confident. While stupidly making a phone call as he blissfully rode his bike toward a green light, he had suddenly encountered a life or death moment. In that moment, it seemed to Gary that time had slowed down, almost stopped. Every second passed as slowly as a full minute and Gary felt like he had all day to make decisions that were actually being made in a microsecond. His brain was moving at ten times, perhaps fifty times, its normal speed.

In what felt like slow motion to Gary, he had instinctively tapped the front brake and laid the bike down on its left side in a maneuver he had never practiced. While the bike was sliding at almost fifty miles an hour, he somehow had the presence of mind to kick the bike toward the oncoming traffic, which simultaneously propelled his body in the opposite direction to the safety of the shoulder. Even as he tumbled toward the shoulder of the road, his mind had taken snapshots of his bike being hit by one car, then another as it separated into pieces with the larger chunks of shrapnel going airborne and getting broken into smaller pieces as three other cars entered the scene.

For the rest of his life Gary never forgot how he felt after the crash sequence ended when he rolled to a stop in the grass on the side of the road. For the next several seconds time continued to move in slow motion. In that first brief moment, which seemed to last for a full minute, the main portion of his bike finally came to rest as cars in the opposing lanes came to a stop. Smaller pieces of the bike – one of the mirrors, a portion of the rear fender, and the entire front wheel – were still flying or sliding in different directions as they ricocheted among the cars. A few moments later, the driver of the truck came running toward Gary in slow motion, around the front of the cab with his mouth wide open as he screamed something. Gary remembered it all. He could watch the video in his mind whenever he wanted.

But what Gary remembered most wasn't on the video. It was a feeling inside, not something that could have been photographed. The accident had happened in the early spring. A quintessential sunny morning after a soft night rain when trees were budding, birds were singing and flowers were blooming. Gary remembered inhaling it all. After his body rolled to a stop on the shoulder, Gary couldn't immediately determine whether he had survived without any fatal injuries. He had literally been too scared to breathe for fear that his body was too broken to perform that most basic function.

In that first moment, as he lay on his stomach in the grass with his eyes still recording the destruction of his motorcycle, Gary could not feel anything. Was he still alive? Was he going to bleed out in the next minute or so? Were his legs shattered so badly that he would immediately crumble back to the ground if he tried to stand? Maybe his throat had been crushed, or his lungs had collapsed and he just couldn't feel it yet. And then, *Can . . . I . . . even . . . breathe?*

The crash sequence had knocked the wind out of him and emptied Gary's lungs. He had last drawn a breath as the tractor-trailer truck ran the light. That had been nine long seconds ago – in another lifetime. Gary deliberately commanded his lungs to draw air. Cautiously at first, then at mid breath when he felt no pain, his inhale accelerated. He sucked air in through his nose and his mouth at the same time. And he could feel it. He could smell it, and taste it. It was life itself. Gary stood up. He. Was. Alive!

His lungs were at the bursting point when the Paul-Bunyan-sized truck driver squeezed all the air right back out of him. It emerged from his body as a long loud scream of joy. A scream of life. He really was alive! But nobody except Gary heard the scream of rebirth, because the helmet muffled the sound, and Paul Bunyan was also yelling at the top of his lungs.

Winston Churchill once said that there is no more exhilarating feeling than to be shot at and missed. After that day, Gary was confident Winston had never driven a motorcycle under a tractor-trailer truck at fifty miles an hour. To save your life by being missed by a bullet from an unseen assassin, you just had to be lucky. To save your life by doing what Gary had done, you had to be calm, quick, skilled, *and* lucky. And perhaps stupidly inattentive right before the crash.

Gary spent a chunk of the truck company's settlement money on the BMW F650 that he was about to ride to work. He had purchased a slightly used model rather than a new one, and spent some of the savings on the panniers. In the three years since the accident, Gary had not experienced any remotely similar level of excitement during his rides. He intended to keep it that way. The only stress he would feel on his way to work that morning was the worry that he wouldn't get to the podium on time.

At 8:27 AM, Gary put the leathers on over his polo shirt and shorts. He was soon out of the garage and driving toward NYU. Traffic was slow even in the high-occupancy-vehicle (HOV) lane, which permitted motorcycles. When traffic got really slow, or came to a full stop, Gary could, and sometimes did drive the motorcycle on the shoulder of the road, or travel between the long rows of cars by driving on the dotted lines that separated the lanes. These "alternate travel methods" were illegal, but the law was almost impossible to enforce because most cops didn't ride motorcycles, and even if they did, it was almost impossible to catch an offender who really didn't want to be caught. Gary suspected the police tended to look the other way when it came to the various shortcuts taken by motorcycles, because if more people rode motorcycles, traffic would move more quickly.

Gary took the Long Island Expressway or LIE, west to the Brooklyn-Queens Expressway, or BQE. Unlike the LIE, the BQE did not have an HOV lane, so Gary had to travel a little slower, even though he occasionally used an alternate travel method. When squeezing between two rows of slow or stopped cars, Gary carefully watched for a car that might change lanes, or an angry driver who might fling open their door to impede his progress. It was safer and faster to ride on the shoulder, but the shoulder tended to have debris, which could puncture a tire. Vigilant cops also had a much longer and clearer line of site on the shoulder. In the several years Gary had been commuting by motorcycle, he had never been ticketed or gotten a flat tire. When it came to motorcycle riding, Gary considered himself "cautiously reckless."

The speedy and uneventful commute ended at a parking garage near Metrotech center, on Flatbush Avenue. The garage had daily and monthly rates, and discounts for NYU faculty members. Gary quickly walked the short distance from the parking garage to the campus. As an Associate Professor on a non-tenure track, Gary's office was nothing to brag about, but at least it wasn't a cubicle. His eight-by-ten foot office had a door, but no window. The door had a lock and he didn't have an office mate. Gary locked the door and changed from his leathers into slacks, shirt, and a jacket. When commuting on the bike, it was easier just to leave a few changes of clothes at the office. He had the clothes laundered at a nearby cleaners, and rotated outfits when he commuted in the Volvo rather than on the bike.

Gary occasionally took some teasing from the students as he walked from the bike to his office wearing nothing but black leather. Some called him a Ninja, others suggested the leather had something to do with his sex life and asked him if he had handcuffs or a collar. It was all in fun, and Gary played the game by coming up with a variety of responses. He found it a little distracting that many of the handcuffs and collar comments came from attractive female students. His responses to the hallway hecklers this morning were shorter than usual as he hurried to the office. He knew precisely how long each phase of his travel to the podium required, so he knew he was already three minutes late when he opened his office door. If he took the usual amount of time to change his clothes, he'd be three minutes late to class.

Gary could make up the time by almost running to the classroom, but he would also have to choose between no coffee, or no tie. It wasn't a tough call, because Gary was addicted to caffeine and he didn't like ties. It sounded a little crazy, but Gary thought it was stupid for men to tie a rope-like object around their neck. An assailant would have less trouble killing a man who wore a pre-positioned noose. Gary had heard that Secret Service Agents, and other similar professionals, wore only clip-on ties for that exact reason. When an assailant grabbed the tie to commit murder by strangulation, the intended murder weapon would come off in the assailant's hand as the intended victim pulled out a gun or beat the assailant senseless. Clip-on ties made more sense to Gary, but clip-on ties generally looked like, well, clip-on ties. So Gary preferred no tie at all. If somebody wanted him dead, he would rather be shot than strangled.

The more senior students in his classes knew that a no-tie day often meant Gary had been running late that morning. Most of the tenure track professors wore ties, but many of the non-tenure track, or NTT, professors did not. With no hope of tenure, the NTT professors were generally less concerned about their appearances and the opinions of the senior faculty members. They would never be closely scrutinized by a tenure committee.

Gary got to the classroom just thirty seconds late, and then spent a couple of minutes reviewing his notes for today's lecture on his laptop. He looked up from his notes as the last of the "on-time" students trickled in. At 9:33 AM, it was time to start class, three minutes late as usual. The class was a ninety-minute, Tuesday-Thursday class. Had it been a Monday, Wednesday, or Friday class, it would have been just sixty minutes long. At the one hour and ten minute mark, Gary really wished it had been a sixty-minute class because he was presented with a conundrum. At the start of every semester, Gary gave a stern warning to his students that all electronic devices had to be muted before the start of each class, and cell phones usage was not permitted. The rule was tough to enforce, but students knew if they got caught and the interruption was not a genuine emergency that they would pay a price. The punishment might be a bad class-participation grade, or a two-point deduction from their final-exam score.

At 10:40 AM Gary's cell phone rang loudly. In his hurry to get to class, he had forgotten to switch the phone to the vibrate or silent setting. In front of the class, Gary was forced to sheepishly pull out his phone and silence it so he could continue the class. He knew at that moment many of his students, particularly those who had already been caught violating the rule, were anxious to judge him negatively for breaking his own rule. Gary glanced at the phone number as he hit the mute button. He was slipping the unanswered phone back into his pocket when his gut said, *Take the call.*

Gary looked at the phone number again, and then looked up at the half empty classroom as he said, "Ladies and Gentlemen, I'm sorry for the interruption but this call is an emergency and I have to take it right now. I'm going to end the class twenty minutes early, but don't feel cheated. At the beginning of our Thursday class I will quickly summarize what we didn't cover, and I will tell you the exact question you will see on this topic on the final exam."

The offer was too good to pass up. Even his potential critics began packing up their laptops before he finished speaking. It was good to be the king – of the classroom. As he pushed the talk button on his phone, Gary admitted to himself that he had lied. The call was not an emergency call from his wife, the baby sitter, a hospital emergency room, or the police. Gary could think of no legitimate reason for ending the class early. His instincts had told him to answer the unexpected call, so he did.

At a random moment days later, however, Gary recalled a story that he read in a book called "Blink" by Malcolm Gladwell. The story was about a firefighter lieutenant who led his team into a residential home to put out a kitchen fire. The team went through the front door and crossed the living room to get to the kitchen in the back of the home. They doused the fire, but it didn't go out. They doused it again, and got a similar unsuccessful result. The team retreated to the living room as the kitchen continued to burn. A moment later, the lieutenant thought to himself, "There's something wrong," and for no reason other than gut instinct, he immediately ordered his crew out of the dwelling. He and his crew fled, and moments later the floor in the living room on which they had been standing, collapsed into a fire that was raging in the basement below.

Had the fire fighters not immediately run away, they would have been killed or seriously injured. At the time of the hasty exit, the team leader could not explain why he had told his crew to run. The living room had not even been on fire, and the lieutenant had been in dozens of similar situations, but had never before left in such haste. Years later, when he was questioned at length by an expert, the lieutenant was able to articulate why his "gut instinct" had been triggered. The kitchen fire had not gone out as it should have. When he retreated to the living room, the house was too hot and too quiet. His unconscious mind put those facts together and he had ordered his team out of the house. Analyzed from afar, long after the fact, it all made sense. The fire hadn't gone out in the kitchen because it was centered in the basement. The living room was hot because the flames were already burning through the floor beams. The house was too quiet compared to the heat level, because the floor was muffling the sound of the fire below.

People like the firefighter, who suddenly changed their behavior without waiting for their conscious mind to understand the data, are said to have "good instincts." People who often make sudden, inexplicable changes in their behavior, without later being able to explain it, are said to be fools; particularly when the building doesn't collapse after their hasty departure.

Like the firefighter, Gary took the phone call and released the class without being able to explain his choice. If he had been interviewed later by an expert, he might have been able to explain why he took the call. His smart phone indicated the call was an overseas call from Russia.

Gary didn't know any Russians, and he had very few friends or acquaintances overseas. However, his unconscious mind immediately recalled that Andrew Blake, a fellow NYU professor was teaching a semester abroad at Lomonosov Moscow State University in Moscow. Gary's unconscious mind quickly went one step further. Other than someone calling the wrong number, Blake was the only person overseas who was likely to call Gary's personal cell phone. And if Blake was calling while Gary was teaching a class, *the call must be urgent.* Blake would have waited until the end of the academic day for any other type of call.

Gary didn't analyze any of those factors when the call came in. He just followed his gut feeling, dismissed the class and took the call.

Gary and Blake had been undergraduates together, and had been more acquaintances than friends. When they both got teaching positions at NYU, they became "work place friends;" people who spent time together during the workday, and occasionally went to lunch, but very rarely saw each other outside of work. The two professors each found the other man's specialty to be an interesting topic of conversation. Gary taught civil engineering, and Blake taught astronomy. They enjoyed having great conversations, and testing out cockamamie ideas that they'd be embarrassed to share with someone else who just wouldn't understand.

Gary said, "Hello this is Gary," as he watched the students file out the door. He nodded to a few of the students who made eye contact with him as they left. He knew some of them, particularly those that had already gotten in trouble for using cell phones in class, thought he was a hypocrite for taking the call. As Blake began talking, Gary thought, *This better be good, because I'm definitely going to pay a price for it later.* To retain any credibility, Gary figured he would have to grant cell-phone amnesty to the entire class for the rest of the term. By the time the call ended, Gary was convinced that *not* taking the call might have cost him his life.

"Gary, it's Blake, Andrew Blake." Blake had always gone by his last name. Nobody who knew him called him Andrew or Andy.

"Blake, I can't tell you how relieved I am that it's you, and not someone who dialed the wrong number. Do you know that I was in class when you called? Remember how we both implemented a rule that requires students never to use–"

Blake cut him off. "Yeah, sorry about that. Now shut up and listen, I don't have much time."

Gary was surprised. Blake was a mild-mannered guy. Gary couldn't recall a single time when Blake had rudely interrupted him, let alone told him to shut up. Gary shut up and listened. It was almost eleven o'clock in the morning in New York, which meant it was almost six o'clock in the evening in Moscow. Blake was not his usual cheerful self. He sounded worried.

"Gary, I'm glad I got a hold of you. I have to tell you something quite serious and I have to say it quickly. If this call gets cut off, do not try to call me back. Do you understand?" Blake was terse.

"Um, yeah, sure. I shouldn't call ba–"

Blake interrupted again, "Gary you and I have talked about some crazy stuff over the years. I've always liked talking to you because you could discuss whacky ideas with me, without thinking that I was whacky."

"Yeah, well I feel the–"

Blake interrupted again as his hurried pace continued, "Gary what I'm about to tell you is whacky, but it's true. You have to believe me. You've got to do what I tell you to do."

"Sure Blake, anything you–"

"Gary, I'm calling because there is a crisis coming your way. In fact, I think this crisis is going to hammer all of North America and maybe a big chunk of the rest of the world. And by crisis, I mean millions of Americans are going to die. Maybe tens of millions."

Had he not known Blake as well as he did, Gary would have hung up. Blake really did sound crazy, but Gary knew Blake was one of the most levelheaded people he'd ever met. Blake didn't drink, well not heavily, and he didn't do drugs. Gary knew Blake was stone cold sober but he sounded, well, he sounded a little out of his mind. Could it be fear?

"Gary, this is the proverbial 'big one.' The big CME is heading to Earth right now."

"What?" Gary had heard and understood Blake just fine. His brain just needed more to time absorb the information.

"CME Gary, The big CME. We've talked about this before."

Gary knew that CME stood for Coronal Mass Ejection, and he remembered some of the conversations. But the conversations had been wide ranging and included many topics including asteroids, comets, and even time travel. To Gary, the conversations had been just a step or two removed from fantasy. The *reality* of a CME was something his mind hadn't embraced then, and desperately wanted to reject now.

Blake continued. "Coronal Mass Ejection, Gary, you know, a huge solar flare, a massive electromagnetic shock delivered to Earth much like the EMP from an airburst of a nuclear bomb."

Gary interrupted, "Yeah, yeah, I know what an Electro-Magnetic Pulse is. I know what EMP means, but you just said this CME–"

Blake finished the sentence, "– is going to hit the United States. Yes, that's what I just said. It's the big one Gary, and it's not going to miss us like most of the big ones do."

"Blake I know you wouldn't joke about something like this, but say it out loud. Tell me this isn't a prank."

When Gary spoke, his nervous voice was almost a whine. He sounded like a child asking for a pinky-promise. Gary looked around. He was relieved to see the entire lecture hall was empty. It took a lot less time for students to leave a class early than it did for them to file in when class started.

Blake slowed down a little. He had already delivered the big news. Now he needed to provide enough of an explanation so Gary would believe the big news. "It's not a prank, Gary. Let me explain. You know I'm teaching abroad here at Moscow State University. The university has access to some of the most sophisticated astronomy equipment in the world. My doctoral students do research for the Keldysh Institute and the Sternberg Astronomical Institute, and we get access to astrological data from both the International Scientific Optical Network or ISON, and the Geostationary Operational Environmental Satellite, or GOES.

"Gary, one of my graduate students was monitoring the instruments when the largest solar flare in the last hundred and fifty years popped. This thing came out of nowhere. The sun was in a relatively quiet period of solar activity, and the spot that gave birth to this flare wasn't particularly huge. Well, not on the surface anyway. I was teaching an undergraduate class when it happened. The grad student called me, and I came in and checked the data. Then I checked it again. Then I called a colleague to have her come in and check the data. We were all stunned by what we saw."

Blake paused for a second, but Gary had nothing to say. Blake continued. "After my colleague came in and confirmed the data, we followed protocol and contacted the department chairman who contacted the university president. At some point the Russian Academy of Science, or RSA and the Russian Federal Space Agency, or FKA were notified, and then the Russian Ministry of Defense was informed. Because of our initial disbelief, we were more than two hours late in complying with the protocol. But shortly after the initial notification to the department chairman, representatives from the RAS, the FKA, and Defense Ministry showed up to check our analysis of the data.

"Nobody wanted to believe what we were showing them, but eventually the representative from the Defense Ministry, Colonel . . . um . . . oh hell, I can't remember his name and it doesn't matter. Anyway, the Colonel called his boss, and after that the most senior leaders of the Russian government got the news, including the President himself. A couple of more hours went by while the military and the politicians argued about what to do. Both groups finally agreed that this enormous solar flare could be an extinction level event for about half the world. The research facility is now being flooded with military personnel. I'm sure they're going to kick me out soon and I wanted to tell somebody back home what was going on. The Russians don't intend to release this information to the public any time soon. Apparently, all the other nations that have access to the GOES data have also decided to withhold the information, at least for now. I'm making this call to you because, well, you know just in case I don't get a chance to make it later."

Gary was a little stunned. Blake felt he needed to tell something important to somebody in the United States, and he had called Gary? Why not call a family member? Gary recalled both of Blake's parent's were dead, and he was recently divorced. Still, why not call his ex-wife; wasn't she still raising Blake's two sons? What was her name, Betty?

Blake continued as if he could read Gary's thoughts. "Gary, I tried calling Becky, but she wasn't home. I left voicemail messages on both her home and cell phones, but I wasn't able to speak to her like I'm speaking to you now. She and the boys are in Colorado, and I think they'll be relatively safe. I think the big cities will be the most dangerous places."

"Dangerous?"

"Gary, the last time North America got hit with a CME was 1989. The CME was caused by an X-15 class solar flare and it shut down the electricity in the entire province of Quebec for nine hours. The inbound CME is about five times bigger than that. How would you like to be in the middle of New York City when the entire state of New York has a blackout that lasts for days, or weeks, or longer?"

"I wouldn't."

"Well it looks like you and a whole lot of other people are not going to have a choice. Look, Gary, I need a favor. Please call Becky and make sure she got my messages."

Blake gave Gary Becky's phone number and he wrote it down. Blake continued with his bad news. "The sun spot that threw off this flare was one of just a few spots that we were tracking. Three days ago, one of the smaller spots threw off a small flare. Yesterday, the effects of that flare impacted Earth, but they went almost unnoticed. Some minor interference with radio and cell phone reception occurred, and people in the far north observed a delightful aurora borealis display, but it hardly got mentioned by the media so almost nobody knew about it."

"At about 11:00 AM today here in Moscow things suddenly got more interesting. One of the other larger sunspots sent out a huge CME. The size and speed of this thing are just staggering and out of proportion to the size of the spot. I almost think that this CME blew like a volcano from far beneath the surface. I've never seen anything like it before. My guess is this flare is about an X-70 on the GOES X-Ray Spectrometer or XRS scale.

"Blake, I'm not familiar with the XRS scale, but you're telling me an X-70 on the X-whatever scale is big?"

"An X-70 flare is almost fifty percent bigger than the Carrington flare of 1859."

"Carrington? What's that?"

"Gary, I don't have time to give you a history lesson. The Carrington Event was the biggest CME to hit North America. It happened in 1859, and there was so much electricity in the air, that telegraph wires in the US were able to function without the use of batteries. If you want to learn more, research it on the internet after I hang up."

"So when is this CME going to hit the US?"

"Nobody knows for certain, Gary. This thing is massive and it's moving faster than any previously recorded CME in more than a hundred years. I estimate that it will travel to earth in less than twenty hours."

"How could it get here so fast? I thought you said the smaller flare took three days to get here."

"Yes Gary, the smaller CME did take about three and a half days to reach earth, and that's about how long most CME's take. We think this super CME is moving much faster than most other CMEs because the smaller flare cleared the way for the big one. We can't get precise measurements on the size or the speed of the super CME because some of the instruments have been affected by the two CMEs and could be giving us bad data."

"What do you mean, 'cleared the way'?"

"The super CME left the sun's surface at about 1,500 miles per second. Ordinarily, the speed of a CME is greatly reduced when it encounters the solar wind, which travels toward earth at about 250 miles per second. Two hundred and fifty miles per second is really fast, but it still acts like a brake when something moving six times faster slams into it. This super CME is going to hit Earth in record time because it's following right behind the smaller CME that left the sun just three days ago. The speed of the solar wind on that particular path is significantly higher because the smaller CME, which left the sun at a respectable 900 miles per second, just blew through it."

Blake continued, "Ironically, a similar thing occurred during the Carrington event. A small CME hit the US on August 28, 1859. Three days later on September first, a much bigger CME hit earth, but it completed its journey from the sun in less than eighteen hours."

Gary said, "Alright so the second CME is moving faster than most, and will get here in twenty hours, that means it will hit sometime tomorrow at about–"

Blake interrupted. "No Gary. The twenty hours is the total travel time. This thing left the sun seven hours ago, that puts the arrival time in New York at about, um, let's see, midnight."

"Midnight? Tonight?" Gary was just now beginning to absorb the magnitude of Blake's bad news.

"Well, that would be the front edge of the arrival window. I don't think it will hit before midnight your time, but I also don't think it will arrive more than three or four hours after that. Look Gary, I already told you that we're not getting accurate data from the sun-monitoring satellites. This super CME is also almost too big and too fast to measure. Nobody alive today has ever seen or felt the devastation we are about to experience. Well you really, much more than me."

"Blake, you're scaring me. What the hell am I supposed to do? And what do you mean by 'you not me' will experience this?"

"Gary, due to the rotation of the earth, North America will rotate into the blast zone and get most or all of the CME effects, while the opposite side of the world, Russia, China, etcetera, suffer little or no damage."

"So it sucks to be us, and by that I mean the US, the United States?"

"Yes, but the Russians have been saying that for decades, you capitalist pig." Blake gave a cynical chuckle as he spoke. If the US were brought to its knees by a CME, while its two Communist rivals remained undamaged, the geopolitical and military implications would be staggering. The US might never have an opportunity to recover. The competition between the two ideologies would end, but not because one had been proven superior to the other.

"That's not funny."

"You're right. But I don't think I'll be coming home soon, maybe not ever. So it's either laugh or cry for me. I might never be back in the good ole USA, but I'll have electricity, and I probably won't be eaten by a roving herd of cannibals."

"What the hell are you talking about?"

"Gary, the shit really is going to hit the fan. Did you read the book, *One Second After*? The government has known for years about the threat of a big CME, and done almost nothing about it. If the electrical power in America goes out for a couple of months, an enormous percentage of Americans are going to die. There will be few if any tractor-trailer trucks delivering food to the grocery stores. When the one hundred million people who depend on food stamps stop getting food, will they stay in their homes and quietly starve to death? Or are they going to visit your home and take what you have?"

"What do you mean the trucks will stop delivering food?"

"Gary, we talked about this before. A large CME would shut down the grid, and it might fry electrical devices that have microchips. That would include every automobile that was manufactured after 1987, which includes all the tractor-trailer trucks that deliver food to the grocery stores. Even if some of the vehicles still run, where would they get fuel after the grid shuts down?

Gary probably had heard some of this before, but only as part of an abstract academic discussion. It had not left an impression. Gary was now struggling to believe it would soon be his personal reality.

Gary said, "No electricity and no functional automobiles? If that's true, then our standard of living will go back more than one hundred years. We'll be living in the eighteen hundreds."

"Yes and an eighteen hundreds standard of living, means an eighteen hundreds population level."

Gary thought about that for a second and then asked, "What was the population of the US in the eighteen hundreds?"

"A hell of a lot lower than it is now. As a Civil War buff, I can tell you that the US population in 1865, was about thirty five million. By the end of that century, the population was, I don't know, maybe about seventy-five million."

"Blake, the current population of the US is around three hundred and thirty million. You're telling me that two hundred and fifty million Americans are about to die? That would be a population reduction of more than seventy-five percent."

"Yes, Gary it might get that bad. You need to take appropriate action right now. Get out of the city and find somewhere to hunker down for at least a few weeks, maybe longer. Maybe a lot longer. Does Mae still work at the law firm on Madison Avenue?"

"Yes."

"When news of this CME reaches the public, Manhattan will be one of the most dangerous places in the world. Millions of commuters will want to leave the city immediately, before the CME actually hits. When the electricity goes out, then the subways will go out, and the elevators too. Anybody who is still in Manhattan at that point, will probably spend the rest of their life there; which of course will be reduced to just a few hours or days. Gangs will rule the city for a brief period as city dwellers flee or starve to death. After that, the city will be a–"

Blake interrupted himself for a moment, and Gary could tell Blake had partially covered the mouthpiece of the phone with his hand. He was talking to someone else. Then Blake came back on.

"Look, this call is about to end whether I want it to or not. A student just told me a colonel is heading in my direction. All of the academic personnel are about to get shoved out the door."

"What the hell am I supposed to do?"

"Gary, that's for you to decide. If it were me, I'd grab Mae and get her out of the city right now. You don't want her to be stuck in the city when the rest of the population learns the CME is coming. You also don't want her to get stuck on a train halfway between your home and her office. If the cell phones stop working, you won't have any idea where she is. When news of the CME goes public, it's likely the cell phones will become useless as people jam the circuits with calls and text messages about the end of the world."

Gary's mind was racing, but he couldn't think of anything to say.

"Look, Gary, I believe this is the proverbial big one, but there's a chance that it's not. Maybe the instruments are wrong and the solar flare isn't as big as an X-70, or maybe the impact calculations are wrong and North America, particularly the east coast of the US will not experience the worst of it. But if I were you, I'd shift to panic mode right now. I'd get Mae out of the city right now.

Gary could hear background voices and noises getting louder on Blake's end of the line as Blake raised his voice a little and continued to speak.

"In a few hours you might not be able to get out of that city in a car, on a bike, or even on foot. Just imagine if Hurricane Sandy's devastation had covered all of New York City, and a big chunk of the east coast. What would you do if you had even five hours notice that a storm like that was coming?"

"I guess I would say thank you for the warning, even though right now I feel like throwing up. Then I'd run like hell."

"Well, you're wel—" Gary heard somebody yelling at Blake in Russian. Blake yelled back in Russian. Then the line went dead.

Chapter 4:   Mae goes to court.

Gary stared stupidly at the phone for a few seconds as if he expected Blake to come back on the line.   It was 10:54 AM.   The conversation had taken less than fifteen minutes. Gary called the number that Blake had called from.   He got a busy signal.   Maybe Blake was trying to call him back, but it was more likely the phone was disconnected.   The screen on Gary's laptop had gone into sleep mode. He punched in his password and spent a couple of minutes searching for news of a solar flare.   He found nothing, and couldn't decide what to do next.   He trusted Blake, but even Blake had said the CME information was almost unbelievable.   Maybe the instruments had malfunctioned and the data was incorrect.   Gary thought, *Should I really go into a full panic for something that might not be true?   How stupid would that be?*

Gary thought about the firefighters in Gladwell's book, *Blink*. Gary was about to run away from the building and the campus.   How stupid would he look and feel if the building didn't explode? When Gary recalled what Blake had said about Becky, it gave him an excuse to stall his decision on what to do next.   He called Becky, and she answered on the second ring. The conversation was brief.   Gary introduced himself and explained the reason for his call.   Becky had already listened to Blake's voice-mail message, so the news wasn't new. Still, she seemed very calm throughout the call.   She and Blake had ended their marriage, but she had the utmost respect for Blake's intellect.   Blake had often told her to expect the unexpected.   Such expectations required common-sense preparations.

Becky's home included a few acres of land several miles from Colorado Springs.   She and her sons, Blake's sons, were well provisioned to survive for weeks, even months, without leaving the property.   To a person like Becky, a crisis like Hurricane Sandy was an opportunity to spend quality time with her kids.   Becky thanked Gary and ended the call quickly.   She had a checklist of things to do when a disaster was imminent, and she intended to get them all done.   Gary wished he knew what was on her checklist.

With the phone call over, Gary was again confronted with the decision of what to do next.   *Should I leave the classroom and the campus at a run?   What if nothing happens?   Or what if the CME hits, but it's not strong enough to knock out the power?   Maybe the satellites malfunctioned, or the information was inaccurate.*   As all the arguments against taking action ran through Gary's mind, another thought popped into his head.   *What if the information is accurate and Blake's assessment is correct?   I might be the only person on campus who knows about the solar flare. Heck, Becky and I might be the only two people in the country who know about the CME, but don't have a top-secret clearance. Well great, then who the heck am I going to call to figure out what I should do next?*

Gary needed to share this information with somebody who could absorb the shock of it all, and then have something intelligent to say. He went through the names of dozens of people he knew, and came up with a very short list of candidates. Aside from Blake, there were only one or two people to whom Gary could talk about a catastrophic CME. Gary called his brother, and was transferred to voice-mail. He left a brief message, "Hank it's me, Gary. Call me. It's urgent. Actually it's . . . um, very urgent."

Gary glanced at the contact information for Hank and called the second phone number listed there, Hank's home phone. A recording said the phone had been disconnected. Gary's mind began to race, as he terminated the call. He hadn't gotten through on either phone. *Was the CME already affecting certain parts of the grid? No, with Hank it was far more likely that the phone was off the hook, or the bill hadn't been paid.* He wondered how his brother was doing. *Hank got laid off when? A while ago, maybe a long while ago. And I haven't seen or heard from him in what, maybe two months?*

10:24 AM

In the Wrightlinger conference room, Mae caught herself thinking about Johnny and his gift rather than the deposition at hand. The firm was defending a client on a products liability suit. Opposing counsel was taking the testimony of Mr. Roger Phillips, the manufacturer's Chief Financial Officer. Discovery had been going on for months, and Mr. Phillips was testifying on the reasons why the company had taken so long to recall their defective product from the market.

The product was a self-propelled lawn mower that sometimes propelled itself when the drive lever was in the stop position. The plaintiff was the daughter of a man who lost control of his lawn mower. The daughter had been seven at the time of the accident. She lost two toes and a chunk of her left heel after the lawn mower overtook her in a brief chase. According to the father and the girl's attorney, the lawn mower had ruined the girl's ambition to become a professional ballerina. During the discovery process, Mae had seen the girl and was certain the girl would never have been a ballerina even if she had kept all ten toes. Still, the story would be a good sell to the jury. It was Mae's job to ensure the case never got that far.

Mae looked at her watch; it was 10:24 AM. She needed to leave the deposition room for about twelve minutes, so she could be present for the start of the mediation session. While she was gone, the deposition would be in the capable hands of Tom Ellis, a fourth year associate who had been working the product liability suit from the start.

He could handle it. Defending a deposition was less challenging than taking one.

The mediation involved a slip and fall claim against Mae's client, a regional grocery store chain. The plaintiff, an overweight fifty-two year old woman, was claiming huge damages, but Mae knew some of the medical expenses were for ongoing treatment of pre-existing conditions, which had not been exacerbated by the fall. Mae also believed the plaintiff had been assisted by an accomplice who intentionally broke a jar of pickles shortly before the plaintiff slipped in the pickle juice and broke her hip. The store's video tape was helpful, but not conclusive on this issue.

The broken hip and its associated medical expenses were real. The extent of the grocery store's liability, however, was being hotly contested. Today's mediation session was the third attempt to resolve the case. Mae's client had attended two prior settlement conferences, but would not attend today's mediation. The client had given Mae a best and final settlement offer, and would simply take the case to trial if this third effort failed. Mae didn't mind taking cases to court and winning them there. That's why clients hired her. When she said she would see an opposing client in court, it was a credible threat. Her courtroom win-loss record was the envy of many litigators, which enabled her to get more favorable settlements.

Mae pretended she had gotten a call and excused herself from the deposition. She stepped into the hallway and walked just a few yards to the Middleman conference room next door. Sam Roberts, a second year associate, would assist her in the telephonic mediation session. Some members of the firm criticized her for choosing male associates as her assistants, rather than being a mentor to the firm's female associates. Mae preferred to work with men. It gave her more control. Besides, she was something of a mentor to Perky, who would one day be an associate.

Mae had chosen the nearby Middleman conference room for the telephonic conference so she could easily move back and forth between the deposition and the mediation. Plaintiff's counsel and his client, would participate via a speakerphone at his office in White Plains. The mediator would participate from his office in the new Tower Seven of the World Trade Center which, after its collapse on September 11, 2001, had been rebuilt from scratch in 2006.

Sam would stay put for the entire mediation. He would use the firm's landline phone to participate in the mediation which left his cell phone free to send Mae texts, while she was out of the room. From her cell phone, Mae could listen to the progress of the mediation on her Bluetooth earpiece, and also receive texts from Sam. If necessary, she could rejoin the mediation within a couple of minutes. If the deposition ended at its scheduled time, Mae would be absent from the slip and fall mediation for only twenty minutes or so. Mae joined Sam in the

Middleman room and he initiated the conference call. A minute later, Mae exchanged pleasantries with opposing counsel and mentioned that Sam Roberts would be assisting her with the mediation. Three minutes later, she quietly left the room without excusing herself. As she was carefully closing the conference room door, she was met in the hallway by Johnny Davis.

Johnny said, "Mae, I need a favor."

From his tone of voice, Mae knew Johnny was about to ask for help with a case. Johnny called it a professional favor. Johnny often asked for such favors on short notice, and Mae sometimes wondered if he flirted with her just so she would be more likely to say yes to such requests. If he was pursuing a co-worker just for sex, he'd get faster results by pursuing a less competent and unmarried younger associate. The two strategies were not mutually exclusive, and Mae was fairly certain Johnny was doing both.

"What do you need Johnny?" Mae glanced at her watch, it was 10:36.

"I need you to be in court in front of Judge Varroe at 11:15."

"Johnny, that's impossible. I'm in a deposition right now and an overlapping mediation session. I'll be tied up until noon. Sorry. No way."

"Mae, this will take only ten minutes. Besides, you know how Judge Varroe usually runs late and breaks early for lunch. He probably won't start before eleven thirty, and you'll be gone by eleven forty-five."

"No. Plus I'm not dressed for it. This pink blouse and short skirt are not appropriate courtroom attire. I'm wearing a 'catch-a-new-rich-male-client' outfit, which is what I'll be doing after lunch."

"Mae, come on. It's Judge Varroe. You know he likes you, and you know he'll like you even more while you're wearing that outfit."

Johnny was right on both counts. Some judges enforced a strict dress code that required a suit and tie for men, and pantsuits or skirts at least two inches below the knee for women. They threatened contempt for litigators who didn't follow the code. Judge Varroe was a dirty old man who had an obvious preference for attractive female litigators who flaunted the code.

"Johnny, I really can't. Sorry." Mae moved to take a step around Johnny. Her cell phone was in her hand, and she was listening to the progress of the mediation as she talked to Johnny and tried to get back to the deposition.

"Mae, you'll be gone from the office for barely an hour, and I'll let you bill my client for two hours."

Mae paused. It was an attractive offer. The mediation seemed to be going well, and when the deposition ended, there would be nothing that tied her to the building. She could continue to participate in the mediation via her cell phone, except for the time when she was actually in front of the judge. Still, she didn't want to make her morning more complicated by dashing to the courthouse for just two extra billable hours.

Johnny responded as if he could read her mind. "Three hours Mae. You can bill three full hours for doing me this favor. I'll have to give you one of my hours that I earn somewhere else to do it, but that's the deal."

Mae thought about the new offer. For the amount of time the task required, she would earn more than most escort services charged, and she wouldn't have to take off her clothes to get it. Not bad at all. Mae loved the legal profession. Every dime she earned at the firm would increase the payout from her father's trust fund; it didn't matter how she earned it. Mae thought briefly about a mansion in the Hamptons, and smiled.

"Okay, I'll do it. But why me? Why not send an associate?"

"Well, Mae you've already agreed to do it, so I'll tell you. Judge Varroe prefers you to the female associate who is already on the case with me. If I give him what he wants, he's more likely to give me what I want."

"So I'm a prettier piece of meat? My litigation skills don't matter?"

"Yeah, something like that."

Mae took Johnny's admission as a compliment. She was well aware of her physical attributes, and she actively used them to her advantage. It was nice to know that she was holding her own against younger women.

"What am I supposed to do when I get there? I mean is there something related to a case that I'm supposed to present to the Judge?

"Yeah, it's an evidence suppression motion. All the motion paperwork has already been filed, but the Judge indicated he had some follow-up questions. He's the one who scheduled the hearing, not me. Besides, you know how Judge Varroe likes to conduct business face-to-face." Johnny ended with a suggestive tone.

"Did you bring me a copy of the paperwork?

Johnny handed Mae a thin accordion folder. "Yeah, it's all in here. You can read it in the car on your way to the courthouse. I'll send my paralegal with you. She knows the case inside out. If you get stuck during the hearing, give her a moment to whisper something in your ear."

Mae quickly glanced through the paperwork. Johnny was defending a Chief Financial Officer charged with embezzlement. The folder contained Johnny's motion to suppress key evidence, the prosecutor's response, and Johnny's reply to the response. There seemed to be no reason for a hearing. Most judges would have "ruled on the papers" without a hearing.

Mae said, "Do you think the judge called the hearing just to leer at the women?"

Johnny smiled. "I don't know Mae, but he knows you'll be there."

"How could he know, you just found out yourself!"

"Mae, I thought I could get you to take it for the price of two billable hours, but I knew you would take it for three."

Mae was a woman with a price tag, and certain men knew her price. Mae again accepted the compliment as she walked back into the conference room. "Thanks, Johnny. I assume you've already reserved a limo to take me to the courthouse."

Mae glanced at her watch. She had been away from the deposition for eighteen minutes; three tenths of a billable hour. Mae would bill the first six minutes to the deposition client, and the last twelve minutes to both the deposition and mediation clients.

Johnny said, "Of course, Mae. My paralegal made the arrangements. She'll be waiting for you outside with the limo at eleven."

Mae said, "Okay," as she re-entered the deposition room. She looked at Tom who gave a slight shrug. Mae hadn't missed anything. With her cell phone's Bluetooth device, she continued to listen to Sam's progress in the mediation next door. With her hair down, the device was hardly noticeable.

At 10:54, Mae collected her things and excused herself from the deposition for the last time. She stopped briefly at the Middleman room to tell Sam she was going to the courthouse. Sam placed the phone on mute to have a one minute conversation with Mae as the mediator talked to the plaintiff about the high cost of litigation and realistic outcomes. Even if Mae had to terminate her participation in the mediation while she was in front of Judge Varroe, Sam could handle the rest of the session. The mediator was doing a good job of educating the plaintiff, and Sam was now confident the case was going to settle today; for less than the maximum amount Mae's client was willing to pay. Mae would of course, get the credit.

At 11:02 AM, Mae stepped outside her office building and found the limousine that was waiting to take her to the federal courthouse in Foley Square for the motion hearing. En route, Mae didn't bother to read the material Johnny had provided. Instead, she had Johnny's paralegal present the material verbally as Mae fixed her hair, freshened her make-up, and adjusted her cleavage.

Chapter 5: Two marshals, a blonde, and a biker.

Gary closed his laptop absent-mindedly. He walked out of his classroom for the last time at 11:06 AM. Whatever he was going to do next, he'd be doing alone. In a country of 320 million, a state of 19 million, a city of 8 million, a university of fifty thousand, and a college campus of almost five thousand, he was alone. Alone with the knowledge – well, possibility? Probability? That disaster was about to strike.

"Good morning Professor Adams!"

Gary looked in the direction of the voice. It was Sharon. She was a junior engineering student. Rumor had it that she would trade any sort of favor for a good grade. If true, her physical attributes would tempt any heterosexual male professor. Gary looked at her long black hair, smooth brown skin, seductive white smile, tight low-cut blouse, and short skirt. His brain processed none of it. Instead, almost unconsciously, his brain delivered a different message: *If the CME is real, she's not going to make it.*

Gary said, "Good morning Sharon," with a lot less enthusiasm.

Gary's eyes shifted away from Sharon before he finished his greeting. He looked at the other students in the hallway. They were all . . . what? The walking dead, like zombies? Was he looking at the zombies of the real world? Not the dead coming back to life and leaving their graves, but young, healthy people who would stumble around for a few weeks looking for food as they went toward their graves? Would they even get graves?

How long would Sharon last? She was already trading sex for academic success, but what would she barter for in the New World? Food? Shelter? Protection? Would people with an excess of those items trade them for sex? Probably. But how many people who had excess food would be willing to make that trade, and for how long? On the other side of the transaction, how many women would be competing with Sharon to make the same offer? Gary concluded there wouldn't be enough transactions to keep all the prostitutes, and wanna-be prostitutes alive.

Gary was crushed by two additional thoughts. If Blake was right, then a lot people in the hallway, indeed the entire campus, would probably soon be dead. And there was nothing Gary could do to change their fate. If he told them what was coming, the vast majority wouldn't believe him. The only thing that would *make* them believe would be the event itself. They wouldn't believe the potential crisis was real until the lights went out. Prior to that, any effort to convince them would be wasted, and Gary had no time to waste. Even if he could make some of them understand what was coming, how many would be able to increase their chances for long-term survival? How many had the skills and tenacity to survive in a world where all of life's necessities were not sitting on a nearby shelf? How many city dwellers had prepared for the possibility of a post-apocalyptic world? One in a hundred? One in a thousand?

Gary continued to walk, and Sharon gave him an odd look as he passed by. She hadn't slept with him yet, but she still had Gary on her list of possible partners. His eyes usually gave her a signal that said his body was contemplating something that his brain had not yet approved. Professor Adams was definitely a heterosexual. But just now, he had looked at her with all the lust he would have for a rotting corpse.

In the three minutes it took Gary to reach his office, he had almost come to grips with what he had to do. Almost. He paced in his small office for a couple of minutes and then plopped down in his chair. His only option was still too radical, too insane to absorb. *I'm going to call Mae and tell her to leave work early so she won't be in the city when the largest solar flare in one hundred and fifty years hits North America.*

The fact that Mae had never left work early at Gary's request wasn't the hardest part. The hardest part would be trying to explain *why* she needed to leave early. Gary hadn't fully convinced himself that the alleged catastrophe was real. How was he going to explain it to Mae on the phone? Like everybody he had just passed in the hallway, Gary had done nothing to prepare for even a much smaller crisis like Hurricane Sandy or Katrina. If he could get to a grocery store before everybody else figured out what was coming, then maybe he could get enough food and supplies to hunker down for a few weeks. Then what? What if the crisis lasted more than just a few weeks? What if the catastrophe was far more widespread than a hurricane, and affected the entire state, or the entire eastern seaboard? What if all or most of the United States got thrown back into the pre-electrified world of the eighteen hundreds?

Blake's warning was unsettling. In his mind, Gary tried to negotiate for less horrific terms. *What if there wasn't a CME? No deal? Okay, what if the CME did happen, but the electricity didn't fail? What if I take some precautionary measures, but do not go to full panic mode? Still no deal? What if I just get Mae to come home early, and wait to see what I should do next? That way if the CME doesn't strike, or it does strike but doesn't cause a widespread blackout, Mae and I can laugh about it in the morning. She could go to work the next day and make up a story about a family emergency to explain her hasty departure the day before. Something along the lines of, "My husband was home alone with my kids and all hell broke loose."* For people who knew Mae, that story would be hard to sell.

Gary knew he was lying to himself. Mae would *not* easily be persuaded to leave work early, and she wouldn't laugh it off the next morning if the crisis turned out to be bogus. Gary felt an overwhelming urge to do *something* but he wasn't ready to call Mae. How could he convince her a CME was coming when he had absolutely no proof to back it up? Mae was, after all an attorney. She would want to "review the evidence." Gary had only one witness, Blake, and he was unavailable for cross-examination. Gary finally hit on what he thought was a good solution. Instead of calling Mae, he would drive to the city and take her home on his motorcycle. If news of the CME went public, Mae wouldn't get stuck somewhere on a train, and Gary wouldn't be relying on a cell phone to find her. She'd be right there with him; pressed up against his back.

On the motorcycle, Gary figured it would take less than twenty minutes to get to Mae's Madison Avenue office. That would give him time to think. Who knew? Maybe by that time, news of the CME would be on the television and Mae wouldn't argue about leaving work early. Gary guessed correctly that his last thought was pure fantasy. The news would not break so quickly. The difficult conversation with Mae could not be avoided. Gary's effort to choose a course of action was clouded by his doubts as to whether the CME was real, and his simultaneous contemplation of the numerous devastating consequences of a super CME. Gary realized his busy mind was paralyzing him. He was still sitting on his ass in his office.

If the CME wasn't real, then taking no action at all was the best option. If the CME was real but the severity was low, taking no action at all would still be the prudent thing to do. If the CME was real and the severity was high, then why bother taking any action? He'd be dead soon anyway! Gary cut off his thoughts by telling himself to "Stop it!" outloud. By itself, no amount of thinking was going to get him out of his conundrum. At that moment, Gary hit upon a philosophy that would guide him through the New World chaos and govern the rest of his life; be it hours, days, or years.

He could not predict or even contemplate the magnitude of the potential crisis. Thus, he could not make a detailed plan to navigate the weeks and months ahead. He simply had to determine what he needed to do *now*, and then do it. After he completed that one best, smartest move, then he would be in a new "*now*" and he'd pick a new "one thing to do." Multi-tasking was a myth, and the future might not happen. "*Focus on one thing to do now,*" was Gary's new mantra.

Gary got up out of his comfy office chair. His last act of participation in his "Old World" academic life was to call the Administration Office and tell them he was too sick to teach his afternoon class. The Admin Office would either find a teaching assistant to babysit the class, or put a class-canceled sign on the classroom door. It somehow seemed appropriate that his exit from the Old World was a lie. In some ways, the Old World itself was a lie. A lie about cradle-to-grave government care in one country, while most of the world's other residents struggled to survive from one meal to the next. Were the realities of hunger, even starvation, about to take up long-term residence in America?

Gary put his laptop in its carry bag, and grabbed his motorcycle helmet and leathers from the closet. He didn't change into the leathers. If Mae did agree to leave her office – and that was a big if – she'd be leaving on the motorcycle. For her safety, Gary would ask her to wear the leather jacket and pants. His leathers would be too big for her, but they wouldn't fall off her while she was sitting on the bike. Gary was glad he kept a second helmet on the bike. He would not be wearing leathers for the ride home, but he and Mae would both have a helmet. Hopefully, he wouldn't have to lay the bike down and slide it under a truck.

Gary left his office and walked quickly to the parking garage. As he left the campus, he noticed dozens of students outside enjoying the warmth of what might be autumn's last sunny day. Some were playing Frisbee, others were kicking soccer balls, but most were sitting in the sunlight with their heads bent over their smart phones. Gary caught a glimpse of one of the phone addicts getting blindsided by an errant soccer ball. It made him smile. Students who were constantly preoccupied with a smart phone were annoying, particularly on a day like this.

A few minutes later, Gary was on the bike and moving fast. Now that he was doing the "one thing to do *now*," he was more calm and able to think more clearly. He persuaded himself that Blake was probably correct, a massive CME was coming. Gary decided he would take radical steps to protect his family. He would do this, and if he was wrong, then so be it. In *this* "now," he was "all in." Gary drove his motorcycle across the Brooklyn Bridge, then he went north on FDR East River Drive. Then he went west on 42nd Street to Madison Avenue. As he drove, the world outside of his own frantic mind seemed normal. Gary thought, *This CME is either a fantasy or a well-kept secret. Nobody is acting as if the world is about to end.*

The sunny reality clashed with Blake's dire warnings. The beautiful weather was like a Siren song beckoning Gary to terminate his frantic activity and simply enjoy the day. Gary was once again overcome by doubt, simply because he had gone outdoors. He closed his eyes for a brief moment as he shook his head. He had already chosen a course of action, and willed himself to stick with it. Gary opened his eyes and said to himself out loud, "Focus on one thing to do now." Gary was in fact already doing 'one thing now.' He was driving. Was there anything else he could do as he drove to Madison Avenue? Gary called his brother Hank using the helmet's intercom. The intercom allowed him to receive a phone call, listen to music from the bike's radio or a portable device, or talk to a passenger on the bike, when their helmet was connected to the system.

Hank didn't answer. Gary left another message, but this time he said his call was very urgent and he begged Hank to call him back. Gary didn't bother calling Hank's disconnected home phone. When he hung up, Gary decided to call Mae, and at least warn her that he was coming. Maybe he would save most of his doomsday sales pitch for a face-to-face meeting when he got there. For now, he just needed her to agree to leave her office and meet with him for a few minutes. Mae did not answer her cell phone, so Gary left a message that said, "Call me."

Gary deliberately focused on his driving to preserve his peace of mind. Soon, he was turning onto Madison Avenue. He drove a few hundred yards, and then pulled to the curb outside Mae's office building. He again tried Mae's cell phone without success. Then he called Mae's private office phone number. If Mae didn't pick up, her assistant would. As the ring tone sounded in his helmet, Gary tried to recall the assistant's name. He had only met her briefly on two occasions, and he rarely called Mae's office phone.

11:23 AM

"Hello. Able, Davis, and Donaldson. This is Amanda. How can I help you?"

Ah, Amanda. Amanda . . . Perkins! And her nickname was . . . Perky! Gary remembered. Gary used the assistant's nickname, hoping it would suggest a familiarity with Mae's workplace that might get him faster results. In reality, Gary had almost no knowledge of what Mae did all day. He knew she claimed to be a litigator, but it seemed she rarely appeared in court.

"Hello, Perky, this is Gary Adams. I am trying to contact my wife, Mae Seymour."

"I'm sorry, Mr. Adams, Mae is at the federal courthouse right now. Can I take a message?"

Gary hesitated for a moment, *Mae isn't in her office? I wasted precious time driving to the wrong place. Crap!*

"Uh . . . she isn't there? I mean are you sure she isn't in her office?"

Perky was too professional to chuckle out loud at Gary's consternation. "I'm very sure she's not here Mr. Adams. Can I take a message? I expect her to be back in about an hour."

There was another long pause before Gary asked, "You said the federal courthouse, right? The one in Foley Square?"

"That's correct, Mr. Adams. But as I said, she'll be back here soon. I can tell her you called when she gets in."

"Um, yeah that would be great. Please tell her to call me back."

Perky said she would, but she never did.

Gary said "Thank you," and "Goodbye."

Gary went north on Madison Avenue, turned left onto a cross street, and then turned left again onto Fifth Avenue to go south toward

Foley Square. As he tried to focus on the "now" he was kicking himself for somehow not knowing Mae was not at her office. He had wasted precious time driving to the wrong location. Expecting to get her voicemail again, Gary called Mae's cell phone. He was caught off guard when Mae answered.

Mae had arrived in Judge Varroe's courtroom at 11:25, which was ten minutes after the specified start time for the hearing. The Judge, however, was in the middle of a hearing for a different case. Johnny had been right; the judge was running late. Mae sat down next to a colleague who was also waiting for Judge Varroe. In a short whispered conversation, Mae learned that after the current hearing, there was one other motions hearing in front of Mae's case. Mae estimated it would be another forty minutes before she would see the judge.

Judge Varroe was further behind schedule than usual, which was something Mae had not included in her own scheduling calculations. Johnny was paying Mae triple time to attend the hearing, so ordinarily she would not have cared about the length of such a delay. However, today's delay might make her late for the new-client meeting at one o'clock. If the Judge took lunch before he called Mae's case, then Mae would definitely be late for the client meeting. Being late wasn't an option. Mae decided it was time to call Johnny and tell him to find a different piece of meat to attend the hearing.

Mae also needed updates from Tom on the deposition and Sam on the mediation. When she entered Judge Varroe's courtroom, Mae's cell phone lost reception. Mae whispered goodbye to her colleague and left the courtroom. She walked down the hall toward the windows where she knew she would regain connectivity. As she was walking, her phone vibrated and she answered without looking at the incoming number. She assumed it was Sam trying to reestablish her connection to the mediation.

Mae said, "Hello, Sam?" and then she heard her husband's voice.

"Mae. Hello. This is Gary."

Mae was all business. "Gary, I thought I told you never to call me at work unless it's an emergency."

"Mae, it's an emergency."

Mae paused. "Are the girls okay?" She didn't sound concerned as she said it.

"Yes. They're fine." As an afterthought, Gary added, "For now."

"Gary, I'm very busy. I have no time to talk. Get to the point."

"Okay, here's the point. There's going to be a blackout in New York City later today . . . I mean tonight. I think it would be a good idea for you to leave work now."

"A blackout? What? How . . . ? Are you serious? The biggest client meeting of my career is going to happen this afternoon. I am NOT going home."

"Mae, please just give it some thought. Things could get dangerous in the city. There might be riots. If you don't leave soon, the roads and even the trains could slow down or stop."

While Gary was speaking, Mae recovered from the surprise of Gary's call and the subject of the call. Without pausing for even a second, Mae responded. "It's a clear sunny day and you're predicting what? A blackout? Caused by what, a hurricane? Gary I don't know if this is supposed to be a prank, but I don't have time for this crap, and I'm going to hang up. Good–"

Gary spoke quickly, "Mae, I know it sounds crazy. It even sounds crazy to me, but you've got to consider–"

Mae interrupted. "Gary I have considered it. I just very carefully considered all the crazy stuff you said, and I am not leaving. If my attendance at the new client meeting this afternoon means I have to walk all the way home through a riot, then I am prepared to do that. I will take off my heels and walk barefoot the whole way if I have to, but I will NOT miss that meeting."

"Mae where are you now? Please just let me talk to you face-to-face before you decide to stay here in the city?

"Talk face-to-face? Where are you Gary?"

"I'm driving South on Fifth Avenue, and heading toward the courthouse."

"You're what? How did you know I was–"

"I drove to your office first and called your assistant. She told me you were at the courthouse. Mae, when I get there, please just come down and talk to me for a moment. I'm on the motorcycle, and I'll be there in just a few minutes."

"You're driving the motorcycle, not the Volvo?! What was your plan to get me home? Put me on the train?"

"Mae, I've got the second helmet with me. Come on, you've ridden the bike before. You have to listen to me, this is a serious situation."

"Gary, I've never ridden the bike in a short tight skirt and heels, and today will not be an exception. Your one minute is up. If there is a blackout, I'll just walk home, or sleep in my office until the lights come back on. My new client meeting is going to happen today, and I'm going to be there for it. Goodbye." Mae hung up before Gary could interrupt her again.

Gary turned left onto a cross street, then turned right onto Broadway Avenue and continued going south toward the courthouse. He was about to call Hank a third time, when his helmet headset buzzed with his phone's text-message tone. Gary didn't like reading text messages while he was driving the bike, but today would be a day of exceptions for lots of things. He glanced around at traffic, slowed down a bit as pulled his phone out of his jacket pocket. Gary didn't recognize the phone number, but when he read the message, he knew it was from Blake. It said, "Everything I told is true. Scenario is worst case. Get the hell out of the city. Good luck." It was the last text message Gary received from his friend Blake.

The news hit Gary like a punch in the stomach. He didn't realize he had stopped looking at the street in front of him until he almost hit the rear bumper of a car that had stopped at a traffic light. He suddenly didn't feel like driving. The crisis was real, but Mae refused to believe it. What was he supposed to do? Physically drag her out of the building, past the US Marshals who guarded the building, and tie her onto the motorcycle?

Gary steered the bike to the side of the street, and parked it. He shifted the bike into neutral. He left the engine running and his helmet on, as he tried to collect his thoughts. After a long moment, it occurred to him that he should send a return message to Blake. Gary quickly typed, "Call me if you can!"

As soon as he pressed the send button, Gary knew Blake wouldn't call back or send a text. Once again, Gary felt all alone. He was surrounded by millions of people, but still isolated by information he couldn't share. Most people wouldn't believe him, and the ones who did wouldn't be of any use to him. In fact, anyone who believed him would probably just make his situation worse. At a certain critical mass, the believers would overflow the telephone networks, streets, and subway stations and make a retreat from the city more difficult or impossible.

Gary struggled to determine what "one thing" he should "do now." With Mae's angry words still ringing in his ears, he had little hope of getting her onto the bike. His plan now seemed silly. Finally, with little hope of success, Gary again called Hank's cell phone. He was pleasantly surprised when Hank answered on the third ring. His estimated arrival time at the courthouse would be postponed.

Gary said, "Hey brother, didn't you get my messages?"

"Yeah, kinda."

"Why didn't you call me back?" There was a pause, during which Hank decided he would ignore the question.

"Why'd ja call?"

Hank sounded as if he was hung over, maybe even drunk, but it seemed too early for that. It occurred to Gary that the person he thought most capable of handling a doomsday phone call out of the blue, was a borderline alcoholic. Even while intoxicated, Hank still had more common sense than the vast majority of sober Americans.

"Hank, you don't sound well."

"No I'm . . . um fine. I'm fine, I just um . . . I just woke up."

"Hank, it's almost noon. What did you do, sleep in or take a nap?" Gary smiled and almost chuckled.

Hank again ignored his brother's question. "Why'd ja call?"

Gary got right to the point. "Hank, this is a lot to take in, particularly since you're hung over or drunk, but I really think there is a big crisis coming. It's coming today, and I wanted to call and warn you."

"Warn me? . . . About what? . . . What crisis?" Hank's words were slurred with long pauses between them.

"Hank, I'm convinced a CME is going to hit us. A CME is a coronal–"

The pace of Hank's speech picked up a little as he cut Gary off. "Gary, I know what a CME is. It's a coronal mass ejection. A huge . . . um, solar flare that could deliver an electromagnetic pulse an um, EMP to earth."

Gary said, "I um, I wasn't sure how much you knew about CME's."

"Look I might not be a professor, but I do know a few things. Heck, CME's get reported in the news . . . every once in a while. So how bad is this one supposed to be? Why did you bother to call me about it? I haven't heard from you in . . . almost three months."

Three months?! Had it really been that long? Gary wanted to avoid that topic.

"I don't know for certain how big the CME will be. The media hasn't picked it up yet, but I've got a friend who gave me an advanced warning. He thinks it will be bad enough to cause a blackout. A wide spread blackout that will hit the east coast and maybe a big chunk of the rest of the country."

Gary paused, and then said, "Hank, look, I'm sorry for not checking in sooner, I know you're going through a rough patch right now–"

Hank interrupted again. "Rough patch? Is that all it is to you? Brother, I've got two convictions, two ex-wives, no job, and the Sheriff is coming to throw me out of my house at the end of the month. This isn't a rough patch, it's a pit. A deep dark pit. My entire life has amounted to nothing. It's shit!"

Gary was a little shocked by the emotional pain in Hank's voice. Hank's situation was bad, but why the outburst now? Everything Hank had just said was old news. Well, almost everything.

"Come on Hank, your house has been heading toward foreclosure for over a year now. We even talked about you getting an apartment, and finding a new job."

Gary had known for a while that Hank was going to lose his house. Gary hadn't known until just now that the process would reach a final conclusion by the end of the month. Maybe Hank's certain knowledge that he was about to be forced into the street had triggered Hank's outburst. It occurred to Gary that he hadn't actually done anything to help Hank find an apartment or a job.

"Yeah, we talked about it. But now it's here and it's real. I'm supposed to pack up all my shit and be gone by the end of the month. Guess what? That ain't happening. What I'm supposed to do? Steal a moving truck? Then what? Get an apartment with no money for rent or a deposit? I suppose I could live in my SUV until the repo man finds me."

Gary was surprised by the mention of the SUV. *Hank was going to lose the house and his car?* "Look Hank, I'm sorry. I just . . . didn't know all this stuff was happening now. I guess I thought you were still a few months away from um . . . moving out."

Gary paused, then continued. "Look, I've got money. If life as we know it continues, I can set you up with a moving truck and an apartment."

Hank thought a man who couldn't provide for himself wasn't a man. Hank had never been a beggar, and he would rather die than ask for his brother's charity. So why had he brought up his financial problems? Maybe he'd gotten soft as he got older, or the booze had made him weak.

Hank shifted back to the CME as if he'd never mentioned his personal problems. "Tell me again about this end-of-life-as-we-know-it scenario. Tell me everything your friend told you, and why you would believe this guy."

Since the mention of the CME, Hank had started putting sentences together more easily. Paradoxically, he sounded sober and almost hopeful when he talked about the end of the world.

"My friend, Andrew Blake, is an astronomer so he knows what he's talking about. He's not a nut job when it comes to conspiracy theories. Blake says the east side of North America is going to bear the brunt of the CME. As the Earth rotates through the blast, the effects might diminish. So the more western parts of the U.S. might get a smaller dose."

When Hank spoke again, he sounded like he had just consumed two cups of strong coffee. His questions started coming rapid fire. "Do you believe this guy?"

"Um, yeah."

"Why?"

"Well I know him pretty well. I have worked with him for years. He's an honest guy, and an expert astronomer. He was very serious on the phone. He even made me call his ex-wife to warn her. She has custody of his two kids. He wouldn't mislead her about something like this."

"How big did he say the CME will be?"

"Big enough to cause a blackout in New York City, all of New York, and maybe a big chunk of the United States. I guess there was a CME that hit Canada several years ago. It caused a blackout for nine hours. This one is supposed to be much, much worse than that. He said it might be as bad as the Carrington Event which occurred in–"

Hank cut him off. "I've heard about the Quebec blackout in 1989, and the Carrington Event in 1859. What I meant was, how big is this CME on the GOES scale?"

"The what?"

47

"The GOES scale. To be a huge CME, it would have to be in the X class, but X what? X-40? X-50? How big is this CME going to be? Scientists rate the size of CME on a thing called the GOES scale."

Gary didn't remember everything Blake had said, but he did remember the X rating. "Blake said a lot of stuff, and he said it really fast so I don't recall all the details. But I do remember he said the flare was bigger than X-50. He said it might be an X-70. Our phone call got cut off, so maybe he didn't get a chance to tell me everything."

Hank's tone deepened. "Whoa. An X-70. That's huge. Wait, did he say the CME *was* an X-70 or *might* be an X-70."

"He said might be. He couldn't be sure. He said something about the data-gathering satellites not functioning properly because of um, well I guess because of the CME. That's kind of ironic when you thi–"

"So maybe the CME is smaller than an X-70, or maybe it's bigger?"

Gary said, "I don't know, like I said, the phone call got cut off. Oh yeah, after the phone call ended, he later sent me a text message. I just got it, in fact."

"What did the message say?"

"It said the CME was going to be a 'worst case scenario.'"

As Hank tried to absorb the information, he slowly repeated out loud what Gary had just said, "He said the CME was going to be a worst case scenario?"

"Yeah, but I don't know–"

"What do you think that means?"

Gary said, "Like I was just about to tell you, I really don't know what it means."

"Don't you think it probably means that the CME is at least an X-70, maybe bigger?"

"I, uh . . . . I really have no idea, Hank. I suppose it could mean that, but if–"

Hank interrupted again. "Why did the phone call get cut off?"

"Blake is a professor here in the US, but he's teaching overseas for a semester in Russia. Some of Russia's best astrological equipment, you know telescopes and such, are shared between the universities and the military. Blake was in one of those facilities when the equipment detected the solar flare on the sun. A colonel or somebody made him hang up."

Hank said, "If the military stormed the place and started shutting down outbound information about the CME, then my guess is this thing is real and it's huge."

After a short pause, Hank added, "What are you doing right now? I can hear an engine running."

"I'm in the city right now. I'm going to get Mae and bring her home. If there is going to be a blackout, I don't want her to get stuck in an elevator or a subway train."

Hank paused for a few seconds. Even with the alcohol-addled brain, Hank was thinking more clearly than Gary. "Say you get her home, then what?"

"I figure we'll hunker down at the house until the lights come back on. I don't have a stockpile of food or supplies, so I'm going to the grocery store as soon as possible. I figure Blake's advanced warning will let me beat the rush."

"You plan to hunker down with Mae and the kids at your house in the middle of suburban Long Island?" Hank's tone made it sound like a bad idea.

"Um, yeah. Why Hank? Is there something wrong with that?"

"Yes, there is something very wrong with that. If this CME is real, your plan will get you killed. We'll discuss that later. Did NASA confirm the information that your friend provided? I mean what if your buddy was smoking dope or the satellite information is bogus? "

"NASA?" Gary knew what NASA was, he just couldn't recall NASA coming up in his conversation with Blake. *Why hadn't Blake mentioned NASA?*

Hank said, "Yeah, NASA. They publish lots of details about CME's. CME's are almost common, but most of them are small. Even when they're big, they don't matter if they don't hit us. Solar flares are directional like bullets, and they usually miss us. What did the NASA web site publish about this big solar flare?"

"Hank, I had no idea you knew so much about NASA and CME's."

"Well uh . . . I had a lot of time on my hands when I was, uh . . . . I mean during the period of my unfortunate incarceration. In pris– . . . . I mean inside. If you take classes, you can get limited access to the internet. You know, to do um, research. So I researched a lot of conspi– I researched a lot of theories. When I got out, I kept at it for a while until . . . well, I guess right up until my internet connection at the house was cut off."

Gary said, "I wish Blake had called you instead of me, so you could have asked him all your questions directly. After his call ended, I did a couple of quick internet searches. I found nothing about the CME, but I didn't go to the NASA web site."

"I'll do some checking and get back to you." Hank hung up abruptly before Gary could say another word.

Gary was surprised by Hank's sudden termination of the call. He was also pleasantly surprised by Hank's transformation during the call. *Hank had listened! He had taken the news of the CME seriously!* Gary paused for a moment feeling satisfied he had finally done something positive with Blake's warning. Hank had taken in the information about the CME, and he was now taking action to get more information. Gary was no longer alone in his struggle. It was true Hank was probably not even sober right now, but it felt good to have shared the news with someone that could handle it. Someone who might assist rather than resist Gary's effort to survive the CME.

Gary looked at his watch and realized the call had taken a full five minutes. It had been an important call, but Gary hadn't gotten any closer to Mae while he had been talking to Hank. Gary couldn't put it off any longer. With a successful call to Hank out of the way, the next "one thing" was to face Mae, and try to get her to leave the city. Gary called Mae again. She didn't answer, so he sent her a text. "Call me now."

With renewed resolve, Gary eased the bike back into traffic and again headed south toward Foley Square. Traffic was heavy and Gary again used the motorcycle's small size and flexibility to reduce his travel time. As he drove, his thoughts shifted from Hank back to Mae. *Crap! Why didn't I call her earlier? Why did I assume she would be at her office?*

Gary turned left off of Broadway and took Canal Street, Lafayette Street, and Duane Street to get to Foley Square. When he was a few hundred yards from the courthouse, Gary found himself instinctively looking for a parking space. But that was an "Old World" instinct. Gary began the process of exterminating those instincts. He drove the bike over the curb, and across the sidewalk toward the high and wide staircase in front of the courthouse.

The Thurgood Marshall United States Courthouse has a wide irregularly shaped base that is six stories tall. Near the center of the base is a thirty-seven story square tower. The courthouse was built in 1936 and its outward appearance is similar to that of the US Supreme Court in Washington D.C. Both buildings were designed by the same man, Cass Gilbert. The building has a massive granite staircase that matches the staircase in front of the iconic and slightly older New York State Supreme Court Building, which is to the immediate left or north side of the federal courthouse. On the right side of the federal courthouse is the forty-story Manhattan Municipal Building. Cases for both the US Second Circuit Court of Appeals, and the US Southern District Court are heard in the Thurgood Marshall Courthouse.

Gary showed no appreciation for the iconic architecture as he gunned the engine and drove the motorcycle up the massive granite staircase. At the top of the stairs, Gary shifted the bike into neutral and turned the bike around on a wide concrete area in front of the columned entrance. When he was done, the bike was facing back down the staircase toward the street. With his back to the courthouse, Gary was a few yards to the left or south side, of the building's front door.

At 11:50 AM, Gary almost shut off the bike before his "New World" instinct asked, "*What if the bike doesn't start back up again? What if the marshals try to arrest me and I have to make a quick exit?*" Gary left the bike engine running.

Gary checked his phone. Mae had not responded to his text. He called her, and was surprised when she picked up on the first ring. Mae was also surprised. She again answered quickly because she thought Sam was calling her about the product liability mediation.

Mae said, "Sam, I'm going to be delayed at the courthouse. Judge Varroe—"

Gary interrupted. "Mae it's me, Gary."

Mae's tone became hostile. "Gary, stop calling me. I already told you I'm not leaving. I'm still in the middle of a deposition and a mediation. I'm also waiting to participate in a hearing here at the federal courthouse. I don't have time for you, and I'm hanging up now."

Gary knew she was serious, and he had to get her attention now. He spoke quickly. "Mae, I'm sitting outside the courthouse right now on my motorcycle at the top of the staircase just a few steps from the main entrance. It looks like a marshal is heading in my direction."

"You're what? Gary that's illegal! You're probably going to be arrested, and when they find out who you are, I will be professionally embarrassed. If you want to get a divorce TODAY, stay right where you are! Otherwise, hang up and leave now!"

"I'm not leaving until you come talk to me."

"Gary, that's bullshit! I'm not going to play this game. Get off the stairs and leave now!"

"If you want me to leave, then come talk to me for just two minutes. If you still want me to leave when we're done talking, then I'll leave."

"Gary, I'm not—"

"Mae listen to me for one second. You know me, and I'm not crazy! I wouldn't pull a stunt like this without a good reason. Give me two minutes to make my case."

"Make it one minute and you've got a deal. I'm leaving the building right now, but I'm hanging up to take another incoming call. If you're not in handcuffs by the time I get to you, I'll give you one minute to speak. But I'm probably still going to file for divorce."

"Mae, do you have your purse and laptop computer with you?

"Yes."

"Good, bring them with you." Mae didn't respond. The line went dead.

The short, stocky, fifty-seven year old US Marshal had been inside processing visitors. He heard Gary's motorcycle and caught a brief glimpse of the bike climbing the staircase. For a moment, the Marshal thought he was delusional. Marshal Stevens walked out the front door and looked to his left. Nope, it hadn't been his imagination. The Marshal took a couple of steps in Gary's direction, then stopped. What was he thinking? The biker might be a suicide bomber. Who else was crazy enough to violate the security of a federal courthouse by driving a motorcycle to the front entrance?

Tony Stevens, the short chubby marshal, concluded he was in over his head, and made a quick call on his portable radio. Inside the building was another marshal who had the training and the brawn to handle this kind of situation. Tony wanted to live long enough to collect his pension. He would let Marshal Madison deal with the biker. Tony had stopped walking when he made the radio call. With the brief call ended, Tony now just stood and stared at the biker. He was hoping the biker would simply drive away. The biker stared back wondering who was on the receiving end of the radio call, and what would happen next.

After a very long minute, the staring contest ended when Mae emerged from the building. She looked right, then left. She saw Gary and marched toward him. Marshal Madison emerged from the building a few seconds later and almost comically repeated what Mae had done by looking right, and then going left. He was four strides behind Mae.

Mae stormed past Marshal Tony without noticing him. Tony saw Mae and his demeanor changed immediately. "Oh Miss Seymour, what a surprise. How are you? Do you know the man on the bike?"

Mae kept marching without saying a word. She was angry. Her carefully planned day had been interrupted by Johnny and now her husband. Of the two, her husband was the bigger problem. He had made a fool, and possibly a felon of himself, by driving his motorcycle up the courthouse steps. Marshal Tony had just figured out that Mae was somehow connected to this idiot biker. Mae wondered if her career would survive. It wouldn't, but not for the reason she assumed.

Four strides later, the much taller, thinner, and younger Marshal Madison reached Tony's location. Tony held up a hand signaling Marshal Madison to stop. Thirty-two years of service had given Tony some rank, and rank had its privileges.

Tony said, "Let's give them a minute or so and see what happens."
Marshal Madison said, "Tony, I already called the police."

"Well then, maybe a minute or two will be all the time they'll get. If the NYPD gets here before the biker leaves, we'll let them handle it. If the biker leaves before the cops get here, my plan is to let him go. I know Ms. Seymour, and she apparently knows the biker. Maybe the biker is here to deliver an important court document." Tony's theory died almost before he finished saying it.

Mae yelled, "What the hell do you think you're doing?!"

Even with his helmet on and the bike running, Gary had no difficulty hearing Mae. Neither did the marshals. Gary was still astride the bike. He popped open his visor, but did not remove the helmet. Mae was on his right, between the bike and the building's main entrance. The two marshals were standing frozen about ten feet behind Mae. Gary noticed that she was not so angry that she had disregarded his instruction to bring her purse and laptop. On the other hand, maybe she brought it with her because she couldn't leave it anywhere in the courthouse unattended.

"Mae, there's an emergency. We have to get the hell out of here right now. I can explain everything while we're driving. I've got the second helmet with me, I brought a leather jacket, and leather pants for you. You've got to put that stuff on and come with me now!"

Mae's expression perfectly matched her words. "Are you insane?! I'm not going anywhere!" Gary tried to think of a time that he had seen her this angry, but could not. Mae wasn't finished.

"I thought I made it clear on the phone. I. Am. Not. Leaving!" "I've got three things going on right now and the biggest client meeting of my career this afternoon. I'm not going anywhere with you." Mae glanced around for a second, lowered the volume of her voice and added, "You're embarrassing me!"

The pause that followed was not intended to be an invitation for Gary to speak. Mae just wanted to take a moment to kill Gary with the two laser beams that were located where most people had eyes. She expected Gary's body to quiver in agony, then fall from the bike and die before it hit the pavement.

Gary didn't quiver, or fall, or die, so Mae said "I'm calling the cops. Don't be home when I get there tonight."

As she began to turn away, Gary yelled. "You promised to hear me out for one full minute, but you've done all the talking since you got here. Now shut the fuck up and give me my one minute."

The F-bomb was a tactic he had rarely used during their relationship. He knew he wasn't the dominant member of the relationship, and rarely tried to act like he was. The curse word made her stop, but something else made her turn back to listen. Lawyers hated to be caught breaking an agreement. Credibility was the coin of the realm. If Mae had to remain silent for one full minute to retain her credibility and win this, or any argument, she would do it.

Mae turned around, glanced down at her watch and said, "Go."

Gary thought for the briefest of moments. He didn't have time to explain the CME and the phone call from Blake. He had to boil the whole thing down to its essence. Just enough to convince Mae to get on the bike. If she did that one thing, then he would have time later to provide the details. Gary's new philosophy echoed through his head, *Do just one thing now!*

Gary began speaking quickly, "Mae, I know you don't want to believe this, but this entire city is going to lose electrical power in a few hours, and the power will stay off for days, maybe weeks. But long before the electricity goes out, this place could become a war zone. You – we – have got to get out of here now!" Gary paused, and then added, "It's going to be a lot worse than Hurricane Sandy!"

Gary could see a shift in Mae's demeanor, when he mentioned Hurricane Sandy. The Super Storm had hit New York on October 29, 2012 and done twenty billion dollars of damage to New York City and Long Island. The stock market had closed for two days, and the subway system had flooded and closed as well. All road tunnels into Manhattan except the Lincoln Tunnel had also flooded and closed. Gary and Mae's home was in an area that had been subject to a mandatory evacuation order. The home had survived relatively unscathed, but the disruption to their lives had lasted for weeks.

The storm remained a significant emotional event for many New Yorkers. Mae was one of them. The hurricane had forced Mae to stay in a hotel for two weeks where she had a reliable internet connection that permitted her to continue working. The storm had reduced her billable hours by almost ten percent for that two-week period. Gary and the girls had returned to the house as soon as possible. Mae returned later, after the home had been restored to its former condition.

"Hurricane Sandy? How could you possibly know that a hurricane is coming? I haven't heard or seen anything on the news. Nobody is talking about it. Besides," Mae said as she glanced at the sky for a moment, "the weather is fine."

"Mae, it's a little more complicated than that. It's not actually a hurricane, it's something far worse, and it will knock out the electricity. The whole story will probably be on the news within a couple of hours, but when that happens, it might be too late for you to get home. The roads could get jammed with traffic, and the subways might be overwhelmed as well. Eventually the subways and everything else will stop when the electricity fails."

Mae glanced at her watch. Gary's minute was not quite over so she couldn't walk away yet. "Gary, I told you on the phone, that I could live in my office until the lights came back on. This meeting is a bigger deal to the firm than a blackout would be to the city. Besides, how can the electricity get knocked out without a storm? How could you know something that CNN doesn't know? If it's going to be worse than Hurricane Sandy, then why isn't the Governor on the television right now issuing emergency orders?"

Gary reached out to take Mae's left hand in his right hand. It was a long reach. Gary pulled her close to the bike. It was better for her to ask questions than to walk away, but she was asking too many questions. There wasn't *time* to explain. He knew his minute was up.

"Mae, we don't have time for logic and reason. Do you love me? Do you trust me with your life?"

Mae's glare softened to a more quizzical expression. This was an argument she had never heard before. The answer didn't come automatically. She had to think for a moment. Her first thought was no, she didn't love him that much. In fact, at the moment, she was still thinking about killing him, or at least divorcing him.

Gary was studying her face with what he hoped was a sincere and pleading expression. Gary's torso was turned to the right as he looked at Mae. Behind her right shoulder, Gary saw one of the marshals approaching. The Marshal was tall and fit looking. Marshal Madison had decided to intervene the moment Gary took Mae's hand. To hell with Tony's seniority. The biker had escalated the exchange from verbal to physical. Perhaps it would continue to escalate. Marshal Madison wasn't going to let a woman get beaten up or shot while he watched from a couple of yards away.

"Ms. Seymour is there a problem?"

The Marshal's close proximity surprised Mae. Her demeanor changed completely as she pulled her hand from Gary's and turned to face the Marshal.

"Good morning . . . uh . . . Matthew." It had taken Mae only a moment to recall the name of one of the little people who worked in the Courthouse. She had seen him perform what she thought must be roving guard duties when she occasionally encountered him inside the building. Mae had never seen him outside the courthouse before, but Gary had also never before driven a motorcycle up the courthouse steps. Today would be a day for many firsts.

Mae smiled as she said, "Thank you so much for coming outside to check on me. No, there's no problem. Can you give us another couple of minutes? This crazy man is my husband," Mae faked a little laugh to show everything was fine between them, "and he's not threatening me or anything. He's telling me about an emergency . . . that um . . . occurred at our house. And he is, well, he is just about to leave."

"Ms. Seymour, I'd like to give you all the time you need, but this building is under federal jurisdiction and I've already called the police—"

Mae's mood shifted. The fake smile and honey-sweet routine hadn't worked. It was a rare defeat for Mae. She glared at Marshal Matthew Madison for a moment as he spoke, and then held up a hand to cut him off. He stopped talking instantly.

Marshal Madison was huge, but obedient. Like a Doberman. Pissing off the wrong person could get him fired, or transferred to a less desirable assignment. The Marshal determined he didn't need to assert his authority. *The police are on their way,* he thought. Marshal Madison glanced toward the street and saw a police officer standing on a step about halfway up the staircase. *In fact, a cop was already here. Fine. Let the cop take the blame for pissing off a prissy overpaid litigator. Wait, why is the cop just standing there? What's he looking at?*

Neither Gary nor Mae had seen the cop. Gary wondered for a second if Mae would give the Doberman a kill command, but Mae suddenly reached for her phone. Gary hadn't heard a ring tone. Maybe he hadn't heard it over the noise of the bike, or maybe Mae had the phone set to vibrate. Mae pressed the phone to her ear with her right hand. She put her left hand over her other ear so she could hear the call over the bike's still-running engine.

The caller was apparently someone Mae knew well. Her contribution to the call was seven words. When she answered she said, "Mae here," then "Are you sure?" and "Thank you." Then she hung up while the caller was still talking. The call lasted less than a minute, but Mae's body language had changed completely in that time.

Mae gave her husband of six years a long steady look before saying, "That's odd." Then Mae went silent, as she continued to look intently at Gary. He knew the look. He called it the "processing data" look. The content of the phone call must have been quite unexpected, and it was causing her to think. And think hard.

Gary couldn't wait for the silence to cure itself, so he said the obvious, "What honey, what's odd?"

"That was Perky on the phone –"

Gary interrupted, "Who?"

"Perky Perkins, you know, Amanda Perkins, my office assistant, we call her Per–"

Gary interrupted again, "Oh yeah. I spoke to her earlier. What did she say?!"

She said, "The meeting was just canceled."

This time it was Gary who filled the silence with several rapid thoughts. As soon as he could put his jumbled thinking into a coherent stream, he launched it at her. "THE meeting? You mean The MOST IMPORTANT MEETING of your career? The one that was CRITICAL to the future success of the law firm? THAT meeting just got canceled?"

Even as he vented, it occurred to Gary that his motorcycle rescue mission and the canceled meeting might have one key thing in common.

Her response wasn't defensive, just matter of fact. It was a professional, analytical tone that she often used in the workplace. The kind of detached clinical voice lawyers adopted when they were forced to backtrack on something they had just said.

"Yes, canceled. But there's more. Perky says she overheard part of a discussion between Mr. Donaldson, the firm's managing partner, and two of the firm's other senior partners, Mr. Able and Mr. Davis. Something big is happening. She says the firm's helicopter is flying in on short notice, and every senior partner that can fit into the helicopter is leaving the building as soon as possible."

As she finished speaking Mae looked up. Gary's eyes followed hers. A Sikorsky S-76 helicopter was flying low and fast going north up the Hudson River. Gary widened his gaze and saw another helicopter in front of the one he first spotted, and two other helicopters to the south of it. All were flying toward various destinations in the city. Again, the thought came to Gary. *Could this mean what I think it means?*

"Mae, I can't explain it all to you now, but I think those senior partners are running for their lives. I think they just found out what I already know – what I've been trying to tell you. We need to leave now! Anybody who is still standing where you are now when the rest of the city discovers what I know – and what those senior partners know – is going to be in the middle of the biggest riot this city has ever seen."

Gary paused, but Mae was still "processing." Gary plunged on hoping to finish the argument with something that would persuade Mae. "Mae I love you. Please trust me just this once."

Gary paused again before adding, "Mae the meeting has been canceled, so you're not really leaving work anyway. You just got the afternoon off."

Gary pulled the leather pants and jacket out of the bike's pannier and said, "Here put these on, and let's get the hell out of here!"

Mae was looking at him with surprise, almost wonder. It occurred to her that for the first time in their relationship, he possessed as much, or more knowledge than the people she respected most. *And he had acquired that knowledge before they had.* She was examining him like she examined clients, judges, and opposing counsel. It was not about *who* he was right now. His status as child-care provider, housekeeper, professor, and occasional lover didn't matter. It was about *what he knew.* He possessed information that was suddenly important to her.

Mae continued to study Gary intently as she processed the data. Boiled down to its essence, her job as an attorney was to think. She was a highly paid professional thinker. As a litigator, she was also expected to *do* something with the products of her thoughts, but if the thoughts weren't right then the deeds couldn't be right. Thinking was the most important part, and she was very good at it.

Gary was silent as Mae's beautiful brain took in all the data and processed it. He knew she was considering every fact, issue, angle, argument, and counterargument. From the newly acquired facts, she would develop several possible explanations and run each of them to ground. It was like having several conversations with different experts and pursuing every potential scenario to its logical conclusion. It was the kind of analysis that few professionals could do in their head without any assistance. For most of those who could do it, the task would have taken several minutes to complete.

After Gary's last comment, it had taken Mae eleven seconds to finish processing the data. She had arrived at the most intelligent, most logical conclusion that any human in her exact position at that moment could have achieved. Now that Mae was done thinking, it was time for action. It was time to execute the best course of action, in the smallest amount of time without hesitation. Even if it later turned out to be the wrong course of action, she would have no regrets if she had made the best decision she could from the information available at the time.

With her decision made, she took a quick look around at the people on the street who, if Gary were right, would soon be victims. There was nothing she could do for them. They were moving to and fro in their usual fruitless haste to accomplish the meaningless tasks they did every weekday as they struggled to pay their bills and retire from the workplace a few hours before they died.

With her now cold, professional eyes, Mae looked at her husband in a way that let him know that she believed him, and she might even still like him. She was now convinced Gary knew what he was doing. He was not like the hoard of pedestrians passing by. Gary had somehow determined some sort of disaster was coming, and he had come to save her. He had taken radical action, broken traffic and perhaps federal law, and put himself at risk to get her out of harm's way as fast as possible. Unlike the firm's senior personnel, Gary didn't have a helicopter at his disposal, so he had come to get her with the fastest, most agile vehicle he possessed. Everything was clear to her now.

Gary was a survivor. He knew what to do when the proverbial shit hit the fan. In that moment, she made a decision; one on which she never reneged. *She would be a survivor too.*

Mae handed Gary her phone, and put her purse and laptop computer into the recently emptied pannier. Then she kicked off her B. Brian Atwood shoes, and unfastened her Armani Collezioni skirt. The skirt fell neatly from her hips and legs and landed around her ankles on the sidewalk. As her skirt was falling, she slipped out of her jacket and tossed it toward the pannier. Then she picked up the skirt, and it followed the jacket.

Her husband, as well as dozens of passersby, who were unknowingly frittering away the last day of their serfdom, got one good look at a beautiful woman, standing at the top of the iconic courthouse stairs. It was a warm cloudless September afternoon, and she was wearing nothing below her waist but a red lace thong. It was the kind of thong a woman wore for her lover.

Mae took the oversized leather pants and slipped them on. She was equally fast with the leather jacket. She retrieved her phone from Gary and she put it in a jacket pocket. Gary handed Mae a helmet and then stuffed the Armani jacket and skirt into the pannier on top of Mae's purse and laptop. By the time the latch snapped closed on the pannier, Mae had the helmet fastened on her head. Her entire transformation, from consummate professional to biker chick, had taken less than a minute. And she'd done it all without saying a word.

Mae held the heel straps of her shoes in her left hand as she slid onto the bike, barefoot, behind her husband. Like most men, Gary had given no thought to his wife's footwear. But he also had not had a spare pair of her sneakers in his office, and he wouldn't have stopped to buy her a pair if he'd thought of it. Screw it. She would ride barefoot. Mae put her arms loosely around Gary's waist. She was still wiggling down into the seat when Gary shifted into gear and released the clutch.

As Gary looked to his front at the path his bike was about to travel, he was surprised to see a uniformed police officer almost directly in front of the bike near the top of the steps. As the bike lunged forward, the cop deftly stepped to his left, and Gary veered the bike to its left. A second later, he barely missed the cop.

Gary thought, *Where the heck had the cop come from?!*

As the bike made the sudden turn away from the cop, Mae's weight shifted unexpectedly, and Gary nearly dumped the bike.

Gary yelled, "Hang on, damn it!"

Mae didn't need to be told. She had already shifted her butt back to the center of the bike, and dropped her eight-hundred-dollar shoes so she could tighten her grip around Gary's waist. She turned her head to the right and squeezed her head and torso tightly to Gary's back. The bike's sudden departure had taken her by surprise. She had been a little out of practice, but now, they rode as one.

Gary righted the bike, hit the throttle, and shifted gears. Then he bounced down the stairs with the front wheel in the air for half of the journey to the sidewalk below. As Gary downshifted to take a hard right turn onto the street, one thought filled his mind.

He had never seen that red thong before.

Chapter 6:   The Beemer has landed.

Gary went north on Centre Street and continued onto Cleveland Place. As he drove, he took a moment to connect both helmets to the bike's intercom system. He set both helmets to "hot mike" so neither of them had to push a button to talk.

"Mae, can you hear me?"

"Yes, I can hear you."

"How are you doing?"

"Under the circumstances, fine I guess. Now that we're moving, perhaps you can tell me more about the big crisis, and your plan to deal with it."

Gary turned right on Kenmare Street, which would take him to Delancy Street and then the Williamsburg Bridge. "The plan is to get out of the city, and hunker down at home until the CME blows over, and the government can get things up and running again. Like I said, that could take a lot longer than it took for things to get patched up after Hurricane Sandy. As soon as we get home, we should hit the stores and stock up on essentials."

Mae said, "Gary, what's a CME?"

For the next few minutes, Gary relayed to Mae the information he had gotten from Blake. By the time he was done, he had already traveled across the Brooklyn-Queens Expressway and the Kosciuszko Bridge. Gary was now going east on the Long Island Expressway, or L.I.E. Gary increased his speed as he left the crushing congestion of Manhattan behind. There was a long stretch of silence between Gary and Mae as he aggressively steered the bike through traffic and Mae was left alone with her thoughts as she clung tightly to her husband.

Gary had intended to stay on the LIE until he got to the Sagtikos Parkway at Exit 53. However, shortly after passing Exit 38, traffic quickly slowed to a crawl and then stopped. Gary drove the bike onto the right shoulder, and then kept going east for almost a mile to see what the problem was. When he got to the point where he could see the flashing lights of multiple police cruisers and emergency vehicles, he decided that no cars or motorcycles would be permitted to pass through the crash scene anytime soon. Gary did a U-turn on the shoulder and drove back to Exit 38. Had he been in a car, rather than on his motorcycle, Gary would have been stranded in the traffic jam for more than an hour. He gave himself a pat on the back for having the clairvoyance to drive his bike to work that morning. Gary took the exit ramp off the interstate, and went south on the Wantagh Parkway. He got off at Exit W4E, and went east on the Southern State Parkway. With no commercial vehicles, and less traffic density, Gary relaxed slightly as he continued to speed east toward Islip.

After several miles of uneventful driving, Gary's phone rang. It was Hank. Gary told Mae he was going to plug his phone into the intercom system and take the call. She could listen in if she wanted. Mae said she would definitely rather listen to something else. She disconnected her helmet's audio jack from the intercom system and plugged it into her smart phone. Given his rate of speed and the fact that he was still occasionally weaving through traffic, Gary would have preferred not to take the call. However, getting Hank earlier had been difficult. Gary didn't want to start a game of telephone tag.

"Hey Hank have you had any coffee yet?"

"Yeah. Two cups."

"How are you feeling?"

"Still a little drunk, but I don't think I would blow above the limit on a breathalyzer, so I'm good."

Spoken like a true functional alcoholic, Gary thought, *if Hank was below the legal limit to drive, then he must be sober.*

Hank continued, "I checked the NASA site like I said I would."

"And?"

"And nothing. NASA's got nothing on their site about a huge CME, or any CME at all. I also couldn't find anything official on any other web sites." Hank was still under the influence of alcohol, but he was working hard to stay focused.

"Maybe NASA doesn't know about it because it was only visible from the other side of the world, when Russia was facing toward the sun."

"Gary, don't be stupid. NASA's sun-monitoring systems are on satellites in space. They collect data no matter where the earth is in its rotation. They've got one system called the Solar Dynamics Observatory which takes videos of solar flares. I watched a video of a small flare that occurred just a few days ago, but NASA has not released any data on the flare described by your Russian friend."

"Hank, he's not a Russian, he is an American professor who— never mind. Okay, so no data on the NASA site means what? That there's no CME and Blake was wrong about everything?" For a moment, Gary felt hopeful, then scared. If there was no CME, Mae would kill him.

Hank said, "No. If the CME happened, NASA definitely knows about it. But if the CME was so huge that it would inflict massive and widespread devastation, it's possible that NASA wouldn't just toss that information onto their web site. The federal government probably doesn't want to put everybody into a panic, just before most of them die. So the absence of information about the CME doesn't prove your friend was wrong."

Hank paused for a moment, then added, "It wouldn't be the first time our government lied to us, or withheld critical information. For some conspiracy nuts, the lack of proof is all they need to prove something exists. You know, like NASA didn't release information about the CME, therefore there must be a huge CME that's about to wipe out mankind."

"Well if NASA isn't going to release the data, then how do we know whether it's real or not?" Gary was glad Mae wasn't listening to the call.

Hank said, "Well . . . uh, for now we . . .uh . . we don't. If this thing is as big as your buddy Blaine said it was, then somebody else will –"

"Blake."

"What?"

"My astronomer friend, my buddy the American, his name is Blake, not Blaine."

"Um, yeah, whatever. Like I was saying, if this thing is really big, somebody is going to leak it. I mean, there must be several NASA guys who know about this. Those guys have families and friends who they are going to want to warn." Hank paused for a moment, it sounded like he was taking a drink. Gary hoped it was water, but suspected it was not. Before he continued, Hank let out a soft "ahh" sound, indicating he had enjoyed whatever he had just consumed.

"If this thing is going to end life as we know it, then the fear of being fired won't be enough to keep them quiet. I'm guessing that a few of those NASA guys are going to tell somebody, then those people are going to tell somebody, and eventually somebody is going to put it on their blog or tell a reporter. A little while after that, one of the networks will do a special live report on TV to the whole country. I mean look at you; how many people have you told?"

Gary paused for a second. "Um . . . nobody. Well I guess, just two, you and Mae. This information is not going to get released to a bunch of other people through me." Even as Gary spoke, he was being proven wrong.

"Okay, so maybe not through you, but at some point, one of the networks is going to say something. The first reports won't provide the whole story, but will instead say it's a rumor, or an unconfirmed report. They won't go whole hog initially, just in case it later turns out not to be true. But they'll still try to bump their ratings by being the first to release some information on what might be the biggest story of the century."

"So how long will it take for that to happen?"

"I'd say a couple of hours at most. Your friend Blaine said the CME was going to hit at about midnight tonight, right?"

"Yeah. And it's Blake not Blaine." Gary was having a hard time concentrating on both the conversation and his driving. Traffic seemed to be getting heavier and crazier by the minute. Some of his responses to Hank were deliberately delayed, as he forced himself to keep his eyes scanning to the left, right, front, and rear as he continued to drive as fast as he dared.

Hank said, "If the CME is going to hit tonight, then this story is going to go public today. At some point the networks, hell even the President, will be forced to say something."

Gary asked, "So what do we do in the meantime?"

"I don't know, prepare for the end of the world I guess."

Gary heard Hank take another drink. After another pleased "ahh," Hank continued, "The smart thing to do would be to grab some food from the grocery store before everybody else figures out what's coming, and hunker down. I haven't really thought that far ahead, but the odds are I'm not going to do the smart thing."

Gary said, "Well I have thought about it a little, and I'm doing exactly what you said. Mae and I are going to hunker down. I just picked her up early from work. I figure we can hunker down at the house – even for a couple of weeks if necessary. I'm on the bike, but as soon as I get to the house, I'll switch to the car and go buy some –"

Hank interrupted. "Gary you told me about your hunker-down plan during our earlier conversation. I've got to tell you it's a really stupid idea."

"You just told me that getting some groceries and staying put was a good idea. You just said that's what a smart person would do. So why is it stupid idea for me to do it?

Hank laughed, but it wasn't a ha-ha funny kind of laugh. "Gary, it's all about location, location, location. You still live on Long Island, right?"

"Yes of course. In Islip. We haven't moved recently."

This time Hank's laugh was more of a groan. Gary didn't have time for Hank's drunken antics, particularly since he was driving as fast as he could on a motorcycle through moderately heavy traffic. "Hank, what the heck is your problem?"

"Sorry, Gary. Let me tell you how I see it. You told me there's going to be a CME-induced blackout for a few weeks or maybe a lot longer. Now you're telling me you plan to ride it out in a suburb on Long Island that's what, about fifty miles east of New York City?"

"Hank, I don't have time for this crap. Get to your point."

"My point is you are stupid or crazy or both. What if Blaine is right? What if the lights go out, and they don't come back on for months? Hell, even if it's just for two or three weeks, how does the food get to New York City and Long Island? What if the CME knocks out cars as well as the lights? The store shelves will be empty in a day or two. What makes you think all those nice gang members in the city and on the Island are going to sit still in their dark Section Eight apartments and quietly starve to death? Why won't they go to your house, kill your family, and take what you've got?"

At the moment, Hank was saying some of the same things Blake had said; things that Gary hadn't fully processed. "Hank, like you said, my house is quite a distance from the city. You might be overreacting. Blake said it would be bad, but he also said he didn't have perfect data.

Besides, I have to go back to my house because that's where my daughters are. It's not like I could have left NYU, grabbed Mae and immediately fled west without my kids. I guess I was planning on staying at the house for a couple of weeks. Then, I guess, I don't know, maybe leave Long Island if things got really bad."

"You think I'm overreacting?" Hank burped before continuing. "Gary, there are eight million people in the city. If the blackout lasts for even three days, there will be no food on any store shelf. No food, no milk, no baby formula, and how are they going to get water? Doesn't water pressure require electricity?"

"Hank, I know it's going to get a little rough in the city, but how are they going to get to my place in the suburbs? Walk?"

"Yes, if they have to. But even if the folks in the city don't visit you, it's not going to be a picnic in the 'burbs either. Does your neighborhood have stockpiles of food and water on every corner, or in every household? Why does it have to be a gang member from the city who comes through your front door with a shotgun? Isn't there a gang problem in Central Islip? That's what, maybe ten miles away from you? Maybe they'll pay you a visit. But what if it's not a gang member at all? What makes you think your neighbor down the street isn't going to try to take your food by force?"

"Hank, I just don't think –"

Hank interrupted. He was almost having fun as he drove his point home to his dear stupid brother. The one who hadn't bothered to call him during the last three months as Hank went through the worst crisis in his life. "Gary, you're a fool. Eight million people are going to drive, walk, or crawl if they have to, to find food and water. Some of them will think the rich people out in the Hamptons will have food and water. But who knows, by the time they pass your place on the way to the Hamptons, maybe you, Mae, and the kids will have already been killed by someone on your street."

"Hank, I don't belie–"

Hank pressed on. "If you really think . . . even just suspect . . . that there is just the tiniest possibility that the CME is going to be huge, you need to get off Long Island *now!* Grab the kids first, but cross a bridge or get on a boat within the next couple of hours or," – Hank hiccupped – "or you're a dead man."

Hank hiccupped again, and then added, "When you get west of the city, keep running."

Gary spoke fast to finish his comment before Hank interrupted again. "Hank, I just don't think it will get that bad."

"You don't know how bad it's going to get. You have absolutely no idea. Nobody does. And by the time you figure out how bad it really is, it will be too late to leave. You must remember the first rule about panic."

"I thought the first rule of panic was 'don't panic.'"

"No. In a real survival situation, the first rule of panic is, 'He who panics first, panics best.' If you don't panic now and get your family off the Island in the next couple of hours, then it might be too late. After the roads are jammed with cars – cars that might stay parked on the road for months if their electronics get fried by the CME – you won't have the ability get off that Island. But if you panic now, and leave the Island, then what's the harm if the CME does *not* happen?"

Hank paused for a moment, but Gary had nothing to say. Gary was beginning to understand his brother's point. Perhaps, in this instance, it was better to overreact, than under react.

Hank continued, "Suppose there's no blackout, and hungry people don't come banging on your door? So what? What's the downside if you're not home when they don't come knocking? Hell, my place is west of the city. You can come here and stay the night. If nothing happens, you can drive back to your place in the morning. There's no downside to leaving the city before a potential life-ending crisis arrives. But if you don't leave now, and your buddy Blair is right, you and your family will probably be dead in a few days."

Hank's house was in Monroe, New York, about an hour northwest of New York City. In non-rush hour traffic, it would take Gary less than two hours to get from his house to Hank's. Maybe Hank was right. Maybe traveling to Hank's place before the CME hit was a good idea. Hank was, however, dead wrong that there would be no downside if the CME didn't hit. Mae had stripped out of her Armani skirt outside the front door of a federal courthouse. Comments about her exhibitionism were probably already on Facebook; perhaps photographs as well. Could Mae really go back to the firm with no repercussions? Would any client want her as their attorney? How could she possibly explain stripping down to a thong in public?

If the CME didn't happen, Gary would die. Mae would kill him. Her career would be the second fatality. If she applied all her lawyerly cleverness to Gary's demise, she would make his murder look like an accident. Then she could survive on the life insurance money until people forgot about her public striptease. Maybe she could go to school, learn a new profession, and change her name, or maybe she would continue to practice law by moving to a different state or country. In every scenario Gary could think of, Mae would be a widow.

Gary was having second thoughts about his reaction to Blake's warning. Taking Mae from the city on a motorcycle had been kind of extreme. Gary had accepted Blake's words as gospel truth, but according to Hank, there was no evidence anywhere to confirm Blake's warning. *What if Blake was wrong? What if Blake's message was a joke? What if someone had hacked Blake's phone just to . . . just to get out of class early?* Suddenly it occurred to Gary that there were students in his classes who had the talent, the resources, and the mendacity to do exactly that. *Have I been punked?* Gary replayed Blake's call in his mind. *It had to have been real. The voice was Blake's voice. How could a prankster fake the sound of Blake's voice?* On the other hand, the connection for the overseas call hadn't been the best. With the static on the line, maybe the voice really wasn't Blake's and Gary just assumed it was Blake because the caller said he was Blake. Blake was an NYU professor and plenty of students had heard him speak. What if one of them was a good impersonator, and the static had been faked? Gary had similarly assumed Blake's wife was who she said she was, but Gary hadn't found the phone number in a directory. He had simply called the number that the man who claimed to be Blake had provided.

Gary felt like he was going to puke. *Wait, what about the helicopters and the canceled meeting?* But Gary had no idea why senior members of the firm had left suddenly. Maybe they had just decided to hold the meeting at a different location, and Mae wasn't in the building so they left without her. *Crap, I can think of half a dozen reasons for the sudden departure of the partners, other than a CME.* Gary continued to drive, and his doubts continued to plague him. Then he caught himself thinking, *Man, I sure hope this CME is real and huge, because if a lot of people don't die, then I'll be – Wait, what? Would I rather have millions of people die, than suffer the embarrassment of a good practical joke by a student?* A small voice inside his brain whispered, *"Yes."*

It took effort for Gary to answer the question firmly in the negative. He even said the word out loud, "NO!" Convincing himself that he would rather be the victim of a practical joke, than a CME, was difficult. Even if he was a victim of a joke, Gary decided he would have to assume it was not a joke until he received hard evidence to the contrary. He needed hard evidence like the sun coming up tomorrow morning on a perfectly normal day, with all electrical devices fully functional.

Hank said, "Gary, what do you mean 'no'? No to what? Man, I thought you had hung up on me."

Gary had been so lost in thought he'd forgotten he was still on the phone with Hank. "Um, nothing, I was just thinking out loud. I was just trying to figure out why NASA hasn't posted any information on the CME. You were saying that if the CME is real I should not hunker down at my place in Islip. Instead, I should go to your place? If the CME is real, will your place be any safer? I mean do you think that being just one hour west of the city will be far enough?

"Will my place be safer?" This time Hank's laugh was full and loud. But it had a dark and ugly sound. "Let me tell ya something little brother. If this CME is real, and it's as big and bad as your buddy Blanch says it is, then all bets are off. I'm *not* gonna run. Your place on the Island will be in a kill zone within a day or two. But some of the city gangs will move west toward me, at the same time other gangs are moving east toward you. My place will be in the kill zone within three or four days, maybe a week at the most."

"So, your place isn't safe? Why would I go to your place if it isn't safe? Are you going to have to flee your home as well?

"I told you Gary, I'm *not* gonna run away. I'm gonna load my guns and wait for them." Hank hiccupped, then burped. "If they come through my door, maybe I'll take a few of them with me when I go."

"What?! Wait, that's sick . . . crazy! If you think you're place is going to get overrun, why don't you take the same advice you've gave me and bug out to someplace safer?"

Hank said, "Where would I go? And why bother? You've got a wife and kids. They are worth fighting for. I mean, well, the kids are anyway. What have I got that's worth fighting for?"

Gary noted Hank's dig at Mae, the "rich bitch" as Hank called her. Gary pressed on, "What do you mean, 'why bother'? You're still alive. Anything is better than dying."

"Maybe for you it is."

Hank's statement hit Gary like a punch. What the heck was Hank talking about? Hank sounded like . . . well, he sounded like he didn't care whether he lived or died.

Is Hank suicidal? I thought this was a conversation about the CME! What the hell did I miss? Gary had gotten completely absorbed in the conversation, particularly Hank's last comment and he wasn't paying attention to the increasingly bad traffic.

Gary's mind was abruptly bought back to reality when Mae screamed, "GARY!!"

Mae wasn't on the helmet intercom, but Gary could still hear her scream. She had been holding her phone in front of his chest. She had connected her helmet's audio cord directly to her phone so she could talk to Perky, her assistant back at her office. She was now punching Gary's chest with both hands trying to get his attention. As she thumped Gary, she let go of the phone.

Gary looked up, but it was too late. *What the . . .?* An "Oh shit!" escaped his lips as he turned the bike to the right and absorbed the impact.

A few minutes earlier, when Gary had connected his phone to the bike's intercom, Mae had connected her helmet's audio cable to her phone. Gary had assumed she was going to listen to a music play list. Mae had instead called Perky.

During the first quiet stretch of the ride, Mae had struggled to absorb what Gary had told her. Intellectually, she could understand how such a doomsday event could occur, but emotionally, it was very difficult to believe that such a thing was actually happening, here and now, *to her.* But *if* such a thing was about to happen, she felt obligated to warn the people she knew. At the same time, she was still worried that Gary and his friend were wrong, and she'd make an ass of herself if she warned somebody about something that didn't happen. After going back and forth on the issue, Mae had finally decided she could warn someone without taking ownership of the doomsday prophecy. She'd phrase it as a "'what if" scenario or a "have you heard" rumor.

Mae thought of all the people she should warn and came up with a very short list. Gary, and therefore her entire family, already knew. Mae's parents were dead, and she had no siblings. It finally occurred to Mae that almost all of the people in her "social network" were "professional associates" connected to her place of work. Mae thought about calling Johnny, but after some reflection, second thoughts, and hesitation, Mae decided to call her office assistant. Mae had invested more of her personal time in Perky, than anyone else at the firm. If the crisis was real, but Mae, Perky, and the firm survived it, Perky would have some hard questions for Mae. Questions like why didn't Mae give Perky a warning? And why didn't Mae call her back after Perky told Mae about the hasty departure of the senior partners?

Mae had taken that call on the courthouse steps before she got on the motorcycle, and ended the call abruptly with no explanation. If Perky was still at her desk, she was probably wondering what the hell had happened to Mae. Why had Mae not returned from the courthouse? It was settled. Mae would call Perky and tell her about the CME. If Perky deemed the warning worthy, she could warn others. However, if Perky was going to tell others, Mae would make sure Perky didn't reveal Mae as the source of the information. Mae decided that one call to one person would be enough; one call to one person with one message that would not be linked back to Mae. If people chose to take the doomsday message seriously, then fine. If not, then Mae had "done her duty" to warn others.

When Mae got Perky on the phone, she sounded more petrified than perky. Ironically, Perky picked up the phone at almost the same moment that Gary had told Hank he had told only two people about the CME. Mae was in the process of passing the news to what was left of the office staff.

"Miss Seymour, thank God you called. I . . . I didn't know what to do. After you and the senior partners left, a few other attorneys also left. I . . . and some other paralegals were . . . well we were thinking of leaving work early. We thought . . . we didn't . . . we don't know what to do. We think something big . . . something bad is about to happen."

"Perky, calm down. I'm calling because –"

"Miss Seymour, I've been talking with Gilbert, Tameka, and Elba. They're with me now. We don't . . . we're scared . . . I mean we're worried and we don't know what to do. Why did you leave? Why did the senior partners leave? Can I put you on speaker phone?"

Gilbert was the office mail clerk. Tameka, like Perky, was an assistant, and Elba was a paralegal who specialized in contract law research. The three of them plus Perky went to lunch together whenever they could, and occasionally socialized outside the office. Mae figured if Perky didn't put her on the speakerphone, she would just repeat everything to Perky's friends as soon as Mae hung up. Perky wouldn't be able to conceal the source of the information because Perky's three co-workers already knew Mae was the caller.

Reluctantly, Mae said, "Put me on speaker phone, and I'll tell you what I know . . . I mean, what I heard."

There was a short pause, then Perky said, "You're on," in a voice that sounded far away.

Mae didn't know Perky had been less than completely candid when she said there were three other people at her desk. The statement was true, but it was also true that there was a total of seven people at Perky's desk or standing close by. As Mae's voice went out on the speaker, all seven stepped closer. They used urgent whispers and hand motions to signal others to join them. They had finally found someone who was "in the know" and was willing to tell the minions what was going on. By the end of Mae's call, fourteen people were close enough to Perky's desk to hear Mae's final words.

Mae started with her pre-planned disclaimer. "Look, I really don't know what is going on, but –" Mae could hear an audible groan from the group assembled on the other end of the phone. It sounded like more than four people were listening, but Mae continued.

"But I'll tell you . . . I'll tell you what I heard." Most of the group were familiar with "lawyer-speak", and knew that Mae was about to tell them what she *knew,* and her opening comment had been the typical, "I-don't-want-to-get-blamed-for-what-I'm-about-to-say," disclaimer. The groaning stopped and they listened intently. Mae could almost see the group press in closer and lean toward the phone. They were listening more attentively than they would have been if Mae had skipped the disclaimer.

"Okay, guys, this is complicated. Well the *cause* of the problem is complicated, but the results on the ground won't be complicated. On the ground, it will be . . . I mean, I *heard* it will be bad. But I don't know anything about the science, and I didn't even hear this information directly from the guy who said it. And the guy that said it is *not* the same guy that talked to the senior partners before they all took off in the helicopter. At least I don't think he was because –"

For the first time in the six years that Perky had been working with Mae, Perky interrupted her. "Miss Seymour, please get to the point. Tell us about the problem – the bad stuff that you heard might happen. We know we can't tell anybody the information came from you."

Mae was stunned by Perky's blunt interruption, but it conveyed the anxiety the office staff was feeling. Mae's effort to distance herself from her message lessened. "I was told that all of New York City will experience an electrical blackout. This thing, this CME flare thingy, whatever they call it, is coming from the sun. It might hit an area a lot bigger than the city, and it might last for days, maybe weeks . . . maybe even longer than that."

There, I said it! Mae stopped talking. There was a pause of a few seconds as the group by Perky's desk looked around at each other. They were almost embarrassed. They figured some sort of crisis was about to happen, but they couldn't imagine something of this magnitude. Had Ms. Mabel Abigail Seymour, lost her mind? They'd seen other attorneys crack under pressure and turn to the bottle or drugs, and then be forced to leave the firm. Crazy talk by itself had never been grounds for termination, but Perky and her friends had never heard an attorney talk this crazy.

The group members were all looking at Perky. It was her desk and her phone. Without a spoken word, the group selected Perky as their spokesperson. It was time for her to say something. Anything. Perky said what 98% of people would have said in the same situation, "Miss Seymour . . . are you . . . are you sure? A blackout that lasts for weeks? That's never happened before. What you said sounds . . . well it sounds crazy. And you're scaring me, I mean us."

"Well like I said, I didn't actually talk to the guy who talked to –" Suddenly, Mae thought, *Screw it. In for a penny, in for a pound.* It was something her dad used to say. As a young kid, she hadn't understood it because she hadn't known the pound was a British dollar.

Mae gave it to them as straight as she could. "My husband is convinced that a long-term blackout is going to happen. He believes it will be widespread throughout New York City, and if it goes on long enough it will lead to extensive looting and riots. This event might make the September 11th attacks look like a walk in the park. I'm not trying to scare you, but that's what my husband believes. He got a call from a guy who is an expert in this kind of stuff. My husband has known this guy for a long time, and he got an advanced warning from the Russians. We're getting out of the city right now. I guess we're going to hunker down at home until tomorrow morning. By then we should know whether this thing is real. Frankly, Perky, I'm scared too."

Mae was espousing Blake's credibility at about the same time Gary was feeling like he would puke because he had been punked. Mae was almost as shocked as her listeners to hear her own words. Had she overstated the case? Did she even believe what she just said? Mae had never "hunkered down" in her life, and she didn't want to start now. When Hurricane Sandy hit the south shore of Long Island, Mae had reserved a room at the first Hampton Inn she could find that was unaffected by the storm. Mae left Gary and the girls in Islip, and used the hotel room as an office until normal operations in the city and at the firm resumed. This time around, she apparently was going to hunker down, because that's what she had just said on the phone. In reality, Mae didn't know what to think or do. Since she had gotten on the bike, she had been alternating between believing the CME was imminent, and believing nothing at all would happen. Perky and a couple of the other listeners who had daily interaction with Mae were beginning to take Mae seriously. They knew Mae was not crazy, or at least she'd never been crazy before. Mae might be wrong, or she might have gotten bad info, but Mae must have believed what she had been told, or she would not have said it. Perky tried to remember a time when Mae had been dead wrong about something. She couldn't come up with anything; not one single thing.

This time, the group didn't need to take another silent vote. Perky jumped in, "When is this supposed to happen? How can we protect ourselves? Where should we go? Why isn't the media talking about this? What is the government doing about this? Can't they prevent it somehow?"

Mae now regretted making the call. She didn't have any answers. She hadn't thought through what she was going to say before she called, and hadn't anticipated this reaction. *What did you think you were going to do, Mae? Tell your assistant the world was going to end, and then hang up on her? Um, yeah, that's pretty much what I thought. Well, how's that working out for you?* Mae stalled for a moment as she tried to think of what to say.

Mae sat up a little straighter on the bike, and glanced over Gary's right shoulder. She hadn't been glancing over his shoulder very often, because he was driving like a maniac, and it tended to make her ill to see it. When she was slouched behind his back, the engine noise was muffled by the helmet, and she had been trying to pretend they were out for a normal bike ride. The sudden accelerations and decelerations made the fantasy difficult. She might have had better luck imagining she was on a radical carnival ride.

She looked up occasionally only to get a fix on the bike's location and then estimate how much longer the gyrating ride would last. When she looked up this time, she screamed "GARY!"

Gary didn't need an intercom to hear his wife scream his name. But he needed a miracle for what was coming next. Gary was driving too fast, but he'd been doing that since they left the courthouse, and that's not why she screamed. As they were driving on the Southern State Parkway traffic volume had increased, while traffic speed decreased. The number of vehicles in the three eastbound lanes of the parkway was building to rush-hour levels, but rush hour was still more than three hours away. Unlike rush hour, however, the drivers were not moving with a single-minded purpose.

Some were driving as typical, midday drivers running errands. The exits with a shopping center were getting a lot of on-and-off traffic. Other drivers were changing their driving style as they drove, and becoming more aggressive. Gary saw more than one driver contentedly driving in the right lane, and then suddenly move to the left lane, accelerate and then get frustrated by drivers moving too slowly. More and more drivers were becoming increasingly erratic. More and more of them were driving recklessly, like Gary.

As Gary watched the traffic, he started to think that he wasn't the only person who knew an astronomer, or somebody else "in-the-know." Perhaps the CME was real and news was starting to spread. Perhaps people like Gary were telling lots of other people about the CME. Gary didn't know yet that his wife was one of those people and she just announced the apocalypse on a speakerphone to a crowd of fourteen people. If he had known what Mae was doing, he would have told her to hang up. How many people would those fourteen tell, and how many others would *those* listeners tell?

Gary's uncertainty about whether the CME was real was still making him queasy, but he started to feel like he hadn't been punked. Or maybe he had been punked, but a lot of other people had been punked as well. How many people heard the news from the senior partners in Mae's firm, who left in the helicopter almost an hour ago? How many of those messages eventually reached the drivers on the road with Gary?

To Gary, it seemed that the news was apparently spreading exponentially, even as the mainstream media remained silent. Gary had not been listening to the radio so he didn't know that a local talk show host had recently told his small but dedicated audience that a doomsday CME was coming. The host had gone rogue. Like Gary, the host had a friend who had access to the raw solar satellite data. The host felt he owed his listeners a warning, so he had given them one without bothering to tell his producer what he was about to do.

When ordered to stop speaking and to recant what he had just said, the host refused. The host ranted about the CME for almost two full minutes, before the station manager was able to pull the plug. There was almost a full minute of dead air time before the station cut to a lengthy unscheduled commercial break. When the commercials ended, the host was gone and the station manager explained the doomsday CME announcement had been a hoax. More of a pre-emptive retaliatory act really, according to the manager, because the host had somehow figured out that he was being investigated for a terrible crime and was about to be fired. The manager implied, but did not explicitly say, that the terrible crime involved the molestation of little children.

The manager was lying. The host hadn't been under investigation. In ordinary times, the manager would have been sued for slander within weeks of making his announcement. The slander was not the manager's idea. He was reading from a script provided to him by a federal agent under the authority of a Presidential Executive Order, the existence of which had been previously unknown to the manager. The agent had been disappointed by the manager's response time. He had contacted the manager when the host was just twenty-two seconds into his doomsday rant. Under the President's authority, a department within the National Security Agency monitored all radio and all television content all the time.

There were just six companies that owned over ninety-two percent of all radio and television stations in the United States. When the White House wanted to influence the content of the information that was being fed to the public, it took only six phone calls. In this case, the agent contacted the station manager directly. Afterwards, calls were made to the CEO's of all six companies. The CEO's were ordered to shift to previously recorded programming if they had the slightest concern that a host might go rogue. Any future rogue announcement regarding a doomsday CME, or anything else that might panic the public, from any station could result in criminal charges, and the cancelation of the company's FCC license to broadcast. If there was a doomsday crisis, then the President himself would announce the news to the masses when he was damn good and ready.

As usual, the six companies complied without complaint. But on Long Island, the damage had been done. Within the small dedicated fan base on central Long Island, the host was popular and credible. The manager's claim that the doomsday warning had been a hoax, was ignored. Had the host himself recanted the story, many listeners might have dismissed the CME story as fiction. But the host had refused to recant even after he had been threatened with a lengthy jail sentence. He was in handcuffs and being taken out of the station shortly after the manager's scripted slander message ended. The talk show was not syndicated, and the listening audience was not large, but some of the listeners passed the message to their friends and family. Some of those message recipients called, texted, and e-mailed additional recipients, who in turn told others.

Gary was completely unaware of the rogue radio message, but he was seeing its effects on the highway in front of him. Some drivers had heard the broadcast directly, while others got the message in a phone call. A few other drivers got the message in violation of state law as they received and sent text messages on their hand held devices. One way or another, many drivers were now thinking the unthinkable as they struggled to come to terms with the unexpected message. *Life as you know it is about to end, and you're probably going to die.* The effect of the doomsday news on the highway traffic, was determined by how each driver responded to the news, if they had heard the news at all.

Some drivers heard the doomsday news and believed it almost immediately. Some arrived at their conclusion logically because they were fast and effective thinkers, others got there with almost no thought at all, because they were predisposed to believe the unbelievable. In normal, everyday life, the predisposed Believers were quick to believe whacky conspiracy theories. Most of their friends called them kooks right to their face. But when something extraordinarily unbelievable really happened, their low normalcy bias enabled them to embrace the abnormal rapidly. They almost *wanted* big, crazy, even deadly things to happen. It would somehow justify their existence as well as all the kooky crap they'd been saying for years. Most Believers took immediate action in response to the news.

Other drivers did the opposite. The Deniers heard the news and rejected it. The story must be false, ridiculous even. *There's no way such a thing could happen in America! Well, not to me anyway.* Deniers rejected the bad news, but were still distracted by their attempts *not* to think about it. Denial of such an enormous event could not be accomplished in one fell swoop. It took ongoing effort for Deniers to avoid the unavoidable.

Deniers tended to pay less attention to their driving and slow down in whatever lane they were in. Some moved to the middle lane on the three-lane parkway to let cars stream by on both sides as they decreased their speed by several miles an hour. Some changed the radio to a music station, or turned the radio off and hummed their favorite tune. Deniers overcame their denial very slowly, or not at all. If they survived, it was usually by accident or good luck.

Slow thinking Ponderers were also on the road. They heard the news, and took a long time to think about it. Some of the Ponderers would eventually believe, others would not. The defining characteristic of the Ponderers was the lengthy amount of time it took them to arrive at either conclusion. Regardless of what lane they were in, the Ponderers' speed of travel tended to decrease so they could focus on their thinking. With such an immense issue to contemplate, some Ponderers reached out for assistance with phone calls and text messages. This made them inattentive and erratic, as well as slow.

A fourth type of driver was those who panicked. The Panickers heard the news, thought about it and believed it, but they didn't know what to do about it. They tended to choose a course of action, but then change their mind and choose another. Some went fast then slow, while other Panickers did the opposite. Some went left then right, as others did the opposite. The Panickers were like wild cards and they provided random pockets of insanity in all the lanes. Some Panickers were so overwhelmed, they chose to do nothing at all. They drove to the side of the Parkway and came to a full stop. They treated the situation like a bad thunderstorm, and parked their car hoping the crisis would pass in a few minutes.

The fifth and final type of driver was the Oblivious or Obliviants. The Obliviants did not receive the doomsday news prior to the massive parkway pile-up that was about to occur. They tried to keep driving as they normally would, but they couldn't. Some of the drivers in the first four groups had radically changed their driving style after getting the bad news, and it was forcing the Obliviants to make changes as well.

The Believers who were traveling near Gary began making one of two choices. They either continued to drive east but now at a faster pace, or they reversed their direction of travel to go west. The Believers made their choice quickly, and attempted to execute it even more quickly. After events like 9/11 and Hurricane Sandy, many Believers had prepared "bug-out" locations in upstate New York. It was now bug-out time! Some eastbound Believers quickly reversed their direction of travel, so they could get off the Island and away from the city. Some of them went to the right, got off at an exit, and then got back on the parkway going west. Others took, or attempted to take, a more expeditious route by moving into the left lane, slowing almost to a stop, and then crossing the median at a "No U-Turn" point, or any relatively flat stretch of ground that was not obstructed by vegetation or a guardrail.

Other Believers, like Gary, wanted to flee west, but were first forced to go east to retrieve loved ones, bug-out supplies, or both. The eastbound Believers increased their speed, but they also wanted to warn others. So the fast-moving Believers made phone calls and sent text messages as they drove. This made them inattentive and erratic, as well as fast. Some of the Believers, who first needed to go east before fleeing west, were on the other side of the Parkway and driving west when they got the news. Some of those Believers waited for an exit to reverse their travel direction. Others took the more immediate option and attempted to cross the median – where they were met head on by eastbound Believers pulling the same stunt in the opposite direction. At the very few places where it was possible to cross the median, cars were crossing chaotically in both directions, and entering the left lane at very low speeds. Things went to hell in the left lane first.

Fast-moving Believers who were already east bound, initially moved to the left lane to hasten their trip home. But as the median-crossing cars suddenly began entering and exiting the left lane, the fast-moving Believers moved back toward the right. At the moment, the right lane was moving faster. Gary was listening to Hank on the phone as the highway havoc began to unfold in front of him. Fast movers in the left lane were being forced to suddenly screech to a halt, or quickly bail into the middle lane without checking their mirrors. In the middle lane, Deniers and Ponderers plodded along at speeds below the limit, and made it difficult for anyone to cross from one outer lane to the other. The right lane was jammed by Obliviants exiting at their regular destination, and by a crush of Believers who were seeking to use an exit, rather than the median, to reverse their direction.

The Southern State Parkway has no shoulders. However, for much of its length, on the right side where a paved shoulder could have been, there is a sandy grass strip about the width of a car. As the speed of traffic suddenly slowed in all three lanes, accidents began to occur. Some Believers took to the grassy strip to pass other vehicles, or to avoid rear-ending a car which had suddenly stopped in front of them.

The highway turned into hell on wheels. As Obliviant fast-movers went left and slow-movers went right, they crisscrossed with Believers through the Deniers and Ponderers in the middle. The parkway traffic that had been moving at ten miles an hour above the speed limit a short time ago, disintegrated into deadly chaos. Accidents simultaneously occurred in all three lanes. For some drivers, the doomsday news became a self-fulfilling prophecy. They died before midnight.

When Mae screamed, Gary was steering the bike onto the grassy strip behind a fast moving Believer, just as a Panicker in a Prius swung onto the side of the road and came to a full stop right in front of the Believer. The Believer slammed on the brakes of his full sized Ford sedan, but he still hit the Panicker's Prius at 45 miles an hour. The Ford's airbag deployed and the driver was uninjured. The impact of the Ford launched the Prius like a kicked football. The punted Prius did a half turn to the left, and hit the ground perpendicular to the grassy strip. The Prius flipped onto its roof, and slid to a halt completely blocking the width of the strip.

Gary had followed the Ford onto the grassy strip at a high rate of speed, and then become distracted by his brother's suicide ideation. When Mae screamed, Gary looked up. He had only one chance to save his life and Mae's. Gary couldn't go left because bumper-to-bumper cars in the right lane were like a wall. He could have gone straight for a few yards by squeezing past the Believer's car, but then he would have driven into the overturned Prius. Locking up the bike's brakes on the sandy grass prior to hitting the Prius would not have prevented the deadly effect of the impact.

Gary's only option was an immediate right turn. He leaned hard and made the turn. As he righted the bike, he suddenly wished he had taken his chances on the locked-brake option. There was a three-foot berm immediately in front of him and thick brush on the other side of it. Gary leaned slightly to his left as he attempted to aim the bike between two tree trunks on the far side of the berm. Then he hit the bottom of the slope like a ramp in an extreme motor-sport event. Some of the slow moving Deniers and Obliviants glanced right and caught a glimpse of the flying motorcycle.

The impact of the slope caused the motorcycle's suspension to compress hard at the bottom of the slope and release near the top. The suspension's release and Gary's high speed launched the bike skyward. For Gary, time slowed to a crawl. The bike's flight lasted mere seconds, but to Gary, it felt much longer than that. He had ample time to take in his surroundings. He thought about what was happening, and what was going to happen.

His honest-to-God first thought was, *Man what a ride!* After the first second of flight, Gary noticed he was flying over the top of the brush. The flight path he had chosen between the trees turned out to be a good choice. Branches from the trees rubbed his shoulders on both sides, but didn't knock him off the bike. He saw a small clearing to his front, but whether he could land in it was not something he could control. As the ground rushed up beneath him, Gary thought, *This is going to hurt!* With his brain working at hyper-speed, Gary raced to think of how he might survive the landing. He wasn't a novice rider. He had landed a few small jumps before, but nothing, *nothing* like this one. Then, *Crap! Mae is on the bike with me! Would she survive? Would she even be able to stay on? Is she holding on tight enough? What is she doing back there?*

Mae was imitating glue back there. She was squeezing herself tight to her husband with both arms, just as she had done for the bumpy flight down the courthouse steps. When Gary had stood up a little on the foot pegs just before hitting the ramp, she had too. With her additional weight, the landing was a lot harder than it would have been, but her weight had probably saved their lives. It kept the tail end of the bike lower than it would have been, which made the rear wheel hit first. Unlike a professional stunt jumper, Gary had taken none of the required preparatory steps at the bottom of the ramp to ensure the landing would go well. All he had was the glue-like, almost dead weight of his lovely wife. *Would she be enough?*

The spine-crushing jolt of the rear wheel was immediately followed by the forward-projecting impact of the front wheel. It took every bit of Gary's strength to keep himself and Mae from going over the handlebars. As soon as his center of gravity was back behind the handlebars, he hit the rear brake hard for a full second with his right foot. Then he made a quick left turn to avoid hitting a tree in front of him as he exited the far side of the small clearing. On the bumpy ground of the forest-like environment, Gary slowed to a stop and put his left leg on the ground. His thigh was quivering with adrenalin. For a moment, he thought his leg would give way and he, Mae, and the bike would fall over.

Gary braced for the screaming fit he knew was coming from Mae, but there was nothing much for her to say. He'd been driving too fast, shit happened, and they nearly died. *Nearly* died. Which meant they were *still* alive. And uninjured. And the bike was still functional. Beemers could take a beating, and keep on being. Mae had not yet reconnected her helmet to the intercom. She lifted her visor so Gary could hear her clearly.

"Loving, dear husband of mine, whatdoya say we slow down a bit, and maybe think about driving a little slower when traffic gets crazy?"

"Yes dear. Good idea."

We have to keep moving if we want to stay alive. Gary put the bike in gear, and slowly threaded his way back through the brush toward the road. When he got to the top of the berm, he paused and looked to his left. He estimated that at least thirty cars had participated in what turned out to be a massive pile up. Fender benders and far more serious impacts littered the highway for more than two-hundred yards. Steam and smoke were rising from several of the wrecks, and loud car alarms on some of the mangled vehicles covered the anguished cries of the injured and dying.

Some drivers had stopped and gotten out of their cars to help, while other drivers were still attempting to drive through the accident scene. The moving vehicles beeped their horns at the do-gooders and walking injured who blocked their way. Gary drove east along the top of the berm until he got past the overturned Prius. The driver had been the only occupant. She had exited the vehicle and was now leaning against it as she looked west, toward the noisy accident scene. Her right hand was pressed against a gash on her forehead that was bleeding profusely. She was in her thirties and wearing jeans and a gray sweatshirt with a blue SUNY College logo. The upper third of the logo had been obliterated by her still dripping blood.

She briefly made eye contact with Gary as he drove past her on the berm. Her face was expressionless. She was shocked, but not going into clinical shock. Gary wasn't worried. He had heard that even superficial head wounds bled profusely. Gary turned left and drove down the berm and back onto the parkway. A long stretch of clear pavement had been created on the east side of the Prius by the roadblock effect of the accident scene. The time between Gary's departure from the pavement and his return to it, had felt like an entire lifetime or two, but it had taken less than three minutes.

Back at the firm, Mae's phone call had ended less than three minutes ago. Mae had dropped her phone to grab her husband, glue-like, with both her hands, just before the bike hit the bottom of the berm. The phone had fallen to the side of the bike, and dangled by the helmet's audio cord for a second before it got sucked into the spokes of the rear wheel and destroyed as the bike launched into the air. The fourteen listeners at the firm had heard Mae's scream, the crash of the Prius being punted by the Ford, and a hard grunt from Mae when the bike hit the ramp. After that, there was dead silence.

The firm's employees were convinced they had just heard Mae die. The entire group panicked immediately. By the time Gary got the bike back onto the pavement, not one of the fourteen employees was still within twenty yards of the phone. All of them were exiting the building as fast as they could. Perky was among them. Mae no longer had a phone, but even if she had called to tell the minions she was still alive, nobody would have answered.

As he drove away, Gary looked over his left shoulder at the accident scene. From the amount of damage, he knew many vehicle occupants were severely injured. Some might die from their wounds before help arrived. Like some of the drivers in the wreck, some of the Emergency Medical Technicians and rescue crews had also heard the talk show's doomsday warning. As a rule, First Responders don't respond when they're in a life or death crisis of their own. Gary accelerated away from the scene. The victims were either going to live or die, and there was little he could do to alter the outcome. For one brief moment, Gary was thrilled by the mayhem. Perhaps the crazy driving and the god-awful wreck meant the CME was real! *Maybe Mae won't murder me!* It was a selfish thought, and Gary forced it from his mind. *Or maybe the CME isn't real, and a lot of other drivers are as gullible as I am.*

Gary reverted to his plan. *Act as if the CME is real, at least until tomorrow morning.* If the CME was real, and affected New York and the United States the way Blake had said it would, then the victims behind him were just the first of many other casualties. Gary couldn't save even a few of them, but if he was fast, and competent, and smart, and very lucky, he might be able to save his wife and daughters. To a remote observer, uninvolved in the coming catastrophe, Gary's decision might seem brutal and inhumane; which it was. But it was also the law of survival that most Americans never experienced, while many of the world's other residents confronted it daily. Many Americans would not survive the coming disaster. Many do-gooders who tried to assist the doomed might instead join the doomed. Gary wasn't going to take that chance.

Like Gary, Mae had also looked back on the accident scene. She knew people at the scene needed help. When Gary didn't go back to help, she started to yell at him to stop. Then a sudden thought cut her off. *Daddy had been right!* When Mae had met the good-looking young professor while she was in her third year of law school, it was an attraction of opposites; Mae was a "type A" personality. Her father was a partner in a prestigious firm. He had gotten there with hard work and no connections. When he was a child, Mae's father had been abandoned by his father. It was possible that her father's parents had never married. Her father had been raised by his mother.

As a single mom, Mae's grandmother supported her son with two part-time jobs, church charity, and occasional public assistance. While he was growing up, Mae's father had been told everyday by his mother that he was special, and he would someday make something of himself. She required him to study hard, and made him promise her that he would *be somebody.* She needed to believe there would be a payoff for her sacrifices. The boy made the promise to his mother. To himself, he promised he would *never* again be as poor as he had been as a child.

His mother died before he graduated from college. The dead mother's son kept his promises and grew up to be Mr. Ellis Anderson Seymour, Senior Partner and Director of the Litigation Division of Sullivan, Hopkins, and Moore in New York City. It wasn't the biggest or most renowned firm, but in the international business community, the firm had a reputation for excellence. The relatively small firm had a habit of taking on seemingly unwinnable disputes, and snatching victory from bigger, better-known firms. Eventually, the law firm of Sullivan, Hopkins, and Moore was able to pick and choose their cases, and they charged whatever they wanted.

Mae was her father's pride and joy, the apple of his eye, and the son he never had. It was a good thing that Mae's intellect and personality predisposed her to the legal profession, because that's where Mr. Ellis Anderson Seymour's "son" was going, predisposed or not. Unlike her father, Mae grew up in the lap of luxury. Her dad put himself through mediocre schools with a combination of loans, a full time job, and grants for the impoverished. Mae, on the other hand, attended expensive schools, received no financial aid, and arrived each fall in a current model year car.

Mr. Seymour was convinced *nobody* was good enough to marry his Mae. But he wanted grandchildren to carry on his bloodline, so he knew he would have to compromise at some point. The initial meeting between Gary and Mr. Seymour was very uncomfortable for Gary, but unlike several other suitors, Gary came back a second and third time. And he kept on coming. Gary wasn't intimidated by Mr. Seymour's gruff manner, or his penetrating, insulting questions like, "How could an Assistant Professor at NYU ever make a mark in this world?"

Gary answered such questions with questions of his own like, "It depends on what kind of mark you want to leave; do you want to spend your life keeping up with the Joneses? Or do you want to achieve something more meaningful like shaping hundreds, perhaps thousands, of young minds whose collective mark would be incalculable?" Mr. Seymour wasn't offended by Gary's implied insult that his entire career had been nothing more than a contest to see who could die with the most loot. He was thrilled to come across a young man who wasn't easily intimidated. Someone who could take it, and dish it back out. It didn't bother him that his potential future son-in-law was an academic idealist. He knew his daughter would wear the pants in the family.

Gary didn't have the blue-blood background and social connections of the elite New York community, but neither did Ellis Anderson Seymour. So Seymour did not hold that against him. For his little girl, Seymour was much more interested in a man who would do *anything* to keep his daughter – his bloodline – alive and well, and if possible, happy. Growing up, Seymour had seen this quality demonstrated by his mother almost every day. Her tenacity, and Seymour's imitation of it, had kept Seymour off the streets, in school, and eventually landed him near the pinnacle of the New York legal community.

Most other observers did not detect Gary's tenacious streak. He was not athletic. He was handsome, but still something of a geek. He tried to avoid stressful situations, and he had a laid back "Type B" personality. All of that was true right up until Gary was forced to defend someone or something that was dear to him, which was almost never.

Seymour had discovered the well-concealed trait during his cross-examinations. Where most people saw a sleeping pussycat, Seymour had detected a crouching lion. In the practice of law, Seymour had often seen hidden characteristics of people and legal disputes, and it made him the success that he was. Seymour was confident of his assessment of Gary.

On his daughter's wedding day, he heard the oft whispered, and sometimes not whispered question, "Why is she marrying him; what does she see in that guy?" Seymour just smiled as he handed out cigars and free drinks at the very expensive reception at a five star hotel in Manhattan. Throughout his legal career, he'd heard similar critical questions in courtrooms and from colleagues. Such criticisms usually reached a crescendo shortly before Mr. Ellis Anderson Seymour got the verdict he was looking for. Verdicts few had believed were possible.

Four years later, when Mr. Ellis Anderson Seymour dropped dead of a heart attack while working late at his office one night, nobody still living believed Seymour's judgment of Gary's character would prove to be correct. Not even Mae. Mae liked Gary a lot. Love seemed like too strong a word. Gary adored her, and her father had a high opinion of Gary. Daddy had also wanted grandchildren. After all the things Daddy had done for her, it didn't seem like too much to ask. Especially since Daddy had left a structured trust fund that provided massive financial incentives for Mae to marry and have children. Mae figured the domestic partnership and the kids would not interfere too much with her more important long-term goals of a law-firm partnership, and a mansion in the Hamptons.

Dropping a couple of kids along the way would make it more difficult to maintain her perfect figure, but she thought she could handle it without too much trouble. She was right. Her law firm had its own state-of-the-art gym, sauna, and locker rooms for both genders. They gave Mae an additional excuse to spend time away from home as she twice got her body back to its pre-pregnancy shape. During the last phone call with her father before his sudden death, she had voiced her usual suspicion that her husband was a little too good at playing Mr. Mom. Mr. Seymour had responded with the same assessment he had provided to her in dozens of previous conversations.

"Mae, that man does for you exactly what you need for him to do for you. Right now, you need a Mr. Mom to take care of your two young girls – girls who have Seymour blood in their veins. But believe me sweetheart, if you ever need something truly extraordinary from him, he will deliver. If I were in a foxhole, I'd want Gary next to me. It gives me great comfort to know that if your survival is ever at stake, Gary will be there to pull you through."

To Mae's amazement, she was now thinking seriously for the first time, that Daddy had been right! Gary was driving away from the dead and injured. He had to do that to increase *her* chances of survival. It's exactly what Daddy would have done if he'd been driving the bike. Of course, if Daddy had been driving the bike, her broken body would probably be in the tangled wreckage near the overturned Prius. There was no way Daddy could have avoided the accident as Gary had done. Mr. Seymour had hated motorcycles and had never driven one. For the second time since she got on the bike, Mae thought, *Gary is a survivor. I will be a survivor too.*

With the crash scene behind them and a clear highway in front of them, the last few minutes of riding had seemed almost boring. Gary drove fast, but more attentively. His realization that nearby first responders, who were still responding, would be occupied for the next several hours, encouraged his caution. Gary reconnected both helmets to the intercom and asked, "How are you doing back there?"

Mae said, "I'm fine. I've got no broken bones, and I'm still breathing so I'm fine. My cell phone wasn't so lucky. It was in my hand when we left the road back there. I dropped it and it got destroyed."

"Well we probably won't have time to get it replaced today, and by tomorrow, who knows? Maybe all the cell phones won't work. I guess we'll have to get through the rest of today with just my phone."

Mae said, "No we won't. The phone that got crushed was the law firm's phone. My personal cell phone is at the house. I almost never use it. It's probably not even charged up."

"We'll have to remember to charge it when we get home, or more likely we'll charge it in the car while we drive."

Mae said, "Drive where? I thought we were going to do some shopping and stay at the house."

"Look Mae, before the um . . . before the bike left the road back there, Hank told me some stuff that we need to talk about. We might need to change our plan"

"Why? What stuff?"

"He said if the CME is real, we shouldn't hunker down in Islip. He said we should leave the Island and get west of New York City as fast as possible. He thinks if we don't leave right away, we might not get a chance to leave later. The blackout effects of the CME might last too long for us to be able to survive in the suburbs."

"So we should go west? To where?"

Gary said, "What if we went to Hank's house today? If we stayed the night, then we could reassess the situation in the morning. If the CME causes a widespread blackout, then we'll be glad we're not trapped on Long Island. If the CME's impact is not severe, then we could just go back home. If we decide to go to Hank's, we should leave as soon as possible. We should pack the car and utility trailer with food and other essentials, because if the devastation is severe, we won't be returning home anytime soon." Gary had already decided that he, Mae and the girls *had* to go to Hank's. He was hoping Mae wouldn't put up a fight.

"Gary, you want to pack the car and utility trailer, and leave Islip because your drunken brother said so? That's a lot of work and panic for something that might not happen."

"Mae, I know this is a difficult decision. We have no solid proof that the CME is real and that it will cause widespread devastation. But think about your meeting getting canceled, the senior partners leaving in a helicopter, and that huge crash on the highway that nearly killed us. What do you think all of that was about? Don't you think there are already a lot of people who think this CME is going to deliver a knockout blow to New York?"

"Sure Gary, a lot of people might think that, but back in the 1930's a lot of people thought the Earth was going to be invaded by aliens because they heard a story on the radio. The point is, all of the CME believers could be wrong." Mae was referring to Orson Welles' *War of the Worlds* radio show, which was broadcast on the CBS network in October of 1938. Many people apparently tuned in late to the realistic, but fictional broadcast, and panicked because they thought they were hearing a live news broadcast about a Martian invasion of New Jersey.

Mae continued, "Gary, I got on this bike, because you convinced me we needed to get out of the city. Fine, I agree that leaving work early and waiting to see what tomorrow brings is a good idea. But now you're telling me we should pack up all our worldly possessions and leave Long Island today? To do that Gary, we would have to go back through the city we just left! That makes no sense. Let's stick with the plan and stay at the house until we *know* whether the CME is real!"

When Mae argued from emotion rather than fact, she tended to exaggerate. Gary knew there was no way to fit all their worldly possessions into one car pulling a small utility trailer. "Mae, I understand what you're saying, but if the CME is real, we don't want to be –"

Mae cut him off. "I don't think you do understand. I don't think you could possibly feel the same way I do. You spoke directly to your friend, what's his name, Blake? And he told you about the CME, but I've only got one witness, namely you, and all you can tell me is something that somebody else said. That's called hearsay, and it's not admissible in court. You can't count Hank as an independent witness. He's a drunk who only knows what you told him."

Gary said, "What about the executives from your firm who left so suddenly? Don't you think they fled the city because the impact of the CME will be huge?"

"I'm convinced they left, but Perky couldn't tell me why they left. The meeting was canceled. Meetings get canceled all the time. Maybe one side or the other simply backed out of the deal. Or maybe one of the key players got an urgent call, and left to participate in a more urgent deal. Who knows, maybe they decided to change the location of the meeting, and I wasn't in the building so I didn't get to go along. The possible explanations are endless."

"Mae, don't you think there are other Blakes out there? Other people with hard evidence, who called their friends and family and started spreading the news? Don't you think the big crash we just survived was the result of drivers getting phone calls that told them about the CME?"

"Gary, I've seen a lot of stupid drivers on this road, do a lot of stupid things. I've even seen a couple of pile-ups that were almost as big as the one we just left. That's why I usually take the train. Yeah, the drivers did seem to get weird all at once, but again, it's not evidence I could use in court, and it doesn't prove what they may have heard is true."

"Okay, counselor, let's play your game. Suppose I call Blake as my first witness and he testifies to what he told me. Mae, he *saw* and examined the raw data on the solar flare that's going to hit earth! It's an X-70 flare; which means its way bigger than any flare ever recorded. He's an expert. He knows what he's talking about."

"So what, Gary? Suppose he's right, and the sun tossed off a flare. When you explained this CME stuff to me at the beginning of this ride, you said most CME's miss Earth, or cause no damage when they hit Earth. So maybe this flare is no big deal. Or how about this; what if a big flare did happen, and a *really huge* CME is going to bitch-slap the world, but it explodes on the other side of the planet? Maybe it takes out China or Russia instead of the United States. Just because Blake is an expert in CMEs doesn't mean he can perfectly predict that *this* CME will wipe out New York City."

"So what are you saying Mae? Do you want me just to assume the CME isn't going to cause us any problems at all? Do you want me to take you back to your office, and we'll just forget the whole thing?"

"No. I just think we should stay at our house until we get enough evidence to figure out what we should do next. Getting out of the city was a good idea. I agreed with you on that, and that's why I told Perky, and some others back at the office to get out of there. The city could become a pitch black war zone by toni–"

Gary cut her off. He sounded angry. "You did what?"

"I called Perky to explain–"

"When did you call her?"

"I called her after you disconnected from the intercom to call Hank. If the city is going to become a war zone, then I wanted to let Perky know. I don't want her to, you know, die." Mae hesitated for a second and then said, "You know Gary, it just occurred to me that when you did your flying motorcycle trick back there, my call to Perky got cut off. God knows what she and the others think happened to me. They probably think I'm dead. Oh, crap. What if I'm wrong – what if *you're* wrong about this CME? I'll never be able to look Perky in the eye again. I wouldn't even be able to go back to the firm. Perky wasn't the only one who heard what I said about the CME."

So that was it, thought Gary, *with the CME just several hours away, Mae's biggest fear was she had misinformed Perky, and Mae would be too professionally embarrassed to go back to work.* Gary almost laughed. A little while ago, that had been *his* biggest fear as well; that Mae might kill him, if Blake's predictions proved to be incorrect. Mae had just confirmed his fears. If the CME didn't happen, Gary would have to wake up before Mae did, grab a toothbrush and some clothes, and rent an apartment for a few months. He didn't want to hasten his demise by sleeping next to his assassin.

"Mae, I've got good news for you. Blake would not be wrong about something like this, which means I'm not wrong, and neither are you. So the good news is that Perky, like most of the other city dwellers, will probably die very soon. The city will become a large ghost town, and you will never have to look her in the eye again and be embarrassed by what you said."

Gary didn't mention to Mae that a small part of him still worried that Blake's call had been a prank. The crazy driving and multi-car accident had temporarily suppressed his fear. If the call had been a prank, a lot of other people must have been pranked as well.

"Gary, you're an ass!"

"Actually Mae, I am a little ticked off, because your stupidity increases the odds that we – you and me and the girls – will not survive this experience."

"Gary, I am many things, but stupid is not one of them. What the hell are you talking about?"

"Mae, for the next twenty-four hours or so we have to act like this thing is real and it will have devastating effects. If we don't, and the CME's effects are horrific, then it will probably kill us. But here's the tragic part, and it's really two tragedies. First, the more people who get the news, the less likely we are to survive. As you mentioned earlier Mae, we are traveling east, which puts us further and further on the *wrong* side of the city."

Mae had no quick rejoinder. She had excellent litigation skills, but her real-world survival instincts sucked. Gary continued. "The point is, Mae, that if we don't go home as fast as possible, grab the kids and a few essentials, and leave again, then we might not be able to get back through the city. We can't afford to stay in Islip tonight, and wait to see how bad things are in the morning. If the devastation is really bad, then everybody else will be trying to leave as well, and at that point, we might not have a functional car. We've got to bug out to the west and put as much distance as possible between us and the city. If too many people find out about the CME this afternoon, then the roads might be impassible before tomorrow even comes."

"Gary, I'm not stupid. I get it."

"I don't think you do Mae. How many people did you just tell about the CME? How many people are they going to tell? And how many others will *they* tell? It's possible that just by word-of-mouth alone, half the city could get the news within the next couple of hours. And what are they going to do Mae? Many of them are going to do what we are doing, and a lot of them are going to do stupid stuff that results in accidents like the one we just left."

"Gary, how was I supposed to know that we were going to go home, and then go back through the city? Huh? Prior to Hank's call, you told me the plan was to hunker down at our place in Islip. Now the plan is changed, and you want to hunker down at Hank's. Well I didn't know that. I didn't know I was supposed to keep everything a secret."

Gary wasn't finished yet. "I said there were two tragedies. The first is the possibility that we will not get off the island alive because the roads are jammed. The second tragedy is that warnings don't help most of the people who get the warning. Who did you warn, and what will they do with the information you provided?"

Mae thought this was about the longest lecture she had ever received from Gary. He might be right, but she still didn't like it. If she had been in his classroom, she would have been looking at the clock and praying for the minutes to move faster. "Well duh, Gary, you already said they will empty the store shelves. So I guess they'll hunker down, or more likely get the hell out of the city, just like us."

"Will they Mae? Do they have that much common sense? How many residents of New York and New Jersey voluntarily got out of the way of Hurricane Sandy before the storm hit? How many stayed put, and did not have the ability to survive the aftermath with no help from the government or anyone else? For this CME, how many people are going to be able to survive for several weeks, or longer, without electrical power? What percentage of the population can think clearly in a crisis, and perform even the most basic life-sustaining functions like staying warm and dry without electricity?"

"Get to your point, Gary. Your condescending lecture does have a point, doesn't it?"

"The point is that your warning would be wasted on at least ninety percent of the population. Your warning merely panics people who have no viable survival option. They'll just spend more time being scared before they die tired. Is that your intent? Would you visit a slaughterhouse to inform all the sheep that they were about to become lamb chops? Warnings are a waste of time because the vast majority of Americans do not have the capability to respond effectively to a crisis."

"Gary, maybe I would visit the slaughter house to warn the sheep. You said the warning would be wasted on ninety percent of the recipients, but what about the other ten percent? Doesn't that minority benefit from the warning? We are here on this motorcycle right now because you received a warning from Blake. Are you saying that he should not have warned you? All I did for Perky was the same thing Blake did for you."

Gary hadn't seen his situation as similar to Perky's until Mae explained it to him. Occasional sloppy thinking had a short life expectancy when your mate was a litigation attorney. Gary thought, *Mae's got a point. If I hadn't taken Blake's call, I would still be on campus right now and oblivious to the coming CME. Am I among the ten percent who will benefit from a warning?*

Gary's tone was a bit softer when he said, "I hadn't thought about it that way Mae. Your warning to Perky was like Blake's warning to me. I also still don't know whether you and I are in the minority that will benefit from a warning, but that takes us back to my earlier point. I hope we are in the ten percent that can do something to increase our chances for survival, and I wish all the best to other members of the ten percent. But right now I am selfishly thinking about what is best for us personally – you, me and the girls."

Gary paused but Mae said nothing. He had already said she was right, what more was there for her to say? Gary continued. "So yeah, I guess I do think the masses are entitled to a warning, but not if that warning reduces my chances for survival. If I were in a movie theater that was on fire, I would probably get myself to the exit before I told other people about it."

Gary paused to think about what he just said, *Am I really that selfish?* Then he continued. "Mae, what we need to do for *us* – to increase *our* chances of survival – is not to give anymore warnings. Many of those who receive a warning at this point will panic, others won't. Others will do the smart thing like we are. Both groups could cause our escape route to get blocked, just like the Parkway behind us is now blocked. The truth is, we might not be in the ten percent that effectively respond. If the CME is as bad as Blake said it was, then everything we do might not be enough. But our chances for survival are better if nobody else finds out about the CME until after we get off the Island."

"So screw everybody else until we get what we need; is that it?"

"Yeah, pretty much."

"Gary, I didn't know you could be such a cold, hard son of a bitch." Mae's tone was analytical, not judgmental or critical.

"Your dad did. That's why he let you marry me."

Mae scoffed. She heard the comment, but said nothing. She thought, *Yes, I'm beginning to believe Daddy saw more in you than I did, but I'm not quite ready to admit that out loud.* With all the talk about warnings, Mae began to wonder if there were now sources other than Blake for CME information. As a lawyer, Mae never voluntarily relied on the testimony of just one witness for any significant issue.

Mae said. "Gary if the senior partners at the firm, and the drivers on the highway were told about the CME, then Blake can't be the only one who knows about the CME. Is there somebody else you could call about this?

"Yeah, maybe." It was a good idea. Gary began thinking about who he could call next.

"Well, do you have somebody in mind?"

"I'm thinking, Mae. Give me a moment."

"Well, while you're at it, do you know anybody who can give us a better offer than the one you got from Hank? Getting out of the city might be a good idea, but depending on your brother for our survival isn't. I mean, I know he's your brother and you love him and all, but Gary if you could be objective for just one minute you'd have to admit that your fat, ex-convict brother is an alcoholic loser, who can't hold a job, and he probably has PTSD. We need a better option. Do you know anybody else who lives west of the city who might put us up for one night? In a doomsday scenario I'm guessing we'd have better luck with someone we randomly picked out of a phone book than your brother."

"Mae, you're being unfair. My brother doesn't have PTSD. In a tight spot, I would absolutely trust him with my life. He spent ten years in the Army and deployed five times. He's the only guy I know who has been shot at several times and lived to tell about it."

"Well you just talked to him Gary. How does he sound right now? Is he in fighting shape and ready for a domestic deployment, or drunk off his ass?"

Gary thought about his brother's slurred speech, and knew he wouldn't win an argument with Mae about Hank's current physical and mental toughness. Gary changed the subject. "Actually Mae, there is one person I can call whose name isn't Hank or Blake. Why don't you stay on the intercom, and I'll connect the phone so we can both hear what he has to say. His name is Ralph. He's an NYU professor I know."

Chapter 7:   Goodbye Ralph.

Gary decided to call Ralph Forester, a history professor. Most of the people who knew Ralph thought he was a conspiracy nut, and they thought he was obnoxious. Gary agreed with the conspiracy nut assessment, but he thought obnoxious was too strong a word. Ralph just really believed the things he said. He called them "conspiracy facts," not theories, and told anybody who would listen, "to do their own research," which almost nobody did. Ralph had an assertive, some said aggressive, manner of speech, and he seemed to phrase things deliberately to shock the listener. There was no easy give-and-take with Ralph. He fired "conspiracy facts" like bullets from an automatic weapon, bang, bang, bang! Then he'd say things like, "Now what do you think of that?!"

If Ralph had spent more time listening and less time talking, he might have won more converts. But Ralph always appeared to be in crisis mode, like something bad had already happened, and immediate action was necessary now! Most listeners looked around, saw no emergency, and wrote Ralph off as a kook. Gary had been born and raised in New York. He was accustomed to obnoxious people. He also didn't mind the occasional dose of Ralph's rapid-fire "facts." They sometimes served as an entertaining distraction for Gary. Gary sometimes went to lunch with Ralph, when Blake wasn't available. Gary respected Ralph's passion and high energy level, but the constant intensity made a meal less enjoyable.

The students loved Ralph. Like Ralph, the classes Ralph taught were high energy. Nobody fell asleep in Ralph's classes, and few students ever skipped. Ralph wasn't an easy grader, but his classes were fascinating. Ralph did an excellent job of teaching the curriculum while weaving in his "conspiracy facts." The students loved the facts and occasionally got an extra point by mentioning them on the exams. Gary knew Ralph was a "prepper" even though Ralph didn't openly advertise that fact. Like Hank, Ralph could probably handle himself well in a crisis. Gary briefly wondered why he hadn't called Ralph earlier, but the answer came immediately. Like the infrequent lunches, Gary suspected that a phone call to Ralph would be unsettling. On the other hand, what did Gary have to lose? Besides, Mae needed another witness. Gary scrolled through his phone's contact list, and called Ralph.

Ralph answered on the first ring. "Hello, Doug?"

"No Ralph, it's uh, Gary, Gary Adams." Gary didn't mention that Mae was on the line.

"Oh." Ralph sounded disappointed. Clearly, he had been expecting a call from someone else, and hadn't looked at the number when his phone rang.

"Look, Ralph, I know this call is unexpected. I apologize for that. You see um, well something has come up. Something *big*. You're one of the few people I know who would um, understand. This thing is um, well it seems kind of kooky, but –"

Ralph interrupted. "Gary are you talking about the CME that's going to hit the East Coast?"

Gary was stunned. "Um, yeah, but how the hell did you –"

"Gary, I've got contacts in lots of places, including NASA. I'm not a lone conspiracy nut. Sometimes we run in a pack." Ralph chuckled before continuing. "We talk to each other and trade information. I have multiple sources who say this CME is the proverbial big one. They're talking about a widespread blackout that starts on the east coast and covers fifty percent or more of the United States. It will last for months. Now look Gary, I'm kind of busy right now and expecting an important phone call so –"

"Ralph, wait! Don't hang up. I could use . . . I could use some advice."

Ralph's tone changed. It was the first time Gary had asked him for advice, with the intention of following it. After the brief exchanges in the hallways, and the longer lunchtime conversations, Gary was now, for the first time willing to take Ralph seriously? Well, it was a little too late for that, and Ralph's tone conveyed that message.

"So you know about the CME Gary, and you're wondering what you ought to do, right?"

"Yeah. I'm taking Mae out of the city and we're going to hunker down –"

Ralph interrupted. He often didn't let people finish their boring sentences. "Great idea Gary. So you're all prepared for a crisis like this?"

"Well, um, no, not really, but it's never too late to –"

"You've done nothing, right? After all those conversations we had over the last few years, you still did nothing?"

"Look, Ralph, it's nothing against you, but that shi–, I mean that stuff you said seemed a little crazy. I mentioned some of it to my neighbor one time, and he laughed at me."

"That's called normalcy bias. People are so used to everything being normal, that they can't conceive of things becoming abnormal very, very, quickly."

"Well, I'd like to think I was not a victim of normalcy bias, but the truth is all I've got is about a week's worth of food at my house, and a few flashlights and batteries. How about you Ralph are you prepared?" Gary was trying to get back to the purpose of his call. He needed to get his family to a safe place.

Ralph's tone got serious. "Yes, Gary. I, my family, and some close friends have made extensive preparations."

Gary wasn't surprised, but he wanted to know the depth of Ralph's preparations. Did Ralph have room for four more people? "So um, how prepared are you?"

"Well hopefully we can survive completely off the grid indefinitely. We've got canned goods and other stuff that should last at least a year. But we've also got gardens, chickens, and fruit trees to provide us with a perpetual food supply. The canned food is just a back-up plan. You know it wasn't too long ago when the majority of Americans could and did provide their own food supply. Now it seems that everybody expects the government to fix every problem and take care of them. Well those folks are going to learn the hard way the government can't and won't do that." Ralph seemed to be having fun talking about the topics he loved most. He no longer sounded anxious to end the call.

"You can be self-sufficient, indefinitely? Really? Where?" Gary didn't add, "Tell me where you're going, so I can take my family to your location," but that's what he really wanted to know, and Ralph knew it.

"Gary, what my wife Jean and I have done is not particularly difficult. Anybody can do it with a little practice, and a lot of time. We've got a few acres in the country and we work with some like-minded people to produce vegetables from raised-bed gardens, meat from rabbits, and a steady source of protein from laying hens."

"But you still need machines, right? Won't the CME shut down your tractor and whatever else you're using?"

Ralph laughed. Now that it was too late, he finally had an attentive audience. "No Gary, we don't need any machines at all. Just a few hand tools. That's one of the benefits of raised-bed gardens. They're five hundred percent more productive than a traditional garden, and they don't require a roto-tiller. We do have a small tractor, but if it breaks, we'll still survive. Besides, the tractor is so old that it will be unaffected by a CME or EMP. It doesn't have electronic fuel injection, or microchips."

"Ralph, I don't know anybody – except, you I guess – who even thinks that they can be self-sufficient. I guess this modern world made us rely on the big corporations and the government. Maybe Mae and I could come by, and you could show us how –"

Ralph interrupted. He knew where Gary wanted to take the conversation, and he wasn't going to let him go there.

"You're right, Gary. Americans pissed away their collective inheritance of liberty and individual responsibility, and turned themselves into sheep. I call them sheeple. Ignorant parasites who are ripe for the slaughter. But we didn't do it by ourselves; we had a whole lot of help. More accurately, we were manipulated."

"Ralph, I'm more interested in the few acres you mentioned." Gary thought if he could keep the conversation going, Ralph might give him what he wanted. Gary felt like a hostage negotiator, except he wanted to be taken, not released.

Ralph ignored Gary's comment. "Gary, who do you think runs this country, Congress? The President?"

"Ralph, where are you going with this? What's this got to do with the CME and staying alive?"

Ralph again ignored Gary's response. "You've heard me talk about central banks before. Did you ever visit *ZeroHedge.com, or TheEconomicCollapseBlog.com*? What about the book, *The Creature from Jekyll Island*, by Ed Griffin? I gave you a copy, did you read it?"

Gary remembered the book. He could even picture it on the shelf where it sat in his campus office. There was a layer of dust on it. "Sure, I remember it."

"I didn't ask if you remembered it. Did you read it?"

"Ralph, that book is more than 600 pages long! I mean, I already have a lot of regular reading to do, just to stay current in my field. But that book –"

"Gary, I told you it was a long read, but an easy one. It reads like a good novel. It even has pictures for goodness sake. And you would have known all that if you had bothered to read a couple of chapters. The book is the most shocking 'who done it?' of all time."

"Okay, so who done it? And what's this got to do with surviving the CME?"

If Gary wasn't desperate to find a safe place for his family, he would have hung up by now. He was starting to suspect that Ralph wasn't going to do anything for him; except perhaps give him the adult-equivalent of, "Nanny, nanny, boo-boo. I told you so!"

Ralph said, "Well first you have to understand that our nation's currency supply is owned by a private banking system, called the Federal Reserve. The private bankers literally create currency out of nothing. Through the fraud of fractional reserve banking, every bank in the country can loan out nine make-believe dollars for every dollar they have on deposit."

"Ralph what's all that got to do with the CME?

"I'm getting to that. Over the last one hundred years, the private central bank of the United States – the Federal Reserve – has been deliberately ruining our country. Their whole purpose was and is to make the United States progressively more socialist. They made citizens progressively more dependent on the government by design. Very few Americans realize that the same globalist oligarchs who own the banking system and our currency, also own the mainstream media companies. The media is not just biased, it is *owned*. And the propaganda networks want the sheeple to be ignorant and easily exterminated at the appropriate time."

"So that's your point? The globalist elite want lots of Americans to die, so they blew up the sun to deliver a devastating CME to the United States? Ralph, you're right. These bankers really are powerful." Gary's sarcasm was obvious.

"Gary, I understand your sarcasm, but I want you to listen to me very, very closely because unless you've got a ham radio, this is the very last conversation we are ever going to have. The elite globalists, our ruling class, *never let a crisis go to waste.* They will use this crisis to increase their control. The oligarchs did not create the CME, but if it hadn't come along by an act of God, they would have created something like it eventually. Something like a nation-wide EMP. In fact, they still might detonate some EMP devices, if this CME doesn't cause enough death and destruction."

"So you knew a CME or EMP was somehow going to be delivered by the um, elite globalist oligarchs, and that's why you set up a farm for yourself in the countryside?" Gary had tried to keep the incredulity out of his voice, but he knew he hadn't been completely successful.

"Yes."

Gary was shocked. Gary could not – would not – believe that any group of people who lived in the United States would deliberately destroy their own country. Yet that's what Ralph truly believed! Now, Crazy Ralph was in a much better position to handle a natural disaster that was real, because he believed in a crazy conspiracy theory that wasn't.

For the sake of his family, Gary could not tell Ralph what he was thinking. *Ralph was insane. Lucky, but insane. I've got to tone things down a bit if I'm going to get something, anything from Ralph that might be helpful.*

"You know what Ralph? That's a lot to take in, and it does sound a little crazy, but I believe it all. I admit it has taken me longer than it should have to get here, but I believe you now, and I believe in what you are doing – have done – about it. Why don't I travel to your location, and Mae and I will work with you – for you – to make your farm a success. We'll bring –"

"Sorry. It's too late. We don't have room for you and your family."

"But Ralph, my kids, my wife –"

"Gary, I've been telling you about this stuff for years. I even gave you a free copy of *Jekyll Island*, which would have been a massive wake up call, if you had read it. I've spoken passionately to you about the need to get prepared for a crisis more than a dozen times. Why do you think I was so passionate? I *knew* this moment would come. I *knew* that I did not have the time and the resources to make preparations for you and others like you. You are responsible for you. I am not your keeper. You had plenty of time, and plenty of money to do what I did. But you chose not to. You and others like you, wrote me off as a kook, a conspiracy nut. Now it's too late."

"So that's it Ralph? You're taking a little victory lap here, knowing that my wife and kids are likely to die? You're not going to share some of your stuff to keep us alive?"

In a steely tone, Ralph said, "What happens to your family is your responsibility, not mine. If you and your kind had listened to me, then together we could have educated others and perhaps gotten enough taxpaying citizens, to work together and fix the problem before the entire system exploded."

Gary wanted to ask, "How the hell could we have stopped the sun from exploding?" but didn't. Instead, he said, "But now it's too late for that Ralph? We can't somehow still work together to get out of this mess? You're going to hog all your resources for yourself?"

"Gary, don't you dare give me that shit! If you had prepared for *any* crisis, then you would be at least partially prepared for this one. I've been working my ass off for years to be debt free and to prepare for whatever the oligarchs and Mother Nature might throw at us. In addition to my full-time job, I've worked nights and weekends, seven days a week for years. Jean did too. She worked right alongside me and got her share of blisters and backaches. During that time I also, quite unselfishly, spent hundreds of hours – away from my family and my preparations – to warn and educate people like you. Almost all of that time was wasted!"

Ralph paused for a second, as if he needed to catch his breath. "You ignored me. Not even five percent of you listened and took appropriate action. When I told people to prepare for a crisis, they refused. Some people told me that if the crisis ever came they were going to come to my place. Really? They got the warning, chose to do nothing, and their 'survival plan' is to steal my stuff? I'm not going to let that happen. All of you were too busy doing what? Watching football? Playing video games? You know what I was doing? I was shoveling shit, turning over compost piles, and building raised-bed gardens and a chicken coop. I enjoy football as much as the next guy, but I haven't watched a game in three years. Now your ignorance, stupidity, and sloth are my fault?! That's bullshit! You made your choices, and I made mine. So be a man and deal with it!"

Gary started to speak, but Ralph cut him off.

"You people are like the lazy animals in the story of the little red hen. You did nothing to prepare. The little red hen tilled the soil, planted the wheat, raised the crop, harvested the wheat, and ground it into flour while you did nothing. Now you want a slice of the bread. That's not going to happen, Gary. I don't have any bread for you. Even with all my preparations, I don't know if I'll have enough food for myself, and those who worked alongside me. The easy living is over, and many, many people are going to die. They ignored me to their peril. By the grace of God, and my extensive preparations, I hope that my family is not among them."

"But my family will die, and you're okay with that?" Gary was furious. Ralph was ignoring Gary's pleas, and pursuing his own agenda. If Gary had known of any other potential lifeline, he would have terminated the call after telling Ralph to fuck off.

"Gary, I have no idea if your family will survive or not. But if your family dies, they will die by your own hand; the lazy uninformed hand that failed to prepare for the inevitable catastrophe. You chose to fiddle in a world on fire. A world that was surely going to explode one day. And now it has. But who knows? Maybe you'll get lucky. Every disaster has a few lucky survivors. But realistically? Realistically, the vast majority of the unprepared people will probably die in the next few months."

Gary again struggled to keep his anger in check. If he hadn't forgotten, in the heat of the conversation, that Mae was listening to the call, it would have been harder for him to say what he said next. Gary swallowed his pride, and his voice quavered as he said, "Ralph, I'm begging you – for the sake of my wife, my kids – please give me something, anything that might help us to survive this thing. You know so much! Please give me something to help me save a few lives without any further assistance from you."

"Okay Gary, I'm running out of time here, but I'll throw you a bone. Build a Faraday cage to protect your sensitive electronics."

"Huh? What's a faraway cage?"

"Gary, I really don't have time for this, so I'm going to tell you just once. When this CME hits our electrical grid, every sensitive piece of electronic gear, particularly those pieces that have microchips in them like computers, phones and cars, might get fried and become useless-"

"But how –"

"Shut up and listen. I really am going to say this just once. A Faraday cage is a metal box or screen that prevents electrical pulses from getting into the cage or container. Anything inside the cage that is not touching the exterior metal should be protected from the electrical pulse. If you had a shipping container, you know the eight-by-forty foot steel containers that are used to ship goods across the ocean, then you could make a few modifications and protect one or two full size automobiles. If you have a functional automobile after the CME hits, you are far more likely to reach a good bug-out location. For small stuff, you could build a Faraday cage by putting a plastic garbage can into a metal garbage can and then put small electronic items into the plastic can. Ideally, the metal can would be grounded."

Gary was dismayed. *I literally begged Ralph for help, and this is what I get? A freaking Faraday cage?* "Ralph, this may come as a surprise to you, but I don't have a forty foot steel shipping container in my back yard."

Ralph laughed. "Of course you don't, that would have required some prior planning. But you could wrap your car in aluminum foil."

"What?!"

"Sure, if you want to protect any electrical item, big or small, from a car to a radio or a cell phone, you just need to wrap a layer of insulation around it, like cardboard or plastic, and then wrap it in aluminum foil. If you don't believe me, you can do your own experiment. Get a battery operated radio, turn it on, put it in a paper or plastic bag, and then wrap it in aluminum foil. Trust me, the signal will die. You'll get nothing but static. This is simple stuff. It's amazing how ignorant you sheeple are."

"But how –"

"Sorry Gary, we're done here. If you really need to know more about anything I've said, Google it before the lights go out. Right now, I've got another call coming in. It's the call I was expecting from Doug. He's heading this way right now with his family and his overloaded pickup truck and trailer. He started working with me on his disaster prep more than a year ago. Unlike you, Doug listened to me. Good luck Gary. If you successfully protect your cell phone with a Faraday cage, and the towers ever start working again, maybe you can give me a call."

Ralph didn't have to add, "Fuck you," because his tone had adequately conveyed that message. The line went dead. *Protect my cell phone?! What about me? How do I keep myself and my family alive?!* Gary looked at the time. The call had taken ten minutes. *What a complete waste of time*, he thought. Gary hated Ralph, even though Ralph really had told Gary on several occasions to prepare for a lengthy crisis. Gary had been too busy to prepare for such an unlikely event. Gary had gotten off the parkway before Ralph had hung up on him. He and Mae were just a few minutes from their home in Islip.

Over the helmet intercom system, Mae said, "So I guess Ralph believes this thing is real."

Gary was a little startled by Mae's voice, he'd forgotten she was on the intercom. "Yeah, that was pretty clear. Ralph's a fanatic, but he's not stupid. If Ralph says this thing will cause huge devastation, then it will. You could tell by listening that Ralph is kind of an asshole, but he has spent a lot of time studying disaster scenarios. We are almost certainly completely screwed."

"What do you mean by "completely screwed"?

"Blake's last message to me was a text that said the CME would be a worst case scenario. He got his information from the Russians. Ralph just told us the same thing based on information he got from NASA. They both said the CME would cause a widespread blackout that would last for months." Gary paused for a moment as he absorbed the significance of his own words. "Mae, we can't stay on the Island tonight. We've got to go Hank's today, if we can make it that far."

Mae had listened to everything Ralph had said without saying a word. Now, there was nothing left to debate. Gary had already said the obvious. Leaving Long Island before the lights went out seemed like the best option.

Mae said, "I agree."

With those two words, Gary won the argument about going to Hank's house that had started before the phone call to Ralph. It didn't feel like a victory. Gary silently seethed as he replayed in his mind portions of what Ralph had said. For a moment, Gary was gripped by a cold, dark, paralyzing fear. He was afraid for his daughters. *What if people like Ralph survive, but my daughters don't? If my daughters don't make it, whose fault will that be? Mine, all mine!* Gary felt a stab of nausea and swallowed hard to keep it down.

Gary concentrated on his driving for a long minute as he pushed the terror of losing his girls from his mind. But after the paralyzing fear left, Gary struggled not to think about what might have been. *What if I had listened to Ralph? What if I had prepared? What if I had a well-stocked truck and a trailer like Doug, or a few acres with a garden and some chickens like Ralph?*

If he could travel back in time, or somehow send a message to a date just a few months earlier, what message would Gary deliver to himself and others? *Pay attention to the kooks, especially the ones you think are smart enough to know better, because maybe they do know better. What's the downside of preparing for a really bad catastrophe by stocking up on canned food and other essentials? If nothing happens, just rotate the canned food into your regular diet.*

Gary forced himself to stop. That line of thinking would take him nowhere. Even if he could send a warning, who would believe it? *What kind of message would a time traveler have to write to entice people to read it, understand it, and then do something about it?* Like Gary, most people were too uninformed and distracted to understand a credible warning written in black and white, and placed right in front of their nose; even if it was somehow crafted into an entertaining read.

Chapter 8:   Goodbye Ana.

1:06 PM

Gary drove the motorcycle up his driveway. He hit the automatic door opener, and parked the bike in the garage. He and Mae got off the bike in silence. They were both still a little shocked by Ralph's blunt comments. Gary felt inadequate. Ralph had spent years preparing for a disaster. Gary had done nothing. Now he was in reaction mode. His only advantage was the warning he'd gotten from Blake, and confirmed by Ralph. Would it be enough to save the lives of his daughters? With every passing second, the advantage shrank as more people got similar warnings. Getting back through the city alive meant he had a lot to do, and do quickly.

Gary said, "Mae, let's make a deal. Let's assume that everything Blake and Ralph said is going to happen. We've got to assume it's real, because if we don't and it is, it will kill us. Let's work together to get west of the city. Hopefully, we can make it all the way to Hank's place. If midnight comes and goes, and nothing happens, then and only then, will we try to figure out how to recover from the huge embarrassment of being wrong."

Mae looked at Gary for a long moment and said nothing. Less than two hours ago she was enjoying one of the best days of her legal career and didn't even know what a CME was. The stuff she had just heard from Ralph was beyond her worst nightmare. The biggest part of her wanted to sit and do nothing. Stay home and see what tomorrow would bring, and maybe cry while she waited. That would be the easy thing to do. It was taking all of her will power to contemplate the apocalyptic reality.

Mae had been through seven years of elite schooling after high school. She had been trained to be an expert thinker. If it was this hard for someone like Mae to wrap her gifted mind around this god-awful reality, what were the odds that far less talented people could accomplish the task? Mae's mind still rebelled. She closed her eyes, and thought about her office, her assistant, and her Armani business suit. Then her eyes popped open when she remembered Johnny Davis and the red lace thong. *Holy crap! That's what I was wearing on the courthouse steps when —"*

Gary interrupted Mae's thoughts. After waiting for Mae to make a comment, and getting nothing, Gary continued. "Mae, every minute counts. We need to get out of here before the roads become impassable. So please work with me Mae. Please help me pack a few things fast, and get the girls into the car and on the road."

Mae thought packing in a hurry would not be easy. She would have to sift through her things and decide what to take in less than an hour. She felt drained, and wanted to postpone the task. When she spoke, she didn't say what Gary wanted to hear. "What about my car?"

"Huh?"

"My Mercedes. You know, the car I drive to the train station every morning on my way to work? It's still there. Shouldn't we bring it back here before we leave?" Mae owned a very nice, current-model year Mercedes C-Class Sedan.

"No Mae, we will leave it there. We don't have time to go get it."

"Gary, getting the car back to the house would take only a half hour or so."

"We don't have a half hour to spare"

"So we just abandon my car? What if thieves –"

Gary interrupted. "Yes Mae, we abandon the car. Please use that magnificent brain of yours in a more practical fashion to consider our options. When we leave here, we're not taking two cars. We need to be in the same car so one of us can mind the girls and perhaps even navigate while the other one drives. If we leave your car at the train station overnight, and the CME doesn't happen, we'll pick it up tomorrow. If it gets stolen or vandalized overnight, we'll file an insurance claim. If we leave it overnight and the CME does happen, the car will probably be non-functional, and we might never see it again anyway. So no, I'm not going to take you to the train station to pick up your car."

Mae moved on. "Okay Gary, so what about Jane? She's in school right now. Don't you remember? She started kindergarten two weeks ago. Are you going to leave her at the school overnight?"

Gary had almost forgotten. For the last few years, Ana, the nanny, had taken care of both girls at home and even taught them a pre-K curriculum. But this year, for the first time, only Josephine was at home. "Crap! I've got to go get her." Gary grabbed Mae's helmet from her hands and started getting on the bike.

"What are you doing? You can't bring her home on that thing! Take the car. You need a car seat."

"I intend to get her back here quickly. If traffic gets crazy here in town, like it did on the Parkway, the flexibility of the bike could save a lot of time. Besides, you'll be packing the car while I'm gone."

"Pack it with what, how?"

"Pack it like we were going on a camping trip. If the end of the world crap scares you too much, just pretend we're going camping."

"Good idea Gary, except we've never gone camping."

She was right. The two of them never had gone camping together. Gary used to go camping with friends, and he had once even been bold enough to take the girls with him. Just once. But Mae had never gone along. As far as Gary knew, Mae had never slept overnight in the great outdoors with or without a tent.

"Mae we don't have time for this. We have to get packed and get out of here fast, and we don't have a lot of room. We can pack the back of the Volvo and the utility trailer. That's it. If it doesn't fit in those two places, we're not taking it. That means we're going to leave behind a lot of stuff that we'd like to take. We've got to focus on essential stuff like canned goods, and leave behind the sentimental stuff like photo albums. You're smart, put your thinking cap on."

Gary had already locked the second helmet into its carrier on the bike. He was now straddling the bike and walking it backward out of the garage when he stopped. "One more thing, Mae, don't forget to find your personal cell phone and put it on the charger."

Mae agreed and Gary started backing up the motorcycle again when he noticed the door from the garage to the house was open. Ana was standing in it. *How long had she been there?*

Gary said, "Um, hi Ana. Is uh, everything okay?"

"Yes. Mr. Adams. I heard the garage door and thought it might be you, but I didn't expect you to be home so early, so I came out to check. Hello Ms. Seymour."

If Ana was a little surprised to see Gary, she was stunned to see Mae. Mae *never* left work early, even when one of the girls got ill. Mae always left in the morning before Ana arrived, and got home after Ana left. The two women almost never saw each other. Mae wasn't just home, she was home before two o'clock in the afternoon, and wearing black leather pants and a jacket that were obviously too big. *Had Ms. Seymour arrived on the motorcycle with Mr. Adams? But Mr. Adams and Ms. Seymour did not work at the same place. That meant –"*

Gary could see the surprise on Ana's face, and almost hear the questions racing through her mind. *How much had she overheard?* Gary was trying to stay focused on the urgent need to get Jane from school, but he was also trying to figure out how to deal with Ana. Should he make up a false story about why he and Mae were home early, or had Ana already heard enough to know the real reason?

Gary decided to tell her the truth, because he simply didn't have time for distractions or subterfuge. *No that wasn't it. I don't want to lie to Ana.* Gary now understood why Mae had warned her office assistant. *But warnings to others might interfere with our hasty exit from the Island! On the other hand, who would Ana tell? It's not like I'm going to give her the bad news on a speaker phone with a dozen other people listening. Ana lived alone – no wait, she lived with her daughter, but her daughter was what? A derelict? An alcoholic? Something like that. Could Ana keep a secret, just for a couple of hours? Would she?*

Without discussing it with Mae, Gary decided he *had* to give some kind of explanation to Ana. But he had to do it fast. "Ana, we didn't come home early to take the girls camping. I'm sorry to surprise and scare you like this, but I believe New York is going to get hit with huge, unexpected disaster. The prudent thing to do is to evacuate."

Ana was surprised, but not panicked by the news. Ana had been a child when her father had fled Cuba with his family in 1960. She had seen people killed in the street. She wasn't too upset by Mr. Adams' news because she didn't think he had any idea what a real disaster looked like. "Mr. Adams, why do you believe a disaster is coming? I've seen nothing on the news."

"I got some information from a friend that I trust. He knows things before the people on TV know. It's like being the first person to arrive at the scene of an accident or a crime, before the police or the reporters arrived. He saw something that will cause an electrical blackout here in New York. The blackout could last for weeks, maybe months."

"Something like Hurricane Sandy?"

"Yes, but probably worse. Much worse. It will make Sandy and even 9/11 seem like no big deal. It's kind of technical, because it involves the sun rather than just bad weather. And it won't be just the city. It will probably affect the entire state, and maybe a big chunk of the United States."

"If it's going to be that bad, why leave? Why not peacefully spend the last few days with God and the people you love?"

It was a tough question, but Gary had been thinking about it off and on since he had spoken to Blake. Gary's survival instincts were very strong. At age thirty-five, he was still young, with a lot of living left to do. But his paternal instinct was even stronger. If it had been just he and Mae, Gary probably would still have fled the city in an effort to prolong their lives, but with Jane and Josie in the picture, there was no doubt. He would do anything to protect them.

"I've got my daughters to think about. I have to do what's best for them. Mae and I are going to pack some things, and get off Long Island as fast as possible to protect our children."

For Ana, the calculation was entirely different. "My daughter is now my only child and she is as old as you are."

It was hard for Gary to give Ana thirty seconds of his attention. As he forced himself to listen, he recalled some details of her situation. Ana's daughter Isabella was a former heroin addict who had never fully recovered. Isabella was Ana's only child, because Ana's two sons were dead. One was killed by gang violence in his teens, the older brother died soon after in an unrelated car accident. Gary couldn't recall either of their names, and wasn't sure Ana had ever told him their names. They were simply "her boys" and they had died less than six months apart. Isabella had no children of her own. She survived on her mother's generosity and tireless love.

When Gary tuned back in, Ana was still talking, ". . . . I'm sixty-six years old. Caring for your beautiful daughters is the most physically demanding task that I can perform." Ana paused for a moment before stating her conclusion. "Mr. Adams, I will go home to be with my daughter. If this disaster comes as you think it will, then I will be with my Isabella until the end, but perhaps it won't be that bad. Before I go home, why don't I help you pack? If it's possible to survive this blackout, I want you and the girls to make it."

Gary thought, *Wow. There was a lot to say, but no time to say it.* Ana and her daughter would likely be dead soon, but Ana was going to face that reality, and offer assistance to someone else. She wanted to help younger folks, who at least had a chance at survival, get on their way. Then she planned to go home and do what? Just wait for the end? It was a clarity of thought and purpose that came easily to those who had lived in the third world. .

"Um, . . . thanks Ana. Yeah, we could use some help packing."

Was there anything Gary could do for her? If the CME damage was significant, then a lot of the sheeple, as Ralph called them, were going to die. Some of the sheeple, like Ana, were going to go quietly into that long last night. Ana's acceptance of the shocking reality was so smooth and fast it made Gary think she had already been comfortable with her own mortality before the CME was mentioned. Still, Gary felt like he had to offer Ana a lifeline, so he did.

"Look Ana, Mae and I could get both you and your daughter out of the city. There's room in our car for both of you." That was an exaggeration, because the Volvo wagon only had seats for five, not six.

Ana's mind was already made up. "Mr. Adams, everybody dies. When you get older, and hopefully you'll live to be at least my age, you'll realize that dying is part of living. And if you know it's coming, then be an adult about it. Do it well."

Ana sighed, then continued. "I wasn't kidding when I said my daughter and I are not worth saving. We could contribute nothing, and neither of us could produce offspring. We would just consume scarce resources that are better left to those who have children and the wherewithal to raise them to adulthood. I also know you don't have room in the car. Not for both of us." Ana was already turning back into the house when she finished. "Mr. Adams, go get Jane from school. Ms. Seymour why don't you change out of your husband's clothes and help me pack? You two don't have much time."

Ana, a woman who left school before she finished the eighth grade, appeared to be in charge. Gary did as he was told to do. He put his helmet on, maneuvered the bike into the driveway, started it and drove away. As he left, Mae meekly followed Ana into the house. Jane's school was less than three miles away.

By running two red lights and driving down one long sidewalk, Gary was there in five minutes. Unlike his arrival at the courthouse, Gary made his arrival at the school as subtle as possible. He shut off the bike's engine several hundred yards from the school, and coasted it to a parking space behind a full-sized pickup truck. He was confident his approach had not been heard inside the building, and the bike could not be seen from the school building.

Gary left both helmets on the bike, so nobody would guess how he intended to transport Jane. Gary knew that certain school officials would not hesitate to overrule a parent's decisions about his own child. There might also be a state child-seat law that Gary was about to violate. Signing Jane out of school, and getting her from the classroom to the bike seemed to take forever, but he and Jane were walking out the building nine minutes after Gary had entered. Jane had been going to school for just two weeks, and it was the first time she had been signed out early. She was bubbling with excitement. "Hi Daddy! Why did you come to school? Isn't my school nice? Where are we going? Will I get in trouble for leaving early?"

Gary held her hand and kept walking without attempting to interrupt the steady flow of questions. Jane had also never ridden the motorcycle. When she was standing next to the bike, and realized that she'd soon be riding on it, she stopped talking, and her eyes went wide with fear.

"It's okay sweetheart. You're a little scared right now, but in a couple of minutes you'll be having fun. Remember when you rode a pony at the fair during the summer?" Of course Jane remembered. She had talked about it for weeks afterward, and Gary had thought about getting her riding lessons, but then thought better of it.

After a long moment, Jane said "Yeah," in a voice Gary could barely hear.

"Well riding the bike is a lot like riding a pony." Gary thought, but didn't say, *Or a whole bunch of ponies all at once!* Gary had no more time for pleasantries. If Jane had been screaming and crying, he still would have stuck her on the bike and bolted.

The helmet was too big for Jane, which meant it would provide little protection in an accident. After sticking it on her head, Gary looked around to see if anyone might try to prevent him from leaving. He was in luck. There were no helmet or child-seat Nazis in sight. Gary placed Jane on the very front of the seat. When he got on behind her, she was sitting up against the gas tank. His arms on the handlebars formed guardrails to keep her from falling off. If necessary, he could lean forward and squeeze his elbows together. It would be impossible for her to fall off – as long as Gary remained in control of the bike.

Gary left the parking lot and drove slowly for the next two minutes. Jane loved it, so Gary increased his speed. It really was a lot like riding a pony, or perhaps a triple-crown winning thoroughbred that could weave through slow suburban traffic at forty miles an hour. Jane screamed with delight. By the end of the ride, Gary's biggest concern was that Jane had enjoyed the ride *too* much. Maybe he had created a monster; an adrenaline junkie. The return trip took six minutes. Gary parked the bike in the garage. He took Jane off the bike, and took the helmet off Jane. She went running into the house saying, "Guess what, Ana, I rode the motorcycle!"

Gary got the keys to the Volvo, backed it out of the driveway, turned it around, and backed it into the garage so he could attach the utility trailer. The five-by-eight trailer was in the back corner of the garage's second bay. Gary moved the lawn mower and other items that were in front of the trailer. Then he pulled the trailer forward by hand and hooked it to the Volvo.

He had purchased the trailer from a neighbor whose job had been transferred overseas. The trailer had been almost new condition when Gary bought it for half its retail price. Gary got a tow hitch and light kit added to the Volvo, but rarely used the trailer. Now, the trailer acquisition seemed like an enormous good fortune. Gary would rather have had a full-size pickup for his bug-out vehicle, but since he was stuck with the Volvo, he was darn glad he had the trailer.

When Gary entered the house, he saw that Mae and Ana had made piles of stuff in the living room. Mae saw him looking around at the piles when she came in with another armload of stuff. She created another pile by emptying the armload onto the couch.

Mae said, "This is the stuff that Ana and I think needs to go with us. If you do the loading, then you can make the final decision on what goes and what stays."

Gary nodded. "That's a fine plan, but how do we know we're not forgetting something essential? It's helpful to think that we are going on an extended camping trip, and pack accordingly. But in certain critical ways, this is *not* a camping trip. We need a checklist."

"Okay, but neither of us has done this before, and you're the one who said we don't have a lot of time. How do you propose we quickly figure out how to pack the stuff we haven't even thought of?"

"While I start loading the stuff you and Ana collected, why don't you do a few Google searches? Find out what the survivalists recommend for a bug-out packing list. All of a sudden, those crazy preppers don't seem so crazy."

Mae started walking toward the garage. She said, "Well then, get busy. I'll have a bug-out packing list in a couple of minutes. I'm going to the garage to get my laptop. It's still in the pannier of the motorcycle. You left to get Jane, before I could take it out."

Gary said, "While you're at it, grab my laptop too. It's in the pannier on the other side of the bike. I almost forgot that I brought it with me when I left work."

Ten minutes later, much of the stuff in the living room was in the utility trailer. Gary didn't have time to load the car and trailer in an organized fashion. He put the most critical items in the back of the Volvo, and almost literally threw everything else into the trailer. If they got all the way to Hank's house, then maybe he would have the time to reorganize the trailer. When the trailer was nearly full, Gary walked back to the living room just as Mae entered the room from the opposite end. She was holding her laptop in her hand.

"Gary, I found a couple of websites that have the information we're looking for. On SurvivalBlog.com, they have excellent prepper and bug-out lists, and they even sell a downloadable Survivalist Manual, but I haven't tried to download it yet. There's another blog called shtfplan.com; the 'shtf' stands for 'shit hits the fan.' I've already downloaded a bunch of stuff to my laptop. While you drive, I can probably continue to download more stuff."

"Mae do me a favor, while we're driving save all that info to at least one thumb drive, and my laptop. That way, we'll have all the valuable information saved to three different devices. My laptop is packed right behind the driver's seat."

Mae said, "Okay," and Gary asked, "So what's on those lists that we forgot?"

"Well, let's see. Food, water, and medicine are at the top of the list. Then he lists some stuff we never would have thought of, like a road atlas, hand tools, and propane tanks. We've already packed a bunch of clothes, and emptied the pantry and medicine cabinet, but we should also pack all our gas cans even if they're empty. Did you know that during Hurricane Sandy, empty five-gallon gas cans were sold for fifty dollars each, and full ones went for a hundred?"

Gary did remember it because he had stayed on the south shore while Mae continued to rack up billable hours in a nice hotel many miles away. "Yes Mae, I did know that but I worked hard to forget all the hassles Sandy caused. Now I'm thinking it was a wake-up call that I should have heeded. Do you know where our road atlas is?"

"Gary, I don't drive very often, and when I do, I use a GPS system. I haven't seen a road atlas in years."

"Well, we used to have one, and I don't recall throwing it away, so look in the front hall closet and the den and see if you can find it, and I'll get the barbeque propane tank, the spare tank, and any empty gas cans I can find."

"While you're doing that, keep an eye out for any of the smaller sixteen-ounce propane cylinders that are used for propane lanterns and cook stoves."

"We might have a couple of those. I'll look around. What else?"

"Well if we have any hand tools we should grab them. Things like a bow saw for cutting firewood, a hatchet, a hammer, a shovel and mechanical tools like wrenches and screwdrivers."

"We've got a few of those things as well. I'll grab 'em. What else?"

"I'm going to gather all the really valuable stuff, the jewelry and our small cash stash. If we don't come back to the house any time soon, then I also need to pack our passports, birth certificates, social security cards, and other stuff like that. Fortunately, most of that is in our fire-proof safe, and I'll just empty it into a bag or something."

"Good. Anything else?"

"Bicycles. The preppers say if the cars stop running, then bicycles will get a lot more use than they do now."

Gary thought about it for a moment. He and Mae had each purchased a bike several years ago, but they had not used them as regularly as they thought they would. Eventually, the bikes ended up in the shed where they had been gathering dust for a long time. The tires were flat and probably dry rotted. *What would Mae and I do with two bikes anyway? Each of us would strap a kid to our back and start peddling? How far could we get? If we added the necessary food and water to the load, even new tires wouldn't be able to take the weight.*

Gary said, "I understand the bicycle idea, but it's too late for me to make it work. You and I are not going to pedal to Hank's house with the girls on our backs. Even if we wanted to try that, our bikes aren't in any shape to be used right now. We also don't have room in the trailer or the car to bring them, and I don't have the time to buy some rope and tie our broken bikes to the trailer roof. So forget the bikes, what else is on the list?"

"There are several other small items, like matches, cigarette lighters, toothpaste, soap, toilet paper, bleach, thumb drives, external hard drives, extension cords, and the inverter so I can use my laptop in the car. I'll gather those items while you're chasing the stuff outside."

Gary said, "Okay." Then he selected another armload of stuff from the greatly diminished piles in the living room and took it to the trailer. It was nearly full. Gary was trying to figure out what items should come out of the trailer to make room, when he remembered the rooftop carrier.

Gary had purchased it before he had acquired the trailer. He used it occasionally to go on rock-climbing trips with college friends, and later, fellow professors. With three or four adults inside the car, the rooftop carrier was needed to haul tents, and other gear. The carrier still looked new because it had been used less than half-a-dozen times. Gary installed the carrier on the Volvo, and filled it with the lightest stuff that had been loaded into the trailer. This left room for the heavier items that Mae had mentioned like canned goods, the propane, and the tools.

Gary went to the shed for the hand tools, and an extra propane tank he had purchased after he'd once run out of fuel in the middle of grilling some steaks. On a second trip, he removed the propane tank that was connected to the barbeque grill. He put the items into the newly cleared space in the trailer. Then he loaded the additional items Mae had gathered inside the house. She had found the road atlas that was seven years old. Gary placed it on the Volvo's dashboard.

Gary found the family's fifty-four quart cooler in the garage. He took it into the house, moved a chair close to the fridge, and put the cooler on the chair. In less than two minutes, he emptied the most valuable items from the freezer and refrigerator. The frozen items included two large steaks, sausage, hamburger meat, and shrimp. Items from the refrigerator included boneless chicken breasts, cheese, bacon, several containers of yogurt, a bag of apples, a gallon of milk, and two dozen eggs. Gary tossed in condiments like ketchup, mustard, barbeque sauce and Italian dressing. He crammed in some fresh vegetables, but decided not to take two pints of Ben & Jerry's ice cream. Then he emptied the freezer's automatic ice tray on top of the contents of the cooler. Gary put the full cooler into the back of the Volvo.

Gary stopped packing when there was no more space left in the trailer, the car, or the rooftop carrier. He was confident of two things. First, the car and trailer were carrying far more weight than the manufacturers intended. Second, if he had had a bigger vehicle and trailer, he would have taken more stuff. He made a mental note to purchase a full-size, four-wheel drive pickup truck and a larger trailer before the next apocalypse.

Gary and Mae had made some tough decisions as they packed. Many cherished items had to be left behind to make room for those things that were essential for life. Gary wanted to believe that he was not permanently abandoning his house, but he couldn't. He was more convinced than ever that he'd never again see the house and its contents in its normal state. Walking away from his motorcycle for the last time had been hard. In a post-apocalyptic world, a functional motorcycle would probably be very useful, but he had no room for it.

Gary closed and locked the trailer doors. The packing process had been brutal and messy, but it was done. Gary knew he and Mae had packed some stuff that was useless, and forgotten to pack other stuff that would later turn out to be vital. There was no time to fix that. A particular decision on whether a specific item should stay or go didn't matter as much as getting the job done now, and getting on the road. When Gary walked into his house for the last time, Ana was in the living room with Josephine in her arms, and Jane at her feet. She had kept both girls preoccupied in the playroom, away from the commotion in the living room. Of the five people in the house, Ana was by far the calmest.

She said matter of factly, "Alright kids, it's time to get in the car for the big adventure." Even that process was brutal. Each of the kids got to take their two favorite toys to their car seats. None of their other toys was making the trip. The girls knew that most of their stuff hadn't been packed. They didn't know they were not coming back for it. As Mae put the kids in the car, Gary kicked into the garage a few items in the driveway that left the house, but didn't survive the final cut of things to pack. Gary locked the doors to the house and garage. He was mostly convinced he wouldn't be back for weeks or months, if ever, but he wasn't going to invite the looters in by leaving the house unsecured.

Ana was now standing in the driveway, with the few items she had brought with her that morning to her nanny job. Gary walked over to her. On the spur of the moment, he took the house key off his key ring and handed it to her. "Ana, if things go badly, so badly that we won't be coming back any time soon, take whatever you need from the house."

2:32 PM

Ana looked even calmer than she had when she had first gotten the news that her life was soon going to end. She spoke quietly but firmly. "Thank you Mr. Adams. Thanks for thinking of me, and thanks for trusting me with your house key. But most of all, thanks for telling the truth about what you think is coming. I still hope and pray you're wrong. But I know you are a smart man, and what you say is probably true."

Gary was anxious to leave, but Ana was firmly holding his forearm. She knew she might be talking to him for the last time. "I'm glad I could help you and your beautiful daughters prepare for your journey. I'm a woman of faith. I believe there is something better waiting for all of us in the next world. But I also believe surviving as long as possible in this world is a good thing, especially for your girls."

Gary felt her squeeze his arm more tightly. "Listen to me Mr. Adams. I don't know what is going to happen in the next few weeks or months, but I know as surely as if God had spoken to me that your girls are going to live a full life. To my age or older. Neither one will remember me, but I'll be smiling down at them from heaven just the same."

There were tears in her eyes when she said it, and Gary knew Ana truly believed the information came directly from God. Gary didn't know what to say. After a moment, he said a quiet "Thank you."

She said, "Peace be with you," and kissed Gary on the cheek. "You don't have time for a long goodbye. Get in that car right now, and drive away fast. There's nothing more to say. God be with you."

There really wasn't anything more to say. It was time for Ana to go home and probably die, while Gary ran away to try to save his family. Gary gave Ana a quick embrace, and mumbled awkwardly, "Peace be with you too, and um, good luck."

Then he got in the car and drove away. The car and trailer were overloaded. It wasn't a fast exit.

Chapter 9:   Two bridges.

As they drove down the street, Mae's first words were, "So how much important stuff did we forget to pack?"

"Hopefully not much, but we can't think about that. In the short amount of time we had, we made the best decisions we could, with the best information we could get. We must never second-guess those decisions. That's our new rule, Mae. Never look back on the things we might have done differently."

Mae nodded without speaking. He was right. When she had been a young associate, a senior partner had told her something similar about the practice of law. *"To make a lot of money in the practice of law, you need to practice it quickly. To practice law quickly, you will necessarily make mistakes. That's what malpractice insurance is for. So go make us rich, kid, and don't worry about all the mistakes you're going to make."*

The girls, especially Jane, were asking questions. "Why did I have to leave school early today? Where are we going? How long will we be driving? When will we get there?" And finally, before they had traveled two miles, "I'm bored."

Mae did what many parents do when trapped in a car with inquisitive young children. She put in a Disney video. Within a few minutes, the girls were fixated on the two video screens that were attached to the backside of the front seats. Their trance-like state was occasionally punctuated by laughter.

Gary said, "We need gas. Gas and cash." He felt stupid. Like a lot of people, he had enough sense to know that he should have prepared for emergencies like a big storm or a power outage, but he hadn't done it. He had packed two five gallon gas cans that he found in the shed, but they were both empty. A moment ago, he looked at his gas gauge and got more bad news. The tank was only one eighth full. He was now forced to spend valuable time buying gas.

Despite his new rule, Gary couldn't help thinking he should have been more prepared. He should have had half a dozen five-gallon gas cans and they should have all been full. He also should never have let the car get below half a tank – enough fuel to leave Long Island even if traffic was slow. He could have kept the gas in the cans fresh by using a fuel conditioner like Stabil. As the fuel aged, he could have rotated the stock by putting the old, but still usable gas into his car's tank, and refilling the cans with fresh gas. Preparations and stock rotation like that would have been tedious and time-consuming, but they would have saved him precious time when it was time to leave; perhaps an hour or more. Now, every minute of delay increased the odds that he and his family would get trapped on the wrong side of the city. Sometimes, one hour was the difference between life and death.

The list of things Gary wished he had done was long. It included a good bug-out vehicle, bug-out bags for each family member, a stockpile of food, medical, and hygiene items stored in stackable plastic bins, and a laptop loaded with everything he would want to know after a crisis arrived. Gary's thoughts violated the rule he had just given to Mae not to think about what might have been. He stopped thinking about his regrets when he saw a gas station he had often used in the past. He said to Mae, "I've got to stop for gas, and I'll fill up the two gas cans while I'm at it. Why don't you hit the ATM and withdraw the limit?"

Mae said, "Okay, but do you think the almighty US dollar will still have value as our civilization collapses?"

"Yes. When the lights go out, credit cards will die. Cash will be king for a few days, perhaps even a week or more."

"Then what?"

"Well if Blake and Ralph are correct, then people will start starving to death after the tractor trailer trucks stop delivering their daily bread. When it's obvious to everyone that things aren't going to get back to normal any time soon, a barter system will emerge. Things of real, keep-a-human-alive, value will be traded for other things of value. Silver and gold might reemerge as currency, but people who lack food, water, and shelter probably won't have any of it, and they won't be interested in accumulating any of it. They'll only be interested in getting the stuff that will keep them alive. Silver and gold will have value only to those who already have all the food, water, and shelter they need."

"So we should get as much cash as we can, and then spend it as fast as we can?" To a frequent clothes shopper like Mae, it sounded easy.

"Yes, but we've got another urgent problem. We have to get out of the city before all the departure routes become parking lots. We might have a couple of minutes to grab cash, but we won't have any time to go shopping until we get past the bridges and are west of the city."

Gary slowed the car to turn into the gas station on Saxon Avenue. All the pumps were occupied, and Gary had to wait a few minutes behind one car. Mae went to the ATM where she had to wait behind two people.

Gary looked around as he pumped the gas. The majority of the gas station's patrons seemed clueless about the coming disaster. He saw two people filling five-gallon gas cans. They appeared to be stocking up, but not fleeing the Island. Gary identified two vehicles that appeared to be doing what he was doing; bugging out. A sedan at the traffic light was pulling a trailer almost identical to his. At the gas station, an overloaded pickup truck pulled away while Gary was still pumping gas. The truck was an older model, perhaps from the late 1980's. It had a half-ton suspension and a regular size cab. As it drove past, Gary could see it held an adult couple and two young children. The kids should have been in car seats, but there wasn't enough room or even individual seat belts for all four to sit on the bench seat with two car seats. The kids were in the middle, probably sharing one belt.

The woman, sitting in the passenger seat, gave Gary a meaningful glance as the truck left. As if to say, "Yeah, we know what you know, and we're getting the hell out of here too. Good luck." She looked terrified.

After the massive car accident on the highway, Gary wondered why more people were not leaving like he was. If the news of the coming disaster was still spreading exponentially by word of mouth, why weren't more people leaving? Clearly some people didn't run, because they hadn't gotten the news. Gary surmised, however, that many people who had gotten the news had chosen not to run. Most of the people – that Ralph called sheeple – probably wouldn't believe the catastrophe would be horrific until after the undeniable evidence was right in front of their eyes. By that time, of course, it would be too late. Maybe Ralph was right. Sheep don't take proactive measures to deal with a future wolf attack; they just panic and die when the wolf shows up for a meal.

Gary smiled. If most of the sheeple who were told of the CME did nothing until the hard evidence arrived, then perhaps Gary and his family could get west of the city before it was too late. Gary didn't blame the sheeple who planned to sit tight on the Island until after the evidence arrived. Both he and Mae had thought that was a good idea until just a short while ago. Gary felt like he was separating himself from the flock. It remained to be seen whether that would increase his odds for survival. Gary finished pumping the gas before Mae returned. When the machine asked if he wanted a receipt, he hit the "no" button. He didn't anticipate needing a lot of paperwork in the near future.

Gary was about to go into the store to see what Mae was doing, when she came out the exit. She was carrying two plastic grocery bags. Mae walked quickly, and almost jogged to the car. Gary buckled in before she got there, and the car was rolling before Mae had buckled her seat belt. The time was 2:50 PM.

"How did you do at the ATM?"

Mae said, "Everything was fine. As you could see at the pumps, things were a little busy so I had to wait in line for a few minutes. I got the maximum amount of cash the machine would provide. So we now have five hundred dollars in twenties."

"That's a good start, but I'd like to get more if we haven't already hit our ATM withdrawal limit for the day. If the banks sense a crisis, they might lower the withdrawal limits. If – I mean when – we get west of the city, we should stop at a bank. What's in the two grocery bags?"

"I got some bottles of water and some snacks for the trip, crackers, candy bars, and a couple of yogurts."

Gary asked, "How did you pay for the snacks, cash or credit."

"Credit."

"Good thinking. If I had been thinking, I would have told you to buy a lot more stuff. The card will be probably be useless by tomorrow morning. Did the clerk object to your use of the card?"

"No. He was a kid, not a manager or anything. He seemed to know things were abnormally busy, but he didn't appear to know why. Like you, I think most of the people who know, are not anxious to educate others until they get out of the city. I saw a few people in the store, including two people who got in line at the ATM behind me, who seemed to know what we know. Like me, they withdrew the maximum. That machine will probably be out of cash within the next hour or so."

Gary said, "I saw two drivers that seemed to be doing what we're doing, bugging out. Let's hope we get to the other side of the bridges before too many people figure it out."

In the back seat, the girls were still happily occupied with their video screens. Gary had left the car running as he filled the tank so the video's power supply wouldn't be interrupted. They had only been driving for a short time, so Jane didn't need a potty break, and Josie who was in the process of being potty trained, was wearing a pull up. As they fled for their lives, Josie's potty training would probably be put on hold. Mae would have given the girls a snack if they had asked, but they didn't so she saved the snacks for later. Videos and snacks were almost the full extent of Mae's motherhood skill set, even when the kids weren't strapped into car seats.

Traffic on Sunrise Highway was heavier than normal, and the same was true for the westbound Southern State Parkway. It wasn't quite as bad as rush hour traffic, but it seemed like it was getting that way. As Gary drove on the parkway, Mae got out her laptop. She connected the power cord to an inverter, and connected the computer to the internet by using her cell phone as a hot spot.

Mae said, "Okay, I've got an internet connection, what do you want me to download?"

"Get as much survival stuff as you can, from wherever you can. Things like how to find edible stuff that grows in the wild, how to trap small game, and how to purify water. Stuff like that."

"Gary, if it comes down to skills like that, I think we'll both die quickly."

Gary responded a little curtly, "Mae you can't talk like that. You can't even think like that. If you and I die, then the girls die too." After he said it, he quickly looked over his shoulder, but the girls hadn't heard him.

Gary continued, "We're not going to quit. Not ever. If we do our best and still lose the game of survival, then fine. But as I exhale for the last time, I don't want to be regretting all the things I could have done to protect our daughters. We've already done many things wrong, because we did nothing to prepare for an event like this. Even after Hurricane

Sandy, I did nothing to prepare for the next catastrophe. That's the last regret I'm going to have."

Mae was a little surprised by the intensity of Gary's tone. Her comment on their lack of survival skills was intended as a joke. Her mind still couldn't comprehend the life-threatening enormity of their situation. Perhaps midnight would bring a cure for that.

"Gary, calm down. I was trying to be funny. I don't need a lecture about our situation every five minutes. Survival skills, got it, I'll do some searches on that topic."

Gary said, "Thanks," in a distracted tone. Traffic had slowed down and drivers in front of Gary were looking to their left across the median. Gary realized he was passing by the accident scene in the eastbound lanes that he and Mae had narrowly avoided by jumping the Beemer over the berm. Gary was relieved to see emergency vehicles on the scene. First responders were still responding. One eastbound lane was open and traffic was moving very slowly through the two hundred yards of wrecked vehicles. Gary felt a little clutch in his chest when he saw white sheets draped over the driver compartments of two different vehicles. There might have been more, but Gary couldn't devote his full attention to the scene, and his view was partially blocked by vegetation on the median.

Mae looked over at Gary, and then looked across the median. After a long moment she said, "It's good to see the ambulances. I hope everybody comes out of it okay."

Gary knew everybody hadn't come out of it okay. Maybe Mae hadn't seen the white sheets. Gary said, "Yeah, me too."

Traffic in front of Gary began to accelerate as the rubberneckers passed the bulk of the scene and stopped looking across the median. Gary struggled for a second to recall what he and Mae had been discussing prior to encountering the distraction in the eastbound lanes. *Oh yeah, internet survival info.*

Gary said, "I'll feel better when we get past the bridges, and New York City is in my rear view mirror. If we make it out of here, and the CME is as bad as Blake and Ralph said it will be, then we'll need lots of skills that we don't currently possess. Maybe you can find and download some YouTube videos on how to do anything and everything without electricity."

"Anything and everything? That's a pretty broad topic."

"Yeah, well the problem is that we don't know exactly what we'll need or where we'll be when we need it. But this might be the very last day that we can download stuff from the internet. So anything with the slightest usefulness, even stuff that we might not need for several months, is worth downloading. Hey, here's something I just thought of. Download a couple of videos on small-engine repair. Small engines, like lawn mowers and generators don't have much in the way of electronics, so they might survive the CME."

"Okay, I'll get busy."

"If you run out of topics to download, start downloading Wikipedia."

"You want me to download all of Wikipedia?" Mae sounded surprised.

"When you run out of other stuff to download, sure, why not? What if the power stays out for a couple of years? Where are you going to go to get the information that's on Wikipedia? Do you think we'll have access to a public library, or a hardcopy set of the Encyclopedia Britannica books? I don't know if they even make hardcopy encyclopedias anymore."

"Gary, I'm sure I don't have enough room on this hard-drive to get *all* of Wikipedia, so where do you want me to start?"

"How about topics like survival, farming, and food? Is Wikipedia alphabetized? You could download everything under the letters S and F.

"Gee, Gary, that's helpful. So I download everything that starts with F, and later, as we starve to death, I'll be sorting through hundreds of pages on topics like forensics, flatulence, and Figaro while I try to figure out which tree bark we should eat to stay alive. But that life-saving information won't be available because it was filed under T for tree or B for bark instead of F for food, so we'll die anyway."

Gary smiled. Mae was right, one lecture every five minutes was enough. He decided not to snap back at Mae. Over time, her cutting sarcasm had become the closest thing she had to a sense of humor. Humor, even bad humor was better than panic attacks. If the CME was real, Mae would not be away at her office for twelve to fourteen hours a day, five or six days a week. If they were both lucky enough to survive, Gary would have to become accustomed to much larger and more frequent doses of Mae and her sarcasm.

"Well, if you download big chunks of Wikipedia at least we'll have something to read while we starve to death. If you have a better idea, I'm all ears." Gary tried to match Mae's dark humor.

"Instead of filling the hard drive with useless stuff from Wikipedia, why don't I find one or two good survival blogs and download their archives of previous posts? While we were packing at the house, I got some good stuff from SurvivalBlog.com on critical items to buy or acquire before a crisis. Why don't I troll their archives and maybe download big chunks of that?

Actually, that is a better idea, thought Gary. "Yeah, Hon, why don't you do that? Oh wait, one more thing. See what you can find on Faraday cages or containers."

"Fara-who?"

"I think it's pronounced fair-a-day. It was something Ralph very graciously mentioned toward the end of his very pleasant wake up call. Don't you remember?"

"Um, kinda but I wasn't listening closely. Frankly, that guy was obnoxious and I tuned him out toward the end. But okay, Faraday, got it."

When Gary turned north and got on the Cross Island Parkway, traffic got worse. The further north he got, the heavier it got. When he got close to the I-495 overpass, traffic slowed to a crawl. A significant amount of traffic was apparently exiting the interstate to go north across the Throgs Neck Bridge. At Northern Boulevard, more vehicles joined the crush of northbound traffic on the parkway.

There were no shoulders on either side of the Cross Island Parkway, and no "off-road" options because the parkway had a concrete barrier on the left and a steel guardrail on the right. Gary was frustrated as he looked at the paved bike path that skirted Little Neck Bay to his right. The path could have accommodated two cars side-by-side, but access to the path was prevented by a steel guardrail. With the Throgs Neck Bridge across the East River in sight up ahead, most of the Cross Island traffic got into the two right lanes for the exit to the bridge. Gary figured that even some of the traffic that stayed on the parkway was probably leaving the island. The Whitestone Bridge on I-678 was an alternate route across the East River, and it was just two miles away.

Gary turned on the radio and selected a local station that gave frequent traffic reports. He didn't know why he bothered to listen. He was committed to his current route of travel across the Throgs Neck, and then the George Washington Bridge. Any attempt to change his intended path of travel, would almost certainly lengthen his travel time. As for traffic conditions, he already knew traffic was heavy because he was in it.

On the exit ramp going up to the bridge, the two lanes narrowed to one lane just before merging onto Interstate 295. Traffic was stop and go on the ramp, and when Gary got to the top of the ramp he knew why. The traffic on I-295 was stop and go as well. It was worse than peak rush hour traffic. The merge point was on a pier-supported section of the highway that was over the water. Gary could see the suspension portion of the bridge less than a mile ahead. But it took a long time to cover that mile. The bridge was three lanes wide with no shoulder on either side.

During the four o'clock news broadcast, Gary heard the first radio report of anything that could be attributed to the CME, even though the announcer didn't mention the CME. Instead, the information was presented as a "disturbing rumor on the internet." The rumor had something to do with a potential "wide-spread blackout." Reading from a script, the news announcer said the rumor was baseless. The rumor was blamed for increased volumes of road traffic, internet traffic, cell phone calls, and text messages.

The announcer conducted a short interview with the Assistant Deputy Manager of Operations for the electric company that provided power to New York City. The assistant deputy assured the public that the company was having absolutely no problems with the production or distribution of electricity. All generators, sub-stations, and other equipment were functioning perfectly. No power interruption of any kind was anticipated. In the wake of Hurricane Sandy, the company had spent millions of dollars to upgrade and harden its most vulnerable equipment. Even another hurricane wouldn't cause the damage Sandy had caused.

As he listened, Gary thought that everything the deputy manager had said was true – and meaningless. The equipment was functioning normally and another hurricane *would* probably cause less damage than Sandy, but the rumors of the coming CME had nothing to do with a hurricane, so the whole story was crap. Gary was so wrapped up in his thoughts that Mae had to say his name twice to get his attention.

Gary said, "Huh, what?"

"I said this thing has really slowed down. The internet I mean. Actually, the internet in general has slowed down, but the traffic on the specific sites I've been visiting has completely stopped. I think a lot of other people just recently started doing what we're doing. You know, downloading survival stuff. I'll try YouTube and some other sites, and see if I have better luck elsewhere."

Gary said, "It makes me wish I had somehow prepared for this, or any emergency really. I could have downloaded all this stuff weeks or months ago without any trouble."

"I thought you told me that our new rule was 'no regrets.' We don't look back and discuss what might have been." Mae was always quick to use an opponent's own statements against him.

"I have a feeling that in the next couple of days, we're both going to need to be reminded of that rule several times."

Mae almost smiled. "I hope you're right. If we need reminders, it will mean we survived the next couple of days."

When they got on to the bridge, the long pauses caused by cars merging onto the highway ended. Traffic now moved at a pace that was slightly faster than no movement at all. They had at least made it to the first bridge. Gary's goal of getting off the island began to seem at least remotely plausible. It suddenly occurred to Gary that the last time he spoke to his brother, Hank had disclosed his suicidal plan to stay put and exchange gunfire with roving, starving city dwellers. If Gary made it to Hank's house, he didn't want to become part of a Butch Cassidy and The Sundance Kid exit plan.

As the Volvo inched across the bridge, Gary turned off the radio and pulled up his brother's number from his call log. On his first four attempts, Gary got an "All circuits are busy" message. Apparently, the internet wasn't the only thing being overwhelmed by information that had not yet been released by the mainstream media.

On the fifth attempt, his brother answered. Gary abruptly started the phone conversation with the same topic on which the last conversation had abruptly ended.

"Hank, what the hell did you mean when you said you were going to stay put and shoot people?"

"Gary is that you? Dude, I thought you were dead."

"What?!"

"Last thing I heard sounded like a traffic accident. I called back a couple of times, but didn't get an answer, so I figured you got killed along with your phone."

"Hank, I'm fine, obviously I –"

"If you're fine, why the hell didn't you call me and tell me that?

Gary paused for a second, *Why didn't I call? How could I have forgotten about my brother?* Then Gary recalled racing home on the bike, getting Jane from school, and getting out of the house as fast as possible. He had focused on his wife and kids. In his haste, he had forgotten about Hank's situation. *Shit!* It sucked to realize how much important stuff he had missed while doing other important stuff. The events of the last couple of hours raced through Gary's mind; the involuntary motorcycle stunt with Mae, the frenzied ride to get Jane, and the final farewell to Ana. It had been one life or death decision after another. *And they all involved lives of people who are closer to me than Hank.* The thought cut like a knife. Hank's suicidal ideation at the end of the previous call had only just now gotten to the top of Gary's priority list. It was a truth that Gary would not admit to his brother.

"Hank I did call you. Repeatedly. The phone circuits and the internet are both jammed to a standstill." It was a true statement. In the last five minutes, Gary had made four calls to Hank that hadn't gone through. Gary quickly changed the topic so his brother wouldn't focus on Gary's failure to call. Obviously, he hadn't called too late; Hank was still alive.

Gary said, "Look I didn't die, and my phone is still functional, but your calls to me also didn't get through. It's the network's fault not mine." *Okay, well that very last part was mostly a lie.*

Gary kept talking. "Hank, I mean . . . shit man, I didn't know you thought I was dead . . . . Hank, I've been running for my life! *You're* the one that told me to do that. Mae and I hauled ass to the house on the motorcycle – someday I'll have to tell you about that ride and why our phone call ended so suddenly. The short version is Mae and I miraculously lived through it. Then I grabbed Jane from school, we packed a few things from the house, and I'm now on the Throgs Neck Bridge heading toward your place. I've been moving at a hundred miles an hour since we last talked. Well, not literally, I mean not at the moment in this traffic – but . . . ."

Gary almost said, "but I really didn't have time to call you." He stopped himself just in time. "but I'm sorry Hank, I'm sorry I didn't . . . I didn't get through. Hey brother, I'm concerned about you. Are you okay?"

Hank was still a little petulant. "I'm just saying a call would have been nice. Anyway, it's good to know that you and the kids are still alive."

Gary didn't think he should come right out and ask Hank if he was suicidal. Not on the phone anyway. He tried to think of something he could say to get Hank thinking more positively. Something to keep Hank from doing something stupid before Gary could get to Hank's house and intervene.

"Hank, I'm on the road right now and I'm heading your way. Like you said, if this thing is bogus, we'll just stay the night at your place and return home in the morning. What I'm seeing on the road right now tells me this thing isn't bogus. I'm bringing the girls of course, so get the guest room ready. The girls will love to see you." Gary was trying to cheer up Hank so he deliberately did not mention Mae, the rich bitch.

"Whatever, Dude, I'll see you la–"

"Hank, Hank, wait a minute, I need some information from you. What do you think we ought to do next? I mean if this thing is real, what do we do after we get to your place? Do we hunker down at your place forever, or go further west? If we have to leave your place, where would we go next?" Gary was thinking, *Focus on the future. Get Hank to start thinking and talking about the future!*

"Gary, look man, I've got a bad headache. So right now, I don't know what you should do, and I really don't c–".

"Daddy, Daddy, is that Uncle Hank? Daddy, can I talk to him please?"

What the –?! Gary looked over his right shoulder. It was Jane. The video had apparently ended, and she had heard Gary speaking on the phone. *It's obviously time for another video,* was Gary's first thought. Then, *Wait a minute!* On the spur of the moment, Gary handed the phone to Jane. Gary was confident Hank wouldn't hang up on his niece.

"Yeah Honey, it's your Uncle Hank. Why don't you say hi?"

Jane took the phone and began babbling. Mae was looking at Gary like he'd lost his mind. He hadn't. He was negotiating by other means. That was something Mae should understand. While Jane was talking, Gary asked Mae to get another video started and she did. Gary let Jane babble for more than a minute. As the opening credits for Disney's latest animated instant classic came on, Gary took the phone back.

"It's me again."

"You're a prick." Hank sounded a little perturbed, but that was good because he was also sounding more awake. More alive.

"It's a gift Hank. My kids want to live Hank. If this thing is real, then the girls and I will need a lot of help from you. My daughters need you Hank."

"To be more specific, you're a manipulative prick."

"Well, I hadn't meant to be that obvious, but yeah, I'm counting on you to help me keep my girls alive. They adore you, and they're not ready to quit the human race yet. So let's make a plan together."

Hank didn't say anything, but he also didn't hang up, so Gary pressed on. The time Jane spent on the phone had given Gary a chance to think up a strategy for getting his brother re-engaged in the business of life, which now might mean the business of surviving while others perished in large numbers.

"Hank you told me earlier that within a week or so, even your place would be overrun by people looking for food. Do you remember that?"

Gary didn't wait for a response; he needed to get his next idea planted quickly; something that he thought would get Hank thinking productively. "I got to thinking about bugging out to a more rural location, and I could think of only one place. Do you remember that farm upstate that you used to visit while you were still in college?"

The phone call with Ralph had made Gary wonder about long-term survival. What if hunkering down for a few days, or even a few weeks wasn't sufficient? What if a widespread blackout lasted for months? Was it possible for Gary to get his family to a farm, a location like the place Ralph had described, where it was possible to live off the land?

Gary waited for a response. There was a long pause, as Hank reached far back into his memory. His first visit to Grandpa's farm was almost twenty years ago. His last visit had been more than five years ago because Hank had been too ashamed to go back. Five years was a long time. It would be nice to have an excuse to go back, but could he? Would he be welcomed?

"Um . . . yeah, I do remember the farm." Hank's tone was less intense. The summers he'd spent on the farm had been the best summers of his life.

"Hank, that farm is the only place I can think of to run to. Do you think the old man is still alive? Do you know of any rural places other than the farm?"

"Gary, I hunted deer on the place a couple of times when I was on leave from the Army, but I haven't been there in, I don't know . . . I guess five years or so. I just got so busy with −" The thought died without a conclusion. "I don't know what happened to uh, Grandpa. We kept in touch for a while, but um, well, I haven't heard from him in years. Hell, he's probably de−"

Gary jumped in again. Hank's tone had turned melancholy. The conversation was moving in the wrong direction. "Come on Hank, I'm sure that old geezer is fine. You told me he was always as healthy as a horse. He's only what, seventy maybe eighty years old? Grandpa's going to live to be a hundred, easy."

The old man wasn't a bloodline Grandpa to Hank and Gary. He was Frankie's grandfather, and Frankie had called him Grandpa.

Frankie had Down's syndrome, and it would have been too confusing for Frankie if Grandpa had more than one name. It was the same reason half the people in the nearby small town also called the old man, Grandpa; out of kindness to Frankie. Everybody loved Frankie and felt sorry for him, the poor little retarded boy. Everybody except Grandpa and Hank; they treated Frankie like an equal, and expected him to do things for himself.

Gary said, "Hank, Grandpa's place is the only rural property in Upstate New York I know of where we might be able to stay. The truth is I don't even know much about it and I don't know how to get there. I was hoping you still had some ties to Grandpa, and you still remembered how to get there. Why don't you start packing your stuff, and I'll drive to your place and link up with you? If this CME thing is real, then maybe we should go visit Grandpa. Maybe you could try calling him before I get to your place. Hank, here's the bottom line. If your place is going to get overrun, I don't want to die in a shootout when the gangs reach Monroe. I'd rather bug-out to an even more remote location and keep my kids alive."

Hank didn't respond immediately. He was thinking about the late 1990's when he was still in college and in love. He had been happy back then. He and Liz, now his first ex-wife, were in their sophomore year of college when they started dating. Liz had volunteered to be Frankie's guardian ad litem while the state was making a permanent custody determination after both of Frankie's parents were killed in a car accident. As his temporary guardian, Liz took Frankie to the farm during summer breaks so Frankie could be with the only living relative that gave a damn about him, Theodore Clayton Horn, Frankie's maternal grandfather.

Grandpa dearly loved the only grandson he had east of the Mississippi, and considered Liz's willingness to serve as guardian for the summer, a huge personal favor. She could do whatever she wanted, including letting her longhaired boyfriend tag along. Hank and Liz did farm chores for a few hours each day, and made love often. Outdoor activities and sex were Hank's two favorite pastimes. He frequently did both at the same time that first summer; in a field, a lake, the barn, wherever, and whenever. Sometimes at night under the stars after Frankie had gone to bed. Sometimes in the heat of the day during or between refreshing dips in Grandpa's creek-fed pond. There had been two equally good summers after that.

The guardian duties required almost no effort at all for Liz and Hank. Grandpa was the perfect guardian. The state should have awarded him permanent custody, but didn't.

"Hello Hank? Hank, are you still there?" Gary was still on the phone. "You should also hit the bank, and get all the cash out of your accounts."

Hank's thoughts shifted back to the ugly present. Over time, Liz had turned into a nagging bitch. Then she cheated on him while he was deployed to Afghanistan. Hank's violent response to her unfaithfulness had ended their thirteen-year marriage. He had married and divorced Maggie since then, and done a year in prison. Hank hadn't gone hunting in years, and he hadn't been laid in months. The world was about to end, and his brother was giving him orders on the phone.

My brother! The bastard who didn't call me for three months when I really could have used some help. Then he calls me from out of the blue to tell me the world is going to end. While he's talking, I hear the sounds of a horrible accident and I know my neglectful brother just died. Then he returns from the dead, without an apology for the agony he caused me, to do what? To talk about Grandpa? He has no idea what Grandpa meant to me! If it weren't for Grandpa, I probably wouldn't have married Liz. I wouldn't have joined the Army. I wouldn't have gone to combat. I wouldn't have –

"Hello? Hank? Are you there, brother?"

"Goodbye," was all Hank said. He didn't add "Fuck you!" until after the line went dead.

Hank was crying. Partly because he just realized how much Grandpa had done for him while seeming to do nothing at all, and partly because he hadn't seen or spoken to Grandpa in years. The truth was, when it came to the really important people in his life, Hank had been more neglectful than his brother. He had drowned himself in his own self-pity. The truth hurt. Hank settled back in his easy chair and tried to get back to sleep. That took less courage than going back to the den, and finishing what he'd started before Gary's first call.

Hank reached down to the floor, and moved some bottles around until he found one that still had some liquid in it. He removed the cap and took a long pull, then another. One way or another, his headache would soon be gone.

Gary wanted to call his brother back, but he thought it might do more harm than good. He'd just get to Hank's place as fast as he could, and sort it all out when he got there. But looking at the traffic in front of him on the bridge, Gary knew he was still hours away from Hank's place.

Mae was still working on her laptop with an intermittent internet connection when Gary's call to Hank ended. Without looking up from the computer screen, she asked Gary, "What was that stuff you were saying about Grandpa? You don't have a Grandpa."

"You're right, he's not my Grandpa. He's a guy that Hank knows, and that's just what everybody calls him. The guy has a farm in Upstate New York. Talking to Ralph got me thinking about what we do if the CME caused a blackout that lasted a really, long time. I mean, Ralph, you know – he made preparations, and he's got a rural bug-out location, but we –"

Mae interrupted. "Gary stop right there. You're speculating! Isn't it enough that I'm willing to go to Hank's with you? I'm a lawyer, and I want to see some evidence before I make a decision. Even if the CME is real, it doesn't mean it will deal a crippling blow to United States. Nothing's happened yet, but you're already speculating about a blackout that could last months!" Mae drilled Gary with her laser-beam eyes for a moment before she continued. "I'm not going to speculate with you about what we should do after the CME hits, because maybe after the CME hits, the lights will still be on, and we'll just drive back to our house feeling like a couple of idiots."

Mae said the word "speculate" like it was a curse word or a heinous crime. Lawyers and judges hated speculation, especially in the courtroom.

"Okay, Mae. I didn't mean to upset you. You're right, we have no idea what tomorrow will bring, and we should focus on what's in front of us. We'll do just one thing at a time."

At the moment, what was in front of Gary was a lot of parked cars. Gary didn't understand why his brother had abruptly ended the phone call, but he was now more concerned with his lack of progress across the bridge. Traffic in Gary's lane had come to a full stop, even though the traffic to his left and right was still inching along. Gary would gladly have changed lanes, but drivers in the other lanes were leaving only inches of space between the cars to prevent being cut off. With the trailer attached to the Volvo, Gary would have no success.

4:12 PM

After three long minutes with no movement at all, Gary got out of the car and told Mae to change seats and get behind the steering wheel. If traffic suddenly started to move, Mae could start driving and Gary would hop in as she went by. Gary walked forward between the lanes to find the problem. More than a dozen cars ahead, he spotted a tan SUV at the front of the line of parked cars in his lane. In front of the SUV, traffic was still moving. Cars from the lanes on either side of the SUV were swooping into the gap created by the parked SUV. There was a shouting match going on between the driver of the SUV and the drivers of the cars immediately behind the SUV. It was obvious the SUV had run out of gas.

Gary could think of only one option that would get the SUV and his Volvo moving again. He quickly jogged back to his trailer, grabbed one of the full five-gallon gas cans, and jogged a little less quickly back to the SUV. The appearance of the gas can immediately ended the shouting match, and drivers of the blocked cars started going back to their vehicles in anticipation of SUV's movement. Without saying thank you, the SUV driver grabbed the can from Gary, and unscrewed the cap and extended the nozzle. Within a minute, the driver was pouring fuel into his tank.

Another minute passed and Gary said, "Hey, you only need a couple of gallons. Don't use the whole can!"

The SUV driver deliberately moved his body between Gary and the can, and continued to drain the can. Gary thought, *Screw it. What am I going to do, club him on the head? Then what? If I knock him out, who's going to drive the SUV? Fuck it, it's not worth fighting about. I'll just re-fill the can when I get to the other side of the bridge.*

When the can was empty, the driver headed toward his driver's door while still holding the can. He had not said thank you, or offered to pay for the gas. Gary suddenly realized the driver also intended to steal the empty can.

"Give me back my gas can!"

The man kept moving and opened his door. It was clear that whatever amount of civility had existed yesterday among New York City drivers was now even less. Additional pleas for the man to do the right thing would be fruitless.

Gary said, "Give me my fucking gas can, or I'll start smashing all your fucking windows."

The driver paused and looked around at traffic. He wasn't going to be able to make a quick getaway. He couldn't drive away faster than a walking pace, and Gary could easily keep up with the SUV as he bashed in the windows. For the first time, the driver made eye contact with Gary. Yes, Gary was serious. All his windows would get smashed. Without a word, the driver dropped the can, got in the SUV, and began cranking the engine.

Ungrateful bastard! Gary grabbed the can from the ground, and the spout cover from the roof of the SUV where the driver had put it and forgotten it. Gary ran back toward the Volvo. There was no room in the Volvo for the empty can, or Gary would have gotten directly into the car. As Gary ran past the Volvo to the trailer, he yelled at Mae to get back in her passenger seat. He stuffed the can in the trailer and re-locked the trailer door. By the time he jumped in the driver seat, the car in front of him had started moving. Gary just barely managed to prevent a car on his right from jumping into the empty space in front of the Volvo.

Progress was slow and steady for the rest of the trip across the bridge. As the car and trailer did a triple "thunk" over the expansion joint at the far end, Mae gave Gary's left shoulder a little squeeze. It was a rare gesture of affection. In that moment, she was truly grateful that he was by her side. When Gary had jumped out of the car earlier to get the gas can, she had gotten into the driver's seat. The seat had been too far from the steering wheel. After she made the adjustment, she realized she was stuck in a traffic jam in the middle of a bridge. She was alone in a car she rarely drove, with two kids and a loaded trailer. She had never towed a trailer before.

At that moment, Mae had a terrifying thought. *What if Gary doesn't come back?* After the shoulder squeeze, she and Gary glanced at each other and exchanged smiles. Quick, tight lipped smiles that reflected a little bit of joy and a whole lot of stress. Gary assumed Mae was just happy that, unlike thousands of others who would later try and fail, they had successfully crossed the Throgs Neck Bridge.

As vehicles coming off the bridge approached the tollbooths, the traffic fanned out from three lanes to ten. Four of the lanes were for cash payment of the toll, while the other six were for E-ZPass payments. The E-ZPass was an electronic toll collection system, which enabled travelers to prepay their toll bills with a credit card or check. Subscribers were given an electronic "toll tag" to place on the windshield of their vehicle. As the car passed through an E-ZPass tollbooth, the toll tag was read by an overhead antenna to collect the toll. A video camera recorded all toll traffic. Drivers with an insufficient balance in their account were identified and billed for the price of the toll plus a penalty.

Unlike cash payments, the E-ZPass system did not require the car to come to a full stop to make payment, so traffic moved much faster in those lanes. Gary's Volvo was equipped with an E-ZPass toll tag, but he was almost certain the balance on the tag was zero. He drove to one of the E-ZPass lanes anyway. If he ever came back to Long Island, and got an E-ZPass penalty bill in the mail, he would gladly pay it. Gary got through the tollbooth without incident.

To leave Manhattan they still needed to cross the Hudson River. With Monroe as their destination, the two obvious options were to turn sharply north on I-695, and then take I-95 to I-87, the New York State Thruway. Staying on the Thruway, Gary could cross the Hudson River on the Tappan Zee Bridge near Tarrytown.

Gary chose the second option, which was to go west before going north. Gary went left on I-295 so he could take I-95, the Cross Bronx Expressway, to the George Washington Bridge. The state line ran down the middle of the Hudson River. The east end of the bridge was in New York, and the west end was in New Jersey. After crossing the bridge, Gary would take I-94 to New Jersey State Route 4. Going west on Route 4 would take him to New Jersey Route 17 north. About fifty miles later, he would enter New York near the town of Suffern. From there, it was less than thirty miles to Monroe on NY State Route 17 and I-87.

Gary hated New Jersey for almost no other reason than he was a New Yorker. However, today he was more worried about getting across the Hudson River, than he was about the awful smell of the "Garden State." If he had chosen the first option and gone north on I-695, he would have stayed on the wrong side of the Hudson River for an additional twenty-five miles, and perhaps another hour. What if traffic got significantly worse during that time? What if the Tappan Zee Bridge was a solid traffic jam when Gary got there? What if the CME came early and the bridge was plugged up with disabled cars?

Gary didn't want to swim his family across the river so he went west through the Bronx toward the George Washington Bridge or the "GWB" as the locals called it. Yes, he would have to spend some time in New Jersey, but hopefully, the journey would be quick and the smell wouldn't be too bad.

4:21 PM

Gary took the Cross Bronx Expressway from the Throgs Neck Bridge to the George Washington Bridge. The distance was only thirteen miles, but traffic was bumper-to-bumper and slow. Few cars got off at the exit ramps, and the entrance ramps all seemed to have newcomers wanting to go west across the GWB. With the incoming traffic slowing down the right lane, Gary decided he needed to get into the left lane. With the trailer it was difficult. By the time he got to Bronx River Parkway, he was in the middle lane, but that was as far as he got. When Gary got on the four-lane upper level of the GWB, the Volvo was in the second lane from the right.

There were pedestrian paths on both sides of the bridge that were separated from vehicle traffic by a metal barrier. As he slowly progressed across the bridge, Gary saw several motorcycles speed by on the pedestrian path. It was of course against the law, but the riders obviously didn't care. Having enjoyed the flexibility of two-wheeled transportation earlier in the day, Gary concluded that a motorcycle was the ultimate bug-out vehicle. If he had possessed the foresight to prepare a bug-out location, perhaps he and Mae could have traveled light, and left the city on two motorcycles; with each bike carrying one adult and one child. On motorcycles, their travel time would have been reduced by half, maybe more.

Near the mid-point of the bridge, traffic in Gary's lane again slowed dramatically. Traffic in the two lanes to his left was inching along at a faster pace, but traffic in the right lane was even slower than Gary's lane. When traffic came to a full stop for about half a minute, Gary got out of the car to see what was ahead. He wasn't high enough to see over the minivans and SUVs ahead of him. The car in front of the Volvo moved a few yards ahead. Gary got back in the Volvo, and moved it forward.

When traffic stopped again, Gary got out again. This time he immediately climbed onto the hood of the Volvo where he was able to see the problem. His shoes were probably scratching the car's paint, but car paint was one of many previously important things in Gary's life that no longer mattered. From his new vantage point, Gary could see that the right lane had been closed off with construction barriers from the mid-point of the bridge all the way to the far end. The construction seemed to involve painting or other light-duty work because the lane's concrete surface appeared to be intact. There were a few small pieces of equipment including light kits, generators, and solar powered flashing lights, but there were no trucks or other large items blocking the lane inside the construction barriers. There were also no workers. Perhaps they had heard the CME rumor and left the job site.

Ahead of him, Gary could see drivers in the blocked right lane trying to change lanes to the left. In the bumper-to-bumper traffic, the only drivers who were succeeding were creating their own gap by driving into the fender of a car in Gary's lane. Gary had a different idea. He got back in the car, and crept forward with traffic. When he got close to the barrier at the construction site, Gary left a gap in front of the Volvo. Two cars from the right lane moved to the left in front of the Volvo. With a quick warning to Mae and the girls, Gary hit the gas, and turned into the right lane through the gap where the two cars had been. He deliberately hit the concrete construction barrier with the front end of the Volvo.

Gary's plan failed. With only the short run up, the Volvo had only moved the barrier about a foot, and the hit had not been hard enough to deploy the car's airbags. Gary slammed the car into reverse backed up until he hit the car behind him, and rammed the barrier again. The barrier moved another foot. At this rate, Gary figured he would have to hit the barrier about four more times. That process would probably kill his radiator, and without a radiator, the entire car would be useless. Gary had expected the barrier to move more easily.

The Volvo was mostly in the far right lane, but the trailer was still partially blocking the next lane over, the second lane from the right. Drivers in that lane didn't quite have enough room to squeeze by the trailer, and they were angry. However, drivers in the third lane from the right were gleeful. Some of them smiled and waved to Gary as they passed him, and gained several yards of quick movement by turning into the second lane from the right, which was obstructed by Gary's trailer.

The driver behind Gary in the right lane, with the newly smashed front end on his car, was not happy. He got out of his car. He was waving his fists, and he was huge. Within seconds, the big, unhappy driver was banging on Gary's window and screaming curses at him. Outside Mae's window, a passenger from the same car, who could have passed for the driver's similarly sized twin brother, was delivering a similar tirade. The girls were screaming in terror while Mae was yelling helpful things like, "What the hell did you do Gary? What the hell are you going to do now?"

The cacophony was painful to his ears. Gary felt like he was going to vomit. What the hell had he been thinking? On the first bridge, he had given away five gallons of gas to clear an obstruction, but now he had created an obstruction that was blocking two lanes of traffic. He might also have disabled the Volvo by crushing its front end. His idea to exit the bridge hastily, by opening the construction lane, now seemed like a very bad idea.

Gary didn't dare open either window to strike up a conversation with one of the two huge angry men. His plan had not worked. If it had, the two men from the car behind him would have been happy. They would have been the second vehicle to gain access to a previously barricaded but now open lane. The rest of the trip across the traffic-jammed bridge would have taken less than two minutes. It was obvious that the twins were not interested in discussing Gary's failed plan. They wanted some form of compensation for their damaged vehicle, and Gary's severed head seemed to be the preferred payment.

So what now? Abandon the plan? If Gary backed into the other car one more time, he might get enough room to go forward, and swing the Volvo back into the lane he had just left. Then, if the Volvo was still functional, he could continue his journey across the bridge. But like the SUV driver who stole his gas, Gary's getaway would not be quick. He'd still be in bumper-to-bumper traffic and moving at a walking pace. The big angry brothers would probably smash all his windows. Still, there appeared to be no other option. Gary shifted the car into reverse.

Before he released the brake, Gary saw movement out of the corner of his right eye. He glanced to his right and saw another man approaching. This man was as tall as the screaming Sumo twins, but while twins were mostly fat, this man was mostly fit. Fit Man walked past the cursing twin on Mae's side of the car without doing anything. It wasn't his fight – yet. He hopped on top of the barrier that Gary had hit twice without much affect. Fit Man looked down the long open construction lane. Then he looked over at Gary and smiled. Gary smiled back. Gary knew he was looking at his savior.

The man was the driver of a double-cab, dual-wheeled, pickup truck that was immediately behind the car that Gary had backed into. Fit Man whistled back in the direction he had come from, and made a "come here" motion. Three other big men exited the pickup truck and joined the first man. The truck was owned by a contractor, and the men were obviously a construction crew. After hearing the doomsday rumor, all four men had abandoned their project so they could rejoin their families on the other side of the bridge. The four big men were soon heaving together to move the barrier out of the way. When they were done, Gary knew he could easily move into the construction lane by backing up a few feet, and turning to the right as he went forward again.

Gary didn't move immediately. He was waiting for a signal from Fit Man to proceed. The fat twins were still pounding on the Volvo. They had not grasped the significance of Fit Man's actions. The fat men were so intent on getting retribution from Gary that they had forgotten why they were on the bridge. With the barrier out of the way, Fit Man walked over to the fat man who was near Gary's window. He was about to solve the fat man's memory problem. The truck driver grabbed the fat man by the throat and squeezed hard. Hard enough to shut off the fat man's words, and his breathing. On the other side of the car, the other three members of Fit Man's crew were standing very close to Fat Man's brother. He shut up without getting his throat squeezed.

In the relative quiet, Gary heard the truck driver say, "Get your sorry ass back in your car, and follow the Volvo through the gap. If you don't move now, I will knock you and your chubby buddy unconscious. I will throw both of you off the fucking bridge, and one of my men will drive your car. If you choose to live and drive, but don't drive fast enough, I'll ram you with my truck. If you stop for any reason, I'll probably toss your entire car off the bridge with you inside. Do you understand?!"

To Gary, a professor with some verbal prowess, it was the sweetest, most eloquent presentation he had heard in years. The fat man, his eyes wide with fear, nodded the half inch that Fit Man's grasp would allow. When he was released, Fat Man held his throat as he wheezed and waddled back to his car. The truck driver gave Gary another smile, and a nod. Gary gave a little salute with his left hand. Then he took his foot off the brake, and backed up. He hit fatso's car with the trailer one more time; partly because he needed a few more inches of turning room, but mostly because he felt like it. Then he shifted into drive and hit the gas.

He was soon moving at thirty miles an hour and maneuvering around the occasional piece of construction equipment. Fat Man's car was never more than two feet behind the back of Gary's trailer. It was clear the bloviating brothers had no desire to go swimming while they were unconscious. The girls settled down considerably before the Volvo reached the far end of the bridge. Even after the bridge ended, the construction lane continued down the shoulder, with concrete barriers along the left side all the way to the first exit. At the first exit, Gary steered left through a gap at the end of the barriers and joined the flow of traffic. All lanes on this side of the bridge were now moving at about fifteen miles an hour. It wasn't highway speed, but it felt wonderfully fast.

Fat Man's car continued to follow Gary. The pickup truck with the construction workers took the exit ramp. Gary figured that some of the crew must be pretty close to home, or they were going to a parking area to reclaim their personal vehicles and go their separate ways. Gary extended his left arm through his open window and gave a little wave above the roof of his car. After he gave the wave, Gary remembered that the Volvo had a luggage carrier on roof that had probably blocked his wave from the truck driver's sight. The pickup disappeared quickly, and Gary couldn't tell if the driver had seen his wave or waved back. Without the construction crew's help, Gary knew he'd still be stuck on the bridge, and his car's windows would probably be broken. Gary owed a debt he could never repay.

Chapter 10: The road to Monroe.

5:02 PM

When Gary hit the pavement that was on dirt rather than bridge decking, he breathed a sigh of relief. The two bridges were behind him. Traffic speed increased, and it seemed that more cars were getting off at the exits than getting on. Perhaps some of the drivers were commuters who were going to their homes in the nearby suburbs. Maybe some of them would do what Gary had done by going home, packing up some food and other necessities, and getting back on the highway. Gary thought the decreased traffic volume might be a sweet spot created by the amount of time those drivers were off the highway and packing.

Gary didn't care why it happened, he was just happy to be moving a little faster. To celebrate, and perhaps in an effort to restore some sense of normalcy, Gary turned on the radio and selected an all music station. But the radio wasn't broadcasting normalcy, it was broadcasting the President of the United States.

". . . White House earlier today, at a press conference regarding the ongoing Chinese military exercises, a reporter went off topic and asked the President about the civil unrest in New York, Baltimore, and other east coast cities. The President made the following statement."

The radio cut to a clip of the President speaking. "The uh stuff . . . I mean rumors that some of you are hearing from um . . . urban cities in the uh eastern shoreline . . . are just rumors. Let me be clear, there is nothing to worry about. There is no uh . . . catastrophe about to happen. Folks should stay home. Don't panic. It wouldn't be prudent. We're uh . . . gonna laugh about this tomorrow."

The station commentator cut back in. "In other news . . . ." Gary turned off the radio. His celebratory mood was gone. He said, "Civil unrest? Those are strong words. We just came through the city; did you see any civil unrest?"

"No Gary, but how could we? We were on the highway. How could we know what's going on in the residential neighborhoods and business districts?"

"Well you're right, I was focused on the traffic and didn't spend any time studying the neighborhoods, but I didn't get any sense that riots were already in progress. Clogged highways and ticked-off motorists yes, but I didn't see any civil unrest. But hey, if civil unrest in the city is really happening, then I'm glad we're already across the two bridges."

Mae just nodded as she continued to look at her computer screen. Gary reviewed in his mind what the President had said, and compared it to the information he had received from Blake. The two messages could not be reconciled; both men could not be correct. A short time after the President's message, the volume of westbound traffic seemed to increase. Maybe Gary was imagining things, but the President's approval ratings had been in the toilet for months. Perhaps when the President told his subjects what to do, many of them now did the opposite.

Gary couldn't disagree with the people who rejected the President's instruction to stay home. He just wished the President had kept his mouth shut for another hour or so. Traffic again slowed to a crawl. Gary suddenly remembered that he and Mae wanted to get some more cash before the banks stopped handing it out. He also had an empty five-gallon gas can, and a car that had burned through a quarter of a tank of gas. With traffic moving so slowly, now might be a good time to leave the highway, because he wouldn't lose much forward progress while he was gone.

"Mae, what's the next exit that has a Wal-Mart store?"

"Gary, what if the President is right, and we're panicking about nothing?"

"Huh? What?"

"You heard me. I don't think the President of the United States would say something to the entire country that would be proven wrong in a matter of hours." Mae and Gary had different opinions about the President. Politics was a topic Gary tried hard to avoid, but Mae had just raised it.

"Mae, I know you like the guy, but what was he supposed to say? At this point, nobody knows with 100% certainty how bad the CME will be. Maybe it will deliver an EMP that is big enough to fry every electrical circuit in the entire country. Or maybe the effects will be confined to the eastern third of the United States, and a big chunk of the grid will survive. If the President grossly understated the danger in his recent message, then tomorrow he'll just say, 'Oops, my expert advisors were wrong, and nobody could have predicted the CME would be this bad.' He could say that even if his experts *did* accurately predict how bad it would be."

Mae still looked skeptical. "I don't know, Gary. I just think –"

"Mae, look, we have already had this discussion. There's no use second-guessing ourselves right now. We're hoping for the best, and planning for the worst. We're going to Hank's house tonight. If nothing happens, we'll drive back home in the morning."

"I'm going to feel like an ass if this turns out to be nothing, and I have to go back to the law firm tomorrow and admit I panicked for no good reason."

"Mae, we covered this already. We don't know what will happen tonight. The mention of civil unrest on the radio means a lot of other people believe the CME is real. Let's stick to the plan."

Gary's thoughts were less firm than his words. He knew that Blake and Ralph believed a super CME was going to hit North America, but what if the President was right and the CME was no big deal? At this point, several hours after Blake's phone call, the President probably had more accurate data. Gary recalled a quotation that Churchill or Franklin Roosevelt had said during World War II, "The only thing we have to fear is fear itself." Maybe that was the only real threat the CME presented, "fear itself." *What if the panic caused by the fear of a calamity caused more death and destruction, than the calamity itself? What if there were city-wide riots in New York tonight, but tomorrow morning the lights were still on and the cars were still functioning? How many people would die, and how many businesses would be destroyed, by a disaster that didn't happen?*

Gary thought about his mad dash out of the city on the motorcycle, and how he almost wrecked the bike. *What if Mae or I had been killed while I was running away from a rumor rather than a real emergency?* Gary looked out the window. Traffic leaving the city seemed unusually heavy, but it was still a beautiful, clear sunny autumn day in eastern New York. It sure didn't look like the heavens had any deadly surprise in store for mankind. For the third or fourth time, Gary shook off his doubts and re-committed himself to his bug-out plan. The agony of the unknown was acute, but it was impossible to eliminate the unknown, so why agonize over it? *I need to focus on something that will accomplish something.*

"Hey Mae, what's the next exit with a Wal-Mart?" Gary repeated the question he had asked before Mae sidetracked him with her doubts about Blake's information.

"I was hoping you'd forget that question, because if the President's right, you're going to buy a bunch of stuff that we'll have to drag back to the house tomorrow and probably never use."

"Maybe so Mae, because we can't predict the future, but we should stick to the plan. So what exit has a Wal-Mart that's close to the road?"

Mae had been searching the internet since Gary first asked about the closest Wal-Mart. "To get to the nearest Wal-Mart we'll have to take a slight detour."

"How much of a detour?"

"It's only a few minutes out of the way. Instead of going northwest onto Route 4, we'll stay on I-95 south a little longer, and get on I-80 west for a couple of miles. Then we'll take Exit 65 toward Teterboro."

"Teterboro? I've never heard of it."

"Well you've heard of Hackensack, and Teterboro is south of South Hackensack."

Gary said, "We also need to hit the bank. We're not going to be able get any more cash from an ATM, but if we can find a branch office for our bank, we can withdraw additional money directly from the account. Does our bank have a branch at the same exit?"

There was a pause as Mae struggled with the slow internet. Then she said, "Yes. After we get off the interstate, we'll cross over Route 46 to get to the Wal-Mart. If we go east on Route 46 for a little bit, we'll get to a bank, a gas station, a Burger King, and eventually a McDonalds."

Gary thought about the time required to do the errands. He would have preferred to take Mae to the bank and wait for her to finish that errand before going shopping. The girls could stay in the car, and one adult would be with them and the valuable contents of the Volvo. It would, however, take twice as long to do the errands. With the two bridges behind him, Gary was confident he would make it to Hank's house. He was now more worried about the bank running out of cash, and store running out of canned goods.

"Mae, why don't we split up? I'll drop you at the bank, and take the girls with me to Wal-Mart. When I'm done shopping, I'll come back and pick you up." Gary knew he could handle both girls in the store better than Mae could handle even one of them at the bank

"So you'll trust me not to empty our accounts, and then hop on a Greyhound bus with all that cash before you get back from the store?"

Gary laughed. "If the CME is as bad as Blake and Ralph think it will be, a Greyhound bus full of strangers is about the last place you would want to be. Especially if you have several thousand dollars in your pockets."

Mae scoffed. "Actually, I was thinking Hank's house is the last place I want to be. How long has it been since his wife left him? It's just a wild guess, but I have a hunch Hank hasn't been keeping up with the house-keeping."

Gary gave a short laugh, but said nothing. Mae wasn't much of a housekeeper either. But she still had a spouse who did some of it, and a well-paid cleaning service that did the rest. Gary got off at the exit and went east on Route 46 to get to the bank. As expected, the bank was busy. Most of the parking spaces were full. Gary drove to the entrance, let Mae out, and drove away. Mae took her computer so it wouldn't be left unattended in the car when Gary went shopping.

Gary went west on Route 46 and took a left on Industrial Drive to the Wal-Mart store. He parked and got both girls out of the car. He was concerned about the security of the car and trailer. If he never made it back to his house, then the car, the trailer, and the rooftop carrier now did contain all of his and Mae's possessions. He left his laptop in the car, locked the Volvo and checked the rear doors of the trailer, which were also locked. He did not have padlocks on the roof top carrier. He would just have to assume some risk and shop as fast as possible. Gary grabbed an empty shopping cart from a nearby parking space and put both girls inside. He jogged to the store with Josephine in the cart's seat, and Jane kneeling inside the cart. Jane had her hands on the front edge of the cart and was facing forward. She enjoyed the jog more than Josephine did.

As he jogged, Gary wished he had a concealed-carry pistol. It was the first time he had ever made such a wish at a Wal-Mart. While Gary was crossing the parking lot, Mae had reached the front of a line at the bank, and was now speaking to a bank teller.

Mae asked the teller for the account balances in both savings and checking. The savings account had twelve thousand dollars, and checking had seven thousand. Mae earned a lot of money as an attorney, but she sent most of her paycheck and her trust income directly to her investments. Given her doubts about the CME, Mae felt stupid about withdrawing a large sum of cash, but she did what Gary had asked her to do, and told the teller she wanted ten thousand dollars from the savings account. Half in fifty dollar bills, the other half in twenties.

The teller looked awkwardly at Mae for a moment. She was a young woman in her twenties, probably fresh out of college. "I'm sorry Ms. Seymour, I can't do that."

"What do you mean you can't do that? Do I need to take it all in hundred dollar bills or something?"

"Ma'am, the bank has a new policy. You can't withdraw more than one thousand dollars of cash in one day, and that includes ATM withdrawals. I see here on the computer screen that you have already used an ATM to withdraw five hundred from checking today. I can give you only another five hundred dollars. You can come back tomorrow and get more if you like."

"This new policy is ridiculous. I have withdrawn larger sums from my accounts in the past. When did this policy go into effect?"

The teller looked even more uncomfortable, and glanced at her watch, "An hour ago."

"Why? Why did you change your withdrawal policy so suddenly?"

"I don't know. We're supposed to say it's just a new bank policy, but I think it's because of the internet rumor. The world is supposed to end tomorrow or something like that." It was clear the teller didn't believe the rumor.

For a moment, Mae wondered whether the CME was real, or if everyone including her husband was deluded. To the teller, Mae said, "Your new policy is stupid. It's my money, and you have no right to keep it from me. Please give me the ten grand, or I'll talk to your boss."

"I'm sorry Ms. Seymour, I truly am. I can't give you that much money, but yes, you can talk to the manager if you like. He's right over there."

The teller pointed to a desk on the far side of the bank. "As you can see you'll have to wait several minutes because Mr. Lane is already talking to other customers."

Mae looked toward Mr. Lane's desk. A waiting area near the desk had four chairs. All the chairs were full and two people were standing near the full chairs.

Mae turned back to the teller. Bluster hadn't worked, and it made no sense to shoot the messenger. Mae glanced at the teller's nametag. In a more pleasant tone than she had used earlier, Mae said, "Thank you, Lisa. I know the new policy was not your idea. Before I see Mr. Lane, would you please give me the additional five hundred dollars? I'll take it all in twenties."

The teller smiled with relief. "Yes, Ma'am." Two minutes later, Mae was seventh in line at Mr. Lane's desk. She was glad the manager was a male. She figured she would have a better chance at getting the money. It took more than twenty minutes for Mae to get to the seat in front of Mr. Lane's desk. While waiting in line, she adjusted her blouse, unbuttoned the top button, and discreetly used her compact mirror to freshen her make-up. She also watched Mr. Lane as she waited. He seemed to be reaching an accommodation with each customer. The requirement to visit Mr. Lane deterred most customers from withdrawing excess cash. Those who endured the wait, were getting at least some of what they wanted.

Mr. Lane felt that it was his job to comply, as much as possible, with the new directive from higher headquarters. If he slowed the withdrawal rate too much, it might create a panic. People might leave the bank and claim they couldn't get their money out. Mr. Lane knew that at some point, the bank *would* run out of cash and be forced to close its doors. He was convinced that closing the doors early, was inevitable. He was also convinced that he'd like to get home to his wife and kids as soon as possible, particularly if the doomsday rumor was true. From a standpoint of pure, personal self-interest, the faster the bank ran out of cash, the sooner Mr. Lane could go home. Mr. Lane decided he had to slow the withdrawal rate enough so he could later tell his boss that he had tried very hard to comply with the new policy. In reality, Mr. Lane was being more generous with the customers than he had to be. Getting home was his primary goal.

When it was her turn, Mae walked slowly and deliberately toward Mr. Lane's desk. She made eye contact with Mr. Lane, and gave him a smile. Not a big happy-to-see-you smile, but one that she hoped conveyed worry; like a beautiful damsel in distress who hopes the man in front of her can slay the dragon. When she sat down in front of his desk, Mae deliberately leaned forward to give Mr. Lane a good long look at some of her assets. Then she slid her bankcard and driver's license across the desk. She smiled again, and asked for nine thousand dollars in cash.

Mr. Lane looked at his computer screen, entered a few keystrokes and said, "I see you have already withdrawn the daily maximum of one thousand dollars."

"Mr. Lane, even after I make this additional withdrawal, I will still have thousands of dollars left in my accounts. My paycheck is directly deposited to this bank every two weeks. I've been banking here for more than a decade and hope to continue that relationship."

There was no need to state overtly that she would change banks if she didn't get what she wanted. Implied threats were just as effective, and a little more polite.

"Ms. Seymour, most other banks have an identical withdrawal policy right now. Whether or not the doomsday rumor is true, today is not a normal business day. I anticipate this policy will be temporary, and within a few days there will again be no limits on withdrawals."

Mae had already decided not to bully Mr. Lane with her "powerful lawyer" routine. She had chosen what she hoped would be a more effective approach. She glanced around as if she was nervous or upset about something. She put on a distraught expression as if she was about to cry. She couldn't deliver tears on demand, but she could and did get her lower lip to tremble a bit. Then she lowered her eyes and pulled out a tissue.

In a low halting tone she explained that her need for cash had nothing to do with the doomsday rumor. Her husband had thrown her out of the house, and she needed a place to stay. She had to have cash to rent an apartment on short notice. She needed twenty-five hundred dollars for the first month's rent, and another twenty-five hundred for the deposit. The rest of the cash would be for expenses, like getting the utilities turned on. She was also afraid her husband would try to empty the bank accounts, and she'd have no money until she transferred her direct deposit to an account that didn't have his name on it. Mae wiggled in her chair and leaned forward again as she spoke.

Mr. Lane thought Mae was lying, but her act had been a good one, and she was a good customer. Mr. Lane was well aware of Mae's physical assets. As an accountant by training and trade, however, he knew that all assets came with certain liabilities. Mr. Lane hadn't gotten to his current position by fooling around with his clients' assets. Mr. Lane was a professional, and a happily-married family man. He would have given Mae the same amount of money regardless of her physical assets or her bogus plea.

"Tell you what, Ms. Seymour. While I am concerned about your husband emptying the accounts, the bank can't get involved in disagreements like that. I've seen situations where the husband claims it's the wife's fault. I'm not saying that's what's going on here, I'm just saying I don't know what's going on, and the bank can't choose sides."

Mae held her distraught expression as she nodded. She really needed to get better at faking tears.

"Here's what I'll do. I'll give you another five grand. That's enough to get you into the um, apartment. That will bring your total withdrawals for today to six thousand dollars, which is six days worth of withdrawals at the rate of one thousand dollars a day. I'm going to put a hold on your account. If the new policy is not canceled, you won't be able to make any additional withdrawals until next week."

"Oh thank you, thank you Mr. Lane." Mae wasted some effort as she played the role of rescued damsel.

Mr. Lane returned Mae's driver's license and bankcard along with a slip of paper with the authorized withdrawal amount and his signature on it. Then he sent her back to the tellers, just as he had done for the six people before her. Mr. Lane spent a few moments making the necessary adjustments on his computer. Hopefully, the six-day hold on Mae's account would convince his superiors he had complied, as much as possible, with the new policy.

As Mae walked away, the next customer in line was a man in his forties. He was still sitting in the waiting-area. When Mr. Lane looked up from his computer screen, the next customer was staring at Mae's backside. Mr. Lane thought, *What a pig!* But he wouldn't let his personal feelings affect how he did business with the man.

Gary entered the Wal-Mart and saw chaos. No carts were available for shoppers who hadn't bothered to grab one from the parking lot. Some shoppers argued with the greeter about it, others went back outside and got a cart. Gary went directly to the canned goods aisle where other shoppers were hastily filling their carts. The shoppers appeared to have no doubts about the coming disaster. They were mostly predisposed Believers, and Gary joined the fray. There was an occasional harsh word, when shoppers bumped into each other as they went for the same item at the same time. But no punches were exchanged. The shoppers were assertive, but not yet openly aggressive. With the two girls in his cart, some shoppers even yielded to Gary. A veneer of civilized behavior still existed.

Gary had to take what he could get. He looked at the shelf closest to him and saw pumpkin pie filling. All the other canned fruit, even the apple pie filling, was already gone. Gary didn't even like pumpkin pie, but he put a dozen cans in his cart. Then he pressed his way down the aisle and snagged several cans of condensed soup. Even as he shopped, the intensity of the shoppers seemed to increase. Gary soon found himself grabbing any cans that didn't have somebody else's hands on them. He didn't bother to look at the labels. When he caught people trying to reach past his daughters to pull cans out of his cart, Gary decided it was time to leave the aisle.

With his cart half-full, he started to think of other high-value items to have in a crisis. Jane complained about having to sit on the pile of cans, as Gary hurried to the other side of the store. The camping gear aisles were mostly empty, and he grabbed the last two flashlights. They both required D-sized batteries. Gary went to the front of the store, but the battery displays by the registers were empty. While he was there,

Gary spotted some cigarette lighters and grabbed two packages. Gary went to the back of the store, to the electronics section, where he found another battery display that wasn't yet empty. He took several packages of batteries in every size he could find; C, D, AA, and AAA, and even four nine-volt batteries.

Gary felt like his shopping trip had already taken too long, and he remembered that he couldn't buy too many items, because he had no packing space left in the Volvo or the trailer. Gary again hurried to the front of the store. He stopped at an end cap display that had economy-sized packages of toilet paper. As he grabbed one, he noticed he was near the aisle that had wax paper and aluminum foil. Gary stopped and looked at the boxes of foil for a second. Then it came to him. Ralph had said that anything that was insulated, and then wrapped in foil would be protected from the CME.

If it were true, the fact was not common knowledge, because the store still had an ample supply of aluminum foil. Gary did some quick math using the calculator on his cell phone and determined that five rolls would probably be enough to cover one car. Gary grabbed ten large rolls of aluminum foil, then paused and grabbed two more. Then he went to the hardware section and got four rolls of duct tape, and half a dozen rolls of masking tape.

When he finally got to the checkout lines, they were long and slow. He looked at the carts of his fellow shoppers and saw an abundance of canned food among the carts. Many shoppers had done what Gary had done, and settled for whatever they could get. Well, except for the aluminum foil; few people were buying anything other than food, water, toilet paper, flashlights, and camping supplies. Gary saw just one other shopper, a man about ten years older than Gary, who had six rolls of aluminum foil in his cart. While Gary was looking in the man's direction, the other man briefly looked back, and then looked away.

Very few shoppers were making eye contact or chatting with each other. Everybody seemed to be guarding their carts and a little embarrassed by their assertive shopping spree. Their journey through the aisles had been akin to a contact sport.

Gary didn't turn to look, but he could hear two men behind him talking to each other. They were friends who had traveled separately to the store, and run into each other at the checkout line. Gary heard one say he knew somebody, who had a friend, who knew a guy, who worked at NASA. The other guy talked about information he'd seen on an internet survivalist blog. Both thought the President's message was designed to keep people at home, rather than rioting in the streets, or running for their lives, and clearing store shelves as they went. They complained about the absence of any guns and ammunition in the store.

Gary still had some doubts about the CME, but seeing and hearing the other shoppers in the store caused the doubt to recede. *Could all these shoppers be wrong? There must be other sources of information* out there, other people like Blake or Ralph. Perhaps professional astronomers at NASA, and even amateur astronomers who had somehow figured it out. Could sun flares be observed by telescopes used by amateurs? Gary didn't know. Could all those sources be wrong, and the President be right? At the moment, Gary thought not.

It seemed to take forever for Gary to reach the register. When he got there, he was happy to see the store was still accepting credit cards. While the cashier ran the items through the scanner, Gary looked at what was left in the candy and magazine racks. The racks were mostly empty, and every candy bar was gone. There were still some gum and breath mints left. There were also a few nail clippers, Sharpie markers, Chapstick tubes, and other typical last-minute purchase items. Encouraged by what other shoppers were doing, Gary grabbed an assortment of everything that was available. He put it all on his credit card. He was more than half-convinced that he would never see, let alone pay, the bill.

As soon as his bagged items were in the cart, Gary hurried out of the store. He wanted to get to the Volvo as soon as possible. It had suddenly occurred to him that Mae was probably already waiting for him outside the bank right now with a whole lot of cash. Gary ran across the parking lot with the grocery cart, and neither daughter enjoyed the ride. When he got to the car, he was relieved to see that the car, trailer, and roof top carrier were unmolested and still secure. All three areas however, had already been filled to capacity prior to his shopping spree.

Gary put most of the new items on the floor in front of the kids' seats. He also put several items on the floor in front of Mae's seat. He had to rip open the package of toilet paper and distribute about half the rolls individually into odd places, before he crammed the rest of the package between the top of the pile and the ceiling in the back of the car. The rear suspension was now squashed flat. With the weight of the trailer on the car's hitch, the nose of the Volvo was slanted upward. If he drove at night, oncoming cars would think Gary had his high beams on.

Gary went directly to the bank and got Mae. She was standing outside the bank right next to the front door. If she had felt threatened, she could have been back inside the bank in two steps. As Mae was attempting to get into the car, she encountered the clutter of cans on the floor in front of her seat.

"Gary, what did you do? Do you really think we need all this stuff? Good grief. How many cans of pumpkin pie filling did you buy? Did you suddenly become a pastry chef?"

"Mae, if you had been in the store and seen what I saw, you'd have done the same thing. People are stocking up like crazy. Apparently a whole lot of people think – no, they *know* – the CME is real."

"Yeah, well a lot of people also spent a lot of time and money getting ready for Y2K and the end of the Mayan calendar. They were all proven to be fools. I'll bet that shortly after those two non-events, a lot of pumpkin pie filling went into trash cans, rather than pie crusts."

"Maybe you're right Mae, but some of the store's shelves were empty by the time I left. I don't recall that happening for the two crises you just mentioned. In another few hours, all the shelves will be empty, and I'll bet the same thing will happen in a lot of other stores." Gary continued talking as he started driving before Mae's seat belt was on. "Which way to the nearest gas station?"

Mae recalled the information she had gathered earlier. "Take a left out of the parking lot. We've got to go further east on Route 46."

As Gary took a left out of the parking lot, he asked, "How did you make out at the bank?"

"I got fifty-five hundred dollars."

"That's all? I thought we had twice that much in our accounts."

"We do, but about an hour ago the bank reduced their withdrawal limit to just one thousand dollars."

"Whoa! Just one thousand dollars? Well then you did a good job."

Gary was in a good mood. They were out of the city, and had successfully hit the bank and the grocery store. Just to mess with Mae, Gary added, "Wait a minute. If the limit was just one thousand and you got more than five thousand, then how did you – what did you have to do to get the additional money? I mean, I was at Wal-Mart for a long time. Did you um, do something special for the bank manager?" Gary was smiling, but Mae didn't think it was funny.

"No Gary, I didn't! You're a pig! If I ever have to do favors for a man to get what I need to survive, I'll demand more than five thousand dollars *of my own money* as payment!"

"It's *our* money sweetheart. But yeah, I guess you're right, when you put it that way. You would only be paying yourself for doing the deed."

"Why don't you shut up and drive and I'll see if I can get an internet connection?"

Gary slowed the car as he turned into the gas station. "Sure hon, anything you say. But let's get some gas first."

As Gary got in a line behind two other cars waiting for a pump, Jane said she needed to pee. Gary wondered why Jane hadn't mentioned it while they were at Wal-Mart. Maybe the run across the parking lot back to the car had shaken it out of her.

In a resigned tone, Mae said, "I'll handle it," as she kicked her feet free of the canned goods, got out of the car, and took Jane to the bathroom. Mae didn't want to pump the gas, and she decided she needed a bathroom break as well.

When Mae got back to the car with Jane, Gary was just pulling up to the pump. He left the engine running and paid at the pump with a credit card. He topped off the Volvo, filled the five-gallon can, and didn't bother to get a receipt. When he was done, Mae and Jane were already strapped into the car, and Mae had started a new video.

Gary drove the car out of the station and drove west on Route 46 and then went north on Route 17. In about twenty miles, he would be out of New Jersey. The city of Monroe was another twenty miles after that. Traffic volume on State Highway 17 was high. The pace was steady but slower than usual. Mae checked on the girls. The video was still playing but both girls were sleeping.

As Gary drove, Mae downloaded survival guides and You-tube videos. The internet was slow, and getting slower. Eventually, the process came to a complete stop even though Mae still had a strong signal. Mae told Gary that she'd been able to download lots of stuff since they had left Islip, but she couldn't get any additional material, at least for now.

"Did you find anything good?"

"Gary, I didn't take the time to review most of what I downloaded, so it will take months of reading to figure out whether any of it is good. One item, however, did strike me as potentially useful for our situation. I mean, helpful if the CME actually occurs."

"All right, I'll take the bait, Mae. What item was that?"

"It's a book called *Beyond Collapse*, by T. Joseph Miller, Jr."

"You downloaded an entire book?"

"Yes, it was less than eight megabytes. Here's the thing Gary, the download is free and the author *wants* people to download it for free. In fact, he wants readers to send electronic copies of the book to other people for free. If someone wants a paperback copy, they can order it on-line and pay for it like any other book, but it's completely legal to download the digital version for free."

"Makes you wonder how good the book is, if this guy Miller is giving it away for free."

"That's just what I thought Gary, so it's one of the few items I spent some time reading, and what I read was really good stuff. This guy covers lots of disaster scenarios and several different ways to bug out, then he focuses on how to survive and rebuild after the collapse. If the CME is truly catastrophic, this book would be something every survivor would want to have."

"Well if it's all that, then I'm glad you downloaded it. If it's free, it kind of makes you wonder why everybody doesn't download it. So *Beyond Collapse* was the only noteworthy thing you found?"

"No. While I waited for stuff to download, I read up a little on coronal mass ejections and electromagnetic pulses. Did you know that CME's have hit earth before and caused blackouts?"

"Um, yeah. When this whole mess started with Blake's phone call, he told me a CME hit Canada in nineteen eighty something. He said there was an even bigger CME that hit about a hundred years ago."

"Actually it was more than a hundred and fifty years ago, in 1859. It was called the Carrington event, because it was observed and recorded by English astronomer Richard Carrington. There was another CME in 1921 called the Railroad Storm, but it gets a lot less coverage than the Carrington event."

"Blake mentioned Carrington, but I don't recall him saying anything about a railroad storm."

Mae said, "Well, I guess the Carrington CME was a much bigger event. It says here that it was an X-50. There was no electrical grid back then, but the CME was strong enough to keep the telegraph wires charged even after they were disconnected from their regular power supply."

"Well Mae, it's nice to know that you are now the resident CME expert." Gary smiled as he said it. He knew Mae wasn't at all interested in astronomy or any of the other sciences. Mae made a harrumph sound and said she was going to close her eyes for a bit.

The drive across the bridges and out of the city had been frantic, and a little scary. Now, traffic volume was high, but with fewer population centers and fewer exits, there were fewer variations in the flow. Drivers were mostly staying in their lanes and moving to their destinations at a relatively steady pace. It was akin to the difference between the first two miles of a marathon foot race, and miles twelve through eighteen. The drivers were grinding out the miles with few changes in their placement.

The twenty-mile drive from Teterboro New Jersey to the New York border at Suffern was uneventful. Traffic thinned out a bit as Gary got further and further from New York City. At Suffern, Highway 17 joined I-287 and then transitioned into Interstate 87. When Route 17 split off, Gary stayed on I-87. As the Volvo approached the south-west boundary of Harrington State Park, Gary turned on the radio. There was no new information about the rumored CME. Repetitions of the President's message played on most of the stations as commentators talked in circles, and made guesses about the meaning of the message.

Gary finally found an easy rock station that was still broadcasting music. If this was going to be the last day that he could listen to an FM radio station as he drove down a highway, Gary decided he wasn't going to waste the opportunity by listening to news anchors speculate on topics they knew nothing about. He could have gotten the same quality of information from an Ouija board, or by shaking a magic eight ball.

As the song *Free Falling*, by Tom Petty played on the radio, Gary sang along. The video in the back was still playing, but both girls were still sleeping. Mae wasn't, even though her eyes were closed. She opened her eyes and glanced at Gary, but she didn't say anything. The song was good, but Gary's singing wasn't. Mae put her ear buds in and pulled up a play list from her smart phone. The memory of driving through Harrington State Park with the autumn leaves in their full glory, a beautiful blue sky overhead, and *Free Falling* playing a little louder than it should have been on the Bose speakers, would be seared into Gary's mind. He would look back on it later as one of the very last normal experiences of his Old World life.

Time passed easily for Gary. During commercial breaks, he tried calling Hank. Even under normal circumstances, cell phone reception in the State Park was not good, so Gary was not surprised by his lack of success. On most of his attempts, the network was overloaded. On the one occasion when it wasn't, Gary got Hank's voicemail. Gary didn't mind. It meant he could get back to his music. Gary left a short message asking Hank to call him back.

As Gary put his phone down on the center console, a song that had been a big hit in Gary's senior year of high school started playing. As it played, Gary re-lived some of the highlights from that year. Then, like a punch to the stomach, he recalled the low point. On a cool clear evening in late October, Gary had borrowed his father's car to attend Homecoming. He had borrowed the car before, and gotten "the lecture" each time. The car, a 1965 Chevy Chevelle SS, was his father's pride and joy. His father had purchased the car in a decrepit state a few years earlier, and then spent most of his free time restoring the car to a like-new condition. On each prior occasion, Gary had returned the car without a scratch. It was that excellent track record that convinced his father to loan him the car on Homecoming night.

On the way to the Friday night football game that preceded the Homecoming dance, Gary had one passenger, his girlfriend Tracy Mayfield. The plan was to have a good time, and drive his one passenger back to her home by midnight. At the dance, Tracy spent time dancing with a football player who was credited with winning the game. In the fourth quarter, he had scored two touchdowns almost back to back. By the time the dance music stopped, the relationship was over. Tracy had traded Gary in for a better catch.

When 11:30 arrived, Tracy was in the back seat of the football player's new Mustang, and Gary was driving away in the antique Chevelle with three drunk friends. Gary was, but still not in command of his mental faculties. *How could that bitch dump me at Homecoming!* Instead of going home, Gary drove toward the lake. The official cause of the accident was excessive speed, but Gary blamed his friend Chuck Raymond who was riding shotgun. Sure Gary had been speeding, but he had driven that fast on the lake road several times before. This time his friends were picking on him for getting dumped. As he made the last joke of the evening, Chuck attempted to slap Gary hard on his shoulder.

The blow landed on Gary's lower right arm, which was connected to the hand that held the steering wheel. Gary's hand went down and the car swerved right. In the middle of a left turn on the gravel road, Gary overcorrected to the left, then he overcorrected to the right. At the edge of the road, the pristine Chevelle hit a tree that was five inches in diameter. The tree snapped off at its base, and the car plunged onward. The front end got crunched a second time on a smaller tree before the car rolled over twice as it tumbled down the slope. Twenty yards from the water's edge, the car landed upright.

Every sheet metal panel on the car was bent, broken, or torn. The frame was twisted beyond repair. Only Gary and one of the passengers in the back seat had worn seatbelts. The bumpy roll down the slope had been harsh, but less damaging to humans than driving into a brick wall. Gary had only been doing forty-five miles an hour when he hit the first tree. All occupants had sustained serious bumps and bruises, and the two without seatbelts both got minor concussions.

First responders said their youth and intoxication level had kept their injuries from being much worse. Gary got the worst black eye of his life when his face hit the steering wheel during the initial impact. But nobody died and there were no broken bones. Gary totaled his father's car that night, but there had been no criminal charges, just a speeding ticket. The cops had followed the boys to the hospital and tested their blood alcohol levels. When they learned the driver had a BAC of zero, they released the students to their parents.

Gary could recall all the details of meeting his father in the hospital that night. It was two o'clock Sunday morning. He recognized his father's footsteps coming down the hallway, before his father was in sight. In his younger days, his father had been known for having a quick temper. By the time he reached his forties, it had tapered off a bit, but Gary fully expected to get a tongue lashing at the hospital, and then a belt lashing at home.

Instead, his father had said almost nothing. "Are you okay son?"

"Yeah Dad, I'm fine, but the car is . . . ."

"I know son. It doesn't matter. You're okay and your friends are too. Nobody was killed or seriously injured. That's all that matters."

The trip home took less than fifteen minutes, but it felt like an hour. Dad didn't say a word. To Gary, it looked like his father had aged five years since the last time he had seen him. His father was a little angry, but mostly disappointed. That's what Gary remembered most about the drive home; overwhelming disappointment. Afterwards, his father never brought up the topic of the Chevelle's destruction.

Gary knew that pieces of his father had also been destroyed that night. It was the piece that had trusted his son too much, and another piece that had poured hundreds of hours into the restoration of a classic car that brought him joy every time he drove it. The car and the joy were gone forever. The car could not be restored, and it was not replaced. Gary knew he could never repair the damage to the car or his father, and the thought still nagged him every now and then.

His father had been distant and unemotional during Gary's upbringing. He was a man who provided well for his family by spending a lot of time at work, perhaps too much. Gary and his father had never exchanged "I love yous." For most of his life, Gary knew his mother loved him more than his father. The night of the wreck, Gary decided he was wrong about that. It was just a different kind of love. The man had lost the possession he treasured most, but didn't say an unkind word to his son. His relief over his son's survival far outweighed anything he could ever feel for an inanimate object; he just didn't know how to say that out loud. This new perspective came to Gary when he arrived home unscathed by harsh words or physical violence from his father. Gary's father wasn't the only one who had aged five years that night.

From the time of the wreck until he left his father's home, Gary never again disappointed his father about anything. He got excellent grades, stayed away from his former friends, graduated, got accepted to a good university, and worked part time jobs while attending college classes full time. Gary used his wages to cover some of his college expenses, and borrowed the rest. Later, he paid off all the loans without his parents' help. As the decades-old song finished on the radio and the commercial break started, Gary decided to give his father a call. Gary hadn't thought about the wreck in a quite a while, and he still didn't exchange "I love yous," with his dad, but he was very grateful for all his father had done for him while he was growing up. Gary wanted to talk to him, perhaps for the last time.

Gary's father Bill and his mother Angela were still married, and living in a retirement community in Florida. Gary tried to visit his parents once a year, and he tried to call them once a month. Gary turned off the radio and made several attempts to get through to his parents. He failed. How had his father gone from being one of the most important people in his life to one of the least? Civilization was about to end, and Bill wouldn't even get a phone call from his son.

There's only so much I can do, thought Gary. *It wasn't my idea for them to retire so far away in Florida.* Gary turned the radio back on. But now, as he listened to the music, he thought about the implications of the CME for his parents in Florida. Would the CME blast the United States that far south? Would the devastation in Florida be as bad as it would be in the north? After a few minutes, Gary reached a conclusion that enabled him to drop the subject and get back to the music. His parents were more than a thousand miles away, and if they got hammered by the CME, there wasn't one damn thing Gary could do to help them. *Why should I spend time worrying or wondering about things I cannot change?*

A new song started playing on the radio, and Gary started nodding his head to the beat of *With or Without You,* by U2.

Chapter 11: Hank's house.

Gary got off the interstate, and took New York 17 west to 17M, which took him to the Village of Monroe. The village had a population of less than ten thousand. In Monroe, Gary turned left off the highway into the residential area near Hank's house. Gary drove slowly past the single-family homes on large lots that had been built in the 1960's and 70's. At dinnertime, most people were indoors eating, watching television, playing computer games, or surfing the net. To Gary, however, it seemed that activity outside the homes was higher than normal. Some residents were on the lawn or driveway talking with their neighbors. Perhaps human-to-human contact was vital at a time like this, or people wanted to know what was going to happen and the media wasn't providing the answers. The residents were anxious, and their anxiety gave way to restlessness. *Do something. Talk to somebody. What the hell is really going on?*

It was a nice evening to be outdoors. The sky was clear and there was still plenty of light. The temperature was dropping, but the warmth of the day had not fully retreated. Most people were in shirtsleeves, a few had thin jackets or sweaters. As people talked to their neighbors they would occasionally look up or point to the sky. It didn't look any different. Some people were not standing around or sky gazing. For every fifteen houses or so, Gary saw one or two where the residents seemed to be packing up their vehicles and preparing to leave. Perhaps they owned property upstate, or knew someone who did. From his shopping trip, Gary knew some people were stocking up. It seemed some of the stockers were planning to leave rather than hunkering down.

When Gary finally turned the car into Hank's driveway, it was 6:35 P.M. The trip from Islip to Monroe, which normally took two hours, had taken more than four. Gary couldn't believe how much had happened in one day, and how much more would happen if the CME was real. He put the car in park, and turned off the ignition. Gary had expected Hank's house to be one of the busy "packer houses," but Hank was nowhere to be seen. If Hank's Ford Expedition had not been in the driveway, Gary would have guessed Hank wasn't home. Gary told Mae and the kids to stay in the car. He got out, and walked to the side door of the house facing the driveway.

Hank's ranch-style house had two stories, a ground floor and a walkout basement. The front of the house faced south toward the street. From the street, the driveway and a one-car garage were on the right, or east side of the house. The garage was detached from the house and the front end of the garage lined up with the back end of the house, which put the garage in the back yard. On the ground level, the house had three entrances. The front porch entrance faced the street and opened into the living room. The side door had a four-step stoop on the driveway and it led to the kitchen. The back door was also in the kitchen. It led to a wooden deck in the back yard that was over the top of the walkout basement's patio door. The patio door was the only exit from the basement. The backyard was surrounded by a six-foot wooden stockade fence that badly needed a coat of stain. A four-foot gate between the house and garage led to the back yard. The gate was open. The front yard was mowed, but the grass in the back of the house was three feet tall. It hadn't been mowed in months.

As he walked past the Expedition, Gary looked in a window. The vehicle was a mess inside, and it was clear that Hank hadn't packed anything yet. Gary rang the doorbell. He could hear the chime inside, but Hank didn't come to the door. Gary rang again. Still no answer. Gary knocked and waited. Then he knocked and rang, and waited again. Then he pounded on the door, and tried the handle. It was locked. He pounded again. After two full minutes of ringing, knocking, and pounding, Gary finally heard someone moving inside. Another full minute passed before Hank opened the door. He was wearing boxer shorts, a t-shirt with a Harley Davidson logo, and a dirty bathrobe that was untied and hanging open. His feet were bare. Hank had a full and unkempt beard. *He looks like hell,* thought Gary.

The inside of the house looked worse. It didn't just lack a woman's touch; no human hand had done any cleaning in weeks. Every dish was dirty, empty take-out containers littered the floor, and the house smelled like a garbage dump. Gary almost gagged. Hank had ignored Gary's packing instructions and done nothing to prepare for the CME. Doing nothing had been Hank's modus operandi for months. Gary was angry. He and his family were running for their lives. Their odds of survival would be dramatically better if Hank came with them, but Hank had apparently been napping.

"Hank, what the hell have you been doing for the last four hours? I fully expected you to be packed and ready to haul ass by now!"

Hank said nothing. He turned away from his brother, and walked across the kitchen toward the living room.

Gary pursued him, his anger mounting. "Don't walk away from me Hank! What the hell is going on with you?" Behind him, Gary left the door wide open to let the place air out.

In the living room, Hank plopped heavily into an easy chair. The living room was a pigsty. It was worse than the kitchen. Hank ate most of his meals in the chair and dropped the empty food containers on the floor. The easy chair was a few feet from the television, and it had apparently been the center of Hank's universe. For a brief moment, Gary wondered if his brother even bothered to get up and use the bathroom down the hall. The smell was that bad. Piles of discarded food containers and empty whiskey bottles were almost knee deep on each side of the chair. Several feet from the chair, the piles tapered off to just one layer of debris that covered almost every square foot of the living room. If Hank was paying for curbside garbage pickup, his money had been wasted. No trash had left the house for several weeks.

"Hank, what the hell is going on?"

"I don't feel well," Hank finally mumbled. Then he tilted the chair back, pulled a large comforter up over his head, and closed his eyes.

Gary felt like yelling again, but thought better of it. It was hard to argue with a drunk who was hiding under a blanket. It was also hard for Gary to draw a breath without gagging. Gary crossed to the south side of the living room and opened the front door of the house, which led to a covered porch. He pushed debris out of the way to let the door swing inward and fully open. The storm door had windows instead of screens. Gary guessed correctly that the storm windows had been on the door since last winter. Gary slid the storm window up as high as it would go. With the lure of a garbage dump, and no screen to stop them, flying insects might soon swarm the house. Gary didn't care. Bugs would be better than the stench. The cooling evening air, however, might keep the swarm to a minimum.

After opening the window, Gary stepped out onto the front porch. His brother had obviously quit the fight. From the looks of things, the surrender had taken place weeks or months ago. Whatever enthusiasm Hank had shown on the phone, had dwindled to nothing while Gary was still driving. If Hank really had consumed two cups of coffee, the effects had been overcome by the contents of one of the whisky bottles, or overcome by . . . by what? Apathy? Depression?

Gary thought about some of the things Hank said on the phone. At the time, Gary had suspected Hank was depressed, maybe even suicidal. Hank's unkempt house and disheveled appearance supported that suspicion. Gary went back inside, and opened the windows on each side of the living room picture window, which faced the street. The air quality was improving.

Gary took a few steps toward the comforter-covered blob in the easy chair. In a low, conversational tone, Gary said, "Hank, tell me what's going on. This place is a disaster." Gary got no response, and tried again to start a conversation. This time he got a response.

"Go away and leave me alone."

Gary let out a sigh. He turned away from the chair and walked down the hall that led to the other rooms in the house. He didn't know what he was looking for, but given his brother's condition, he knew the house would tell him more than Hank would. There were two bedrooms on the left side of the hall, a bathroom on the right, and a master bedroom at the end of the hall on the right. Hank and his two ex-wives had never had kids. The first bedroom on the left was a guest bedroom, while the second one had been used as a den. Gary glanced into the guestroom which hadn't seen a guest in years. It had become something of a storage room, with boxes and clutter on the bed, and the floor.

Gary continued down the hall, and discovered what he didn't want to find in the den. His heart skipped a beat and he felt a little thump in his chest. The room was about twelve feet in both directions. There was a closet to the left of the entry. A wooden desk was under the room's only window, which was on the front wall of the house. To the right of the desk was a table, with the same oak veneer as the desk. On the wall to the right of the entry, there was a four-drawer metal file cabinet, and a small combination safe about the size of a two-drawer file cabinet. There were two chairs in the room, an expensive office chair by the desk that had three adjustment levers, and a similar but less expensive chair by the table with only two levers.

Except for a small neat area in the center of the desk, the room was a cluttered mess. The neat area had apparently been created by simply shoving books, folders, documents, and office supplies off the top of the desk onto the floor. A debris pile about a foot high was on the floor to the left of the desk. The pile contained multiple late payment notices for the SUV, a foreclosure notice on the house, and a termination notice for unemployment benefits. Near the top of the pile was a forcible-detainer notice. It was the last step in the foreclosure process. The notice ordered Hank to be out of his house by the end of the month. If he didn't leave, the sheriff would force him to leave.

It wasn't until later that night that Gary learned about the contents of the debris pile. What captured his attention at the moment were the three items in the clear spot on the desk. An exquisite Mountblanc pen, a single sheet of white paper with a hand written note that covered half the page, and a loaded Smith & Wesson, .357 revolver.

Gary could feel his legs tremble from the flow of adrenaline as he approached the desk. He glanced at the note. It said what a worn out, defeated, emotionally devastated, middle-aged, twice-divorced man would say after he had decided life wasn't worth living. Hank wasn't going to flee the CME; he was going to flee life itself. Gary now knew why Hank hadn't bothered to pack.

Still trembling, Gary picked up the note and the gun, and walked out of the den. *What am I going to do, confront Hank with the evidence? Then what?* As Gary approached the living room, tears were streaming down his face. *My brother was about to commit suicide, and I had no idea. I'm such a schmuck! What if he had killed himself before I got here? How could things have gotten so bad?*

Gary got stuck on that thought. *How could things have gotten so bad for Hank?* Hank graduated college, got married to Elizabeth, and worked for two years as an engineer. Then the terrorist attacks of September 11, 2001 happened, and Hank enlisted in the Army as an infantryman. During his initial four-year hitch, he did two combat tours in Iraq. When he re-enlisted, he transferred out of the 75th Ranger Regiment and went to the Special Forces (SF) Qualification Course. While in SF, he did three combat tours in Afghanistan, and earned the rank of Sergeant First Class, E-7.

His first wife, Liz hated the Army, and Hank was convinced she had cheated on him while he was deployed. When he came home on leave, he tried to patch things up. After one particularly nasty argument, Hank checked his wife's phone and discovered a series of sexual texts, between his wife and one of his college fraternity brothers. Hank went to the man's house and beat him to a pulp.

The Army discharged Hank administratively under "Chapter 14" for misconduct, and the civilian courts gave him a misdemeanor assault conviction and two years of probation. Both the Army and the civilian court would have been harder on Hank if it hadn't been for his stellar service record, and the fact that the victim didn't cooperate. The victim feared his testimony would have lead to a second visit from Hank.

Liz divorced Hank and married the fraternity brother. Hank fell back on his Bachelor's degree, took some refresher courses, and found an engineering job. With his criminal record, and absence of recent experience, he got only an entry-level position in a small company. Six months after the divorce was final, Hank married Maggie, a woman he had met in the Army who was five years younger than he was.

Things had gone well for a while as the two of them worked full time, and bought a house. Just a few months shy of their second anniversary, Hank caught Maggie cheating on him, and he did to that lover what he'd done to the first. He was again convicted of assault, but this time he didn't get the good-soldier discount and the charge was a felony, not a misdemeanor. Hank got a two-year sentence. With early probation, he served only one full year, but he served that time in prison, not jail.

Maggie left him and moved in with her lover, and Hank hung onto the house and SUV by burning through his savings while he was in prison. When he got out, nobody would hire him as an engineer. Hank got a job as a bouncer at a rowdy biker bar. The SF combat service and the prison sentence were job prerequisites. A few months later, Hank found steadier and less violent work as a night security guard for a company owned by a friend.

The economy slowed, the company downsized, the plant closed, and Hank lost his job. He qualified for unemployment, and had collected those checks until they stopped coming. The house went into foreclosure, and the notice of forcible detainer had arrived weeks ago. Hank had decided to give the blood-sucking bank his house and his corpse, at the same time. By the time the Sheriff arrived, his stinking corpse would have been rotting for several days, which would add another distinct odor to the home's already powerful stench.

Gary stopped at the end of the hall a few feet short of the living room. His brother was still in the chair with his eyes closed. He was apparently asleep. The comforter was now tucked under his chin, rather than pulled up over the top of his head. Gary's mind continued to race with questions but no words came to his lips. *How could I not notice Hank's descent into hell on earth? When had Hank cleared the desk, written the note, and loaded the gun? Why was he still alive? Have the note and gun been sitting there for days? Hours? Minutes? What if I had not driven to the house today? Would Hank still be alive? But the only reason I called or visited was because of the CME! I had no idea his life had gotten this bad. What if the CME had not –*

"Uncle Hank where are you? Come on Josie, let's go find him!"

Jane's high-pitched squeal came through the still open kitchen door. The excited tone was immediately replaced with one of disgust. "Pee-yew! Mommy, what's the smell? Mommy, I think I'm gonna throw up."

Mae said, "Jane get out of that house right now! Sit down on these steps next to your sister, and don't move. Keep an eye on Josie, I'll be right back."

Mae came through the kitchen and looked into the living room. She was holding her nose to pinch off the smell. She looked from Gary, to Hank, and back to Gary. The squeals from Jane had jerked Hank out of his coma. Hank pushed the comforter down to his waist and sat upright in the chair. He rubbed his eyes. Mae was standing in the archway between the kitchen and the living room. Gary was to her right and Hank and the chair were to her left. Gary was facing Hank and his left side was toward Mae. With the suicide note in his left hand, and the gun in his right, Mae could see the note, but not the gun. The kitchen lights were on, but the living room and hallway lights were not.

Mae said, "Gary, what the hell is going on? What are you guys doing in here? We've been waiting in the car forever. I thought Hank was supposed to be packing. This place stinks!" Her voice had a high nasal tone because she was still holding her nose.

Gary kept the gun from his wife's view. He had quickly wiped away his tears when he first heard Jane's voice. "Yeah . . . um . . . Hank and I were just talking about that . . . . Hank's not um . . . he's not feeling well."

Actually, Hank was suddenly feeling better, a lot better. He said, "Hey, did I just hear Jane's voice? Are the girls here?"

Hank stood up. Mae was looking in his direction, but turned away quickly from the sight of her brother-in-law's dirty open bathrobe and boxer shorts.

"Are they outside? I'm going to go see them."

Gary and Mae both said, "No!" at the same time. Gary added, "Not like that. You can't let them see you like that. Go get cleaned up."

Mae added, "And you're not going to see them in here; not in this pigsty."

Like an obedient kid who had been reprimanded by his parents, Hank said, "Okay, I'll get dressed.'" Hank stepped away from his chair and wobbled a little as he headed toward the hallway where Gary was still standing.

Gary stepped aside to let Hank pass and said, "Not just dressed. Take a shower, and shave." His brother had just rejoined the living. It seemed kind of sudden.

Hank continued his obedient routine as he said "Okay," and kept walking. As Hank passed by, Gary turned on the hallway light.

"Wait a minute Hank," Mae said as she stepped past Gary to pursue Hank. "Do you have an internet connection here?" Without thinking, Gary turned to look down the hall in the direction of Mae and Hank.

Hank said, "No" as he kept walking. "I lost the house phone and internet when I stopped paying the bills. The TV still works though, because I'm stealing cable from my neighbor."

Mae said, "Never mind, I'll see if I can get a connection with my cell phone again."

Hank said nothing as he kept walking toward the master bedroom. When Mae turned around to go back to the kitchen, she saw the revolver in Gary's right hand.

"Is that a gun? Gary, is that a fucking gun?!" Mae spoke in an intense whisper. She didn't want the girls to hear her.

Gary thought, *No Mae, it's a cigarette lighter; it just looks like a gun. What the hell can I say? Yes, it's a gun. My brother was just about to kill himself when I walked in. Nice day isn't it, I mean with the CME and all?*

"Yeah, it's a gun."

"What the fuck are you doing with a fucking gun?! Have you gone fucking crazy? Wait, is that Hank's fucking gun?!"

Gary thought, *Four uses of the word "fuck" in three sentences? Really?* As an attorney, Mae was rarely at a loss for words. When she was, she sometimes didn't stop talking, she just filled in the blanks with f-bombs.

Gary looked at her stupidly. He too didn't know what to say, and Mae had just used up the "fuck" quota for the entire conversation. Mae saw the note in Gary's left hand. Before Gary knew what she was doing, Mae took a quick step and grabbed the note. Then she walked back into the kitchen to read it. She absorbed the words, and the meaning in a matter of seconds. When she was done, she took a couple of steps back toward Gary.

"He is going to kill himself?!" Mae's voice wasn't as much of a whisper as it had been, and she wasn't holding her nose anymore.

"Was," Gary said. "He *was* going to kill himself. Well at least it looks that way. I . . . we got here in time. The CME . . . ." Gary's voice trailed off. *The CME what? The CME got here in time to save Hank's life? I'm such a shitty little brother that it's only pure luck that he's still alive? Wait, now the CME is a lucky thing?*

"Mommy what's going on? Are you okay?" Jane was standing at the top of the steps just outside the kitchen door to the driveway. She had heard her parents talking and she was worried.

"I'm fine honey." Then suddenly, "Hey, where's Josie?" The spot where Josie had been sitting was empty.

Mae turned toward the kitchen door, but stopped to hand the note to Gary. She said, "This is your plan? We stay in this garbage dump tonight, and if the CME destroys the grid, we rely on your brother to save us? If that's the best you've got, then we are all fu– screwed."

Jane was within earshot, so Mae stopped herself from dropping another f-bomb. Mae left the house with Jane before Gary could respond. Josie was half way down the driveway, but Mae reached her before she got to the street.

Gary put the note and the gun in a high kitchen cabinet above the refrigerator, out of reach of the girls, and probably Mae as well. He went outside to talk to Mae. He pleaded to stick with the plan, and get Hank packed and ready to go. Mae eventually calmed down a bit, but she argued that they should abandon Hank. Having seen and smelled Hank's house, she said she would rather spend the night in a hotel. If no rooms were available, then sleeping in the Volvo or a ditch on the side of the road would still be a better option. Like many lawyers, her colorful arguments were prone to hyperbole.

Gary talked her into sticking around long enough to see the clean fully dressed version of Hank. Waiting half an hour before implementing a half-assed Plan B wouldn't hurt. While Hank took a shower and put on a relatively clean set of clothes, Gary looked around the one-car garage at the end of the driveway to see what useful items Hank might take with him, if the CME forced them all to abandon Hank's house. The girls were playing in the driveway near the side entrance to the kitchen. Mae was several yards away, standing next to the Volvo. Her laptop was open on the hood of the car next to her cell phone. Mae told Gary to watch the girls so she could focus on attempting to download more information from the internet.

An overloaded SUV drove past the end of the driveway. Several minutes later, two overloaded sedans drove past. It was clear that the two cars were traveling together and, like the SUV, they were bugging out. Quick glances were exchanged with Gary, but nobody waved. Maybe there had been another television update, and more people were beginning to believe the CME was real. Some of those who packed would never leave. They had no better place to go. They packed because they thought the government might issue an evacuation order. Like good sheep, they would stay put until told to do otherwise. The order never came.

When Hank appeared in the kitchen doorway, his hair was still wet and he looked much better. He had even trimmed his beard back to something that could be seen in public without drawing stares. He came down the steps into the driveway and shouted, "Where's my girls?!"

Gary couldn't believe his brother's sudden transformation, but anyone who had ever stood on the brink of the abyss, and seriously contemplated the "to-be-or-not-to-be" question could have explained it to him. The presence of young, joyful people who love you wasn't the antidote to clinical depression, but it was a powerfully good step in the right direction. Hank loved his nieces and he hadn't seen them in months.

Hank was also feeling better because Gary was there. To be sure, Gary had shown up for the wrong reason, but he *had* shown up. Hank hadn't really been sleeping in the chair when Gary returned from the den with the revolver. Hank had seen Gary's tears and the trembling. *Gary really did care!* Hank was still convinced that his entire life had been a waste, but if good people like Gary and the girls stayed close to him, perhaps he could stick it out for another few days. Maybe, just maybe things would get better. Well, better for him anyway, the rest of the country was apparently fucked.

Hank walked down the steps, as the girls ran toward him. He scooped up one of them in each arm and then twirled around in the driveway. The girls were laughing and pulling on his beard. They had never seen him with a beard before. "Is it real, Uncle Hank? Is it real?"

Hank soon sat down on the second step with one girl on each knee. The girls caught their breath for a moment and then both started talking at once. "Uncle Hank, Uncle Hank, we drove for *days* to get here! Why did you grow a beard? Are you going to shave it off? It scratched my cheek. Santa has a beard, but his is white. Are you one of Santa's helpers? Why does your house smell so bad? Tell us a story!"

Mae had walked back up the driveway as Hank was scooping up the girls. From the look on her face, it was clear that she would rather the girls played in traffic than played with Hank. Gary walked over to Mae, a few yards away from Hank and the girls, and in hushed tones they continued their earlier discussion about whether to hunker at Hank's house, or find a motel.

Hank was attempting to answer about one out of every five questions from the girls. "Yes, it's real. Yes, I'm one of Santa's helpers so you better be good!"

Mae wanted to find somewhere else to spend the night. She was still hopeful that life would somehow be back to normal in the morning. Gary still felt partly to blame for his brother's condition, and he didn't want to abandon him, but Hank hadn't packed anything. If the CME turned out to be real, and a more rural location would increase their odds for survival, would Hank want to leave? Or did he still prefer to die in place as he had said earlier on the phone? Hank pretended not to know what Gary and Mae were talking about. After a few minutes when the girls had calmed down a bit, Gary and Mae decided it was time to figure out whether they would stay with Hank, or find an alternate hunker-down location.

Mae left the conversation by saying, "He's your brother, it's your job to figure it out. I'll give you five minutes. Then I'm leaving with the car, the trailer, and maybe the girls." It was an empty threat, Mae had never towed a trailer, and she had never been the girls' primary care giver for more than an hour. Gary knew if Mae left, she would leave the girls with him. Gary had rarely seen his wife so illogical. She was a control freak who rarely showed emotion. The doomsday threat was taking a toll. Mae took the girls to the car and gave them some snacks.

7:07 PM

Gary went to where Hank was sitting, and got right to the point. "Hank, I need to know right now whether you're going to face this CME with us. Mae says we should leave you here and go to a hotel. She's convinced everything will be fine in the morning. I'm not. I think we will need to flee to a more rural location, but I want you by my side when the shit hits the fan."

Hank didn't answer. He looked at Gary, then at the girls, then back at Gary. Gary continued his pitch. "If the CME causes the power to go out, then civilization as we know it will quickly grind to a halt. You're the one that told me to get out of the city and hunker-down at your place. Well, I did what you said. I'm here now, but my family will have almost no chance of surviving without you. I need your help. The girls need your help."

Gary deliberately didn't mention Mae. He continued. "A lot of people are going to die. You know more about hunting, living off the land, and getting through tough situations than I'll ever know. If we need to keep running, I need you to come with us, but I'm worried that you'd rather crawl into a hole and die. My daughters . . . we need a fighter, not a quitter."

Hank was still sitting on the kitchen stoop with his feet on the driveway. His elbows were resting on his knees and his hands were clasped. His head was tilted down as if he was staring at his shoes. It almost looked like he was praying.

Hank started talking firmly but quietly without looking up. "Crawl into a hole and die? Yeah, that's what I had in mind. I was in the deepest darkest hole in my life brother, and where the hell were you? You didn't call, you didn't visit."

"Hank, I had no idea you were hurting so bad."

"No idea? Tell me you didn't know about the second divorce, the prison sentence, and the foreclosure. Tell me you didn't know I got fired."

"Hank, I knew about those things, but the economy sucks and lots of people are going through the same crap; well except for the prison part. Besides, you told me your unemployment benefits had been extended and you were doing okay."

"Gary, those benefits ran out more than two months ago. I've had no income since then, and my bank accounts were already empty. I've been eating free food from a church pantry, because I don't even have enough money for pizza. I haven't made a car payment in two months. According to that foreclosure detention notice or whatever it is, I've got to be out of my house by the end of the month, or the Sheriff will throw me out. The car dealer will probably take my SUV before then. I've got no money, no wife, no kids, and no life. I'm thirty-nine years old, and I'm a complete failure. I've worked all of my adult life, and the sum total of what I've accomplished is a negative net worth of about two hundred grand. So thanks for noticing."

Gary paused for a moment, as he thought about Hank's situation. Yes, Hank's life sucked and Gary screwed up by not being fully aware of that, but there was no time for a pity party. Hank needed to start dealing with reality right now, or Gary, Mae and the girls would leave without him. It was a now or never moment. Gary didn't have time to give his brother some tough love. He chose instead the tough shit approach.

"Hank, I'm sorry I didn't call, and I'm sorry I didn't visit, but you've got to pull yourself together. Don't flatter yourself and feel special. About half the people our age have a story similar to yours. The entire country has been going to hell for years. This CME thing is just the coup de grâce. There's nothing you or I, or anybody, can change about any of the stuff that's happened to you. But this is not about you or me. I'm trying to get you to focus on something besides yourself, Hank. You know, something like keeping Jane and Josie alive."

Gary again didn't mention Mae. He didn't think Hank would lift a finger to help her. Gary continued, "Hey, you want to look for an upside to this whole doomsday scenario? Guess what brother? If this CME shuts down the east coast, then the bank isn't going to foreclose on your house. The sheriff isn't going to show up, and the dealership isn't going to repossess your car. Think about it. If the electricity goes out for several months, then almost everything will come to a halt including financial transactions. The downside is that a significant percentage of the American population will die, but you will have the ability and a reason to survive."

Hank had looked up while Gary was talking and his eyes were now drilling into Gary's. Hank had expected more sympathy, and he wasn't quite ready to stop feeling sorry for himself. Maybe Gary and the girls really would leave without him.

Gary continued, "Think about it Hank. Think about the survivors for a second. The survivors will be debt free. I mean sure, they'll also be free of their jobs, their 401Ks, and their health care plans, but all the things you've been bitching about will be gone. You'll have a chance to make one of the most radical fresh starts imaginable. If you've ever dreamed about the simple life that existed in America a hundred years ago, then I've got great news for you, it will be here in about" – Gary looked at his watch – "five hours."

Hank looked away. His mind was racing. He'd been trying for months to come up with a way to get even with the banks, his employer, and others he blamed for his misery. Now it looked like the CME would take care of that for him. Maybe Gary had a point. At midnight, life might get very interesting indeed. And what was the worst that could happen? He had already looked into the abyss and chosen death. If it weren't for his brother's phone calls and visit, he would already be dead. *I really do have absolutely nothing to lose.*

Gary was still talking, "Hank, like I said, it's not about me or even the opportunity for you to use this disaster to ditch all your problems. Think about Jane and Josie. Are those two girls going to survive if all they have to protect them is me and Mae? Hank, I don't even own a gun."

By the look on Hank's face Gary could tell Hank was doing some serious thinking. *Good. Hopefully, he'll stop thinking about his own misery.* "Hank, the girls need you, and I need you. Think of all that Army training you've got. You know more about survival and shooting guns than I will ever know. Hank, please let go of your self-pity and help me save my daughters."

Gary stopped talking. There was a long pause. There was really nothing more to say. Hank would either choose to serve something bigger than himself or he would not. Earlier in his life, Hank had chosen the former when he joined the Army, and things had pretty much gone downhill ever since. Still, maybe it was time for Hank to do another hitch; this time for his nieces.

Hank finally broke the long silence. "You will probably be proven wrong about that."

"Huh? Wrong? About what?"

"About the survival skills thing. I probably don't know as much as you think I know. Obviously, I've never experienced the devastation of a CME before. So you better learn at least as much as I know about staying alive. We're both going to have to learn, and do much more than we think we are capable of, to keep the five of us alive."

Gary was a little relieved that Hank had said the number five. It meant he had included Mae in the count. The two of them, Hank and Mae, in close quarters over the next several days or weeks was going to create some interesting 'group dynamics.'

Hank continued. "If we're all going to be in this together, there's something we need to get straight right from the start." Hank again looked directly into Gary's eyes as he spoke. Gary held his brother's penetrating stare. He had no clue why his brother was suddenly so intense.

Hank continued, "I've been in situations – situations where I led soldiers in combat. Situations where soldiers were fighting, and killing, and some of us didn't make it back." Hank paused.

Gary could tell that the memories of those violent experiences were going through Hank's mind as he spoke. This was the first time his brother had ever made a direct reference to his combat service. Gary knew his brother had done two tours in Iraq and three in Afghanistan. Two tours as an infantry grunt, and three more in the Special Forces. Hank earned a Bronze Star "with V-Device" during one of his tours in Afghanistan. He had the scars to prove his lengthy combat record, but he never showed the scars or talked about the deadly battles. The "V-Device" on the Bronze Star was for "Valor." The award was one-step below a Silver Star. Gary didn't know it, but Hank's unit had put him in for a Silver Star, and if Hank had been an officer, he might have gotten it. Higher headquarters, however, had downgraded the award, so Hank received the "Bronze with a V."

Hank said, "I learned the hard way that the most important thing in those situations is leadership. There can only be one leader. The leader makes the decisions. They could be good decisions or bad decisions, but the leader makes those decisions and everybody else must obey them. That's the way it has to be for most of the troops to have the best chance of living to fight another day. Do you understand what I'm saying?"

Gary nodded.

"While we attempt to get through this crisis, I will be the leader, and you will follow my orders. Later, there might come a time when you will be the leader, and I'll take orders from you. But for the foreseeable future, I will be your boss and you will do as I say. Have you got that? Can you handle it?"

Without hesitation, Gary gave a firm, "Yes." It had taken an act of will power not to add "Sir!" For his daughters and his wife, Gary believed he would and could do anything. He'd gladly follow Sergeant First Class Henry Arnold Adams' orders. To Hell and back if necessary.

Hank said, "What about Mae? If there's a widespread blackout, and we try to get through it together, do you think she'll be cool with that arrangement, at least for the next few days?"

Gary paused, swallowed hard and said, "She's going to have to be. I'll talk to her. She's not as bad as you think Hank. She and I have already been living this nightmare for seven hours, and done some things we've never done before. Hard things." As he spoke, Gary recalled driving on the motorcycle away from the accident on the Southern State Parkway.

Hank nodded and said, "Look, brother, I know you're a little worried about me, and you're right. The gun and the note were real. I was truly on the brink, but I'm not on the brink now. I couldn't care less about the CME. If the world blows up and everybody dies – including me – I'll be fine with that. But if you and the girls want to make a run for it, I'm cool with that too. I'll go with you, and give you the best I've got."

After a pause, Hank continued. "There's one thing I've got to ask you before we get started. Does the bitch really have to come with us?"

Gary knew his brother was only half joking. "Yeah, it turns out Mae really did give birth to the only two nieces you have."

Hank sighed, "I guess the good and the bad are sometimes inseparable. So you really think the bitch will agree to all this? Do you think she'll follow the orders of an old soldier like me?"

"Yeah, sure, why not? I mean if it ever actually comes to that. Which it won't."

The answer startled Hank, because his brother hadn't said it. Hank glanced to his right where Mae was standing and fuming several feet away. She had left the girls in the car munching on snacks; dinner really. Without being noticed, she had quietly walked close to where Gary and Hank were talking. She had heard most of what they had said, and just answered Hank's question.

Mae continued. "But don't get your hopes up Hank, because in the morning when everything turns out to be fine, I'll go back to Islip and I'll probably never see you again. As for this evening, I've got a news flash for you. I am *not* spending the night in that pigsty." Mae pointed toward Hank's house to ensure there was no doubt as to which pigsty she was referring.

Then she said, "Oh, and one more thing Hank. If you ever call me a bitch again, I'll cut your balls off." She said it very calmly, as if she had already selected the knife.

Hank smiled and said, "Well, I'm glad we got that cleared up, um . . . Mae." Hank didn't think Mae was actually quick enough with a knife to cut off both of his balls. Still, he'd have to watch what he said.

Gary shook his head and again wondered what it would be like to travel with the equivalent of an open can of gasoline, and a lit match. He was thrilled that his brother was going to face tomorrow with them, but with that decision made, there was still a lot to do, and do now.

Gary loudly cleared his throat to signal that it was time to change the subject. "Okay, recently self-appointed fearless leader, what do we do now? As your humble servant, I meekly offer the suggestion that you pack your shit now in case we have to haul ass in the morning."

Hank stood up. "Knock it off Gary. Until the shooting starts, we'll probably have time for conversation and make decisions as a group.

Suggestions are always welcome." Both brothers had ignored Mae's edict that she wouldn't stay the night in Hank's house.

Mae said, "I know you guys are trying to avoid the topic, but I'm serious. I'm not going to spend the night in that smelly shit hole that Hank calls his home."

Gary spoke quickly to defuse the situation. "Okay Mae, why don't you make a hotel reservation right now?"

Mae said, "I'll do that."

Gary said, "Hank, is there a hotel nearby?"

Hank said, "Uh, yeah, there's a Days Inn just a few –"

Mae scoffed, and cut him off, "Thanks anyway Hank, I'll handle it."

Mae walked a few steps away as she did an internet search and then made a phone call. She had to try the local number several times because the circuits were busy, but a few minutes later, she had secured a reservation at the Hampton Inn. It was the most expensive hotel in the area. At the end of the call, the receptionist said the reservation would be held with a credit card, but when she arrived, Mae would have to pay cash up front for the room. Mae was a little surprised by the request. She decided not to tell Gary about the cash requirement.

While Mae was busy, Gary checked on the girls and then came back to the steps. Hank remained sitting on the steps by the kitchen door. When Mae rejoined the men, she was more willing to play along with them. She knew she would be leaving soon to get a good night's sleep in a pristine hotel room.

Hank saw Mae coming back up the driveway and said to Gary, "I assume your car and trailer are already loaded to the max. When, I mean if, we leave in the morning whatever I'm taking has to fit in my SUV. But I'm going to leave the back bench seat empty in case we have to abandon your car and put all five of us in the SUV."

Hank glanced around for a second before adding, "Gary why don't you look through the garage and grab stuff that we might take with us and put it in the driveway. I'll go through the house and do the same."

Hank looked at Mae without making eye contact and said cautiously, "Uh, Mae, I know you're watching the girls, but maybe you could look through the stuff in the car and trailer with two things in mind. First, see if you can free up some space by removing items that are not essential to survival. Second, shift the most important items to the car and roof-top carrier, and put the less important items in the trailer; just in case we have to ditch the trailer."

Hank's directives were simple and obvious. Gary said, "WILCO" which he knew was Army talk for "will comply." Almost too quietly to be heard, Mae said, "Okay." In a louder voice, she added, "But I'm planning to leave for the hotel in the next hour or so." Then she went to the Volvo. The girls were bored and restless, so Mae sent them to the garage to be with Gary.

Gary remembered the survival packing-list that Mae had gotten from the internet. He mentioned it to Hank. Hank thought it was a great idea, and asked Gary to get the list, and use it. The three of them split up and went to their separate tasks.

Hank said, "Let's get this done as fast as possible." He had been steady on his feet as he assumed command and gave orders. He was still drunk, but he was more than eighty percent functional. Over the last couple of years, Hank had developed a high tolerance for alcohol. After twenty minutes, there were piles of stuff by the garage, the side entry to the house, and the back of the trailer, as each of the three adults made progress. The scene was similar to the one Gary and Mae had created at their home.

Hank interrupted the progress when he called for Gary and Mae to come inside. Gary asked if he should bring the kids.

Hank responded, "Yeah. This could take a few minutes. There's going to be a special announcement by the President. Maybe he'll tell us he's called off the CME and we can all relax." Hank wasn't a fan of the President, but in this unusual crisis, he wanted to hear what the man had to say.

When they came inside, Hank called them to the living room. He was standing in front of the television. "I turned this on to listen for updates while I packed. He's supposed to be on in a few seconds."

Hank stood in the living room, close to the TV. Gary carried the girls inside and put them down in the kitchen, and joined Hank in the living room. Mae stayed with the girls in the kitchen. She had gone into the house just far enough to see and hear the television. Through the archway between the kitchen and the living room, Mae was looking more at the side of the TV than the front.

The President's arrival was late, as usual, so the picture perfect blonde newswoman said, "We're going to show you some scenes from wide-spread protests in New York City and along the east coast for a few minutes."

Gary scoffed at the mention of protests. Someone highly placed in the broadcast industry apparently had decided the term "civil unrest" was too strong. Gary suspected the images they were about to see would show no protest signs. The television station had recorded interviews of the "protestors," but the interviews would not be aired. The broadcasters didn't want to be blamed for the panic, particularly after the White House ordered all broadcasters not to say anything that gave credibility to the doomsday rumors. The "protestors" weren't protesting anything, they were just scared. The interviewees had all talked about the sun, the earth, a blackout and the end of the world. How does one protest the apocalypse?

The image on the TV screen changed to an aerial view of the Throgs Neck Bridge. The bridge was a parking lot. Gary glanced at the television for a moment, and then kicked some debris out of the way so he could get closer to the TV. The footage, shot from a helicopter, was so high that it was difficult to see the individual cars that were clogging the bridge.

A moment later, Gary was stooped over with his face less than a foot from the screen. "They're walking!" Gary looked back at Mae. "The drivers are leaving their cars and walking off the bridge. The bridge will be impassible for days, even if there is no CME."

Gary paused for a moment as he absorbed the meaning of his own words. "Mae, if we had left even an hour or two later, we'd probably be walking too."

As Gary spoke, the view on the television switched to the Tapinzee Bridge, then the George Washington Bridge, and finally the Holland Tunnel. It was the same view at all three locations. The view of the tunnel was shot at lower altitude or a higher resolution. It was clear to Hank that Gary was right. People were leaving their cars and trying to walk out of the City. It reminded Hank of the images he saw of people walking out of New York City more than a decade ago on September 11th. On this occasion, however the walkers were not just employees trying to get home. Instead, the residents of Long Island and the five boroughs were leaving their homes. Hank saw whole families with moms, dads, and sometimes older siblings, pulling or carrying young children and their luggage. The images were not clear enough to see the terrified expressions and tears, but Hank knew they were there.

Hank didn't say it out loud, but thought, *They're running for their lives, but they'll probably just die tired within the next few days.*

Gary turned back to the TV and the three adults stared in silence at the disturbing footage. Unlike September 11th, it was not obvious that thousands of people had died or would soon die, but if the CME were real, the body count would be far higher.

In the kitchen, Jane walked to the edge of the living room where she could see Gary. "What's wrong Daddy? What's wrong?"

"Nothing honey. We're just waiting for the President to make an announcement on TV."

"Oh, he's boring." Jane turned around and went back to Josie who was a few steps away from the kitchen's door to the driveway.

Images of Baltimore, Washington, and Atlanta came and went. The TV screen showed a lot of activity in those areas, but none were as dire as New York where millions would be trapped on islands with no exit. Just as Gary determined he had wasted too much time looking at tragedies he couldn't fix, the President appeared, and Gary stayed where he was.

"My fellow citizens, I uh . . . am speaking to you today. To address the rumor. That some massive . . . natural disaster. Is about to strike our nation. Many of you. Are probably not aware. Of these rumors. But some . . . news outlets have reported. That there is civil unrest. In New

York City. They also reported. Irresponsibly. That the unrest was related to the . . . a pending uh . . . impending . . . I mean alleged disaster. A rumor really . . . nothing but a rumor."

Gary assumed there was an off-screen teleprompter, but if there was, the President was having a hard time reading it. Maybe the darn thing had stopped working.

"My fellow citizens. Let me be clear. The only thing we have to fear . . . is ourselves . . . I mean . . . being scared. There are some people who want you to be afraid. These people are like the speculators. Who drive up the price of oil and the stock prices. They are trying to manipulate you. And scare you. To them I say. Your time has passed. You know – this situation. It almost makes me want to laugh. Folks, you all have probably been watching too much TV. And disaster movies. And now those uh . . . speculators. Manipulators. Are trying to make us believe. That it's gonna happen for real. Let me be clear. There's no comet or asteroid heading our way. That's not gonna happen. The irresponsible news reports. Might be good for ratings. But it's bad for our country. And it's got to stop. I will appoint a Presidential panel to investigate. I will personally . . . find out why the media and the speculators did this. Bottom line is, don't panic. It wouldn't be prudent."

Jane was still bored, but Josephine was starting to get upset. The anxiety level among the adults and the chatter on the TV were making her unhappy. Josie went to the archway between the kitchen and living room, and called for her daddy. While the president continued to speak, Gary went to the archway, picked up Josie, and went back to the living room as he soothed her.

He whispered, "Everything is going to be alright honey," as he encouraged her to rest her head on his shoulder and relax.

With her playmate gone, Jane went to the living room and stood near Gary. Gary held Josie in his right arm, and stroked Jane's hair with his left as he continued to look at the TV.

The President said, "Make no mistake. We are all going to wake up tomorrow. And we will all probably have a big laugh. It's gonna kinda be like that radio show. Back in the eighteen hundreds when uh . . . Orson Welles said aliens were invading the earth. Some listeners believed it was real. Well, it wasn't. They panicked. We are not going to . . . panic. 'Cuz fear shouldn't make us scared. So let me be clear. You will probably laugh about this tomorrow."

"Now just before I came on . . . I spoke to the leader . . . the uh . . . Director of NASA. And I told her to check her stuff out. You know . . . check the data . . . to see if there was anything . . . anything at all . . . that we should know about. I expect to get that report . . . in a few hours. But let me say again, that NASA has already confirmed . . . that there is no doomsday device . . . I mean no comet, no asteroid that's going to hit earth and kill us all. Folks if you're worried about that . . . you've been watching too much Fox News. Let me be clear . . . it is time . . . time to change the channel."

Hank jumped in. "Doesn't this idiot know that his public address is being broadcast on all the networks, including Fox News? This guy is a–"

Mae cut him off. "Shut up Hank, we're trying to listen."

Gary advised both Hank and Mae to take it down a notch to avoid upsetting the girls. All three adults directed their attention back to the television.

". . . and this will not distract me from the important issues facing this country. Jobs. Jobs and the deficit. Make no mistake. There are no aliens or comets or asteroids heading our way. And in New York City, they've got those protestors. But that's nothing to worry about. No need to uh . . . panic. That wouldn't be prudent. That's all. Now we can all go back to regular programming and uh . . . enjoy our evening. That's all . . . all I have to say. At this time. Thank you." The President left the podium quickly without taking any questions.

Gary turned off the TV. He thought the message had been a waste of time. Keeping his tone level and calm, Gary said, "Well, the images of the bridges in the city were interesting, but I don't think that was a valuable use of our time."

Hank's tone matched Gary's. "Sorry brother. You know I don't like the guy, but I thought under these circumstances, he might have told us something useful."

"Hey guys, why do you assume he's lying? He said the CME wasn't going to happen. What if he's telling the truth?" It was Mae.

Hank was having none of it, and his calm tone evaporated. "Come on Mae, you're a lawyer. You're supposed to be the smart one. Tell me this, did he ever mention the CME, or say the words coronal mass ejection?"

Mae said, "He said the only thing we have to fear is fear itself, and that there was no, um –"

"No comets or asteroids heading our way." Hank finished the sentence for her, and continued, "He said that three times. He even said we weren't going to be invaded by aliens. But what did he say about a CME, Mae?"

"Um . . . well . . . ."

"He said nothing, Mae. Nothing at all."

Mae protested, "He said NASA said there was nothing to worry about."

Hank disliked Mae because, among other things, she was supposed to be an expert at thinking logically and parsing words to determine what a person was actually saying. For some reason she had a blind spot when it came to the President. It seemed to Hank that Mae rarely applied her professional analytical abilities to her political views. Hank considered himself to be a logical thinker, and he found it frustrating that Mae seemed to use that skill selectively.

Hank said, "No Mae, the President didn't say that. He said NASA was going to get back to him in a few hours with a report." Hank was speaking slowly and precisely, but without condescension. He was earnestly trying to make Mae understand.

Mae responded, "Yes, but if the CME was real, real enough for Gary's buddy in Russia to have seen it, then NASA must already know about it. So the fact that NASA didn't report anything, means there's no CME to report."

Hank said, "Mae, are you listening to yourself? I've watched this man enough to read between the lines, and understand the real message behind his obfuscation and misdirection. It's clear to me that the CME is real. The President's message just convinced me of it, even though he didn't tell us that. If he does tell us that in a later message, he will insist that he told the truth in the message we just heard. Well he *did* tell the truth, but not all of it. It's true that there is no comet or asteroid about to impact earth, and we probably won't be invaded by aliens. Well not the kind from space anyway."

Mae rolled her eyes. Hank should have left that last sentence off if he was trying to win her to his way of thinking. Gary noticed that Hank sounded surprisingly sober as he argued with Mae.

Hank continued. "Here's what the President will say in his next message. First, he'll say he told the truth; there really are no comets, asteroids, or space invaders coming toward Earth. Second, he'll say the CME is real. He hasn't said that yet, but he will. It will be his first acknowledgment of the CME. Third, he'll say that he *just* got the report from NASA. Then he'll say the CME will probably cause little or no damage. That part will be false, but he'll later claim, if he ever speaks to the country again, that *nobody* could have accurately predicted the extent of the damage. Finally, he'll say CME's are rare and no prior CME has ever done significant damage to our country. Which will also be true."

"So you're saying that NASA doesn't know what the guy in Russia knows? NASA can't yet see the CME?"

"No Mae, I'm saying that the President will claim that he *just* got the report from NASA, but NASA detected the CME at the same time Blaine did."

"Blake," It was Gary.

"Huh?"

"You said Blaine. His name is Blake. Telling me about the CME may have cost Blake his life, and saved all of ours. You could at least get his name right."

"Okay, brother. Thank you. I'll get his name right from now on, because that's really the most important fucking thing we should be focusing on right now."

Jane tugged on Gary's pant leg and said, "Daddy, Uncle Hank said a bad word."

Gary shook his head and rolled his eyes at Hank. Hank apologized before continuing. "So anyway, NASA and Mr. Blaaaaaake – who had access to some of the same equipment that is used by NASA – both detected the CME as it occurred. NASA certainly reported that to the President immediately. They knew it was the proverbial 'Big One.' But the President won't be lying when he says NASA just handed him a report. He'll say "the report" to suggest that it's the *only* report he got from NASA, but it won't be. It will just be *the latest* report."

"At the request of the President, that latest report will say the CME damage cannot be predicted with certainty. The report will say the CME *might* be limited, even though all the evidence indicates the damage will be huge. Those deliberately imprecise statements will give the President the wiggle room to go one step further and say, 'The CME will probably cause little or no damage.' If he's feeling particularly honest, he might add, 'but it's too early to tell.'"

Mae said, "That's a rather detailed prognostication. You've made a remarkably fast transition from being drunk on your ass, to a mind reader."

Jane tugged on Gary again, and said "Mommy said a bad word."

Gary reminded Mae that the girls were present. He was actually pleased that the conversation between Hank and Mae was as civil as it was. Perhaps the trick was to have the girls present, and to keep reminding the adults to be on their best behavior.

With effort, Hank ignored Mae's insult. "I'd wager anything you'd like Mae, that I'll be proven correct. I know how this President attempts to control people. Mae, if you would apply the analytical abilities you use in the courtroom, to what the President says on TV, then you too could make correct predictions about him."

It was odd, Mae thought, *why did she never deploy her considerable talents to parse the words, deeds, and motives of the man she voted for? If he were a courtroom adversary, would she shred his testimony, or be persuaded by the logic and truthfulness of it?*

Hank said, "Let me make my final point. If the CME is *not* real, the President would have said so. He's right. There is a lot of fear and panic out there right now. News of the CME is probably sweeping across the internet, and traveling by phone, text messages, and word of mouth as well. If all that fear and panic is for a CME that is *not* going to happen, the President would have said so. With clear, direct words he could have shut it all down. But he didn't. He said comets, aliens, and asteroids weren't going to happen. He never said the CME wasn't going to happen. So now I know the CME *will* happen, and the damage will be severe."

Gary decided to make a point while Mae was still in a listening mode. He said, "Mae, do you remember the conversation we had on the motorcycle, after we left your office?" Gary was rocking back and forth as he spoke. He didn't think Josephine would go to sleep, but he was giving it a try. He had already switched her from his tired right arm to his left. Jane was still content to stand next to her big strong daddy, but she was now holding onto his right leg, instead of his left.

Mae said, "Some of it, what part of the conversation do you have in mind?"

Gary said, "The part about not telling your friends about the CME because most of them wouldn't do anything to increase their chances of survival. Don't you think that's why the President doesn't tell the public the whole truth? His goal is to keep people calm. He wants them to stay home and not panic. Why should he bother to tell the masses about a coming disaster, when the masses are unprepared and going to die anyway?"

Hank took the point a bit further. "If you think about it, the United States is always at risk for a disaster of some sort, but the government makes no effort to ensure the population can take care of itself. People are essentially trained to be helpless, and rely on the government to save them. So when something huge like a CME comes along, it's almost guaranteed that the damage and the body count will be unnecessarily high."

Gary said, "Mae, don't you remember your own argument? Even though most of the population doesn't have the ability, for whatever reason, to improve their chances for survival, a minority of Americans do have that ability. When the President understates the severity of the crisis to keep the helpless majority from panicking, it hurts the minority who could have used a truthful warning to increase their chances for survival. You're the one who gave a warning to Perky. Well, your favorite President disagrees with you."

When adversaries used her own arguments against her, it was time to change the subject. Mae said, "I'm surprised you boys have so much time to chat. Aren't you supposed to be packing so we can leave tomorrow morning if the CME turns out to be real? Speaking of tomorrow Gary, are you going to drop me off at the hotel tonight and then pick me up in the morning, or should I just take the Volvo and drive back here when you boys are ready to leave?"

Gary ignored Mae's comment and said, "Okay Mae, it's a topic for another time, because we need to get busy, but Hank made a good point. Ask yourself this, why aren't the American people more prepared for hurricanes like Katrina, and Sandy, or lengthy electrical blackouts? If the government wanted us to be self-sufficient, don't you think more of us would be?"

Hank answered the rhetorical question. "The government doesn't want us to be self-sufficient because it would reduce the size, power, and influence of the government."

Mae was being double-teamed, and she had had enough. "You're right Gary, it's a topic for another time." By which she meant never.

Gary wasn't done. He turned to Hank. "You may have been persuaded by what the President *didn't* say, but I was persuaded by the crowds on the bridges and at the tunnel. The masses seem to be convinced it's real, and they are voting with their feet. They apparently don't agree with the President, and they are not staying in their homes. I'm now even more motivated to get out of here fast. That crowd of refugees from the city is going to be here before too long; perhaps by car and eventually by foot. I'd like to stay in front of them."

As Gary finished he turned away from the television to leave the room. Josie had been quiet and motionless for a while. Maybe she was asleep and he could put her down somewhere for the night.

"Refugees?" The query came from Mae who was still in the kitchen doorway. "You called the people leaving the city refugees."

Gary paused as he was exiting the living room. He was hardly aware he had used the word. *The people walking off the bridges certainly looked like refugees, but . . . but this was America!* "Yeah, um . . . the definition of a refugee is a displaced civilian. Somebody fleeing something. Like a war or a disaster. So yeah, I think the term 'refugees' applies to them."

Mae paused, then said, "Doesn't it apply to you and me as well? Aren't we already refugees? We're just like them, but we left earlier. We've already fled the city and our home."

Gary said, "Yeah, I um, I suppose we are. We're refugees that got a head start of just a few hours, but right now we're squandering that advantage. Based on what we just saw on the TV, I'm with Hank. I'm more convinced than ever that the CME is real. We should stop the chatter, get the SUV loaded, and get out of here."

Gary took another step toward the hallway. When he moved, Jane shuffled along beside him. When he stopped, she stopped. Jane was not happy. Daddy had been holding Josie for a long time, and she wanted to be picked up too.

Mae said, "Get out of here when, now? Before the CME hits? Gary, have you forgotten? I just made a hotel reservation. The plan is to stay in town for the night. Remember?"

For the second time in less than a minute, Mae had asked a question that caused Gary to stop in his tracks. Jane had to back up a step to stay with him. "Well yeah, I mean no. Now that we're convinced the CME is going to happen, why would we stay here for the night? Why don't we get out of town now before the shi–, I mean the stuff really hits the fan? We'd be getting another head start, like we did when we left the city."

Mae responded. "What do you mean 'we' Gary? I'm not convinced. How could you be convinced of anything based on what you just saw on television? Yes, those people are 'voting with their feet' as you say, but they are not scientists. They have no expert knowledge. They are just reacting to stuff they saw on the internet. Are we supposed to do whatever they do, just because they did it? What if they all decided to turn around and go back to their homes in the city? Would you load me and the kids into the car and take us back to Islip?"

Gary hated arguing with Mae. It took so much effort. She never quit. At the moment, he couldn't think of anything to say.

Mae still had lots to say. "Up until a few minutes ago, our plan was to stay here for the night and assess the CME damage in the morning. That will give us time to see if the CME actually occurs, and whether it causes a widespread blackouts. Now you are already talking about leaving and going further west, but the CME hasn't hit yet. What if there is a CME, but it causes little or no damage? Do you really want us to run away now, even if there is nothing serious to run away from?"

Gary still had nothing to say.

"And run where, Gary? You want to flee to a more rural location, but you didn't say where. Have you made hotel reservations at a rural location that I don't know about?"

Gary looked at Hank. During their last phone call, the two of them had discussed the possibility of going to Grandpa's farm. Gary hadn't discussed it with Mae, because she hadn't let him. Hank was the one who had developed a relationship with Grandpa. Gary had visited the farm just once. Hank had spent his college summers on the farm with his girlfriend Liz, whom he later married. Gary's only visit to the farm had been a short one, en route to a salmon-fishing weekend Upstate that had been arranged by Hank.

Gary's left arm was tired from holding Josie, and Jane was loudly asking to be picked up. Gary took a few steps into the kitchen and sat down in a chair. He let Josie slide down a bit so her weight was on his left leg as she leaned against his chest. Jane immediately assumed a similar position on his right leg.

"Well Mae, the rural location that Hank and I have in mind is a farm that's owned by a guy that Hank used to visit. Hank spent summers there when he was in college. It was what, fifteen years ago? The old guy that owns it might still be there. Hank also did some hunting on the property for a few years after that. Right Hank?"

Hank nodded, but said nothing. Gary stopped talking. Mae looked at him, expecting to hear more. She didn't.

"That's it? That's the plan? Why didn't you tell me earlier that you had such a crappy plan? I should have stayed in Islip."

"Mae you asked me about Grandpa's place while we were driving in the car on the Throgs Neck Bridge, but then you didn't want to know the details. You said if the CME hit, it might not cause any damage. You said you wanted to see if the evidence first, and didn't want to speculate about what we should do after the CME hit."

Gary was entirely correct, so Mae changed the subject. "Have either of you spoken to the old guy recently? What's his name?"

"Grandpa," said Gary.

"Oh yeah, I remember, you call him Grandpa, but he's not really your grandfather, right?

Hank chimed in. "Yeah, that's just what we . . . what everybody called him. His real name is um . . . Horn, Theo Horn. I visited him a couple of times after I graduated from college, but I haven't spoken to him since . . . well, since I don't know when."

Gary looked surprised. "Hank, I thought after you and I talked on the phone, you were going to call him and see how he was doing. You know, find out whether he still owned the farm, and if it was okay for you to . . . uh visit him . . . um, tomorrow."

Hank looked at his clueless brother. *Doesn't he know that I didn't do any of the things he told me to do on the phone? After I hung up on him, I sat in the easy chair, did some drinking, and then slept until he showed up.* Hank kept his thoughts to himself. "Um, no. I um . . . I didn't get a hold of him. Yeah um, I mean no. I haven't spoken to him in five years or so. I don't even know if Grandpa even still um, lives there."

Mae jumped in. "You haven't been there in what, ten years, and you haven't spoken to him in five years?! What in the world makes you think he's there, or that he still owns the property? Good grief, maybe the old fart is dead!" Mae's tone was a mixture of sarcasm, skepticism, condescension, and astonishment. It was a gift that she had perfected over the years.

Hank loathed the way Mae talked down to people. If she kept it up, he'd probably strangle her to make it stop. If the CME hit, and Hank was required to be within speaking distance of Mae, Hank estimated her life expectancy would be less than forty-eight hours. With the civil unrest, he could kill her and not worry about being arrested.

Hank felt the need to feed her own tone back to her, but he kept his murderous plan to himself. "Nothing Mae. Nothing makes me think that. Why don't you call him and see if you can get us a reservation. Oh wait, I don't have his phone number handy, and even if I did you wouldn't be able to call him because the whole fucking state is panicking right now and all the lines are busy."

Jane murmured, "Daddy, Hank said –" Gary said, "Shhh."

Mae said, "I don't know about that Hank. I made a hotel reservation not too long ago. It's true I had to try the number a few times before I got through, but I did get through. Why don't you dig out Grandpa's phone number, and we'll make reservations for five at his place?"

Gary looked at Hank. Mae's idea was a good one. Gary had thought Hank made the call prior to Gary's arrival, but Hank hadn't. So why not call now? Gary said, "You know Hank, it's not a bad id–"

Hank interrupted, "Yeah, okay! I got it. I mean I'll get it. The number I mean."

Still in the kitchen chair, Gary shifted his right leg a little. Jane was heavier than Josie, and his right leg was going to sleep. The good news was Jane had just closed her eyes and stopped moving. Maybe she would go to sleep as well. A numb leg would be a small price to pay.

Hank patted down his pockets and looked around the kitchen. "I might have his number in my phone, but um . . . I'm not sure where it is right now."

As Hank looked for his phone Gary said, "I'll call it so we can find it when it rings." It took a few moments for Gary to make the call because his phone was clipped to his belt, and Josie's leg was draped across the top of it.

Mae said, "Good grief, I'll look up the number myself. What's the old fart's name again, Theo something?"

Hank said, "Theodore Horn."

Mae used the internet to find Theo Horn's phone number before Hank found his phone. As she dialed the number, Hank was coming back down the hall toward the kitchen. He had found his ringing phone in his bedroom where he had changed out of his bathrobe before he showered.

Mae got a recording that said the phone number she dialed had been disconnected. She pressed the speaker button so both men could hear the message. The brothers looked crestfallen.

While the recording was still playing Hank said, "Maybe you dialed the wrong number. As Hank pulled up Grandpa's phone number from his contact list, Mae disconnected from the recorded message.

Within a few moments, Hank was listening to the same message. He disconnected without putting his phone on the speaker setting. Hank said, "Maybe all the circuits are busy and we should keep trying."

Mae felt she had won this round. She spoke confidently. "I don't think so Hank. When the circuits are busy, that's what the message says: 'the circuits are busy, try again later.' The message I got said the phone was disconnected. Is that the same message you got Hank?"

Hank didn't nod or say yes. He remained silent. Mae knew the answer was yes. Hank dialed the number three more times. The first two times he got a circuits-busy message. The third time he got the disconnected message again. Hank was now in a really bad mood, which was the usual result of a conversation with Mae.

For Mae, the conversation wasn't over, and she kept the condescension coming. "So you're the self-appointed dictator of our little group Hank, but now you've got no plan. Grandpa Theo is dead or gone, and you have no idea what we'll do in the morning if the CME shuts down the grid. Am I right? Have I summed it up accurately?"

Hank felt like he was being cross-examined on a witness stand. *How does she always do that to me?*

Gary tried to smooth the waters. "Mae you're not helping. You still believe that the CME isn't real, and you'll be going back to Islip tomorrow morning. So you can't be too critical of Hank for not having a detailed plan to deal with an emergency that you don't think exists."

Hank thought, *Good point Gary! Why didn't I think of that?* Some of his confidence returned. Hank drew a deep breath let it out slowly. Then he said to Gary, "I'm not asking her to cut me any slack, even though I'm still not sober. People like Mae make things more complicated than they are. They want to have a detailed plan that will work perfectly if they follow it step-by-step. In real life, life on the ground where people fight, and struggle, and sometimes die, nobody knows for sure what the hell is going to happen next. Every plan turns to crap within five minutes after the shooting starts." Hank's voice had a "been-there-done-that" tone.

Mae was leaning against the frame of the kitchen archway with her hands folded. She was looking at Hank like he was a cockroach.

Hank continued, "So we're going to have a very simple plan, and we're going to be very flexible since we know – since *I* know – *every* plan fails. Pay attention Mae, 'cuz here's the plan. I don't have a lot of friends with apocalypse-proof properties, so if the CME inflicts massive damage, then we're going to go to the only place that Gary and I know about. We're going to Grandpa's farm. Period. That's the plan. I don't give a shit about his phone being disconnected. For all I know, he disconnected it himself and he's living there off the grid."

Jane was still resting comfortably on Gary's lap and had let Hank's last two verbal indiscretions pass without comment.

Hank continued, "How about it Mae, have you got a better plan? Do you have any friends who have, I don't know, say 100 acres of land, who would greet you with open arms during the biggest crisis of the century even if you hadn't seen them in several years? Like me, Grandpa is a combat veteran. As sure as I am standing here, I know *if* Grandpa is still on his farm – and I'm betting he is – that's how he will greet me. With his arms wide open, I know he'll share everything he's got. So how about it smarty-pants, have you got a friend like that? A friend who will keep you alive after the shit really hits the fan? If you do, let's call him right now, and do that trick you just did. You know, put him on speaker phone so the rest of us can hear."

Mae *hated* the way Hank was talking down to her. *One day*, she thought, *I'll probably kill him for it.* Outwardly, Mae only shook her head slightly.

Hank continued, "I can tell Mae that you've got a lot of questions because in your perfect, downtown Manhattan world, plans are discussed for weeks, revised for days, and practiced for hours before the action starts. So here are the contingencies, or alternate plans that should address most of your questions. If we get to Grandpa's and he's not there, or he doesn't own the place anymore, we try to stay there anyway. Hopefully, the place isn't occupied. If it is, we'll have three choices, co-exist with those who are already there, wipe them out and take the place for ourselves, or move on to another place. If we don't get as far as Grandpa's, we'll try to find an alternate location in the countryside that gives us a good chance to survive. That's it. That's the plan and all the contingencies. It's something even a new buck Private could understand."

Hank looked at Gary and added, "The way I see it, almost any rural setting will be better than Monroe. And I agree with you Gary, it would be a lot easier to leave now and travel to Grandpa's farm before the CME hits and the vehicles stop running."

It was obvious to Mae that Hank's plan was missing several key components. She thought this would be a good time to start identifying the shortcomings. "Okay Hank, but what about food and water? Will those things be magically delivered to us in the countryside?"

Gary jumped in to prevent the fireworks from getting worse. "Mae, Hank is delivering bad news, but he's just the messenger. Think about our food situation. All we have is what we packed, and whatever Hank has here. That's not Hank's fault." Involuntarily, Gary glanced around. It seemed obvious that Hank had no food in the house. It was equally obvious that he shouldn't bother mentioning that to Mae.

Gary continued, "The point is, whether we stay or go, the amount of food we have is the same. All we've got is what we've got, and we'll try to get more as we travel. Going to the farm is more for security than food. If we can put some distance between us and the city before the vehicles stop running, then we're less likely to be killed by someone who wants to take what little food we do have. Plus, there's probably more food in the countryside. I mean, they grow it there, and ship it to the city, right? If the CME hits, the food will still be there, but it won't be shipped. Help me out here, I hadn't thought of that until just now."

From the look on her face, Mae also hadn't thought about unshipped crops in the countryside.

In his most soothing tone, which got a lot of use in his household, Gary asked, "Do you agree Mae? Do you agree that the things most likely to kill us are starvation, or other people who want to kill us because they are starving? Monroe has far fewer people than Islip, but it's still a densely populated place compared to . . . ."

Gary looked toward Hank, "Hey, Hank what's the name of the town that's closest to Grandpa's place?" Gary was still stuck in the chair, and now both his legs were going numb. Both of the girls seemed to be comatose.

Hank said, "Sandville Center."

Gary turned back to Mae, ". . . compared to Sandville Center."

Mae got the "processing" look on her face, and Gary knew he needed to wait while she thought it through. Hank didn't recognize the look, but he recognized Gary's effort to calm things down a bit and build a consensus. Hank made an effort to assist his brother.

"Okay, look I know I said some stuff earlier about being in charge, but for this question – the question of whether we stay or go tonight – we're a democracy, not a dictatorship. We'll take a vote. If ya'll want to stay here until after the cars stop working, then fine; I'll go back to my easy chair, and wait for the starving walkers from the city to arrive. If you recall Gary, that's what I was do– . . . . I mean, that was my plan before you guys showed up. I'm single, I've got no kids, and I've got almost nothing to lose. By the end of the month, what little I do have to lose is scheduled to be taken from me by the banks. But if I was you guys, with two young kids, I'd run like hell to Grandpa's right now."

Mae was still processing, so Gary responded. "Hank you and I agree that going further west immediately before the cars stop working, is the best course of action. Let's give Mae a moment to work it out."

Hank and Gary both looked at Mae, who finally spoke. "Even if this is a democracy I've already been out-voted two to one. I guess my options are to go with you, or stay in the Hampton Inn while the two of you run to Grandpa's on a big adventure. Gary, if I stay, are you going to take the girls?"

Mae wasn't ready to stop arguing yet. But then she never was. She was a lawyer. Hank gave a disgusted grunt. Trying to be nice to Mae was a waste of time.

Gary spoke again in a soothing tone. He hadn't realized he and Hank had already cast their votes. "C'mon Mae, don't be like that. Tell you what Mae, I withdraw my vote. You, I, and the girls are a team. I'm not going to break up the team. I love you. I'll do whatever you think we should do. If you want to stay until morning to see if the CME is big and bad, then I'll stay too."

Mae almost smiled. She now controlled two of the three votes. She had just gone from having no vote at all, to having the sole authority to make the decision. She was a renowned negotiator. The two men, boys really, hadn't stood a chance.

Mae responded. "Look, I know you two are convinced we should leave now, but my position hasn't changed. I don't think we should panic and drive to Grandpa's unless the CME damage is so massive that we're not likely to survive unless we're on a farm. Besides, we just got off the highway. The roads are jammed full of traffic. If we started driving right now, we'd probably spend the entire night on the road."

Gary thought back to the things he'd learned from Ralph the conspiracy nut. "Mae, you listened to that phone call I made to Ralph. According to him, we can't afford to try your 'wait and see' approach. If we don't get to our destination before the CME hits, the vehicles will probably stop working, and we'll be forced to travel on foot."

Gary paused as he did some calculations in his head. "If we leave on foot, we could only take what we could carry on our backs. That wouldn't be much, since we'd be carrying the two girls most of the way.

We'd be lucky to travel ten miles a day. Grandpa's place is what, about a hundred miles from here?" Gary looked at Hank. Hank nodded.

"So, if we were lucky, and we didn't get attacked, or hurt, or lost, we'd get there in maybe ten days, but there's no way we'd be able to carry ten days worth of food. And we'd have little opportunity to scrounge for food, if the rest of the state is already scrounging."

Gary looked Mae square in the eye to emphasize his point. "Mae, if we don't leave now, with fully loaded vehicles, we'll probably starve to death on the road, as we attempt to walk to Grandpa's."

Mae wasn't convinced. "I'm staying here in a hotel tonight. Even if the CME hits and causes a lot of damage, I think it's better to stay put for a while, then to leave now and drive to a place that might not exist."

Hank glared at Mae as he thought, *It's funny how quickly my plans shifted from suicide to murder. On the other hand, I was planning to be dead by tomorrow anyway, so what the hell? Staying here will require a lot less effort than running to Grandpa's. Fuck it, I'm done. Let Gary and the bitch sort it out.*

Mae pressed on. "Gary we bought food on the way here, but if you're worried about starving to death in Monroe, why don't you go buy some more food right now?"

Hank had been thinking about his easy chair and a whiskey bottle next to it that might still have something in it. When Mae mentioned food, it occurred to him he was hungry. Hank had almost no food left in his house. What was left wasn't particularly appetizing.

Gary was exasperated, but he paused to consider the conundrum. *How do you convince people to prepare for a crisis before the crisis hits? Mae might be right. The CME might not be a national catastrophe. But what if it was? How often did an 'extinction level event' happen? Once every thousand years? How do you convince somebody to respond to something that has never happened in their lifetime, or the ten, twenty or fifty lifetimes prior to that?*

Hank was thinking too, but he was thinking about what Mae had said. *She and Gary had brought food? And they had cash to buy more food? Now would be a good time to do a shopping trip and get something tasty to eat. Perhaps something good to drink as well! Maybe Mae's idea of staying the night wasn't so bad after all.*

Hank suddenly had another thought. He said, "If we left right now, Gary, how long do you think it will take us to get to Grandpa's?"

"It's what, about one hundred miles or so. It takes about what, maybe two hours to get there?" Even as he finished saying it, Gary knew he had miscalculated.

Hank said, "It *would* take two hours under normal circumstances Gary, but this ain't normal circumstances. You saw the traffic on TV. It's not that bad out here, but it's still a problem. How long will it take us, if a lot of other people are doing what we plan to do?"

"Well I see what you mean, but like you said, the traffic to the west of us can't be as bad as what we saw on TV."

"So make a guess,"

"Make a guess based on what?"

Hank said, "Based on common sense and the best information you have available. Make a SWAG." While serving as an infantryman, Hank made a lot of SWAGs, or "scientific wild-ass guesses." It was surprising how fast certain habits came back to you when you needed them. Soldiers made SWAG's when situations got "FUBAR", or "fucked up beyond all recognition." If the CME turned out to be the king of all FUBARs, the number of SWAGs would probably rise dramatically, even as the number of people making them declined dramatically.

Gary was familiar with the term SWAG. Mae just pretended to know. Gary said, "Okay, I'll say four maybe five hours, but that really is a SWAG."

"Okay, so what time is it now?"

7:34 PM

Gary glanced at his watch. "It's 7:34 PM." Gary suddenly realized where his brother was going. If the CME was going to hit at midnight, then the blackout was less than five hours away.

Gary continued, "Crap! Even if we left as fast as we could, the bad traffic might prevent us from getting to Grandpa's before the CME shuts down the vehicles. Blake said the CME would probably hit between midnight and three in the morning. If we're on the road when the CME hits, then we'll get stranded short of our destination, and have to start walking. We'd probably find ourselves in the middle of a lot of other walking refugees."

Hank said, "I agree that bad traffic might make the trip take longer than five hours, but if we leave immediately, we might make it. Especially if the CME hits toward the back end of the three hour window, instead of the front. Even if we don't make it the entire distance, we might get close enough to walk the last few miles."

Mae repeated her one note argument. "Guys, I've done all the running I'm going to do today. I'm not running off to a farm that Grandpa might have already sold, unless I'm forced to."

By "forced," Mae meant forced to leave because of the crippling blow from the CME. For a moment, however, Gary thought about putting a gun to her head and forcing her to get into the car. He decided against it. There was a least a fifty percent chance that he'd be the one to get shot, and a ninety percent chance that Mae wouldn't get in the car against her will no matter what he did.

Hank was hungry and tired of the back and forth arguments. "The two of you need make a decision. I'm at the point, where I don't give a crap what happens next. In fact, I've been at that point for months. Mae if you get your way, and we stay the night, then you might be stuck in

Monroe for the rest of your life, because the CME might make it impossible for any of us to drive away from here. If you're cool with that, then so am I, but if we stay in Monroe and you get kicked out of the Hampton Inn, I'm probably going to make the four of you live downstairs in the basement. I need my space."

Hank paused and then added, "By the way, is anybody else hungry? I sure am."

Gary ignored the food comment. He was thinking about a way to stay the night and still be able to drive away the next day. Gary was also thinking about his legs, which were numb. He cautiously shifted his legs to try to get the blood flowing again without waking up the girls.

Gary said, "Hank, what if it we could stay here tonight, and wait for the CME to hit, but still drive away in the morning even if the CME causes a widespread blackout?"

Hank was *really* tired of talking in circles. "What if Santa Clause came early this year and gave us a ride to Grandpa's in his sled?"

"Hank, I'm being serious. Have you heard of a Faraday cage? We could protect our vehicles by building Faraday cages around them."

"Sure I've heard of them, but I've never built one or used one. I also don't have any metal boxes big enough to stick my SUV into. So if you or Santa Clause can conjure up such a thing, I'm all ears."

"Me too," Mae chimed in. The brothers glanced at her. It was obvious she was in favor of any idea that didn't require her to leave Monroe.

"Hank, this might sound crazy, but I recently heard that we might be able to protect the vehicles from the CME by um . . . ." Gary paused, what he was about to say, *did* sound crazy. He finished the sentence quickly. "By wrapping them in aluminum foil."

Mae laughed. Hank only grunted.

As she spoke, Mae was still laughing. "Let me get this straight, Gary. This huge CME that is going to destroy civilization can be defeated by aluminum foil? If that were true, why wouldn't everybody just wrap their electrical stuff in foil?"

Gary didn't think it was funny. "Mae, I'm not an expert. I don't know if one layer of aluminum foil is enough to protect a car. I'm just going by what Ralph said during the phone call shortly before he hung up on me. Mae you were on the call. You heard the same thing I did."

Mae said, "Well I guess I did, and I even did the research you requested, but I thought a big Faraday cage had to be, you know, a big metal cage. Like a large metal box. I think Ralph referred to a shipping container."

"He did Mae. But after that, he also said aluminum foil would work. If Ralph was right I can prove that to you in a couple of minutes. I could build a small Faraday cage right now."

Mae wasn't laughing anymore, but she shook her head in disbelief. "Yeah Gary, why don't you prove it to me? Let me see the evidence, because I'm hoping you're correct."

Gary was right; Mae had listened in to the phone call with Ralph, but she was a lawyer, not an electrician. If Gary could prove his point with a demonstration, then let him do it. Mae had proven lots of stuff in court with demonstrations by various experts. Plus, if Gary were correct, it would be another reason for her to stay the night in Monroe and not go looking for Grandpa's farm in the dark on foot. Mae decided she would not treat Gary as a hostile witness.

Gary said, "Hank, this demonstration will work best, if you have a battery operated AM/FM radio. It would also work better, if I could stand up and move around. Can you guys help me with the girls? I can't feel my legs."

Hank said sure, and picked up Jane. Jane settled into Hank's grasp and rested her head on his shoulder without opening her eyes. There was a pause, and both men looked expectantly at Mae. She glanced around for a moment before she figured out what the men were expecting. Then she awkwardly took Josephine from Gary's lap, and tried to hold her the way Hank was holding Jane. The transition wasn't smooth. Josie opened her eyes, and looked around before resting her head on Mae's shoulder. She did not close her eyes.

Gary stood up slowly and leaned hard with one hand on the back of the chair, and the other on the kitchen table. He shook one leg, then the other. Then he repeated the process two more times to get the blood flowing.

Finally, Gary said, "Where were we? Oh yeah Hank, I asked you for a portable radio."

Hank said, "I've got one of those around here someplace, but it will probably take me a couple of minutes to find it. When I do find it, the batteries will probably be dead, and I don't have any replacement batteries. Can't we just use a radio that plugs into the wall? The electricity still works at the moment."

"I don't think so, because the cord from the radio to the wall would leave a small hole in the Faraday cage I'm about to build. That small hole, and the electrical wire itself, would let in an electromagnetic pulse or EMP. In this case, the EMP is the radio signal itself."

Hank said, "Alright I'll look for the radio."

"Tell you what Hank, you find the radio, and I'll go out to the car and get some batteries. What size do we need?"

Hank said, "I'm pretty sure we need two Double-A's. While you're at your car, why don't you bring in some food?"

Gary said, "Why? Do you really have nothing in your house to eat?" As he spoke, Gary walked to the Hank's refrigerator, opened the door and took a quick look inside. He gagged, and quickly shut the door. There was nothing edible inside the fridge.

Gary said, "Don't you have any food at all?"

"Yeah, but not in the fridge. I've been surviving on canned food from the church pantry."

Gary said, "Why don't you get the radio and we'll talk more about food right after our Faraday experiment."

As Gary left, Josie said, "Where is Daddy going?" Mae assured her that Daddy was coming right back.

Hank shrugged and left the kitchen to look for the radio in his bedroom's walk-in closet. He was still carrying Jane, and she was showing signs of waking up. Surprisingly, he found the radio quickly and placed it on the table when he got back to the kitchen. Gary returned from the car with batteries, a roll of the aluminum foil, and no food.

Still holding Jane, Hank sat down in the chair Gary had recently occupied. He turned on the radio. Nothing happened. Hank thought Jane would continue to rest and perhaps go back to sleep, but she took an interest in what Uncle Hank was doing. She rotated around so her back was to his chest and she could see his hands and the radio. Hank opened up the battery compartment and discovered the corroded batteries that he had left in the radio when he stored it. Hank asked Gary to get a knife from the kitchen drawer.

Gary gave the knife to Hank, and Hank scraped off the corrosion. When the contacts were clean, Gary gave Hank new batteries to install. Gary said, "I think we need to wrap the radio in an insulating material before we wrap it in aluminum foil. A small plastic bag would work."

Hank said, "I might have a plastic garbage bag around here someplace."

"A garbage bag would be kind of big. How about a dry piece of paper? That might be good enough for this little experiment."

Hank handed Gary the radio, and then leaned over in the chair as he scrounged around on the kitchen floor for a moment. When he sat back up, he had a paper bag that had contained Chinese take-out a few weeks ago.

Jane was awake, and Hank no longer had the radio. She slid out of Hank's lap so she could watch what her daddy was doing. Josie was still in Mae's arms. She was awake and looking around. She didn't look happy, but she wasn't crying yet.

Gary looked at the radio for a moment. "Hey this isn't just an AM & FM radio. Can this thing also pick up shortwave radio signals?"

Hank got up from his chair and said, "Yeah, before I deployed for the first time, a buddy of mine convinced me that I would need a shortwave radio to get news broadcasts overseas. So I bought one. He was wrong. All the forward operating bases had a variety of radio and television stations. I played around with the ham radio frequencies a couple of times just to see if the radio worked, but I never really used it."

"So, the ham radio receiver on this thing works?"

"It worked fine, the last time I checked it. Go ahead and check it if you want."

Hank looked as if he had suddenly remembered something and took a few steps toward the stove. When he got there, he opened a cupboard and pulled out two cans of stew that he had acquired on a Saturday visit to the local food pantry. Then he cleared a place next to his electric can opener so he could open the cans.

Gary said, "Interesting," as he extended the radio's antenna. Then he turned on the radio and moved the tuner dial through a variety of ham radio frequencies.

Mae asked, "Why do they call it ham radio? Is 'ham' an acronym for something?"

Hank said, "That's one thing I do know. This type of radio is called 'amateur radio' to separate it from the commercial or 'professional' radio stations that broadcast to the public. In the early nineteen hundreds, the word ham started out as a slur to refer to the incompetent amateur radio operators."

Mae said, "It seems kind of weird that the amateur radio operators would refer to themselves with a word that started out as an insult."

Hank shrugged, as he began removing the lid from the first stew can with the electric opener. There were many things about the world that he couldn't explain.

Gary was still fiddling with the radio, and said, "I can hear ham radio traffic on this thing just fine." Then he changed the selector switch to FM and tuned in a strong signal from a local station. When he collapsed the antenna, the station still came in clearly.

Gary looked at Hank. The can opener was grinding away on the second can, and Gary waited a few moments for it to stop. He wanted to ensure that Hank and Mae were both paying attention.

Gary felt like a magician about to perform a trick, except he wasn't a magician and he had never even tried to perform this trick before. He put the radio in the paper bag, and folded the bag tightly around the radio. The music on the radio was slightly muffled, but the signal strength was still strong. A commercial for the local General Motors dealership could easily be heard.

Gary tore off a one-foot-long piece of aluminum foil, and put it on the table. He placed the bagged radio on top of it. There was no change to the signal strength. As Gary folded the sides of the foil over the top of the radio, the signal got weaker, and then stopped. The radio was on, but only static could be heard. The experiment worked. The electromagnetic signal of the radio-station's transmitter did not penetrate the foil.

Gary looked at Hank and Mae with a "Ta-dah!" expression on his face. He got no reaction from the adults so he turned to Jane, who had been watching closely. He said, "Ta-dah! The radio no longer works!"

Jane smiled and clapped her hands, but she didn't know why Daddy was happy about breaking the radio. If she had done that, she would have gotten in trouble. She held out her arms for Daddy to pick her up and he did. It was his way of saying thanks to the only happy member of his small audience.

To the adults, Gary said, "Based on what Ralph told me, we could protect sensitive electronics from the CME's by doing what I just did to the radio. If we built a Faraday cage around a car, we could test it by putting an unprotected radio inside it. If the radio still gets a signal, then the Faraday cage is defective."

Hank had temporarily halted his meal preparation to watch the magic trick. With the show over, he looked around for a clean pot. Finding none, he placed the two open cans on one of the big stove burners and turned it on. He adjusted the heat to a low setting because he didn't want the stew on the bottom of the cans to burn. Mae frowned at Hank's culinary effort. *Isn't food supposed to be put in a pot before it is cooked?* Mae wasn't positive, because she never cooked, or ate canned food, but she thought Hank was probably doing it wrong.

With the stew heating, Hank turned his attention back to Gary. "So all we need to do is go out to the driveway, stick my SUV in a big paper bag and then shrink wrap it in aluminum foil?"

Gary said, "Yes, but heavy-duty plastic would provide better insulation than a paper bag. Also, we might get additional protection if we parked the vehicles inside a building first."

Hank said, "You mean, like the garage? It has a metal roof. Maybe that will help."

"I was actually thinking about a different building; not the garage. Your garage is only big enough for one-car, and we've got two vehicles to protect."

Hank looked confused for a second. He didn't have any other buildings big enough to fit two cars. His shed was too small.

Josie started whining and squirming in Mae's arms. Mae didn't know what to do. She leaned down and placed Josie on the floor in a standing position. Josie immediately walked over to her daddy and demanded to be picked up. Without interrupting the flow of the conversation, Gary scooped up Josie in his left arm. He was already holding Jane in his right. It was apparently time for another one of his regular, girl-induced, arm workouts.

Gary said, "Hank, your house also has a metal roof."

Hank still couldn't figure out where Gary was going.

Gary continued, "And your house has a walk out basement with poured concrete walls. Unlike your one-car garage, your basement is surrounded on three and half sides by dirt. I've already told you I'm not a Faraday cage expert, but I'm guessing the dirt and reinforced concrete would provide some protection from an electrical pulse."

"You want to park both cars in my basement?" Hank was surprised.

"Well, it would be a tight fit and we'd have to tear off the patio door, and probably cut the opening a little bigger. We would also have to get some building materials to cover the enlarged patio door opening, but yeah, why not? We could use sheet metal to cover the opening."

Gary paused for a moment. Hank's alcohol addled brain was trying to keep up. Gary continued. "Don't worry too much about all the damage we're about to do, Hank. As Mae pointed out earlier, it's not really your house anymore. At least it won't be by the end of the month. So how do you feel about doing some destructive remodeling?"

Hank smiled and laughed, "I would feel great about that. But I'd feel even better if I ate something first." Hank pulled a dirty spoon from the pile of dishes that filled both sinks, rinsed it under the tap, and dried it off with his shirt. Then he stirred both cans of stew. He determined the burner's heat setting was too low and made an adjustment.

Mae was pleased by the turn the conversation had taken. Hank and Gary were now both following her plan to stay the night, and not leave until the next morning. This made Mae wonder if leaving immediately was the better option. Like a lot of lawyers, Mae often wasn't happy even when she got what she wanted. As the victor, however, she couldn't show that she was already second-guessing herself.

Mae asked Gary. "What time do the stores close? You said you needed building materials. Where are you going to get them?"

Gary looked at his watch and said he didn't know. Gary looked at Hank expectantly.

Hank said, "The Wal-Mart is open twenty-four hours, but Home Depot closes at nine. It will only take us ten minutes to get there. They might stay open late because of the crisis, but we should leave now and not count on that."

Hank continued. "But even if we get there, and they still have stuff to sell, what are we going to use for money? I'll be honest with you, I don't have any cash, and all my credit cards were maxed out months ago. Surprisingly, I still get offers for new credit cards, but my applications get rejected."

Gary said, "Well you don't have to worry about your useless credit cards, because the stores probably aren't taking credit cards from anybody right now. All my credit cards are equally worthless. Cash is probably now king. By tomorrow, we might be on a barter system."

Hank asked, "So how much cash do you guys have? With purchases of both food and the building materials, we're going to need several hundred dollars. Maybe a grand or more."

Gary said, "We've got no problem in the cash department. We can go right now."

As soon as he said it, Gary looked at his two daughters who were still in his arms, and thought, *Well, not right, right now. I'll have to hand off the girls to . . . Mae.* Gary didn't think the transition would go well, so he postponed it. Gary put Jane down in the chair by the radio so he could check his wallet. The radio was still in foil, and static was coming out of it. Gary had more than fifteen hundred dollars, and he knew Mae had even more than that. Gary later wished he'd taken some additional funds from Mae before he left. Jane began to unwrap the radio.

Hank said, "Let's eat before we go." He pulled a dirty plastic bowl and another spoon from the sink and rinsed them under the tap. He poured half the stew into the bowl and offered it to Gary. Gary rejected the bowl, and took the can instead. Gary noticed that Hank hadn't used soap when he washed the bowl and spoon. He figured Hank was immune to whatever germs might still be clinging to the dishes. Gary put Josie down on the counter for a moment so he could taste the stew. It was warm but not hot. Gary put the can down, and picked up Josie.

To Mae, Gary said, "If you and the girls are going to eat the stew, you should let it heat up for a few more minutes."

Gary said, "Let's go," again to Hank who was still spooning stew into his mouth from the bowl. Gary added, "We'll take your SUV, and we can eat as we drive." Gary intended to hand off Josie to Mae just before he walked out the door. Now seemed like the time. Jane was at the table, and trying to undo the magic trick by pulling the foil off the radio.

Mae said, "Wait. Both of you are leaving? Aren't you two forgetting something?"

Hank and Gary both froze. Gary asked the obvious question. "Forgetting what, Mae?"

"I'm spending the night at the Hampton Inn. Maybe you guys could drop me off when you go shopping."

Gary was befuddled. "Wait, you still plan to leave the house and stay in a hotel tonight?"

"Yes, what's wrong with that? I'm not going stay in this filthy smelly house. I'd sooner sleep in the Volvo."

Hank shook his head and said, "Wow, what a stupid bi–"

Gary quickly interrupted and said, "Shut up Hank, I've got this. Look, Mae, you know what? If that's really what you want to do, then I'll do it. If you want to go to the hotel right now, I'll take you there and you can stay the night. But I'm not sure you fully understand the implications of that decision. Hank and I are going to buy some materials, and then come back to the house where we will wrap the Volvo and his SUV in aluminum foil. Nobody is sleeping in either vehicle tonight because the doors will be wrapped and taped shut."

Mae said nothing. Gary continued. "We're also not sure the whole Faraday foil scheme is going to work. In the morning, our vehicles might not start. That will leave Hank and me here, and you at the hotel."

Gary turned to Hank, "How far is the Hampton Inn from here?"

Hank's response was postponed because the radio started blaring as Jane pulled a large piece of foil off the radio. She jumped, but also smiled. Hank stepped over to the table, put down his bowl of stew, and persuaded Jane to give up her possession of the radio. He turned off the radio and removed the batteries.

He put the batteries in his pocket and said, "The Hampton Inn is about six miles away. It takes maybe ten minutes to get there."

Gary said, "Did you hear that Mae? It takes about ten minutes to get there *by car.* But if the cars don't work in the morning, you'll have to travel back here on foot. That will take you about two hours, assuming you don't get assaulted or murdered as you walk back to the house. It's your decision Mae. What do you want to do?"

Mae *hated* losing an argument almost as much as she would hate spending a night in Hank's house. She processed the data for a few moments. In the final analysis, she was not so confident in a benign CME outcome that she would bet her life on it. Choosing to walk two hours in an unfamiliar place with a non-functional cell phone while surrounded by people who thought civilization had ended or was about to end, would be stupid. Mae was not stupid. She was highly pissed off right now, but not stupid.

"Damn it, Gary, I do NOT want to spend the night in this house!"

Jane said, "Daddy, Mommy just said a bad word." The adults ignored her.

A hissy fit from Mae was a rare thing indeed. Mae almost never lost an argument. When she did, she usually handled it like a mature professional. Mae blamed Hank for her bad mood.

Gary didn't back down. "Mae, it's your decision. We'll take you to the hotel if that's what you want."

"Shit! Maybe I'll sleep in the garage. It can't be worse than this house."

Jane said, "Daddy, Mommy just said another bad word." She tugged on Gary's pant leg this time, but the adults ignored her again.

Gary said, "So that's it, you're staying Mae?"

Mae's expression implied yes, but she didn't actually say yes. She tried for a compromise. "Gary, can you at least take the girls with you while you shop?"

Gary let out an exasperated sigh. "Mae, there is no sense in dragging the girls to the stores. It's already past their bedtime. We're taking the SUV, and it doesn't have car seats. You should stay here and put them to bed."

Gary was right. Taking the girls on a shopping trip when the shoppers might turn into rioters at any moment was a bad idea. Mae had lost two arguments in less than a minute – in front of Hank. She changed the subject.

"Gary, maybe you could at least stop at a restaurant and buy some real food when you're done shopping. I'm not going to eat stew out of a can."

Gary said, "Real food? Crap! I forgot about the cooler."

Gary handed Josie off to Mae so he could go outside and get the cooler. Jane tugged at his pant leg and said, "Daddy that was kind of a bad word."

Gary leaned down and said, "I know, honey. I'm sorry."

Mae said simultaneously, "What cooler?" In Islip, Gary had loaded the cooler with food and packed it in the Volvo so quickly, that Mae had not seen it leave the house.

Gary opened the kitchen door and was walking away as he said, "Mae, I brought a bunch of stuff from our fridge with us, and if the lights are going to go out, then all the meat needs to be cooked tonight." Mae could barely hear the end of Gary's sentence because he was already outside in the driveway. He had left the door open.

Mae looked shocked. She yelled, "YOU WANT ME TO COOK IN THIS FUCKING KITCHEN?!"

Mae was still holding Josie who started to cry.

Jane said loudly, "Daddy, Mommy just said another bad word!"

Mae thought, *Gary's kids are obnoxious brats!*

Gary was outside and almost to the Volvo. He had no trouble hearing Mae, but he hadn't heard Jane. He briefly wondered what bothered Mae more, Hank's filthy kitchen or the fact that she might have to do some cooking. Even though he hadn't heard Jane's comment, Gary knew Mae's curse had been heard by both girls, and maybe the neighbors. If they survived the next few days, the girls were probably going to acquire an expanded vocabulary.

Hank realized he was in the kitchen with a crying kid and a crazy woman. He mumbled something about helping Gary with the cooler as he bolted out the still-open door. Gary and Hank soon returned with the cooler. Each man was holding one handle. Gary could have carried it himself, as he had done when he put it into the Volvo, but Hank insisted on helping. They put the cooler on the counter near the stove.

Mae looked at the cooler as if it was Pandora's Box. She had no intention of opening it. Mae dumped the crying Josie into Gary's arms as she fumed silently and regretted her loss of control in front of Hank and the kids. Jane went to Gary and latched onto his leg.

Gary poked through the cooler with one hand and said, "We've got chicken, sausage, hamburger, bacon, eggs, and some steaks in here. And like I said, if the meat doesn't get cooked now, it will spoil if the lights go out." He had loaded the cooler so quickly he could not have given an inventory from memory.

Hank licked his lips as Gary ran down the list. In the last few weeks, Hank hadn't eaten any of the items Gary had just mentioned. His mouth was watering. He said, "You had steaks in the car that needed to be cooked, and you let me cook the stew instead? Gary, what the hell were you thinking?"

Jane whispered, "That was a bad word." Hank gave Jane an apologetic smile and a wink.

Gary shrugged. He had obviously been thinking about his Faraday demonstration, and it hadn't occurred to him that Hank was opening cans that had a much longer shelf life than the steaks.

Thinking about the steaks, Hank said, "Hey, maybe I could stay behind and do the cooking while you and Mae do the shopping."

Trading cooking for riotous crowds sounded good to Mae, but Gary nixed the idea. "Thanks for the offer Hank, but you need to come along to pick out building supplies and load them into your vehicle. Besides, I'm sure Mae doesn't want to leave the kids alone with you in this house."

Mae looked perplexed. The need to abandon the kids to avoid cooking hadn't entered her mind. Now that it had, shopping seemed like an even better deal. Her last spoken comment hadn't gone well, so Mae kept her thoughts to herself. *Don't they have stock boys or something to load materials? How difficult could this shopping trip be?*

Gary felt like he had stepped between two gunslingers in a standoff. He wanted it to end quickly with no additional shots being fired. He said, "Mae, Hank and I need to leave now. In addition to the cooking, you'll probably have to put the girls to bed."

Mae glanced around at the smelly clutter. Then for the second time that day, she attempted to kill Gary with her laser-beam stare. She sure as hell didn't want to go poking through Hank's filthy, shitty mess to make a bed for the girls. In her opinion, the house needed a few gallons of gasoline and a match. She would be happy to perform the deed.

Hank saw the deadly look on Mae's face, and knew what she was thinking. For him, the show was over. It was time to go. He grabbed his keys and wallet from a kitchen drawer. As he hurried out the door he said, "You know what Mae, you're right. This house is a mess. Why don't you tidy up the place a bit while we're gone?"

Hank was out the kitchen door before Mae could respond. With his back toward Mae, she couldn't see his wide smile. In the driveway Hank added, "Cook my steak medium well."

Gary handed Josie to Mae, and pried Jane loose from his leg. He said goodbye and went out the door quickly. Both girls started to cry. He closed the door firmly, which deadened the wailing sounds.

Mae had won. She had persuaded the men to stay the night, but lost the hotel room in the process. Now she was stuck in Hank's filthy kitchen, with a cooler full of uncooked food, lukewarm canned stew on the stove, and two screaming kids. It didn't feel, smell, or sound like victory.

In the driveway, Hank stopped and asked Gary whether he had a gun. When Gary said, no. Hank pulled a 9mm Berretta from a concealed carry holster inside his belt and showed it to Gary.

Hank said, "Brother, with every passing minute, there is less and less civilization out there. We intend to go shopping, acquire some valuable stuff, and get that stuff back to my place without being attacked. It's quite likely the police will have other priorities. We should each carry a gun to ensure we get back here alive."

Gary said, "I didn't know you had a concealed carry permit."

"I don't. That's why I keep the gun so well concealed."

Gary said, "Well I don't have a permit either, but I just happen to know where I can find a loaded revolver. The guy who owns it, no longer needs it for its intended purpose."

Gary re-entered the house and went to the cupboard above the refrigerator where he had stashed Hank's .357 revolver. Gary moved quickly. He didn't want Mae to see what he was doing, and he didn't want the girls to latch on to him again. Mae hated guns. If she knew he intended to carry one in public, she would make a scene. The girls were already making a scene that was bad enough. Mae was focused on her own misery and didn't see the gun.

Gary again left the house quickly. He stuck the pistol in the front of his waistband. He tried to think about something other than accidentally shooting his balls off. It was the first time he had carried a pistol, but he tried to act cool about it. He wanted to know where the safety switch was, but he didn't want to embarrass himself by asking about it. He'd keep his finger off the trigger, and take his chances.

Gary and Hank got in the SUV. As Gary sat down, the handgrip on the pistol jabbed him in the stomach. He pushed the grip down so the pistol was tipped to the right at forty-five degree angle to his waistband. Now a misfired bullet would take out his hip rather than his balls. The gun was still poking him, so Gary tilted his seat back a little to relieve the pressure.

Hank put the SUV in reverse as he glanced over at Gary and said, "Comfortable?"

Gary said, "Very," with a smile, even though he wasn't. He was smiling because the gun hadn't gone off when the grip had jabbed him in the stomach. They left the driveway at five minutes to eight.

Chapter 12: Mae cleans house and the men shop.

Mae turned off the stove without touching the can of stew. She was hungry, but she didn't want to eat the stew. If the girls got hungry, Mae would get some more snacks from the Volvo. She couldn't remember the last time she had been left alone with the kids. Whenever it happened in the past, she paid Ana to hurry over and assist. Mae missed Ana very much.

The thought of spending the night amidst the debris and foul odor revolted her. If she had to spend the night here, she decided she would make the best of a bad situation, and inflict some retribution on Hank for creating such a mess. She also needed something to distract and quiet the kids. Holding Josie, and with Jane tagging along, Mae took a quick tour of the house.

The cluttered guest bedroom would be the easiest room to salvage for an overnight stay. It was the only room that didn't have moldy take-out food containers. She went through the rest of the house and opened all the windows with screens that weren't already opened. Each time she opened a window, she put Josie down so she could use both hands. Josie didn't like it, but so what? The kid was already crying. Mae closed the front porch door to stop bugs from coming in.

Back in the guest room, Mae opened the window and removed the screen before she picked up Josie again. Then with one hand, Mae started tossing clutter from the room out the window and onto the front lawn. Cleaning house was another skill Mae didn't have, but this was more a dumpster-filling project; without a dumpster. Jane wanted to join in, but thought she and Mae would get in trouble when Daddy got home.

Mae treated Jane like a client and quickly persuaded her to do as Mae directed. Jane was soon tossing stuff toward the window and giggling about it. As Mae had hoped, Josie eventually stopped crying. She wanted to join her sister. Mae quickly put Josie on the floor, and both girls were soon having fun. They took turns holding up an item so Mae could see it and asked, "Mommy, can I throw this out the window?"

Mommy always said yes, and the girls gleefully practiced their overhand throws. Some of their throws caused an object to clear the hurdle of the windowsill and actually land outside the house. Mae sorted through the items before the girls got to them, and found a few things that might have value in a crisis. She took the items to the kitchen and looked for an uncluttered horizontal surface. A small area around the portable radio on the kitchen table was the only clear spot. Mae shoved some counter-top clutter by the stove onto the floor. She put the things from the guest room into the newly cleared space, and then moved the radio from the table to the counter.

When she realized she was now doing what Gary and Hank had told her to do, she felt like throwing up. She fumed as she continued to "tidy up the place a bit." Mae cleared the kitchen table by tipping it over onto its side. The tabletop didn't make a loud thud when she dropped it to the floor, because it never actually hit the floor. It was cushioned by empty pizza boxes and take-out containers. Dishes, plastic-ware, unopened mail, and empty food wrappers from the table joined the pile. Mae righted the table, and removed a ketchup covered food wrapper that had glued itself to the table surface weeks ago. She found a dirty dishrag and rinsed it in hot water for several minutes before wiping down the table.

Mae retrieved the packable items she had placed on the counter, and put them on the kitchen table. She went back to the guest bedroom. She noted that the girls had continued tossing items onto the front lawn in her absence without asking permission. She did not reprimand them. She never reprimanded them. That chore was owned by Gary and Ana.

Mae went back to making the guest room habitable. Books, papers, clothing, Christmas decorations, garbage, small appliances, and an old desktop computer went out the window. Mae took only two more trips to the kitchen with items that might be useful in a crisis. The clutter was gone in less than ten minutes. Mae found a vacuum, emptied its full canister over the rear deck rail into the back yard, and vacuumed the carpet in the guest room. She stripped the bed, and tossed the stained and dusty comforter out the window. She collected the blankets, sheets and pillow cases, and took them to the washing machine where she started a load.

It took her a few minutes to press the right sequence of buttons to make the machine go. Even with her own washer at home, she needed instruction from Gary on the very rare occasions she attempted to do laundry. A minute later, she had to go back to the machine, because she remembered she hadn't put any soap in. She didn't know whether she should have been surprised to discover that laundry soap was one of the very few things Hank appeared to have in abundance.

Mae went to the kitchen with the girls following her. Jane asked if there was any more stuff she could throw out a window. Mae absent mindedly said, "I don't know sweetheart," as she surveyed the kitchen and living room. Even with all the windows open, the stench in the house was not leaving as fast as she had hoped, but why would it? All the truly smelly stuff was in the kitchen and living room, and it was all still there. It was time for all of it to go.

Mae took the girls back to the relatively clean and now uncluttered guest room. She turned on the television that sat on a dresser where it could be seen from the bed. She tried to find a kid's channel, but couldn't find any channels at all. Either Hank hadn't hooked the bootleg cable to this TV set, or Mae was not properly using the remote. Mae noticed the TV had a DVD player. She left the girls in the guest room, and went to the Volvo to get a couple of movies. She brought the disks back to the guest room. The tired and emotionally drained girls soon assumed zombie-like positions in front of a video they had watched just a few hours earlier.

Unencumbered by the children, Mae went to the garage and came back with a blue plastic snow shovel. In the kitchen, she used the shovel to scrape off the countertops. Take out containers, ceramic coffee mugs, eating utensils, and dirty dishes all hit the floor. Some of them broke on impact. Mae was going to push the trash out the side door to the driveway, but thought better of it. The clutter would interfere with trips to and from the vehicles. Instead, she opened the back door that connected the kitchen to the wooden deck at the back of the house. She then pushed the piles out the door and onto the deck. After every second or third shove, she would go outside and push the piles further out onto the deck, and occasionally over the side.

When the girls heard objects crashing on the floor as Mae had cleared the kitchen countertops, they had visited the kitchen with the hope of throwing more stuff out a window. Mae escorted them back to the guest bedroom. She didn't want one or both of them to fall off the deck into the back yard. A dead or injured child would be one hassle too many.

The shovel worked well on the vinyl floor and the kitchen was completely cleared of debris in less than ten minutes. Mae attacked the living room next. It disgusted her to have to use her fingers, rather than the shovel, to pull some of the sticky food wrapper debris from between the cushions on the sofa and drop it on the floor. The shovel didn't work as well on the carpet as it had on the vinyl, but twenty minutes later all the living room trash had been pushed out the front door onto the porch. On the front porch, Mae cleared a path to the front stoop and sidewalk, so the entry to the house was not obstructed. If the house caught fire tonight, she didn't want to burn to death as she struggled to free herself from a pile of Hank's trash.

Mae went back into the house, across the living room and down the hall to the main bathroom, which was across the hall from the guest bedroom. That bathroom was messier than the one in the master bedroom, because Hank spent most of his time in the living room. If Mae had to pee at two in the morning, she would use the main bathroom, so that's the one that needed to be cleaned. Mae figured she would spend the night in the guest bed with the girls. The bed was full sized, so Gary wouldn't fit. He would have to find his own sleeping arrangements.

Mae glanced around the den and the master bedroom, and then closed the doors to both of them. Neither room was as filthy as the living room, but she had no intention of cleaning either of them, and didn't want the girls to wander into them. As Mae was going back toward the kitchen, Josie met her in the hallway.

Josie was tired, and wanted to be held. Mae ushered Josie back into the guest room where the movie was still playing. When Mae tried to leave, Josie started crying. Mae had to pick Josie up to get her to stop. Jane was still contentedly watching the television. Mae decided she would continue working for a few minutes while carrying Josie. Hopefully, Josie's mood would soon change, or she would go to sleep. It didn't happen that way. Josie was away from her home and out of sorts after a long stressful day. Mae would have to carry Josie until Gary got back from the store.

Mae thought about putting Josie to sleep for the night with a little cough syrup, but she had no idea where the contents of her medicine cabinet had ended up. She thought about looking for cough syrup in Hank's house but decided against it. If Hank had any, it would be adult strength and probably long past its best-by date. Mae wanted to put Josie to sleep, but not permanently.

With only one hand available, Mae's efficiency decreased, but she got back to work. She went to the kitchen and emptied the kitchen trashcan off the side of the deck into the back yard. She took the empty can to the bathroom and filled it with porn magazines and other garbage. She made a second similar trip with the garbage can, and again dumped the contents in the yard. All the horizontal surfaces in the bathroom were now visible. Mae found a bottle of bleach in the kitchen, and made a strong solution of it with hot water. She wiped down the bathroom to the point where she'd be willing to sit on the toilet, and wash her hands in the sink. She decided she wouldn't take a shower, and left the filthy tub untouched.

She went to the kitchen and wiped down all the countertops. Then she dried a spot, and sat Josie on the counter. As long as Mae was standing right in front of Josie and touching her, Josie didn't cry. Mae's arms were tired. She had been shifting Josie from one arm to the other and back again, and both arms needed a rest. How did anybody ever get any housework done with two kids present? It was a mystery to Mae.

The bleach helped a lot, but the living room still stunk, so Mae sprinkled the rest of the bleach solution onto the carpet. The stench was greatly reduced, but the blue carpet developed white spots where the bleach had landed. The destruction of the carpet didn't bother Mae in the least. When she was done in the living room, the house no longer smelled like a garbage dump. In fact, the smell of the bleach was a bit overpowering. Mae decided to take a break outside, and let the place air out for a little while. She opened all three exit doors to the house, and told Jane she was going outside. Mae carried Josie, and Jane followed Mae outside. Mae turned off most of the lights as she left. In the driveway with the girls, Mae simply stood there for a couple of minutes as she breathed in the cool night air. If she had been a smoker, it would have been a good time for a cigarette.

Mae's arms were tired from holding Josie. She attempted to put Josie down, but Josie protested. It was past her bedtime, and she and Jane both claimed to be hungry. Mae took the girls to the Volvo and the three shared some crackers and a candy bar. Halfway through the candy bar, Mae's stomach grumbled. She really was hungry and she needed something more substantial to eat. Mae thought about driving the car to a fast food place, but that would require her to back the Volvo and the overloaded trailer out of the driveway. She had never before backed up a car with a trailer, and she didn't know how to disconnect the trailer from the car. She also couldn't find the keys. Maybe Gary had them.

Mae thought about her options. It came down to canned food from the car, or cooking something from the cooler in the kitchen. After some procrastination and some whining from the girls who were also still hungry, Mae decided she would have to do the unthinkable. She would have to take pieces of dead animals from the cooler and attempt to cook them. Reluctantly, she went back into the house with the girls. She thought the chicken would be the most palatable, but decided to experiment with the steaks first, in case something went wrong. If she had gotten some cooking instructions from the internet, the experiment would have gone better.

A few minutes later, Mae had the partially frozen steaks on a cookie sheet that had seemingly never been used by Hank. At 8:55 PM, she put the tray in the oven, set the oven to broil, and closed the oven door.

7:52 PM

An hour earlier, as the men left the driveway in the SUV, Hank turned on the radio. Regularly scheduled programming on most stations had been discontinued as commentators talked nonstop about the riots in urban areas and false rumors of an asteroid about to hit earth. Portions of the President's earlier address were replayed, and listeners were told to go home and get a good night's sleep. There was no new information. Hank left the radio on, but turned the volume down low. If new information was announced, he'd turn up the volume and listen.

While they were driving, Hank and Gary decided to split up when they reached the stores so the shopping would take half as long to complete. Gary would go to Wal-Mart, and Hank to Home Depot. Hank initially argued that they should both hit Home Depot first and Wal-Mart second, because Home Depot was closing in just over an hour, while the Wal-Mart never closed. Gary explained that Wal-Mart was either already out of food, or soon about to be, so he needed to get there as soon as possible. Gary was also worried about finishing the shopping at both stores quickly, before the riots and looting started.

They drove in silence for a while, and then Hank said, "Gary, I've been thinking about the construction of the Faraday cages for our vehicles and I think we need to expand our shopping list."

"Why?"

"In your demonstration with the radio you used the dry paper bag as an insulator. To cover the vehicles, we'll need a lot of insulation. Home Depot sells six-millimeter plastic in one hundred foot rolls that are ten feet wide. One roll of that should be enough to cover both vehicles, so I'll get one while I'm there. We should also buy some more aluminum foil. It's going to take a lot of foil to cover all six sides of both vehicles."

"Okay," said Gary. "I bought some earlier today, but I'll buy another several rolls at Wal-Mart. You can get the plastic at Home Depot."

"And tape."

"Um, yeah. I got some of that earlier as well, but yeah, I'll get a bunch more."

"Don't forget to try to get some food while you're at it."

Gary laughed. No, he hadn't forgotten the original purpose of their trip.

Hank added, "And beer."

"Beer?"

Hank said, "Yeah. Wal-Mart doesn't sell whiskey, and I don't have any beer left in the house. In fact, there isn't much of anything left in my house because I was, you know . . . I mean I hadn't really planned on needing anymore beer if you know what I mean."

Gary said, "Yes Hank, I know what you mean." Prior to Gary's arrival, Hank's anticipated future need for alcohol, food, water, and oxygen had been zero.

Hank didn't mention that he still had two unopened bottles of alcohol in his bedroom. One was a bottle of wine which in Hank's opinion, wasn't worth drinking. The other was a bottle of bourbon which Hank felt unworthy to drink; particularly by himself.

"The point is Gary, that you've now got me signed up for a stint as a survival instructor, and if I quit the drinking cold turkey, I might be completely nonfunctional by tomorrow. I mean, I'm not an alcoholic or anything, but the symptoms of a sudden withdrawal are something I don't want to – what I mean is it might be tough to deal with. Anyway, if you could snag a case of beer, or at least a couple of six packs, then I could kind of taper off, you know?"

Gary thought Hank had made a good point. Hank would be a far less valuable survival asset if he was overcome by delirium tremens, or DTs.

Gary said, "No problem Hank, I understand. I'll get you a case of beer."

"Thanks, brother."

As Hank continued to drive, Gary pulled out his wallet and counted his cash. "How much do you think you'll need for the purchases at Home Depot?"

"I don't know, maybe three hundred bucks."

Gary counted out the money and gave it to Hank.

8:06 PM

When they got to Wal-Mart, Hank let Gary out. The Home Depot was about a quarter of a mile away, in the next shopping center on the same side of the road. Without reliable phone reception, "Plan A" was for Hank to drive back to the grocery store in forty-five minutes. If Hank didn't arrive before Gary was done shopping, then "Plan B" would be for Gary to walk the quarter mile to Home Depot pushing a grocery cart. Gary was concerned about being able to cover that distance without getting robbed, but Hank reminded Gary that he had a revolver in his pants.

Hank said, "Use the gun if you need to, little brother. I really want you back in one piece. I mean if you're gone, I'll do what I can to save your girls, but if Mae is still around, I don't think I could do it. In fact, now that I'm thinking about it, you should tell me right now; would it be okay with you if I had to shoot Mae, just to shut her up so I could save your daughters?

Gary ignored his brother. He knew Hank was only half joking. As Gary walked the short distance to the store, he concluded that panic in Monroe lagged several hours behind the panic in the city. The store was busier than it was on Black Friday after Thanksgiving and the situation seemed tense, but shoppers were still coming and going without violence.

When he entered the store, he determined the mood was not as benevolent as he had assumed. From the angry comments of some of the customers, Gary learned that the store had recently implemented a cash-only policy. Credit cards were useless. There were several customers with full carts near the cash registers, but the customers could not complete their purchases because they had insufficient cash.

Gary came up with an idea, and started closely inspecting each of the carts. Based on his earlier shopping trip, Gary figured there were items in the carts that were probably no longer on the shelves. Gary tried his strategy on the owner of the third cart he inspected. The cart was almost overflowing with food items and most of it was canned goods.

The cart's owner was a young woman in her late twenties. Gary looked her in the eye. "I'm guessing you've got no cash so you can't check out."

"What's it to you?"

"Tell you what. I'll give you five hundred dollars cash, if you'll give me the cart. Then you can grab another cart, fill it with five hundred bucks worth of stuff, and be able to go through the checkout line."

"I don't own these groceries yet, so how can I sell them to you?"

"You're not actually selling me the groceries. I'll still have to go through the checkout line and pay for them."

"That's stupid, why would you pay for the groceries twice?"

"Because it will save me the time of having to fill the cart. Think of it this way. I'm not buying the groceries from you, I'm just paying you for the time it took you to put the groceries in the cart, and bring them to the front of the store."

"I don't know, it sounds weird. Maybe illegal."

"It's not illegal. Do you want the five hundred or not?"

"I don't know, I –"

"What's going on?" The woman was interrupted by a man of about the same age who unloaded a few additional items from his arms into the cart.

"Hey Stan, what took you so long? This guy wants to give me five hundred bucks for the stuff in the cart. Then we can fill another cart and pay for the stuff in that cart with the cash."

The young man's response was immediate. "Get lost mister. My girl and I are leaving this store with this cart of stuff. We'll steal it if we gotta." As he spoke, he lifted up his shirt so Gary could see a large sheath knife.

Gary moved on. He made the same offer to two other shoppers without success. They, like the young woman he'd first spoken to, couldn't understand why Gary would pay for the groceries twice. Even as they stocked up on food items, they were still operating as though a crisis hadn't and wouldn't occur. Their 'normalcy bias' was too high. They hadn't yet absorbed the significance of a cash-only crisis, let alone the doomsday crisis that was about to follow. The little voice in Gary's head said, "*They're not going to make it.*"

Gary was about to give up and do his own shopping, when he saw an older man, in his late fifties or early sixties. The man's cart contained canned goods, and a few items of camping equipment. If Gary had done the shopping himself, the contents would be almost identical. Without introduction or explanation, Gary offered the man five hundred dollars for his cart full of stuff. The man thought for a few seconds, and Gary could tell the man's comprehension of the situation far exceeded that of the three previous cart holders. The little voice in Gary's head remained silent as he studied the man.

"It will cost you two grand," the man said firmly.

The price shocked Gary. "I can't pay you that much, because I still need to go to the checkout line and pay the store for the stuff. I can go as high as seven hundred. This is probably the only cash offer you're going to get. If you don't take it, you'll leave empty handed."

"Fifteen hundred. I won't leave empty handed. I'm waiting for the crowd of cashless shoppers to rush the exits with their full carts. I'll leave along with all of them."

Gary looked at the exit and saw the two police offers he'd noticed earlier on his way in. "That could take a while, because the two cops might use up their ammunition first. If you wait for the ammo to run out, the crowd will be in full panic mode, and you might get crushed as you try to exit. Once outside, the crowd will probably turn on you and take all your stuff. To make it safely all the way to your car, you need to leave before the crowd turns into a lawless mob. Take my offer old timer; it's the only one you're going to get."

If Gary had been in the same position as the older man, he too would have stolen the groceries. But he would have left through the store's back door. The rear door probably wasn't guarded, and when the stampede and shooting started at the front of the store, it would create a nice diversion for anyone leaving out the back. The rear exit would also be safer because few shoppers would have thought of it. In a crisis, normalcy bias was sometimes fatal. Gary didn't tell the man about the rear exit strategy. Instead, he waited a long few seconds for his scary words about cops shooting customers to sink in.

Gary said, "One thousand dollars. That's my final offer. Anything more than that, and I won't have enough cash to pay for the stuff at the checkout counter."

"Most of the stuff I have in this cart isn't even on the shelves anymore. If you grab an empty cart now, the pickings will be slim."

"You're probably right about that, but that's my final offer." Gary turned as if he was going to walk away."

"Wait a second. You've got a deal, with one condition."

"What's that?"

"You get most of what's in the cart, but I get some of it." The man was already starting to remove several items from the cart; flashlights, batteries, pocket knives, a machete, and a propane lantern.

Gary told the man to wait while Gary grabbed an empty cart. It took a couple of minutes because Gary had to jog all the way to the parking lot to get a cart. When he returned, the man unloaded about a third of the items from the full cart to the empty one. In addition to all the camping items, the man took some of the choicest canned goods. Among the transferred camping supplies were six, sixteen-ounce propane cylinders, and four packages of lantern mantles. The sixteen-ounce cylinders could be screwed into a propane lantern or cook stove.

It occurred to Gary that he had a propane lantern with a cylinder attached to it. But he had no idea how much fuel was in the cylinder, and he had no spare propane cylinders. With one small brass fitting from a camping or tractor supply store, Gary could have refilled his empty sixteen-ounce cylinder from his barbeque tank. Neither man knew that, or owned such a fitting.

Gary said, "You can keep all the stuff you just took, but I'm reducing the price to eight hundred dollars, and I'll need two of those propane cylinders and one package of the mantles."

The man looked hard at Gary. "Those were the last six cylinders they had on the shelves, and I took the last of the mantles as well."

Gary replied, "I appreciate what you're saying, but you get to keep most of the propane and the mantles. And if we don't conclude this deal quickly, we might both leave here with nothing. Take it or leave it."

The man looked around. The cops at the front exit were having loud conversations with two customers who wanted to leave without paying for the unbagged items in their carts. The man was still not convinced he should give up the propane.

Gary said, "I've got two young kids and a wife. Every ounce of that propane will be put to good use, and it will be used sparingly. You'd be doing my family a personal favor."

The older man had a wife, but they'd never been able to have children. He said, "You'd better not be lying to me about the kids, or God will punish you." Then he transferred two propane cylinders and the mantles to Gary's cart.

Gary thanked the man and handed him the cash. Gary took the cart and went looking for aluminum foil and tape. The old man went in the opposite direction to replace some of the canned food he had just sold, if there was any left.

At a jog, and narrowly missing other shoppers as he went, Gary acquired the aluminum foil and tape. There was still some foil and tape left on the shelves after Gary took what he needed. Most people, it seemed, still did not know about Faraday cages, or how to build one in a hurry. Gary went to the beverage section, but there was not a single can of beer left on any shelf.

As Gary went back toward the cash registers, other shoppers looked jealously at the contents of his cart. Some even attempted to grab an item from the cart as Gary jogged by. On two occasions, a shopper attempted to stop the forward motion of the cart. Both times, forward motion was restored when Gary revealed he was carrying a gun by unzipping his jacket. After the second incident, he left his jacket unzipped. He had not pulled the weapon from his belt on either occasion. Given the risk that he would shoot himself, his balls were grateful. It was the first time Gary had carried or flashed a pistol. It felt good. He thought, *When you're armed, the world around you is a lot less dangerous – for you.*

8:42 PM

As he waited in the checkout line, Gary looked over the contents of the cart. Even with the propane cylinders, lantern mantles, tape and foil, the contents were still mostly canned goods. Gary was pretty sure none of the cans in his cart contained pumpkin pie filling. With the cash-only rule, and the limited number of customers that had cash, the checkout went quickly. Gary nodded to the officers at the front door as he left. The entire shopping trip had taken less than forty minutes. Gary beat Hank's deadline by five minutes, but the price had been steep. The groceries cost more than three hundred dollars, in addition to the eight hundred dollars he paid to the old man. Gary now had less than one hundred dollars in cash.

Hank and the SUV were nowhere in sight. Gary called Hank's number, but got an "all circuits are busy" message, so he began pushing the cart toward Home Depot. There was a small crowd outside the Wal-Mart entrance, and several cars were parked illegally nearby with drivers still in them. The crowd consisted of the drivers for the other cars parked further away. They were waiting anxiously for friends or relatives to exit the store. They planned to quickly load the groceries and make a fast getaway. Members of the small crowd glanced at Gary just long enough to determine he wasn't the guy they were waiting for. Nobody bothered him.

Several yards after leaving the crowd, Gary transitioned to a slow jog. He was aggravated by a flat spot on the front left wheel of the cart which caused the darn wheel to bump, rattle, and occasionally spin in a full circle. Distracted by the wheel, Gary almost didn't notice that he had left the bright lights of one shopping center, but hadn't reached the bright lights of the next. Off to his left, in a spot where there was even less light, a group of young men watched Gary's approach. There were at least eight of them, and almost all of them wore hoodies that put their faces in shadow.

Gary's instincts told him that the group was up to no good, but they hadn't quite decided what particular 'no good' they were going to do. Perhaps they were waiting for the looting to start, and they planned to steal some big-screen TVs. Gary almost chuckled as he recalled the familiar media image, from other crises, of thugs running from looted stores with oversized TVs. This time around, they'd have no place to plug them in. Gary's attention came back to the present when one gang-member, with his hood down, took a few steps toward Gary, and aggressively made eye contact.

Gary knew that the contents of his cart were an attractive interim target for the gang, while they waited for the looting to start. Gary slowed his pace almost to a full stop so he could remove the pistol from his waistband without accidentally pulling the trigger. He placed the gun on top of the grocery bags in the child-seat portion of the cart. Gary wanted to keep the gun in his hand, but he couldn't jog and push the cart with just one hand. Gary resumed his jogging pace, and hoped his awkward maneuvering didn't reveal him to be the novice that he was. Gary was confident that at least some of the gang members also had guns, so Gary was literally, out-gunned. However, Gary also guessed correctly that the gun-toting gang members wanted targets who didn't shoot back. They could tell Gary was a novice, but a novice with a gun was still a force to be reckoned with. The night was still young. The gang would wait for a softer target.

One of the other young men, who was still concealed by a hoodie, said, "Forget 'em, dawg." The aggressor who had made eye contact with Gary turned around and rejoined the group. Once again, Gary was amazed at what a gun could accomplish even when it wasn't fired. Gary had heard the statistic that for every time a pistol was fired in self-defense, there were five other instances where the potential victim merely brandished the gun without shooting it. It was the kind of statistic the media didn't emphasize.

Gary reviewed his recent shopping trip and came up with the number three. He had already brandished the pistol three times to avoid a conflict. *What's that mean? I've got only two brandishes left before I'll be forced to shoot somebody? Brandishing a gun works fine as long as the other guy doesn't pull a gun and start shooting. What if somebody calls my bluff and I have to shoot back? I really ought to ask Hank where the damn safety button is. If I can pull this thing out of my pants without shooting myself, I don't want to die in the next moment while I'm pulling on a trigger that won't move.*

As he continued to jog, Gary glanced over his shoulder every few yards to ensure the gang members didn't change their mind. A few minutes later, Gary saw Hank's parked SUV. He pushed the cart close to it to unload the groceries. But the doors were locked, and Gary didn't have the key. *Well that was stupid. I'm sure Hank has a second set of keys. Why didn't we think to bring both sets? Crap, if Hank doesn't make it back to the vehicle for some reason, I'll be pushing this cart all the way back to Hank's house. Or not. The revolver has what, only five or six shots? No way would I make it all the back and still have the groceries.*

Gary realized he wasn't following Plan A or Plan B. Well, actually he *had* followed Plan B, all the way to the end. *What now?* Gary called Hank again, but the phone lines were still tied up. He couldn't leave the cart unattended, and he didn't want to just stand in the parking lot with a cart full of goodies and wait for Hank. Gary turned the shopping cart around and started pushing it toward the Home Depot store.

He didn't go to the entrance door, because he worried that Hank might leave through an exit as Gary entered. As he moved toward the exit, Gary paused for a second and picked up the pistol from the front of the cart. He examined it closely as he looked for the safety switch. He couldn't find it. Gary carefully transferred the gun to its former location in the front of his waistband. *If this thing doesn't have a safety, then maybe I really could shoot myself by accidentally pulling the trigger as I pull the gun out of my pants.* Gary wondered why Hank had let him take the revolver instead of the 9mm automatic. He was pretty sure the automatic had a safety switch. Gary again zipped up his jacket half way to conceal the weapon.

Gary waited at the exit for a moment, then as a customer left, Gary entered. The store was almost empty compared to the Wal-Mart. There wasn't much to eat in a home-improvement store, and at the moment, most people weren't focused on improving their home's resale value. The items that might be helpful in a crisis, like portable generators, and flashlights appeared to be sold out. It made Gary wonder whether Hank would be able to get what he needed.

Gary looked at all the checkout lines; no Hank. Then Gary remembered the contractor checkout line on the far end of the store. He began to move in that direction and glanced down each aisle as he went. Finally, in the outdoor gardening section, Gary saw Hank halfway down the aisle. It looked like Hank was talking to, or perhaps arguing with another customer. When he got closer, Gary saw that Hank and the other customer each had a hand on a metal garbage can that was right next to a lumber cart, which Hank had already piled high with stuff. Hank and the other customer were facing each other across the aisle. Hank could see Gary by looking over his left shoulder; the other customer could see Gary by looking over his right.

When Gary got within earshot, he heard the other customer say to Hank, "Alright, I'll give you fifty dollars cash for this can, but that's my final offer. You need to start getting reasonable if you know what I mean."

As he finished speaking, the man shifted his glance to his right where another man was standing a dozen feet away with a half-full shopping cart. The second man had his back to Gary. When the first man glanced at his partner, he also saw Gary, but he ignored him. He didn't know the odds had just shifted to Hank's favor. The man who was trying to take the can from Hank was in his early thirties. He was over six feet tall, and looked like he spent a lot of time at the gym. He was wearing the work clothes of a contractor; a Carhart shirt and jacket, and Wrangler painter's pants. But the clothes were new and unsoiled, as if the man was only dressing the part.

The man's shopping buddy, standing further down the aisle, was almost a carbon copy of the make-believe handyman. Together, they could have beaten Hank to a pulp, stuffed what was left of him in the can, put the lid on it, and walked out of the store without paying for anything. No store employee would have stopped them. Their oversight was to bring their big well-sculpted bodies to a gunfight. But to be fair, they didn't know Hank had a pistol, and when they started the confrontation, it was two against one.

Gary pushed his Wal-Mart shopping cart to the side of the aisle. With both hands free, he unzipped his jacket and stepped to the middle of the aisle where the two Carhart men could both get a good look at him. When Gary moved to the center of the aisle, Hank glanced in his direction. Gary put his right hand near the pistol as he looked back with an expression that said, *"What now, brother?"*

Hank shrugged as if to say, *"I really don't care how this ends."* But then he glanced at Gary's right hand and gave a little nod. Gary knew his brother could be foolishly stubborn. Even if Hank didn't want the can, he'd never give it to someone who had tried to take it from him by force.

Gary wondered why Hank hadn't already drawn his own pistol. Then he remembered that Hank's gun was tucked into the back of his waistband. Hank's right hand was on the can, and drawing the gun with his left hand would have been awkward. To pull the gun out, Hank would have to let go of the can and draw with his right hand. Gary suspected Hank was about to do exactly that when Gary arrived. Gary couldn't believe what was about to happen. *I'm a college professor and I'm about to use an illegally concealed, unregistered gun to force a man to let go of a garbage can that I'll still need to pay for. The end must be near.*

Out loud, Gary said. "Hey guys, how are you doing? Hank, it's good to see you. Are you about ready to check out, because me and my .357 revolver are ready to leave."

After saying the line, Gary felt like an actor in a bad movie. But he also felt his palms sweat as his adrenaline started pumping. The gun and the bullets were real, and he had no idea what would happen next. As he spoke, Gary pulled his unzipped jacket to one side with his left hand, and placed his right hand on the grip of the pistol. He was very careful not to touch the trigger. If the Carhart duo had guns, Gary was counting on Hank to take them both out.

The big man with his hand on the can, looked at the gun and let go of the can immediately. His demeanor changed completely. "Hey guys we don't want any trouble, we just wanted the can for a, a um—"

"A Faraday cage?" Gary was relieved by the man's sudden disinterest in the can, and he finished the sentence in a polite tone that matched the tone the burly man had suddenly adopted.

Based on the man's reaction, Gary was convinced that neither of the two men had a gun. New York State's extremely restrictive gun laws had made almost all of its residents defenseless. With his illegal gun, Gary was now thoroughly enjoying the benefits. Both men looked a little surprised to learn another customer knew what they did about Faraday cages. They had thought themselves clever and unique.

There was no room on Hank's cart for the can, so he held the can in one hand as he pushed the cart a few feet closer to Gary with the other. Then to the recent loser of the can fight, Hank said, "Tell you what, friend, I'll give you some advice. This can isn't going home with you, but you've already got a Faraday cage in your house, and it will probably hold more than this can."

The man took a step back as he looked cautiously at Hank. He couldn't tell if Hank was sincere, or setting him up for a joke. Hank read the man's look and said, "I'm not kidding. It's called a refrigerator. Think about it. A refrigerator is a metal box with a plastic liner. I don't know whether the metal shelves inside the refrigerator make any contact with the exterior metal box. You should probably remove all the shelves, and put the electrical items in a plastic bag before you stick them in the fridge. When you're done loading the gear, you should use a strip of tin foil to cover the gap between the door and the body of the fridge. If you push the fridge over so it lays on its back, that might be easier to do."

When Hank stopped talking, Gary's face showed as much surprise as the faces of the two former trashcan thieves. Not just because the idea was a good one, but because Hank was offering helpful advice to someone he had been about to shoot less than a minute earlier.

The flummoxed man who had just let go of the can said, "That's actually not a bad idea, thanks. I'm sorry about the earlier misunderstanding."

The man then backed up a couple of steps before turning around and walking quickly away down the aisle. His Carhart copycat followed. As they left, Gary heard one of them say, "Lou, I don't think we have enough aluminum foil. Let's go buy a few rolls. We should get some duct tape as well."

Hank pushed his cart closer to Gary and let out a sigh when he got close. "Nice timing. You play the clichéd cavalry role well."

"You're welcome brother, but I know you didn't need my help. When I arrived, you were about to let go of the can and pull your gun, weren't you?"

Gary looked at Hank's overflowing lumber cart; then he took the garbage can from Hank and put it on top of the groceries in the Wal-Mart cart.

Hank said, "Nah. I had already decided to let go of the can and take the fifty dollars."

"Really?"

"Yeah, I know I could have kept the can, but if I had to shoot two guys to get it, then I might not have been able to leave the store with all the other stuff. Sometimes you've got to let go of something you want, to keep something else you want even more. I didn't want to take the chance that there's a Monroe cop who would still go to the scene of a double homicide."

Gary said, "Well I just saw two cops at Wal-Mart trying to stop a riot, so at least some of them are still on the job and trying to make a difference."

Hank shrugged. Gary continued, "So it was only the potential problem with the escape plan that kept you from killing two guys for a garbage can?"

Hank shrugged again and said nothing. While deployed, he'd seen men get killed for less, but he didn't want to start a conversation on that topic.

Gary asked, "Are you done with the shopping? I'm kind of anxious to leave."

Hank said, "To turn this metal can into a Faraday cage, we still need a plastic can that will fit inside it."

Gary said, "Good point," and walked a few steps toward the display of plastic garbage cans.

Unlike the empty metal can display, there were three different styles of plastic cans still in stock. Gary tested the most likely candidate by shoving it down inside the metal can. It fit snugly, but four inches would have to be cut off the top, for the lid of the metal can to fit over it. Five minutes of work with a utility knife would do the trick. Gary put the cans and lids in the Wal-Mart cart. The brothers began walking quickly toward the checkout counter. Gary grabbed a utility knife from an aisle display on the way. He also zipped his jacket to conceal his gun.

Gary tried to sound casual as he said, "Well I'm glad we didn't have to shoot anybody, because I've never fired a pistol. I can't even find the safety switch on this darn thing."

Hank stopped suddenly and looked at Gary as if he was about to laugh or maybe cry. "Gary I've never owned or seen a revolver with a safety switch. Now listen up, you're about to become a revolver expert."

Hank glanced around and backed into an aisle that appeared to have no security cameras. Then right there inside the store, Hank gave Gary a three-minute class on the operation and use of the pistol. Hank made Gary unload and reload the pistol. Gary felt much better after the class. Hank wished he had time for a longer class at a shooting range, but if someone started shooting at them on the way to the SUV, Hank didn't want to be the only one shooting back.

As they again hurried toward the register, Gary said, "That refrigerator idea sounded good. Good enough to make me wonder why you were fighting over a trash can when I arrived."

"I didn't come up with the refrigerator idea until after I started thinking about what I would do if those two bozos got the last metal can in the store. Besides, I'll feel stupid if I empty my fridge, and let my food spoil, and then the CME turns out to be no big deal."

"Hank, I've seen your fridge. It doesn't have any food in it that isn't already spoiled. Besides, don't you have a freezer in your basement that you used to use for venison when you were still hunting?"

Hank said, "Um, yeah." Gary could almost see the light bulb going off in Hank's mind.

"What's in it right now?"

"Um, nothing. It's been unplugged for years."

CREDIBLE WARNING

"Well, Hank since we already have a kick-ass Faraday cage in the form of huge empty freezer, do you want me to return the two garbage cans to their display racks?"

"No. We'd look stupid if we left the can after you played cowboy to get it."

Neither man was stupid, but they wouldn't think of everything. Even a former outdoorsman like Hank was going to miss a few things as civilization collapsed. Most survivors would have a trusted friend or relative nearby to reduce the number of potentially fatal oversights.

"Hank, while we're on the subject of appliances, I just thought of something else that would work as a Faraday cage with no modifications whatsoever."

"What's that Gary?"

"A microwave oven. Think about it. The shielding that keeps the microwaves inside the oven, must also keep electromagnetic waves that are outside the oven from getting in."

Hank said, "You're probably right, but microwave ovens aren't very big, so it would be useful only for small items. Do you want me to go tell our Carhart comrades about your epiphany?"

Gary laughed and shook his head no. Hank looked at the shopping cart Gary had taken from Wal-Mart, and said, "That's a lot of stuff. How did you get so much, so fast?"

Gary smiled, "I took a short cut. I'll give you the details later, but it took most of my cash. Now we probably don't have enough money to buy the stuff on your cart. Speaking of cash, something else just occurred to me. How much gas do you have left in your SUV?"

Hank thought about it for a second and said, "Less than half a tank. It's always got less than half a tank, because I can never afford to fill it up. I also don't want to give the repo man too much free gas when he takes my SUV."

Gary said, "I'm going to set thirty dollars aside so we can top off your tank on the way home. The Volvo is already topped off."

Hank said, "Fine," as they continued toward the register. When they got there, only one customer was in front of them. She was already paying for her purchases with cash. As that customer left, a thin man in his seventies came up behind Hank and Gary with only a dozen or so items in his shopping cart. Ordinarily, both Gary and Hank would have let the man go first, but now time was of the essence. Every minute mattered. The old man would have to wait.

As Hank helped the cashier scan his items, Gary examined the contents of the overflowing orange lumber cart. Gary saw almost two dozen two-by-fours, half a dozen sheets of exterior siding, several pieces of sheet metal roofing, a box of roofing screws, two boxes of three-inch exterior screws, two rolls of copper wire, and six copper grounding rods. The smaller items included an eighteen volt DeWalt cordless drill, two

Eveready headlamps, Duracell double-A batteries, two hand-crank flashlights, three D-cell flashlights with batteries included, and a six-pack of cigarette lighters. The headlamps provided either red or white light. They could be worn like a miner's light with a single elastic strap which kept the wearer's hands free.

Before she started ringing up the items, the clerk confirmed that Hank would be paying with cash. The store no longer accepted checks or plastic. When the total cost of the items appeared on the cash register screen, Hank emptied his wallet. It wasn't enough. Hank looked at Gary, and Gary emptied his wallet of everything except the thirty dollars he was saving for the gas. Still not enough.

Hank leaned over to the woman at the register. She was probably in her early thirties. In a whisper so the one customer behind Gary couldn't hear, Hank asked the woman to take what cash they had, and let him leave the store without paying the full price for the merchandise. The woman shook her head and pointed at the camera immediately above the register. There was no way she could do a favor for Hank, and not get caught.

Hank said, "Well, it was worth a try," and smiled at the clerk. After a moment, Hank said to the clerk, "Okay, cancel two sheets of the exterior sheathing, and cancel six of the two-by-fours." Gary grabbed an empty cart, and transferred the discarded items as the clerk deleted them from the register total. The new lower total appeared on the register. Still too high.

The old man behind them was making sighing noises and saying, "Come on!" every now and then. Hank told Gary to pull the garbage cans in the discard pile. They would have to rely on Hank's freezer for their Faraday needs. Gary looked around. The Carhart duo was nowhere in sight. Gary dragged the cans off the cart. He put the lids on the cans and set them next to the register in a manner that made them look like they were being used by the store.

The new total appeared and it was still too high. Hank told the clerk to remove the cordless drill. As she made the deletion, Hank transferred the drill to the discard pile. When the new total appeared Hank, added a box of screws, and a roll of grounding wire to the discards. It was already five minutes past closing time. If the CME didn't happen, the store employees would have plenty of time to restock the items in the morning. The clerk made the deductions. When the new total appeared, Hank confidently pushed the cash to the clerk. She counted it, put the cash in the register, and gave Hank his change; one dollar and eighty-three cents.

"About damn time!" The obnoxious voice came from the seventy-year-old man, who'd been fuming through all three of the brothers' checkout attempts. The old man would be the last customer to make a purchase from that store while the lights still worked. Even the back-up generator would not survive the CME.

Hank said, "I'm sorry sir," without turning to look at the man. At the same time, the clerk looked at the man and gave him the store's sincere apology phrase that she had been trained to say. It was exactly the distraction Hank had been hoping for. As he moved to the side of the cart away from the register, Hank discreetly pulled the cordless drill from the discard pile and put it on the cart of purchased items. Gary noticed, but said nothing. The clerk and the old man were oblivious. The camera operator, if there was one, either didn't notice or didn't care. They walked through the first set of exit doors unmolested. Hank paused by the rack that held tie-down cord and safety flags for transporting lumber.

Gary said, "That was ballsy."

"Not as ballsy as you think. The clerk had already neutralized the RFID security tag on the drill, because it was among the scanned items that we intended to buy. When we didn't have enough cash, I placed the drill on the discard pile in a spot where I could grab it easily. Also, I'm not positive, but, I think, when I made the transfer, my arms were concealed by the metal roofing. The camera may have seen me bend over, but I don't think it could see me take the drill." Hank grabbed about a hundred feet of tie down cord, and started walking again.

As they passed through the second set of doors, Gary said, "Why do you want a cordless drill anyway? Your hobby used to be carpentry. Don't you already have enough power tools?"

"I still have most of my power tools, but not my cordless drill. I used to have one that was just like the one I just acquired. I loaned it to my neighbor, but he never gave it back. When I asked him for it, he said he was keeping it as payment for services rendered."

"Services rendered? What services?" As soon as he said it, Gary wondered whether he really wanted to know the answer.

"My neighbor mowed my front yard a few times. Actually, it's been more than a few times. He's done it once a week for the last several months. I'm also stealing cable TV services from his connection, but I don't think he knows about that."

Gary said, "So you were already stealing from your neighbor, and now the CME has turned you into a shoplifter as well."

"Brother, if that's the worst thing this CME makes me do, then I'll be thrilled." If the CME became a worst-case scenario, Hank was prepared to do several things that were far worse. It would come easily to him; he'd already done most of it while deployed overseas.

Gary said, "Well, there is one thing that you won't be thrilled about; Wal-Mart was completely out of beer."

Hank said, "Completely out? Not one single can or bottle?"

"Not one, Hank."

Hank said, "Well, I've got no argument with the buyers. Beer is a critical survival item. Well, my survival anyway. Hey, maybe we could hit a liquor store on the way home."

"Hank, except for the money I set aside for gas, we're completely out of cash. Do you think the liquor stores are still taking credit cards?"

"No, I suppose not. Damn! Without alcohol, the next few days are going to suck."

Gary changed the subject. "How the heck are we going to get all this stuff into the SUV?"

9:14 PM

"We'll tie the sheet metal and sheathing to the roof rack, and stuff everything else inside." Hank gleefully held up the large amount of white cord that he had obtained at the store's exit. It took several minutes, but the plan worked. When they were done, the two-by-fours stuck out through the open back door. Hank didn't stick a red flag on the end of them. He correctly assumed the cops would be too busy to write him a ticket. When Hank started the SUV, the radio, which had been on when he parked the vehicle, came back to life. The President was speaking, and it was clear that Hank and Gary had already missed a chunk of the speech.

". . . the report I just got from NASA. So I asked NASA if there is any reason. For normal people. To be worried about these uh . . . rumors. They told me no. They said the sun is in a busy solar period. Make no mistake. This is something that we knew. The sun, comes as no surprise. Sunspots and solar flares that is. As most of us know. Spots and flares sometimes uh . . . send increased energy to earth. And it is beautiful. In fact it gives us the Orion, uh I mean the Azores . . . the . . . . the northern lights. In places up north. Like Alaska. Let me be clear. The northern lights are nothing to be afraid of. Tonight they might be bigger than usual. I plan on watching them. You should too, that is, unless you're afraid. Of the dark." The President laughed at his own attempt at humor.

Hank groaned and said, "If the CME hasn't hit yet, what killed his teleprompter? He sounds like he's making up this stuff on the fly. Did they forget to load the script?"

The President continued, "Folks, I'm telling ya, some of our fellow citizens who live as far south as the equator might be in for one heck of a light show."

Hank groaned again at the thought of "fellow citizens" at the equator. The southernmost point of the continental United States was twenty-five degrees of latitude short of the equator. But maybe the President was talking about "fellow citizens" of the world, not the country.

"Let me be clear. Sometimes those northern lights have caused the lights to go out. Human-made lights that is, you know, like blackouts. Like in Canada a few years ago. Make no mistake . . . small temporary blackouts are nothing to be afraid of. I have already put repair crews on notice. . . . They are standing by to assist. As I said earlier, there are no comets and no asteroids coming our way. That's true. But maybe some blackouts. Can't say for sure. They're hard to predict. Earth will survive. We'll be fine. Solar flares have never caused a permanent blackout. Do not give in to fear. Don't let the rumors and speculators scare you. That um, that wouldn't be prudent."

Hank spoke quickly, "He just said everything I told Mae he would say. I'm more convinced than ever that he's lying, and we are completely screwed."

"Just as a precaution, and nothing more than a precaution, I've taken the following steps." The President began speaking in a steady, unbroken tone. It was clear that he was reading from a document, or the teleprompter had suddenly started to function. "I have federalized the National Guards of every state east of the Mississippi River, and there will be extra security in our towns and cities by tomorrow morning . . . ."

As the list continued, Hank said, "That's called martial law."

" . . . I have imposed a nation-wide curfew of ten PM Eastern Time. All banks will be closed until further notice. All flights from all airports in the United States are canceled until further notice. Okay folks, that's about it. Please stay in your homes with your families. We'll get through this together. Good night and God bless . . . the uh, World."

Hank had started driving while the President was speaking, but now he accelerated. "Gary that settles it for me. Based on what he said, I think the CME will be massive. What did your friend Blake say, worst-case scenario? Well, we've got a lot to do, and not much time to do it."

Gary was shocked. For once Hank got Blake's name right. "Yeah, Blake said the solar flare was probably bigger than the one that caused the Carrington event." Gary paused, then said, "I wonder if the blackout will go as far south as Mom and Dad's place in Florida?"

Hank said, "Well, the President must think so. He just said the aurora borealis will go all the way to the equator. Even if the CME effects don't reach Orlando, we'll have no way to communicate, and Orlando could still experience a shortage of items that are usually imported from other areas. The flow of most food, medication, repair parts, and other stuff will likely slow down or cease. Florida might get relief from the sea, or the gulf, but how much relief will there be and where will it come from? Once it arrives, how will it get shipped inland?"

As Hank was talking, Gary tried his parent's phone number several times. When Hank was done talking, Gary told Hank about the unsuccessful calls. Hank said, "Why don't you send them a text message? Maybe it will get through and they can text you back."

Gary said, "Okay," and wondered why he hadn't thought to send a text message earlier. Gary pulled up his mother's cell phone number and typed out a short message that said, "Hank and I are together at his place. We heard about the CME. Hope all is well with you." He pressed the send button and put his phone back in his pocket.

Gary wondered how his parents would fare if the CME blackout reached them. His parents were in their late sixties and in good health.

They lived in a retirement community and, like most Americans, the delivery of their daily sustenance relied on a functional economy. Gary thought about the older retirees he had seen, when he visited his parents last year. To Gary, some of the retirement communities looked like warehouses for the walking dead. Soon they might become warehouses for the fully dead. Some residents depended on oxygen machines, and other medical devices that required a constant electrical supply. Other retirees didn't need such devices, but they relied on the frequent replenishment of their prescription drugs.

The first group would start dying as soon as the electrical supply was cut off. For the others, the ones who needed daily medication, the number of pills they had on hand might determine whether they died of starvation or a soon-to-be unmedicated condition. Gary recalled his earlier effort to try to contact his parents, and his conclusion that he did not have the ability to help them. He and Hank were just too far away. If telephone communications ceased for an extended period, Gary and Hank wouldn't even know when and how their parents died.

Gary said, "Look Hank, you and I are not going to be able to do a darn thing for Mom and Dad. We also have enough problems of our own to worry about. If we get hammered by the CME, and Florida doesn't, then maybe we'll drive down there in a few weeks and move into their condo. Of course, half the country might have the same idea, and Florida might close their border to keep the flood of refugees out. Let's agree not to talk anymore about Florida until after the CME hits and we have some idea of the CME's effect. There's just no point."

Hank gave a grunt and said, "Agreed." Like Gary, Hank didn't spend a lot of time thinking or worrying about his parents. The CME wasn't going to change that. As the brothers continued their drive, there were more cars than usual on the streets, but many drivers appeared to be driving without purpose. It seemed like they didn't know what to do with their final few hours of civilization, so they drove around to see how other people were squandering it.

Hank wasn't squandering, he was speeding. He ran a red light, and heard a screech of tires as he squeaked through. The only thing that prevented him from going faster, was fear of losing the materials that were tied to the roof. The roof load had also forced him to run the unexpected red light. If he had stopped suddenly, the materials might have landed in a pile in front of the SUV.

Gary told Hank to slow down, and reminded him that they still needed to stop for gas. Hank said, "Crap, I forgot," as he slowed down quickly to avoid passing the last gas station before his house. Gary went inside with the cash, as Hank readied the pump. The process was completed in a couple of minutes, and the SUV's tank was nearly full when they left the station.

9:50 PM

Hank was still in a hurry as he pulled into the driveway, but lost his momentum when he saw the clutter on the front porch and lawn. There was a lot of it. The entry doors to the living room and kitchen were both wide open even though the lights in the kitchen were on. Was Mae deliberately trying to lure bugs into the house? Mae had trashed the house, or more accurately, she had de-trashed the house by putting all the debris outside the house. Gary thought Hank might lose his temper so he started talking fast.

"Look Hank, you know she's a crazy bi–, err, woman sometimes. But please, please don't kill her. If the CME is real, I'll never collect on the life insurance and I'll be stuck with two kids."

Hank didn't laugh, but he also didn't leave the SUV immediately in a murderous rage. Gary tried another approach. "Look, tomorrow morning you're going to leave behind the house and all the stuff that got tossed out of it. What difference does it make whether the stuff is on the porch or in the house when you drive away from it?"

Hank's response surprised Gary. "You're right." Hank said it with a smile. He got out of the SUV and went quickly into the house. Gary followed. He was glad he still had the revolver. In the dim light of the truck, Gary couldn't tell if Hank's smile was happy or homicidal.

When Gary caught up to Hank, he was already in the kitchen a few feet from Mae. She was standing near the stove with Josie in her left arm, and a cooking spatula in her right hand. The kitchen, indeed the entire house, smelled of smoke and bleach. The powerful smells hit the men like a wall. Mae and the girls had apparently gotten used to it. Gary was glad the kitchen doors and windows were open. He stayed near the door and noticed several empty alcohol bottles near the sink. Mae had apparently emptied the bottles down the drain. Leaving the empty bottles on the counter seemed like a deliberate effort to draw Hank's ire. Dumping the booze was part of the price Mae had extracted for being forced to "tidy up the place a bit."

Hank glanced around the kitchen briefly, but his eyes and attention quickly focused on the kitchen table where he saw a blackened pan and two charred and shriveled black objects. Hank's mind struggled for a moment before he said, "Are those the steaks?" Hank spoke slowly and reverently as if he was asking about a recently departed dear friend.

Mae said, "Um, yeah. It turns out you're not supposed to close the oven door when you broil steaks. It also turns out, steaks cook quite fast. I got distracted for a few minutes. By the way, Jane here is quite the accomplished little chef, but I didn't know that when we started this cook-everything-in-the-cooler contest. We did a much better job on the chicken and the burger."

Mae pointed to the stove as she finished. There were two large pans on the stove. One was filled with loose, sauce-covered hamburger meat, the other with chunked chicken. Both were cooked and seasoned.

Jane was standing on a chair in front of the stove between the two pans. She had a wooden spatula in her hand and was apparently in charge of the operation.

Gary also noticed that the cover on the fire alarm in the kitchen was open and the battery had been removed. He correctly guessed that the steaks had not gone quietly to their demise. It was subtle, but Gary could tell Mae was happy; even a little proud. She had tackled one of her demons, and with Jane's help, she had cooked something that was edible. Two out of three wasn't bad.

Gary tousled Jane's hair. Like Ana, Gary already knew Jane was a good cook. He said, "Good girl Jane, it's my fault that we didn't talk about how to cook the steaks before I left."

Gary said hello to Josie, who was nearly asleep in Mae's arm. Josie opened her eyes, realized her daddy was there and immediately insisted on being held by him. As soon as the transfer was complete, Josie closed her eyes again.

Gary said, "So what's this, spaghetti sauce?" as he stuck his finger in the pan with the beef.

Mae said, "Not quite," as Gary put his finger into his mouth and got a taste of the sauce.

Gary said, "It tastes like–"

"Ketchup!" said Jane. "We didn't have any spaghetti sauce so we used up the ketchup that was in the cooler. It's more like Sloppy-Joe sauce."

Gary said, "Well it tastes very good, Jane. I'm guessing we don't have any buns or bread to go with the sauce."

Mae and Jane looked around the kitchen and shrugged. To Gary, Mae's look conveyed the message, *You're the one who just went shopping. Why didn't you buy hamburger buns?*

Gary said, "I'm going to have some Sloppy-Joe sauce anyway. Have you guys eaten?"

Jane said, "No Daddy, but we were just about to." She pointed to the counter on the left side of the stove. The counter was clean, and there was a stack of clean plates, bowls, and silverware. Gary was amazed. He was going to compliment Mae on her previously dormant cleaning skills, but decided Mae might not want to hear it. It was something she had done against her will, and she probably wouldn't want to be reminded of the defeat.

"Well why don't we all get something to eat?" Gary opted for the beef for himself and the two girls, and grabbed three bowls from the stack of clean dishes. Before he filled the bowls, he took a long look a Josephine. Then he put one of the bowls back. Josie was asleep, but probably not far enough gone to be put down for the night. Mae took a plate and had the chicken.

As Gary had been talking and tasting, Hank had mourned over the steaks for a while, and then started looking around. As he moved away from the kitchen table, Mae took a few quick steps and positioned herself in front of the empty bottles. Hank walked across the kitchen and into the living room. To Hank, his walk across the vinyl and the carpet felt a little weird. He could see both floor surfaces, and he didn't have to kick stuff out of his way as he walked. He noticed the obvious and frequent bleach spots on the living room carpet before he walked down the hall and checked out the guest room and bathroom.

When he returned to the kitchen, Hank said to Mae, "I love what you've done with my place. If I had known you were such a good maid, I might have retained your services more often." Hank was smiling. His smile didn't look homicidal. Perhaps he hadn't noticed the empty booze bottles, or perhaps he just didn't want Mae to think she had won this round.

Mae was surprised by Hank's reaction, but she didn't show it. Her rule was always to stay on the offense. "It's not your place Hank. It already belongs to the bank. I know you don't care what happens to it, particularly since you believe the world will end tomorrow. And Hank," Mae paused to ensure Hank was making eye contact, "You'll never be able to afford my services."

Hank laughed out loud. The verbal jousting had been fun. Having Mae around might not be quite as bad as he had imagined. Maybe he'd let her live for another day or two. Things were going so well, that Mae almost felt bad about dumping Hank's alcohol down the drain. She had felt a stab of regret when she stepped in front of the empty bottles to block them from Hank's view. If he hadn't figured out what she had done, maybe it was best to postpone the discovery.

Gary was at the stove dishing out food with one arm as he held Josie in the other. He was amazed. The tense moment between Hank and Mae had passed, and neither one of them had killed the other; yet. Gary worried that the banter might soon take a turn for the worse, so he jumped in and changed the subject.

Gary said, "How's the packing going, Mae?"

"Except for the small pile of stuff on the kitchen table, I didn't find much stuff worth taking."

10:04 PM

Gary said, "We've all got stuff to do that needs to be done before midnight. We need to eat quickly and get to work."

Hank looked at his watch and said, "You're right, Gary, I'm going to grab a bite." Hank went to the stove, and got a bowl of beef.

Gary set Jane up at the kitchen table to eat. He then decided Josie was ready to be go to bed for the night. She hadn't been bathed, and her teeth hadn't been brushed, but Gary decided she was ready anyway. Gary asked Mae if there was a prepared place for Josie to sleep. Mae directed Gary to the guest room. Gary went to the guest room, and put Josie in the bed that now had clean sheets on it. He put pillows on each side of her to keep her from rolling out of the bed. It was just a precaution. Josie was a deep sleeper who never tossed or turned. Gary was confident she wouldn't move or wake for at least eight hours.

When he got back to the kitchen, Hank had already gulped down a bowl of Sloppy-Joe sauce without sitting down. He had also eaten a few pieces of chicken by pulling them from the pan with his fingers. He licked his fingers, wiped them on his shirt, and told Jane she had done a magnificent job on both the beef and the chicken.

Jane beamed and said, "Thanks, Uncle Hank! I like to cook."

Mae almost said, "I helped with the cooking," before realizing how silly it would sound.

Hank said to Gary, "Eat quickly we've got a lot to do." Then he walked out the kitchen door to the driveway and toward his SUV. Gary gulped down the ketchup-covered beef much faster than he wanted too, and followed Hank out the door. On his way out, Gary grabbed the roll of aluminum foil that he had used to conduct his Faraday experiment. He hadn't realized he had gotten used to the smoky bleach smell of the house until he drew a clean breath from the cool night air.

Chapter 13: Covered parking.

To get the SUV to the rear of the house, Hank had to drive it across the lawn to the west side of his house. The four foot gap between the house and garage on the east side of the house was too narrow for the SUV. Hank stopped the SUV when he got to the stockade fence. Gary followed on foot. Hank got out and explained they needed to remove one eight-foot section of the fence so the SUV could get to the back yard. Gary stayed where he was. Hank went to the basement, got a hammer and a crowbar. From the back side of the fence, he started prying the fence section loose from its four-by-four inch vertical supports.

When Hank yanked loose the final nail, the fence section fell forward toward the front yard and dented the SUV's hood. It was Gary's fault for not catching the fence as it fell, but Hank didn't care. The SUV already had several other dents. Hank and Gary flipped the fence section out of the way. Hank tossed the hammer and crowbar into the SUV, and drove it to the back of the house. He parked near the patio entrance to the basement. The men removed the building materials from the roof of the SUV, and stacked them on the patio to the left side of the patio doors. Debris from Mae's hasty cleaning of the house littered the area, and Gary kicked some of it out of the way to make room for the stack of building materials.

Gary asked, "Do you want to unload the other items you bought – well, bought and stole – before you attempt to drive through the hot tub and into the basement?"

Hank looked at the patio doors and the hot tub that partially blocked the pathway to the doors. "Crap. I'd forgotten about the hot tub. But you just reminded me of something else."

Hank opened the side door of the SUV and pulled out the stolen DeWalt. "Before we get started on the vehicles, let's gather all the battery-operated electrical devices we've got, and get them recharged. We'll charge them in the spare room down here because it's the most EMP-proof room in the house. Shortly before midnight we'll unplug the devices, and do what we can to shield them."

The 'spare room' was supposed to be a guest bedroom when Hank and his second ex-wife Maggie had finished the basement. It was in the front, south east corner of the house under the living room which meant two of its four walls were poured concrete that were completely buried. Later, Hank learned the room couldn't be used as a bedroom because it didn't have a second exit, like a window. So he and Maggie never put a bed in it, and they called it "the spare room."

To the right of the spare room, there was a big utility room. The room included ample space for Hank's work bench and large collection of power tools and wood-working equipment; all of which was covered with a thick layer of dust. In the last few months, Hank could have used the money his tool collection would have brought at a pawn shop. He had thought about making the transaction a couple of times, but could not bring himself to part with any piece of his collection. He decided he'd rather die than part with his tools. Yet, with his nieces on the scene, he'd soon be forced to abandon most of it without one dime of compensation.

The truth was, the entire basement remodeling project had been a waste of money. Hank was initially in favor of the plan because he was an amateur carpenter. He had done some of the work himself, mostly as an excuse to buy some new tools. When the job was finished, it turned out that Hank and Maggie hardly spent any time there. They didn't have any kids and they didn't really need the extra space. With the house now in foreclosure, Hank wished he still had the cash from the home-equity loan that he'd blown on the basement remodeling. He was now about to "remodel" the basement again, and turn it into a parking garage. The value of the seven thousand dollar, professionally installed, oversized hot tub with cedar decking, was about to drop to zero.

Hank walked to the spare room with the new DeWalt. The unused freezer was in the spare room. A few years ago, Hank had moved the freezer out of the utility room because he needed the floor space for a drill press. Gary went upstairs, and got his laptop and power cord, as well as the charger for his phone. Mae didn't want to give up her computer just yet, because she was still attempting to download survival information from the internet. A couple of minutes later, Gary joined Hank in the spare room. Gary plugged in the phone and his laptop. Hank plugged in his laptop, phone, the new DeWalt, some other battery powered tools, and a rechargeable flashlight. Gary asked Hank if he had garbage bags or some other plastic container that could be used as an insulator inside the freezer that was about to become a Faraday cage. Hank told Gary there were several eighteen-gallon Rubbermaid storage bins in the attic. The bins were full of stuff, but it was stuff that would have no value in a post-CME world.

Gary offered to go to the attic and get the bins, but Hank decided he would do it. In the attic, Hank found several Rubbermaid plastic bins. He dumped Christmas decorations from two eighteen-gallon red bins, and outdated tax records from two ten-gallon blue bins. Hank stacked the four bins together with all four lids on the top of the stack. On the way back to the basement, he made a detour to his master bedroom. He took a bottle of wine from a box of assorted items that had been left behind by his ex-wife when she moved out. Hank had collected the items in one place thinking Maggie might come back for them some day, but she never had. The bottle of Gallo Red Moscato was now Hank's. He didn't drink wine, and if he did he wouldn't drink Red Moscato, but there was now just one other unopened bottle of alcohol in the house, and Hank couldn't bring himself to open that one. Hank slipped the bottle of wine into the plastic bin that was on the top of the stack. He carried the stack to the kitchen and set it on the table. Hank rummaged through two kitchen drawers to find what he was looking for. He slipped the corkscrew into his front pocket, closed the drawers, picked up the stack of bins, and went back downstairs. Mae didn't ask Hank what he had been looking for, and didn't know what he had found and taken. Jane had finished eating, and Mae was rinsing out the dishes. She had turned the television on loud enough so she could hear it in the kitchen. She was hoping to hear a message saying the CME had been canceled. The beef and ketchup pan was empty and Mae cleaned it. The chicken pan still had some chicken in it, so Mae put the entire pan into the refrigerator. As Mae closed the fridge, Jane said she was tired and wanted to go to bed. Mae was delighted. She turned down the television, and took Jane to the guest bedroom without detouring to the bathroom for teeth brushing or a potty break.

When Hank returned with the Rubbermaid bins, Gary put every portable electrical device he could find into one of the bins including the portable radio with which he had earlier proven the Faraday cage concept. He put the full bin into the freezer, and left the three empty bins next to the freezer. When it got closer to midnight, Hank and Gary would use the other bins to put the DeWalt drill and other electrical items into the freezer. While Gary was loading the red bin, Hank opened the bottle of wine. He took two big swallows, and made a sour face and a gagging sound. Gary looked at Hank, but said nothing. Hank didn't feel like he owed Gary an explanation, but he gave him one anyway.

"Gary, I know Mae emptied the whiskey bottles she found that still had something in them. I didn't mention it in front of her because I didn't want to make a scene. It only would have given her another chance to talk down to me. The truth is, there wasn't much left in those bottles, that's why I asked you to buy beer. But the beer purchase didn't happen, so I'm now forced to taper my alcohol consumption down to zero with this crap." Hank held up the bottle of Moscato as he finished speaking.

Gary shrugged as if to say, "Whatever," and asked Hank if it was okay for him to cut off the two flat prongs of the freezer's three-prong plug. With just the ground wire remaining, the freezer-cum-Faraday cage would be grounded, but not connected to a power supply when it was plugged back in. Hank nodded and took another swallow of the red stuff. He grimaced again, but didn't gag. For the rest of evening, Hank would drink large amounts of water, and small amounts of wine. Gary got a pair of tin snips from Hank's tool bench, cut off the prongs, and plugged the remaining round prong into the wall socket. The Faraday cage was now grounded, but no electricity was flowing to the freezer.

When Gary was done with the freezer, he joined Hank in the main room of the basement. Hank had already started clearing the furniture from the large room. Gary joined in. They shoved the couch up against the east wall, and stacked the love seat on top of the couch. For the smaller pieces of furniture like the coffee table, several chairs, and two bookshelves that had held knick-knacks, the men adopted Mae's method, and dumped the items in the back yard.

As they returned from his last trip to the recently created garbage dump, Gary asked, "What now?"

Hank smiled and said, "Now let's make a vehicle entrance for this two-car garage that used to be a party room."

It was Maggie who had labeled the room a party room. She had finished the basement for the specific purpose of entertaining her friends, but her small social circle had met there only once. It turned out her friends preferred bars, and Maggie preferred another man's bedroom. The room was large enough to accommodate the two vehicles, but Hank and Gary would first have to remove the hot tub, which blocked the SUV's access to the patio doors. Hank decided the Volvo would go in first, because it could more easily maneuver away from the entrance to make room for the SUV.

The basement was rectangular in shape with the long side parallel to the road that ran from east to west in front of the house. It was forty-two feet long and thirty-six feet wide. One girder ran down the middle of the basement, parallel to the road, to support the weight of the house. Four vertical steel columns supported the girder, and they had been boxed with three-quarter inch pine boards when the basement had been finished. The basement ceiling was eight feet high. Where the girder and heat ducts hung down, the ceiling was only seven feet high. Even the lower portions of the ceiling were high enough for the SUV to fit. The entry point, however, was not. Hank went to the patio door and measured the height of the entrance just by eye-balling the distance between the top of his head and the metal frame of the door. Then he went outside and measured the height of the SUV in a similar fashion.

"Gary, we'll check this with a tape measure, but I think the SUV is about six inches higher than the patio doors, which means we'll have to remove the doors, and then rip out the upper part of the metal door frame, as well as some of the wooden framing above the metal frame."

"So what do you want me to do, grab a tape measure?"

"No. Most of my tools are in my workshop. I'll grab what we need in a few minutes. Right now let's get this hot tub out of the way."

Gary groaned. "That job is going to take too long. My neighbor had his hot tub taken out to replace it with a bigger one. The removal alone took a couple of hours."

Hank smiled. "Trust me Gary, it's only going to take us a few minutes. But it will be easier to move if it's empty. Why don't you shut off the circuit breaker, and I'll pull the drain plug? The breaker box is in the southwest corner of the basement."

When Gary returned to the back yard, water was draining from the tub. Hank had the SUV's front bumper just a foot from the hot tub. Hank pulled a length of cable from the winch on the front of the SUV. He wrapped the cable around the tub, and closed the loop by latching the hook back onto the cable on the winch side of the tub. Hank engaged the winch and took up the slack. Then he got in the SUV, shifted into four-wheel drive and hit the gas. With a crunching sound, the tub went backward as its sides were compressed and broken by the tightening of the steel cable Hank spun the wheels in the soft sod of the yard, even though it wasn't necessary, and left two deep ruts. The tubs electrical wires and plumbing were ripped away from the house, and water shot out from the house in a full steady stream from the broken inlet pipe. Hank stepped out of the truck laughing, but then he saw the broken pipe and said, "Oh shit!" He ran into the basement, and the water flow ceased when he shut off the valve that supplied the hot tub.

11:05 PM

"Now for the patio doors," said Hank.

Together they removed the two glass doors from the door frame, and then measured the height of the opening. For the SUV to enter, the doorway needed to be six inches higher and four inches wider. To gain those inches, Hank and Gary removed the metal door frame and then dug into the wooden frame behind it with a pry bar, hammers, and a reciprocating saw. When they were done, the back side of the house looked like it had been hit with a wrecking ball, but the opening was big enough for the SUV.

Hank looked at the mess and said, "If the CME doesn't happen, the bank is going to be upset by the damage we just did to their house." He was smiling when he said it. What would the bank do, sue him? He had no job, no assets, and no money, so the bank wouldn't be able to collect anything. In a civil suit, he would be "judgment proof." Perhaps the bank would find a criminal statute to throw at him.

The Volvo was going into the basement before the SUV, but it still had a trailer attached to it. Gary wanted to secure the trailer and its contents inside the garage for the night. Hank and Gary went to the one-car garage which was more cluttered than the house had been, prior to Mae's radical cleaning effort. The brothers spent a few minutes clearing a space for the trailer by tossing the clutter into even higher piles at the rear of the garage. Gary backed the trailer into the garage, and disconnected it from the Volvo. He moved the Volvo back to the driveway. Hank helped Gary remove the rooftop carrier, which they placed on the floor in front of the trailer.

Hank closed the garage door, and Gary drove the Volvo to the back of the house, across the patio and into the basement. He took a right turn, and then had to move the car back and forth a couple of times to avoid hitting one of the vertical support columns as he cleared the entryway for the SUV. While Gary had been maneuvering the Volvo, Hank had folded in the side mirrors on the SUV. As soon as the Volvo was clear of the entryway, Hank drove the SUV straight into the basement. When he stopped, the Volvo was on his right side, almost perpendicular to the SUV, with its rear bumper toward the passenger side of the SUV. Gary checked his watch. It was 11:11 PM. Gary was amazed at how quickly they had turned the basement into a parking garage. Even so, there was very little time left, and a lot left to do.

Gary said, "Hank we're not going to get it all done by midnight."

"Well Gary, we'll just do as much as we can as fast as we can." As a soldier, Hank had learned that even when human lives were at stake, there was only so much he could do in a finite amount of time. All he could do, was all he could do. Worrying about what might not get done would distract him from doing all he could do. If they ran out of time before both vehicles were protected from the EMP, Hank wouldn't beat himself up about it if he had done all he could have done.

While Gary and Hank had been remodeling the basement and parking the vehicles inside, Mae had gotten over her bad attitude. Jane had gone to sleep as easy as pie, which felt like an accomplishment to Mae. She had cooked, cleaned, and played mother all in the same day. She had no intention of doing such things on a long term basis, but it was good to know she could do them in a pinch. Mae decided she would continue to play along until morning; when she hoped to go back to Islip, and take a long hot shower. She made a final trip through the house, and brought a couple of items that might be worth packing to the kitchen. Then she decided to see what the men were doing.

The television was still on in the living room, and just as Mae was about to go downstairs, she heard that the Director of the Department of Homeland Security was about to make an announcement. Mae went half way down the basement stairs and told Gary and Hank they might want to come upstairs to hear what the DHS Director had to say. Time was precious, but potentially useful information was more precious. Now that the clock was about to run out, perhaps the DHS Director would tell Americans the truth. Both men went to the living room.

At 11:14 PM, the Director of DHS began the live briefing from the White House. He said, "As the President stated earlier, NASA has identified a Coronal Mass Ejection or CME that appears to present a credible threat to the nation's electrical grid. The President has ordered me to take reasonable measures to limit the potential damage that the CME might cause. The measures that I am about to announce are prudent and commensurate with the threat we face. If the CME were a severe hurricane, or a tornado nobody would question the prudence of seeking shelter in a sturdy structure."

"The CME presents us with a different type of emergency, and thus requires a different response, a different shelter if you will. The electromagnetic pulse, or EMP that will be delivered by the CME could cripple the grid and household electrical equipment. If your house were in the path of a severe electrical storm you would probably unplug your computer, television, and other sensitive electrical items to protect them from a power surge. As a nation, we are going to take similar measures on a much larger scale. The Department of Homeland Security will protect the nation's power grid by shutting it down before the CME arrives."

"By Executive Order of the President of the United States, a phased shutdown of the entire electrical grid will begin at midnight Eastern Time. The shutdown will begin on the east coast, and proceed as quickly as practicable to the west coast. The extensive connections between the power grids of the United States and Canada will cause portions of Canada's grid to be affected. My Canadian counterpart will say a few words when I'm finished, and then we'll take a few questions."

The Canadian counterpart had almost nothing to say. She seemed to have been brought in at the last minute and was, like the television audience, hearing about the Executive Order's phased blackout for the first time. Her message boiled down to, "everything is under control," and "please stay calm."

The DHS Director returned to the podium and the first question he got was, "When will the CME hit the United States, and how much of the country will be affected by it?" Like a politician, the Director didn't provide a clear and specific answer, but he did suggest that the worst effects of the CME would probably not hit before 3:00 AM Eastern Time.

Gary said, "That's good news. If the CME doesn't hit until three in the morning that gives us an additional three hours to prepare."

Hank said, "Three o'clock in the morning? Gary, I thought you said the CME would hit at midnight."

"Hank, all I said was what Blake told me. He estimated that the CME would hit between midnight and three AM. So midnight was the front edge of the impact window. What we just learned is that government thinks the CME won't hit until the back end of that window. It remains to be seen whether DHS is right about that. If they really thought the CME wouldn't hit until three AM, why are they going to shut down the grid three hours early?"

Hank responded, "I have no idea, but if we had known the CME wasn't going to hit until three AM, we probably could have made it to Grandpa's even if we left at eight PM. Hell, even with bad traffic we probably could have left at nine PM and still made it." Hank looked at Mae as he spoke. He knew she was the primary reason they hadn't already left for Grandpa's farm.

Gary said, "Maybe. But we stayed because we didn't know when the CME was going to hit. We still don't. We also still don't know if the CME will cause a widespread blackout. Sure, the government is going to take protective measures. That suggests that the CME is huge and presents a serious threat, but if the protective measures work, then the lights will get turned back on tomorrow morning and we'll be glad we didn't make a senseless journey on a crowded highway."

Mae just shrugged when Hank looked at her. It was now too late to go to Grandpa's. The argument was over. She had won.

Hank said, "Well Gary you seem to have a lot of confidence in the future success of the government's protective measures, but I have a different opinion. I agree that the DHS Director's announcement indicates the CME will be massive. What if it's *really* massive? So massive that the government's protective measures don't work? I think we're going to regret spending the night here, rather than bolting for Grandpa's when we had the chance."

Gary said, "Hank that argument is over, and it's too late for us to leave now. Look at the bright side, the three AM arrival of the CME gives us enough time to finish our preparations. Hopefully, our vehicles will still work even if the CME is massive, and we'll still have the ability to drive to Grandpa's. In the long run, protecting the vehicles is probably far more important than an earlier arrival at Grandpa's." Gary's point was debatable, but they had no time for debates.

Hank thought, *Good grief! Did Gary and Mae always talk this much? Why do I keep getting drawn into it?* It occurred to Hank that lawyers and college professors got paid to talk. They made a living out of verbosity. Hank would have traded all their words for the sound of duck or turkey calls, or even finger nails on a chalkboard.

Hank responded as he walked toward the basement stairs, "Like you said, we've got three extra hours to prepare. I don't want to waste them. However, according to the DHS Director, we're going to spend most of that time in the dark, because he's going to shut off the electricity before the CME hits."

Gary asked, "Should we shut off the electricity to the house before the government shuts down the power grid?"

Hank stopped at the top of the stairs and said, "No, leave the lights on so we get every minute of electrical power we can. Once the grid shuts down, we'll have to start using up our battery power. Let's put that off as long as possible.

Gary said, "Hank, I think you're wrong. Even with the grid down, if the power to your house is still on when the CME hits, the pulse could fry the wiring in your house and your appliances."

Hank laughed. "Gary, have you forgotten? On the first day of next month, this house will no longer be mine. If the CME doesn't cause widespread devastation, and civilization continues as normal, the Sheriff will still kick me out of the house. If the CME does cause widespread devastation, then all of us are going to Grandpa's. Either way, I'm leaving, and I don't give a damn about the condition of the electrical system or anything else I leave behind. I'm going to leave the lights on so we can see what we're doing without using up our flashlight batteries."

As Hank was talking Gary's phone buzzed, and he took it out of his pocket. He had just received a text message from his mother. It said, "We're fine boys. There's a NASA retiree here who says the CME is real, but its effects probably won't hit us this far south. Maybe you should come visit. Love you both. Good luck."

Gary quickly typed out a response. "Love you too. Good luck." Gary explained the text message exchange to Hank.

Hank said, "Florida is a long, long way from here. Even if Florida is completely unaffected by the CME, the devastation between us and them might make it impossible for us to get there. But I suppose it's an option we could review in the morning if we, you know, survive the night."

Gary shook his head as he shifted his thoughts back to the here and now. He looked at his watch and said, "Look, I hope Florida and everybody who lives there survives, but for the next few hours we've got more pressing issues to think about. If the government is going to shut the grid down at midnight, then we've got just twenty-seven minutes until the lights go out."

Hank said, "Okay, so let's round up the flashlights so we can keep working after the government delivers us into darkness three hours ahead of schedule. I bought two new LED headlamps at Home Depot, and I have one here in the house that I've had for years, but I don't know where it is."

"Hank, didn't you say you had a propane lantern? I bought a couple of fuel cylinders and a package of mantels."

"I think the lantern is in the basement, I'll go look for it."

Gary said, "The headlamps are still in your SUV along with some of the other stuff you bought at Home Depot. Let's go downstairs, get the headlamps and see if we can get that lantern working. If it works, we can use the lantern down there. I'll give one of the headlamps to Mae."

Hank said, "Okay," and started walking down the stairs. Gary followed and was just a step behind him. Hank stopped abruptly, and Gary almost bumped into him.

"Hey Gary, where is that portable radio that you used to conduct your Faraday cage experiment?"

Gary said, "I think I chucked it into the Faraday freezer with a bunch of other small electrical items."

Hank finished his journey down the stairs and went to the Faraday freezer in the spare room. Gary followed him. Hank opened the freezer and retrieved the radio from the plastic bin inside the freezer.

Hank said, "I'm not going to go upstairs every time the government makes an announcement. With this," Hank held up the radio, "we can listen down here to what the short wave radio community is saying about the CME. Some of the news will be from overseas. What do you want to bet, we'll hear stuff that the US government isn't going to publish?"

11:32 PM

It must have been a rhetorical question, because Hank turned away without waiting for an answer. Hank put the plastic bin back into the freezer and closed the freezer. Then he said, "Follow me." The two men left the spare room and went to the party room, which was now a garage. Within a couple of minutes, Hank found the propane lantern and his old LED headlamp. The lantern was out of fuel, and both mantels were broken. While Hank worked to install the new mantels and a sixteen-ounce fuel cylinder on the lantern, Gary worked on the headlamp. Hank hadn't used the headlamp in a long time. Like the portable radio, batteries had been left inside the device, and corroded the copper contacts. Gary removed the batteries and cleaned the corrosion from the contacts. Then he bent the contacts outward so they would make a better connection to the new batteries. When Gary installed the new batteries, the headlamp worked fine. Gary got the two new headlamps from the SUV and installed batteries in both lights.

When Hank finished the maintenance on the lantern, he tested it by lighting it. Gary suggested keeping the lantern lit at a low setting just in case the government jumped the gun and shut down the grid a few minutes early. Hank refused, and turned off the lantern. Propane was too valuable. Gary delivered the headlamp he had just repaired to Mae, and came back downstairs. Hank and Gary each had one of the new headlamps. Hank placed the lantern, a box of matches, and the radio on the roof of the Volvo without any indication that he cared about damaging the car's paint job. The car's aesthetics had already been destroyed by Gary when he crushed the front end against the concrete barrier on the bridge. At 11:48, the brothers were ready to get back to work.

Mae stayed upstairs as she attempted to eke out additional downloads from the slow and intermittent internet connection. The girls were still asleep. Mae was tired, but knew she wouldn't be able to sleep if she lay down. Waiting to see if the world was going to end made her too anxious to sleep. On the television screen, the DHS Director was still taking questions. News commentators could be seen in an inset box at the top right corner of the screen. They would cut in occasionally to tell the audience what the Director just said. His words were the first government confirmation that the basis for the crisis was a CME.

The story was now official. Regular programming was shoved aside as broadcasters focused on the CME and the blackout. It might be their last broadcast for a long time. When the press conference ended, the main stream media, or MSM, showed graphics of solar flares. News anchors talked repetitiously about the unpredictable sizes and effects of the flares. There were only so many things one could say about a solar flare. The Carrington Event was briefly mentioned, but it was passed off as irrelevant because it had occurred before the electrical grid, and the solar-monitoring satellite system even existed. The government-induced blackout was discussed, but listeners were left with the impression that the blackout would be brief. The grid would be protected, and the lights would come back on shortly after the CME's effects dissipated.

Commentators emphasized that the post-CME blackout of 1989 in Quebec, Canada had lasted only nine hours. They also pointed out that the Canadian grid had not been protected by a pre-emptive shut down prior to that CME's impact. The prevailing message through all of the MSM's chatter was the United States would definitely not experience a long term post-CME blackout, and it probably wouldn't experience a short term one either. There was some discussion of how people should prepare for the brief blackout that would be caused by the executive order, but the coverage was sparse and dismissive.

One female commentator, who had been in sports magazine's swimsuit edition two years ago, said, "Listen, there's going to be a blackout, but it's going to happen at night. So you should just go to sleep like you usually do, and tomorrow you can wake up and turn the lights on like you usually do. But hey, put a flashlight on your night stand so you won't stub your toe when you get up in the middle of the night to pee."

The beautiful commentator gave a naughty smile and her co-hosts tittered, and made jokes about pissing in the dark. One of her co-hosts said, "If you don't have a flashlight, just leave a bucket near your bed."

The commentators tittered some more, and exchanged winks and nods as they made indirect suggestions about things people could do in bed when the lights went out and there was no television, internet, or phone service. Eventually, the subject shifted back to a more direct discussion of CMEs. Viewers saw historical NASA videos of sun spots and solar flares, which were compared to computer-enhanced images of the flare that launched the inbound super CME. The footage was replayed again and again as experts discussed solar cycles, electromagnetic pulses, and the excellent survivability of the electrical grid. Viewers heard nothing about what it would take to survive if large portions of the grid were out of commission for months.

The MSM never mentioned Faraday cages, or other useful things that might increase a citizen's ability to survive. According to the MSM, the largest, fastest, and most catastrophic CME in human history was going to be just a brief and temporary inconvenience. The entire event was covered as though it were a hurricane or storm. The MSM didn't give the CME a name, as it now did for every weather event that got more than a few hours of coverage. It was, "The CME," and it was assumed there would be only one; just as people had once assumed there would be only one World War.

Instead of positioning themselves next to high seas and crashing waves, news announcers, stood with their microphones near urban areas and looked grim as they said things like, "Soon, all these lights you see here are going to go out." The statements and mages were for the benefit of the MSM viewers who didn't know the meaning of the word "blackout." "Live footage" was shown of the sun, as if to say, "Here's the culprit!" But the sun looked the same as it always had, and gave no sign it was aware of Earth's existence, or mankind's predicament. Less than five percent of US citizens had the common sense and wherewithal to use the last few hours of civilization to prepare for the genocidal chaos that would follow. Hank and Gary were in a tiny minority as they worked frantically in the basement to protect their two vehicles.

Hank and Gary decided to disconnect the battery cables from each vehicle's battery, and disconnect every major electrical connection they could reach. If an electrical jolt somehow hit one part of the system, it would hopefully not damage another part of the system. The SUV's damaged hood was easier to open than the Volvo's. On the George Washington Bridge, Gary had repeatedly rammed the front end of his car into a concrete barrier. He had to use a crowbar to pry the hood open. He pounded the latch back in to shape so it would be easier to reopen.

When he was finally able to reach the engine compartment, Gary said, "We should also pull the fuses. Then we should connect the negative battery lead to one of the grounding rods you bought. Then we'll install the plastic and the aluminum foil that make up the Faraday cage." Gary was wrong about the grounding rod, but neither brother figured it out at the time.

Gary worked on the Volvo while Hank worked on the SUV.

Gary took special care to find the Volvo's main computer and disconnected the wires going in and out. He told Hank to do the same. If they had had more time, Gary would have pulled the computers out of the vehicles and shielded them in the same way he had shielded the laptop computers; in a separate, smaller Faraday cage.

Gary was still disconnecting wires under the hood, when Hank said, "Hey Gary, it's 11:58. We've got just two more minutes until midnight when the government will shut down the grid."

Hank went to the Volvo where he could reach the radio that was on the car's roof. He turned on the radio and tuned in a shortwave news station. All the coverage related to the CME and the preemptive blackout that was now less than a minute away.

Midnight came and nothing happened

Chapter 14: Day One.

The brothers listened to the radio for another three full minutes expecting the lights to go out at any second. Nothing happened. Gary and Hank went back to work. Ten minutes later, the lights were still on. Hank and Gary were grateful for what they thought would be just a few more minutes of electrical power.

Hank said, "What the heck is going on? Do you suppose they canceled the pre-emptive blackout?"

Gary joked, "Maybe Congress took a vote and canceled the CME."

Hank responded. "I have no doubt Congress considered such a vote." In a mocking tone that imitated a politician, Hank continued, "My fellow Americans, with the nation's slow economy, we simply cannot afford the luxury of a CME at this time."

Gary gave a short laugh, and then said he was going upstairs to see if Mae had gotten any new information from the television. Hank said he was going to stay downstairs with the radio and keep working. Gary put his headlamp in his pocket because he figured he would need it for the return trip. When he got to the living room, a news anchor said he expected the blackout to start any second. Nobody had any explanation for the delay. At twenty minutes after midnight, Gary gave up on the television. *Screw it. So the blackout didn't start on time. It was a government operation; of course it hadn't started on time! The delay was a gift, and the explanation didn't matter. We can keep working with house lights instead of batteries.*

Gary checked on the girls. They were both fast asleep. When he told Mae he was going back downstairs, Mae said, "There's nothing left for me to do up here. I know you guys are busting your tails down there, so what can I do to help?"

Gary was pleasantly surprised by Mae's willingness to help, but tried not to show it. He thought for a moment, and came up with an idea. "Mae, if you want you could set us up with a potable water supply. You could put water into all the jugs, pots, and other containers you can find including the tub. If we get stuck here after the CME, a tub full of water will come in handy. If the vehicles still function in the morning and we decide to go further west, we'll want to bring every transportable water container that the vehicles will carry."

Mae said, "That sounds easy." Gary went downstairs. Mae went to the hallway bathroom to fill that tub with water. When she was done, she filled the tub in the other bathroom. In the kitchen, she filled all the pots she could find, both clean and dirty. She figured that even dirty water would come in handy for flushing toilets. Then she searched for water bottles and anything else with a lid that could be used to transport water, and found very few serviceable containers.

12:22 AM, Day One

As she was looking around, her eyes fell on the empty whiskey bottles that were still sitting by the sink. Mae had discovered an upside to Hank's drinking problem. Mae thought about the several other empty bottles that she had shoveled out of the house onto the front porch and back deck. Some of the whiskey bottles were glass, others were plastic, but they all had screw-on caps, and they were all designed to transport liquid. Mae retrieved as many bottles as she could find. Then she began the task of rinsing out each bottle, filling it with water, and screwing its cap on tightly. When she finished, she had more than two dozen transportable bottles filled with clean drinking water.

When he got to the basement, Gary noticed that Hank had changed the radio station and moved the radio to a location where he could hear it clearly, while he worked on the SUV. There was a roundtable discussion on the station with three experienced operators discussing CME-related topics as other operators briefly joined and then left the roundtable. Gary got the impression that there were many people like Hank who were content to listen. It reminded Gary of an AM Radio talk show. Helpful information from various locations was being exchanged. Hank had been listening intently as he had continued to work while Gary was gone.

"Fascinating stuff," was all he said when Gary returned.

Hank and Gary disconnected the last few wires under the hoods of the two vehicles. Then they installed the grounding rods Hank had purchased. On the driver's side of the Volvo, they pulled back a section of carpet and pad, and used the sledgehammer to break a hole in concrete. Then they pounded in one of the eight-foot copper rods at a slant. It could not be installed vertically, because there was insufficient space to swing the sledge hammer.

Gary got the spool of recently-purchased copper wire, and used a portion of it to connect the grounding rod to the Volvo's negative battery cable, which was no longer connected to the battery. While Gary was doing that, Hank used the sledgehammer to break a whole in the concrete on the driver's side of the SUV. By the time Hank pounded in the second eight-foot grounding rod, Gary was ready to attach a cable to the rod, and hook it to the SUV's negative battery cable.

At 12:55 AM, the radio announced that the President would be making a short public announcement. Hank didn't want to go upstairs and watch it on TV, but Gary talked him into it. "Come on, you could use a break. When was the last time you had a drink of water?"

Hank was thirsty for something else, but he had only the red Moscato, which was almost half gone. Hank had a headache, and suspected he'd have an even worse headache when the sun came up no matter how much water he drank. Hank agreed to get some water and take a short break. He left the wine bottle in the basement and followed Gary up the stairs.

Gary went to the kitchen, filled two glasses with water, and joined Hank and Mae in the living room. The President was on the screen with his wife standing next to him. She did her best to look somber, but her dress seemed inappropriate for the occasion. The dress, by an Italian designer, had cost thousands of dollars. If the First Lady had set out to draw attention away from her husband, she could not have done a better job without exposing her breasts. Maybe she suspected it was her last nation-wide television appearance, and she wanted to leave a lasting impression.

The President was not in the White House. The podium at the undisclosed location from which he was broadcasting had a presidential seal behind it, but it was obviously a scaled down version of the press room on Pennsylvania Avenue. Most viewers assumed the President was in an underground bunker, but the small set could have been on a plane or a submarine. The announcement would be brief, and the President would take no questions when he was done. How could he? There were no reporters present.

The President read carefully from a piece of paper that he held in his hand. "You probably noticed that the lights are still on. That's because I overruled the decision of the DHS director." The President made it sound as if the Director had not been acting under an executive order from the President. He did not explain the apparent contradiction.

"If the nation's power grid were preemptively shut down, countless lives would be lost as millions of non-functional traffic signals would cause thousands of automobile accidents throughout the country. Oxygen machines and other medical devices would also fail. That vital, life-saving equipment is crucial for those who are most in need of our compassion. I will not be responsible for the loss of so many innocent lives. The speculative nature of the possible danger posed by the CME is not sufficient to order the deaths of so many Americans."

"The only thing we have to fear is fear itself. Like the Americans of the Greatest Generation, and the generations who preceded it, we will face this challenge head on. We will not shrink from what lies ahead, or shirk our responsibilities. We will not choose to stumble in the dark. The lights will remain on because this is America, and that's what we do. We keep the lights on. Even when it's, you know, dark outside. Thank you, good luck, and good night."

The President skipped the "God Bless somebody" part. His terse message was punctuated by his abrupt departure. He walked away so suddenly, that his wife was standing alone by the podium for one long awkward moment, before she lurched to catch up with him. The two of them had not arrived or departed side-by-side, or hand-in-hand. When they were gone, the empty podium filled the screen for almost half a minute. Either the programmers hadn't known how short the script was, or the script had been longer than what the President had delivered. The chattering commentators cut back in, and told the viewing audience what they had just heard. Soon they advanced to meaningful questions like, "How do you suppose the President is feeling at a time like this?"

Bill, a regular TV guest said, "Well no President has ever faced such a challenge. This is one for the history books. If I had to go out on a limb, I'd say the President's courageous handling of this incredible crisis will be the defining moment of his Presidency. It will be his legacy, and it will become part of the historical record for all posterity."

"I couldn't agree with you more, Bill. The country is lucky to have someone with such gravitas at a time like this. You know, the First Lady stood with him during this difficult time. Don't you think the two of them standing side-by-side, portrayed a united front for the entire world to see, as a symbol for our country to unite during this crisis. And I must say the First Lady struck just the right pose with that stunning dress and serious expression."

"Jaime, there is no doubt that the entire country can draw strength from these two magnificent people. We're fortunate to–"

Hank was almost gagging as he turned down the volume. "So half the world is going to explode, and the media is focused on the President's gravitas, his legacy, and his wife's dress? You know what the ham radio operators are talking about? They're spilling all the inside information they can find. They're talking about the size and speed of the CME, the anticipated damage it will cause, and the geographical area that will be most affected. They're also offering tips on what people can do right now to improve their chances for survival."

Hank looked at Gary and Mae. He got no argument from either of them, mostly because Mae was exhausted. Hank continued, "Why does the media provide no helpful information? How about some information on protecting electrical equipment or stockpiling water, so viewers will have something to drink when the municipal pumps fail? If this country were on the Titanic after it hit the iceberg, the media would be talking about window curtains, tomorrow's menu, and the Captain's uniform. There would be no discussion about lifeboats."

Hank left the living room abruptly. He often yelled at his television, but he usually didn't have an audience. Hank went to the bathroom in the master bedroom, refilled his glass with water, and grabbed a bottle of out-dated acetaminophen pills from his medicine cabinet before he went back downstairs. Gary took a bathroom break. Then he went to the kitchen and refilled his glass before following Hank downstairs. Mae stayed upstairs and cleaned whiskey bottles.

It was time to build a Faraday cage around each vehicle. Gary removed the recently purchased plastic, aluminum foil, and tape from both vehicles and put them in a pile on the floor. Then he said, "Hank, is there anything else we need to take out of the vehicles before we wrap them in plastic and aluminum? We won't be able to open the doors when we're done."

Hank inspected the inside of the SUV, and said, "I don't think so."

"Alright, let's work together and wrap one vehicle at a time. Let's do the SUV first."

As Gary unrolled the plastic from its box, Hank stood still and watched. Gary finally asked, "Hank can you help me out here? Is something wrong?"

Hank said, "We're going to put the plastic on first, and then the aluminum foil, right?"

"Yes."

"And the purpose of the plastic is to serve as an insulator between the aluminum foil and the vehicles, right."

"Yes Hank. We talked about all of this earlier."

"Do you think one thin sheet of plastic will provide enough insulation? If this CME is the biggest EMP to hit the Earth in more than one hundred and fifty years, is it possible that the electrical jolt will be strong enough to pass through the plastic?"

"Hank, this plastic is six millimeters thick, which is pretty thick. So no, I don't think it will burn through the plastic."

"What if we could add another layer of insulation that was ten times or maybe even fifty times thicker?"

"Hank, what are you talking about? The stores are closed. Where would we get thicker insulation material?"

"Gary, you're standing on it."

Gary looked down at his feet. "You're talking about the carpet?" The carpet had been installed when the basement had been finished. It had hardly been walked on and looked new.

"Well the carpet would be a good insulator, but I was talking about the rubber pad underneath the carpet. I can tell you that the pad is the deluxe version, which is half an inch thick. Maggie insisted on the good stuff, and I paid the bill."

Gary paused for a moment. Wall-to-wall carpeting covered the entire basement floor. Some of that carpeting and padding were unavailable, because the two vehicles were parked on it. However, the main floor of the house upstairs also had wall-to-wall carpeting, as did many other houses in the Unites States. Many, perhaps most houses in the US had a supply of insulating material ample enough to cover at least two vehicles.

Gary said, "It's a good idea. I hadn't thought of it, but you know what, we've got plenty of plastic, and the plastic will be much easier to install than the heavy carpet padding. My recommendation is we use just the plastic."

Hank shrugged. "It's your call. If you think the plastic is thick enough all by itself, then let's forget about the carpet padding."

From the one hundred-foot roll of plastic, the brothers cut a piece that was long enough to go over the top of the vehicle from bumper to bumper and reach almost to the floor on both ends. When it was unfolded, the plastic was ten feet wide. They taped one edge of the plastic to the top center line of the SUV from front to back. The plastic hung like a curtain and covered the passenger side of the SUV. The brothers then installed a second piece in a similar fashion and covered the driver's side. In the middle, the two pieces of plastic overlapped by three inches. Wrapping and taping the plastic around the tires and underneath the vehicle was difficult, but they got it done with Hank working under the SUV, while Gary assisted from above.

They held the plastic in place with duct-tape strips that ran perpendicular to the length of the vehicle. The silver-tape ribs were about two feet apart, which gave the SUV the appearance of a segmented worm. As Hank rested for a moment and studied the silvery blue worm that was his SUV, he suddenly said "Oh, crap!"

"What?" Gary could tell that Hank thought something was wrong.

Hank said, "You're the Faraday expert, tell me how they work."

"Hank I don't know what you're getting at. I showed you how they work with the radio demonstration I did earlier."

Hank said, "Yes you did but you didn't install a ground wire on your radio faraday cage."

Gary said, "Yeah, so what? What's your point?"

Hank walked over to the grounding rod next to the SUV and put his foot on the top of the rod that protruded a couple of inches above the concrete. "If you had grounded the faraday cage on the radio, how would you have done it?"

"I would have connected the ground wire to – oh crap! The grounding rod is supposed to be connected to the outside of the Faraday cage. We connected the SUV's grounding rods to vehicle's electrical system, which is *inside* the Faraday cage. I screwed up. I'm sorry. We need to ground the cage, not the car. On the freezer we did it differently, but we're not trying to protect the freezer's electrical system, just the stuff in the plastic bins."

"So you agree with me that the grounding rod on the SUV should not be connected to the negative cable that used to be connected to the battery?"

"Yes. We'll have to open the hood and disconnect the cable." The brothers both looked at the hood for a moment.

Gary said, "Well that will take about fifteen minutes since we just covered the hood with plastic and then taped it shut."

Hank thought about it for a moment, and said, "I can do it a hell of a lot faster than that. Where is that utility knife you had earlier?"

Gary gave the knife to Hank. Hank cut through the tape and plastic along the front edge and the two sides of the hood. When he was done, he had a three-sided flap of plastic that could be lifted along with the hood. Hank cut a similar three-sided flap around the driver's door so he could reach the hood's release lever. When he pulled the lever, Gary opened the hood and disconnected the ground cable. The brothers repaired the cuts Hank had made by taping the edges back together. They also put a new layer of plastic over each of the two areas that Hank had compromised. The entire process took only seven minutes.

It was now 1:30 AM, and the brothers felt like they could not afford to rest or even slow down. What if the CME came early? They moved on to the installation of the aluminum foil, and listened to the ham radio as they worked.

There was a spirited debate among the operators over the President's decision not to shut down the grid. It wasn't just a Presidential decision, some argued; it was the imposition of martial law. Others responded that no such thing had occurred. The government order to leave the lights on simply meant the CME was too small to harm the electrical grid.

This response was soon drowned out by operators who claimed to have access to raw data regarding the size of the CME. The CME, they claimed, was truly massive. Its impact on the grid would be severe and widespread. They argued that shutting down the grid and hastily shielding certain key components would significantly reduce the damage to the grid. The President's order would increase the damage to the grid, and increase the loss of life. The angry operators laced their language with f-bombs that would draw the ire of the Federal Communications Commission, if the FCC was still functioning in the morning.

The debate continued as Hank and Gary wrapped the SUV in aluminum foil. They covered the front grill by hanging the strips of foil vertically from the hood and wrapping the other end underneath the vehicle. After the grill was covered, they installed the foil from side to side across the vehicle by going up one fender, across the top of the hood, and down the other side. Each strip of foil overlapped the strip next to it by an inch and a half. The brothers taped every inch of every seam as they installed strip after strip from front to back on the SUV.

As the brother's finished covering the front half of the SUV with aluminum foil, a ham radio operator said the Governor of Arizona had just announced that he was disobeying the President's order. He was going to shut down every piece of the electrical grid in Arizona that he could, and he was asking the governors of neighboring states to do the same. Over the next half hour, similar announcements were made by the governors of Texas, New Hampshire, and Indiana. Other states indicated they were considering similar measures. The process continued, and soon, fourteen governors were openly defying the President's order.

The effort by the Governor of Texas would prove to be the most successful. When it came to the electrical grid, Texas was literally in a class by itself. The electrical grid in the continental United States is separated into three pieces: the Eastern Interconnection, the Western Interconnection, and – all by its lonesome – Texas. The Texas grid is called the Electric Reliability Council of Texas, or ERCOT. Texas constructed ERCOT specifically to avoid federal regulation. With very few federally-approved exceptions, ERCOT's power lines do not cross any state or national borders.

The President did not retake the podium with his well-dressed wife in an effort to halt the defiance. Instead, the White House Press Secretary published a two-sentence written release that stated the rogue governors were unwise. She suggested, in a Chicago-thug kind of way, that federal post-CME disaster aide to those defiant states would be limited or non-existent. Four more states went rogue immediately after the Press Secretary's release. Unfortunately, for the American public, most of the states, which contained most of America's high-population metropolitan areas, complied with the President's order.

It was also unfortunate that the rogue governors in states other than Texas, did not have as much influence over their state power grids as they would have liked. In some states where a defiant announcement had been made, not even one transformer in the state was pulled off line. Most of the grid was an intertwined nationwide system, and most of it was owned by very large corporations. It could not be shut down immediately by order of a governor, or even a group of governors, especially since the corporations were following the orders of the President.

When the top and sides of the SUV were covered with aluminum foil, Hank crawled underneath to install aluminum foil from side to side across the bottom of the SUV. With the split axles, the steering control rods, the transmission and four-wheel drive gear box, it was tedious work that required lots of maneuvering and lots of tape. The SUV's wheels were also a challenge. The rubber tires provided excellent insulation between the vehicle and the ground, but the axles and tire rims needed to be inside the Faraday cage. When they were done with the aluminum foil, the brothers connected the grounding rod cable, which had previously been connected to the negative battery cable, to the exterior of the Faraday cage. They taped the length of exposed copper wire across several feet of the aluminum foil.

Mae came down to the basement while Hank and Gary were covering the axles and wheels. The girls were still asleep. Mae offered to help, but Gary told her there was little she could do to assist. After fifteen minutes, Gary asked her to check on the girls, and Mae went back upstairs. When she came back down a few minutes later, she had her computer with her. She said traffic on the internet was so slow that attempting to use it was a waste of time. She left her laptop on the stairs, and went to the Volvo. She opened the front passenger door, and removed a bag of stuff she had purchased earlier at the gas station.

Mae said, "I thought it would be a good idea to pull this out, before you two shrink-wrapped the car." Hank agreed. Mae pulled candy bars and small packages of crackers from the bag and handed them to the men. Hank and Gary each took a candy bar and some crackers, and wolfed them down. Mae put the bag of snacks on the stairs, and then returned to where the men were working. She assisted them on every occasion where a pair of soft, well manicured, white-collar-professional hands that had never done physical labor, were helpful. Gary occasionally asked her to check on the girls, and she did.

1:51 AM

The installation of the aluminum foil on the SUV had taken half an hour. Hank and Gary finished the job at 1:51 AM. If the CME was going hit at 3:00 AM, they had precious little time left. The men moved on to the Volvo. The first thing they did was open the mangled hood and disconnect the grounding rod from the negative battery cable.

On the ham radio, operators were talking about last minute preparations. Food, water, shelter, guns, ammo, candles, matches, propane, and Faraday cages were all discussed. It was clear that most operators didn't need to scurry around at the last minute, because they were already prepared. That's why they had the time to chat on the radio. For some, it was an opportunity to celebrate. The huge disaster, which they had predicted and prepared for, was finally here. Few had predicted a CME, but their preparations were effective just the same.

The flow of the conversation was interrupted by a female operator who clearly had no radio experience. She didn't use proper transmission procedures, her speech was stilted, and she sounded afraid. Over the next couple of minutes, the female operator explained that she was not a licensed operator. The radio and the license belonged to her husband. Her husband, however, was in the Army Reserve and deployed overseas. While deployed, she had communicated with him twice a day via e-mails and Skype, but she hadn't been able to talk to him for more than forty-eight hours.

Her husband was a prepper so the woman had adequate supplies, but she also had two young kids. She was the only one in the house who could fire a gun, and she didn't trust her neighbors to leave her alone. She was twenty-four years old. After a pause, another female operator chimed in, "Don't worry honey, we'll find a way to send you some help, but we've got to do that without publishing your exact location in the clear on the radio. Do you have a Citizen Band radio at your location?"

The mom, who would never see her husband again, answered in the affirmative. The female operator said, "Good," and directed the woman to a frequency with a lot less traffic.

Hank didn't follow the two women to the new frequency. If he had, he could have heard about the first phase of the rescue operation that the female operator arranged. The single mom, who did not yet know she was a widow, used the ham radio to identify a location that was thirty miles away from her house. The female operator contacted another operator near that location who would establish contact with the single mom, first by ham radio, then by CB radio. A second location much closer to the widow's house would be selected, and if necessary, communications would be handed off to another operator who could communicate using both radios. By transmitting only half of each message on the ham radio, and the other half on the CB radio, the operators hoped to limit the chances of an interloper getting to the widow first.

In the next phase, a meeting location that was a mile from the young widow's home would be selected. An operator and a couple of his gun-toting friends, at least one of whom would be a female, would arrive at the site at a certain time. From a distance, if the single mom liked what she saw, she would make her presence known, and the armed men and woman would ensure the mom and the rescue crew were not followed back to her home. At that point, a decision would be made to either leave guards with the mom and her two kids, or relocate everyone to a more secure location.

There was insufficient time to complete the rescue mission before the CME hit. The success of the mission depended, in part, on the ability of the widow and the rescuers to shield their radio equipment from the CME, and to have power sources for the equipment after the CME arrived. For the majority of the ham radio operators, neither requirement presented a challenge. That was, after all, the pride of the operator community. To transmit and receive, when other more modern methods were disabled. An operator who could not transmit and receive after a devastating crisis wasn't really an operator.

Gary heard the female operator's question about the CB radio before she left the frequency. Gary didn't own a CB radio, and if he had, he probably would not have remembered to bring it.

"Hank, do you own a CB radio?"

"Well I did. It was installed in the pickup truck I used to own before I bought the SUV. I removed it from the truck before I traded it in, but I never got around to installing it in the SUV. I guess, you know with cell phones and satellite radio, I just never saw the need."

"So what did you do with the radio?"

"I don't know. Its gotta be around here someplace. I don't remember throwing it away."

Gary said, "Well, if you could find it, it might be worth taking with us. Unlike cell phones, CB radios don't require transmission towers to operate. If we had a functional CB radio, it might come in handy."

"Good point. I'll have to think about where I put it."

Gary said, "Hank, why don't you think about it right now so we don't forget to find it and put it in the Faraday cage?"

Hank said, "Fine," in an aggravated tone, and went to the spare room to begin the search. A few minutes later, he left the spare room and went to the utility room. A few minutes after that, he emerged with an old, dust-covered CB radio. He went back to the spare room and placed the radio into the Faraday freezer.

While Hank was gone, Gary cut a length of plastic to install on the Volvo. When Hank came back, Gary said, "What about a generator, Hank? Do you have one of those as well?"

Hank thought for a long moment before he said. "I think I do. I can't believe I didn't think of it earlier. Years ago, I bought a real nice portable Honda generator that I used to use on hunting trips. You can carry the darn thing like a suitcase 'cuz it only weighs fifty pounds, but man, I haven't used that sucker in a really long time. It might be in my garage. If I had remembered that I owned that thing, I would have pawned it by now. Even used, it's got to be worth several hundred dollars."

Gary looked amused as he said, "Hank, do you still own it or not?"

Hank said, "If I still have it, it's probably in my garage, but do you want me to spend time looking for it now? It's a sophisticated machine with some sensitive electronics, but there's no room for it in the freezer."

Gary said, "I think it's worth spending five or ten minutes looking for it. If you find it, we can stick it in the Volvo. When we put the Faraday material around the car, it will protect the generator as well."

Hank said, "Fine. I'll give it five minutes, but only if you help me look for it."

Gary agreed and the two men left the basement and went to Hank's cluttered garage. Mae left the basement at the same time to check on the girls. Seven minutes later, when the men returned, Mae was already back. With one hand, Hank was carrying a red, dust-covered Honda EU2000 generator. He opened the front passenger door of the Volvo, and put the generator on the seat. As he closed the door he said, "I'll be surprised if we can get that thing running without the help of a mechanic."

As Hank and Gary cut a second long piece of plastic for the Volvo, a ham radio operator who said he was from New Paltz, New York made the comment that CB radios and other small electrical devices did not need to be protected by a Faraday cage. Instead, he said, they just needed to be disconnected from the grid. Two operators disagreed and a third operator asked for clarification.

The New Paltz operator said the ground effects of a CME were different from that of a man-made Nuclear Electro-Magnetic Pulse weapon, or EMP. He said the shock wave from an EMP had three components, while the CME had only one, and the one component imitated the E3 portion of the EMP. He went on to say that the E3 component would knock out the electrical grid, but it wouldn't pack enough punch to short-out electrical devices that were not plugged into the grid when the CME hit. He repeated his claim that Faraday cages were unnecessary for such non-connected devices, including cars. Other operators said the New Paltz operator was wrong, and they had already protected their sensitive equipment with Faraday cages.

Hank said, "What the hell is he talking about? I mean, if he's right, we just wasted a bunch of time, money and effort putting a Faraday cage around my SUV."

Gary said, "I have no idea. Prior to my conversation with Ralph, I couldn't have told you what a Faraday cage was. I thought the electrical pulse created by a CME was the same as the one created by an EMP weapon. Based on what the other operators said, the New Paltz guy could simply be wrong, and we probably shouldn't take any chances. We already bought the Faraday material, and the SUV is already wrapped. I think we should press on and do the Volvo, too. It's better to be safe than sorry."

Hank said, "Brother, I'll help you wrap the Volvo if that's what you want to do. It's not like I've got a hot date, or anything else to do this evening, but I'd sure like to know if the New Paltz guy is right."

Mae was still on the basement stairs looking for a chance to be useful. She had heard the ham radio chatter, and the discussion between Hank and Gary. She said, "Guys, the internet is pretty much useless right now, but I'll give it a try to see if I can find an answer for you. I can also search among all the stuff I downloaded earlier today."

Hank and Gary looked at Mae, and then looked at each and shrugged. Gary said, "That sounds great Mae, thanks." Then he turned to Hank and said, "So we agree? We should keep doing the Faraday thing, because we don't know if the CME will knock out the vehicles?"

Hank said, "Sure. Like I said earlier, I've got nothing else on my calendar this evening."

Before the men got back to work, Gary explained to Hank an idea he had come up with to hasten the installation of the Faraday cage on the Volvo. Putting the plastic and aluminum foil on the SUV had been a difficult task, but it would be an even more difficult task on the Volvo, because of the car's lower ground clearance. Gary's idea would make the task much easier, and hopefully faster.

To cover the bottom of the Volvo, Gary said they should put a wide layer of plastic on the floor that had foil already taped to the bottom of it. Then they could push the Volvo onto the plastic, lift the outer edges of the plastic and foil up onto the car, and tape it into place. The top of the vehicle would be done in the same way the SUV had been done. When it was finished, the entire Volvo, including its tires, would be inside the Faraday cage.

Hank said the idea sounded good. He was willing to give it a try. The Volvo would have to be pushed rather than driven onto the plastic and foil wrapper, because Gary had already disconnected many of the cars electrical components.   Unfortunately, with the SUV parked just three feet behind the Volvo, and a basement wall less than three feet in front of the Volvo, the Faraday wrapper would have to be unrolled under the car in stages. With the Volvo pushed back until it was only one inch from the SUV, there was six feet of space between the front of the Volvo and the concrete wall.

Hank and Gary had already cut two lengths of plastic for the Volvo. With Gary's new system, they needed a flat surface that was twenty-three feet long and ten feet wide, to attach the foil to the plastic. Gary said they would put plastic down first, and then tape the aluminum foil to the top of the plastic. When they were done, they would flip the two layers over so the foil was on the bottom, and roll it up like a carpet.

Hank explained that his driveway was the best place to assemble the Faraday wrapper, even though it might attract attention from his nosey neighbor. He also explained pushing the Volvo over the rolled up Faraday liner might kink or tear the aluminum foil. Hank said he could build a ramp to protect the roll of Faraday material while Gary and Mae assembled the material in the driveway.

Gary said, "Sounds good," to Hank, and "Let's go to the driveway," to Mae.

Mae said, "Before we do that, can I give you guys the answer to that CME versus EMP question you asked earlier."

Gary said, "Can you do it quickly?"

Mae said, "Sure. The internet was too slow to be helpful, but I found the information in some material I had previously downloaded. The answer comes from a guy named Jerry Emanuelson who publishes stuff on futurescience.com. He says there are three different pulses from a Nuclear EMP weapon: E1, E2, and E3. The E1 pulse has a very high voltage and can destroy computers and other devices that use microchips. The E2 pulse has an impact much like a lightning strike, and it tends to be the least damaging of the three.

The E3 pulse is similar to the effects of a CME. Emanuelson says a CME's impact, like an E-3 pulse, disrupts the Earth's magnetic field. The disruption creates currents in long electrical conductors, which are common in the power grid. The geomagnetically induced currents can destroy the grid's transformers and other critical components. So, like the guy on the ham radio said, the CME is probably going to knock out the grid, but without the E1 and E2 portions of a nuclear EMP, electrical equipment that is not connected to the grid will probably not be affected."

It was a lot to take in. There was a long pause before Hank said, "If Emanuelson is correct, than the grid will go down, but most of the automobiles will still run. I'm guessing we're going to wish we had spent more time buying gas cans and stockpiling fuel, than building unnecessary Faraday cages around our vehicles. With the grid down, most gas stations won't be able to pump gas. The ones that retain that capability will probably get swarmed and emptied in very short order. The loss of the grid could reduce production of fuel by refineries. Even if refinery production isn't reduced, truck drivers probably won't want to deliver gas to areas that are experiencing a long-term blackout. In other words, even if the CME doesn't disable the cars electrically, most of them will stop moving within a few days for lack of fuel."

Hank paused and then added, "Gary are you sure you wouldn't rather spend our final hours of civilization stockpiling fuel?"

Gary said, "We already did stockpile fuel. Both vehicles have full tanks, and I've got two full five-gallon cans in my trailer. That's more than enough to get us to Grandpa's. Once we get there, we plan to stay put, so we don't need a lot of fuel. If we went out and gathered a lot more gas than we already have, we wouldn't have any way to transport it. The hauling capacity of my car and trailer is already maxed out. Once we load your SUV with your stuff, it will be maxed out as well. We've got no need for more fuel, and no place to put it."

Gary continued, "As for the difference between a CME and an EMP, I've never heard of this Emanuelson guy before, and neither Blake nor Ralph mentioned such a difference. In fact, Ralph said Faraday cages were a good idea. Hank, you and I already decided it's better to be safe than sorry. So let's stick to the plan and use the driveway to create a Faraday wrapper for the Volvo."

Hank shrugged and said, "I don't have strong feelings either way. If you want to wrap the Volvo, that's fine with me. I'll start working on the ramp."

Mae said to Gary, "Before we go to the driveway, why don't I shut down my laptop and stick it in the freezer? You know, just in case this Emanuelson guy is wrong."

Gary said, "Okay, but let's hurry. Did you back up the stuff you downloaded to your hard drive to a thumb drive and my laptop?" Mae said yes to the thumb drive and no to the laptop. Gary took Mae's laptop to the spare room and removed his laptop and Hank's laptop from the freezer. He took a couple of minutes to transfer the information on the thumb drive to both laptops, and then put all three computers into a plastic bin in the freezer.

While Gary and Mae were backing up the computers, Hank had started working on the ramp that would protect the rolled Faraday material. When Gary and Mae were ready to go to the driveway, Hank assisted them in carrying the plastic, aluminum foil, and tape outside. With the three of them working together, it took only a few minutes, to stretch out the plastic. They pinned down the corners and sides of the plastic with a hodgepodge of relatively heavy items Mae had tossed onto the front lawn when she cleaned the guest room. When Gary and Mae started attaching the aluminum foil, Hank went back down to the basement.

Hank built a hollow wooden speed bump by placing two long two-by-fours on the floor in front of the Volvo. The boards were parallel to each other, and the inside edges were eight inches apart. Where the front tires of the Volvo lined up with the boards, he bridged the gap between the long boards with three short sections of two-by-four in front of each tire. When assembled, the gap between the long boards was eight inches wide and one and a half inches high. Hank hoped the gap would be big enough for the tightly rolled Faraday material to fit, when the Volvo was pushed up over the two-by-fours. The total height of the speed bump was only three inches, but it was a significant obstacle since the car was already inoperable. The car would have to be pushed over that hump without the benefit of a running start. Hank got a hand-held grinder from his shop and made the hump more ramp-like by grinding a thirty degree slant into the ends of the short two-by-fours, and the edges of the long boards.

When he was done grinding, Hank took a short break. He still had a headache and he was exhausted from the ceaseless frenzied activity. He went to the bathroom in the basement and took a dose of acetaminophen with a glass of water, and a couple of swallows of Moscato. Then he went to the driveway to check on Gary and Mae. When he got there, they had nearly finished constructing the faraday wrapper. Hank helped with the taping for the next couple of minutes, and then assisted in flipping over the material to put the foil on the bottom. When that was done, all three of them rolled up the material tightly so it would fit into the ramp's eight inch gap. Together, they carried the ten foot long roll of material to the basement.

They placed the roll of material against the wall in front of the Volvo, and unrolled it until it was a few inches from the car's front tires. Gary and Hank put the two-by-four ramp across the top of the roll. When they attempted to push the car over the ramp, the tires pushed the ramp across the floor instead of rolling up over the ramp. They stopped pushing. Hank went to his work bench and came back with a hammer and some ten penny nails. The nails were not designed for concrete use, but Hank drove one nail through each of the four ends of the long two-by-fours and into the concrete.

For the second effort, the men enlisted Mae as a pusher. Straining and grunting the three of them got the car over the hump, after which it coasted almost all the way to the wall. They removed the ramp, unrolled the plastic, pushed the car back toward the SUV, and then unrolled the plastic again. With the roll of material a few inches from the rear wheels, Hank and Gary put the ramp into place, and Hank nailed it down again. After another three-person push, the car was over the ramp for the second time. They removed the ramp, and unrolled the Faraday material the rest of the way. Then they immediately began taping the plastic edge of the material to the sides of the Volvo.

When it was time to insulate the top half of the car, Gary asked Hank and Mae to pause for a moment. Gary said, "That lower half went fast because we pre-fabricated the Faraday wrapper in the driveway. I think we'll save time on the top half if we use the same process again."

Hank and Mae agreed. The three of them picked up the necessary raw materials and trudged back to the driveway. Working together, the fabrication process went quickly. Every few minutes Gary would look at his watch and implore the other two to work even faster. The CME could hit at any minute and the Volvo was not yet protected.

Mae would occasionally respond with something like, "Gary, I'm going as fast as I can."

Hank responded with a grunt. With every beat of his heart, his head pounded with pain.

As they were finishing, Hank's curious neighbor Bruce Williams came over and attempted to start a conversation. "Howdy Hank, how are you doing? Have you heard about this CME thing?"

Bruce disliked Hank mostly because he thought Hank was a drunken lazy slob who, among other things, hadn't mowed his lawn in months. Bruce felt forced to take on the unpaid mowing responsibility just to keep his own place from looking bad. Bruce only mowed the front yard though, because the back yard was mostly concealed behind the stockade fence.

Hank didn't hate Bruce, he just thought the man was a pompous disagreeable ass. Hank was also still a little miffed about Bruce's theft of his DeWalt cordless drill. Some would consider the loss of the drill a good trade for all the times Bruce had mowed Hank's front lawn. Not Hank. He didn't care how his lawn looked so why should he pay anything to have his grass mowed? Bruce's lawn mowing services were actually a source of aggravation to Hank. The noise of the mower forced Hank to turn up the volume as he watched stolen cable channels on his television. Fortunately, Bruce's mower was a zero-turn model that finished the front lawn in just ten minutes, so Hank had never gotten up out of his easy chair to complain about the noise.

Bruce was visiting now only because he thought the world might end, and Hank seemed to be doing something useful, or at least interesting, while most of the rest of the neighborhood seemed dumbstruck. Hank smiled and spoke in the nicest tone he could muster. He wanted to get rid of Bruce quickly. Hank lied and said, "Hey, Bruce, good to see you. I'm fine." Then he lied again and said, "Yeah I heard something on the news about a CME, but I don't really know what they were talking about."

Bruce said, "Yeah, I guess it's confusing a lot of people. Me, I figure if the CME was going to be really bad, the President would have shut down the grid to protect it. We'll just have to see what happens tomorrow morning. What's up with the huge piece of plastic?"

Hank knew Bruce had a closed mind that could not understand any concept that was not already inside it. Like many adults, Bruce's brain had reached a permanent knowledge plateau years ago. If Hank had a full month to explain to Bruce the function and benefits of a Faraday cage, he knew his effort would be wasted. Hank didn't have even one full minute to waste on Bruce, so he made up a bullshit story to explain the sudden need for a large sheet of plastic with aluminum foil backing.

Hank pointed to Gary and Mae and said, "Bruce, this is my brother Gary and his wife Mae. They had to leave the city unexpectedly because of the doomsday rumors, so they're going to spend the night here. They have two wonderful daughters, but one of them, Josephine, is unfortunately allergic to just about everything. We've got to put this make shift anti-allergen liner on all four walls of the guest bed room, as well as the floor and ceiling, just so she can make it through the night without going into anaphylactic shock."

Bruce was wide-eyed. Hank had just spoken more words to Bruce than he had in the previous six months. "Wow, what a terrible thing to have to deal with at a time like this. You folks have my sympathies. I guess her allergies explain why you had to get all the garbage out of the house so quickly. Maybe you'll have time to clean the front lawn tomorrow?"

Gary and Mae nodded solemnly as Gary tried to look the part of a concerned parent and Mae tried not to laugh. Josephine didn't have an allergy condition, and she was sound asleep in what still had to be the dirtiest house in the neighborhood. Mae thought, *Is this neighbor really stupid enough to believe the allergy story when both girls had played outside in the driveway earlier?*

Hank smiled. "Bruce, I apologize for the mess on the lawn. You don't have to tell me twice. I promise you that by tomorrow morning, you'll have absolutely no concerns about my front lawn."

Hank spoke the truth. Hank figured that by tomorrow morning Bruce wouldn't care about the trashed lawn because Bruce would be more worried about staying alive. Bruce turned to go, but then turned back. "I understand the plastic, but what's the purpose of the aluminum foil? I'm just, you know, curious."

Hank didn't pause for a second. "I really can't explain it to you Bruce. You'd have to ask the pediatrician about it. The doctor said something about how the res judicata of the heat transfer to the differentially permeable membrane would somehow reduce the likelihood of allergen influxation. It was all Greek to me. I'm just doing what the doctor told Mae we should do. Isn't that right Mae?"

Mae was sure her bewilderment at Hank's "explanation" had already given the game away, but she cleared her throat and tried to look distraught. "Yes Hank, that's exactly what Dr. Prendergast told us to do, but I really don't think we're getting it done fast enough. I'm really worried about poor Josephine. Hank, can you please focus on the task at hand so she might survive the night?"

Mae's mock concern had the desired effect. Bruce scurried away as he mumbled an apology. As Bruce left, Hank apologized to him for having to end the conversation so abruptly.

Hank, Gary, and Mae quickly rolled up the second large piece of Faraday material, picked it up together, and carried it through the gate by the garage to the back yard. The men grabbed the ends of the roll and Mae was in the middle. As they walked, Mae said, "Hank do you have any idea what you said to that man about res judicata and allergen influxation?"

Hank was carrying the front of the roll, and didn't bother to look over his shoulder when he said, "Nope, I just threw together some big words because I knew Bruce wouldn't have the humility to ask me what they meant."

"What if he *had* asked what they meant?"

"I would have referred him to you Mae. You're the kids' mom so you're the one who got the information directly from what's his name? Dr. Pendergast? Like I said, all that medical jargon is Greek to me."

"I've got news for you Hank, that stuff you spouted wasn't medical jargon." Hank shrugged and kept walking.

Mae was almost impressed by Hank's ability to deliver the BS explanation so quickly with a deadpan expression. He had been, she thought, fast on his feet; like a court room attorney. The "fast on his feet" expression caused Mae to remember the note Johnny Davis had sent along with his gift of the red lace thong. The racy gift, and even more racy elevator ride, seemed like distant memory from weeks ago, but it had been only eighteen hours ago.

Mae thought, *Where is Johnny now? Was he frantically preparing for the end of civilization? Will I ever see him again? Would it really matter to me if I didn't? Probably not. Shallow womanizers like Johnny are a dime a dozen. But it had been a fun workplace distraction.* Mae was still wearing the thong.

When they got to the basement, they unrolled the foil and plastic over the roof and hood of the Volvo, and started taping it into place. The application of the plastic and foil wrapper to the top side of the car went faster than the bottom half because they didn't have to mess around with the wooden ramp.

2:23 AM

The combination of their prior experience with the SUV, the smaller size of the Volvo, and Mae's assistance paid off. They finished the installation of the Faraday cage on the Volvo at 2:23 AM. The next project was to cover the wide open area of the patio door opening that no longer had doors. Hank and Gary hoped the installation of sheet metal would deflect any electrical pulse that might otherwise strike the vehicles. Mae went to check on the girls and the men took a water break. Even with the cool air flooding the basement through the patio door opening, both men were perspiring from exertion. Except for the task of pushing the Volvo over the speed bump twice, none of the work was particularly strenuous. It was, however, constant and the pace was frantic.

Hank had left the ham radio on while the Volvo was being wrapped. He missed some of the conversation among the operators while he was outside, but he could hear it fine now. Hank changed the location of the radio so he could hear it better while he and Gary installed the sheet metal. Some of the ham radio operators were leaving the net. They explained that they were shutting down their equipment to protect it from the anticipated electromagnetic pulse. Some said they were probably signing off for the last time because they did not have a back-up power supply, or they had one but didn't think it would survive the CME.

Three operators explained that they were already using their back-up power supply because their state governor had successfully shut down at least a portion of their grid. Two of the operators were in Texas, and one was in Arizona.

For those who had backup power supplies, there was a lot of chatter about how to protect those supplies. The conversation was filled with references to Faraday cages, grounding rods, and aluminum foil. Hank and Gary glanced at each other occasionally. Everything they had done to protect their vehicles was consistent with what the operators were doing to protect their radios. Perhaps they should have tuned in sooner; you know, like maybe a year ago. On the other hand, if the New Paltz operator and Emanuelson were correct, Faraday cages were vital for nuclear EMP protection, and largely unnecessary for CME protection.

Gary leaned the two-by-four boards vertically against the back of the house over the opening while Hank put a step ladder into position. Using the DeWalt cordless drill, and three inch screws, Hank attached the boards vertically to the back side of the house at two foot intervals. Using the shorter screws, Hank and Gary then attached the metal siding to the two-by-fours. Mae returned after checking on the girls, visiting the rest room, and getting a drink of water. She assisted where she could by fetching tools and screws. She knew so little about construction that her assistance did not reduce the time needed to complete the project.

By 2:45 AM, virtually every ham radio operator was off the net. Even those who had a backup power supply didn't have a hardened radio system that could survive a severe CME while the system was on and operating. The radio traffic declined dramatically as it was reduced to only those operators who believed they were outside the CME's impact area. At 2:47, Hank took a break from the construction project, and did what the majority of the operator community had done. He shut off his radio. Hank removed the batteries, and took the radio to the spare room. He put the radio and the batteries in a bin inside the Faraday freezer.

It took another twenty minutes to finish the installation of the sheet metal. When it was done, the recently enlarged patio entryway was completely covered with sheet metal that extended a couple of feet on both sides of the opening. Hank and Gary also covered a window that was on the right side of the entryway. The brothers installed a grounding rod on each side of the sheet metal wall, and connected the rods to the metal with grounding wire.

3:13 AM

Hank glanced at his watch and said, "We're living on borrowed time, it's already 3:13 AM and the electricity is still on."

Gary laughed and said, "Maybe the whole thing was a hoax!"

At that point, Gary and Hank realized that they had effectively sealed the exterior entrance to the basement. The brothers were outside the house on the patio, while Mae was still in the basement. To re-enter the house, Hank and Gary walked around to the driveway side of the house and entered through the kitchen. As they made their way toward the driveway, Gary noticed he could see almost well enough to see his shadow. He looked upward and saw a moon that was full or nearly full, but the northern sky seemed extra bright. Having not lived in the area, Gary thought it might be the glow from a well lit urban area.

"Hank, look at the sky. Is that glow to our north caused by man-made lights?

Hank kept walking as he said, "I don't know, maybe. I mean it could be. Isn't there a shopping center in that direction?"

Hank was exhausted and functioning on auto-pilot. He did not have the mental energy to discuss extraneous topics, and he hadn't looked up at the sky when Gary told him to.

"I don't know Hank, I don't live here. I was just wondering whether the aurora borealis is starting."

Hank said, "I have no idea. Who cares if it is starting?"

"Well I think we care. When the aurora borealis arrives won't it bring the EMP with it?"

"I don't know Gary. I guess we'll know soon enough. Look, we don't have time to stand around looking at the sky. Let's get back inside and finish doing what needs to get done."

Gary said, "Okay," and the brothers entered the house, walked through the kitchen, and went downstairs to the basement.

Mae said, "What took you so long. I thought maybe you guys had gotten lost."

Hank said, "Gary was stargazing." Mae didn't know what to make of that so she said nothing.

Hank and Gary examined the interior side of their recent metal installation without really knowing what they were looking for. It looked like a shoddy job that had been done in a hell of a hurry by a couple of amateurs at night. If they had been contractors, the customer would have thrown them off the property and refused to pay them. Still, they couldn't see anything more that needed to be done to their shoddy sheet metal shield.

Hank and Gary each looked at each other with a "Now what?" expression. Hank said suddenly, "We've forgot to unplug the chargers!"

Hank still had the DeWalt drill in his hand as he walked quickly to the spare room. Gary and Mae followed Hank. Hank opened up the Faraday freezer and put the DeWalt drill into the plastic storage bin. He held the bin open as Gary and Mae unplugged the chargers for the other electrical devices and tossed them into the bin with the DeWalt. Hank put the lid on the storage bin, and shut the freezer. There was a pause as the three of them looked at each other and shared the same thought. *Was there anything else that still needed to be done?*

This time it was Gary who spoke up. "Quick, we should throw our watches into the freezer." In less than a minute the freezer was opened, three watches were tossed into a plastic bin, and the bin and the freezer were closed again.

As soon as it was closed, Hank said, "We need to put a strip of aluminum foil around all four sides of the door to cover the gap in the metal caused by the door seal."

Gary recalled that Hank had said the same thing to the Carhart shoppers at Home Depot. Gary left the spare room and went to the Volvo where the last scraps of aluminum foil were located. He also grabbed two nearly empty rolls of tape before hurrying back to the freezer. Two minutes later, a strip of foil was taped into place around the sides of the freezer door.

When it was done, the three again looked at each other. A long quiet moment passed before Gary said. "That's all I've got. I can't think of anything else to do."

Mae said, "Neither can I."

Hank said, "Me neither, let's go upstairs." He had wanted to say, "Let's go upstairs and get some beers," but he knew there were no beers to get. Moving slowly, Hank trudged toward the basement stairs. He thought, *It's a hell of thing to have to experience the end of civilization without beer, particularly when you're an alcoholic.*

On the way to the stairs, Gary took a detour and grabbed the unlit propane lantern and matches. He didn't bother to turn off the basement lights. When Gary got to the top of the stairs, it was 3:22 AM. Mae sat down at the kitchen table.

When Hank got to the top of the stairs, he went directly to the living room. He had brought the nearly empty Moscato bottle with him and he put it on the floor next to the recliner. Hank went to the television with the intention of turning it off but he couldn't find the remote.

A handsome male commentator with a full head of hair and very white teeth said, "Well folks, it's almost three thirty AM and we're still here. The lights are still on, and there have been no reports of damage caused by the solar flare. If this was going to be the proverbial big one, it sure hasn't panned out that way."

The commentator spoke in the same happy tone he had used two days ago to report the birth of a bear cub at a nearby zoo. The commentator had never believed the CME was going to be the "proverbial big one." In fact, he thought the CME would be nothing at all. However, the non-stop coverage of the CME had been great for ratings, so he had been forced to talk about the CME as if it mattered.

Hank picked up the wine bottle and drained the last two ounces of Moscato into his mouth. The commentator was certain the rest of the night would pass uneventfully, and he'd be back at the news desk tomorrow after several hours of good sleep. He was dead wrong about that.

Hank found the remote and hit the power button. Still feeling dehydrated, Hank walked into the kitchen and said, "I'm thirsty."

Gary was standing at the counter by the sink. He had been tinkering with the propane lantern, but he hadn't lit it.

Gary said, "Me too. I'm also hungry."

The men had left their drinking glasses in the basement after their last water break. Gary went downstairs and retrieved them. He filled the glasses at the kitchen sink and handed one of them to Hank. Gary looked around and spotted the open can of stew that was sitting on the stove where Mae had abandoned it several hours early.

Gary held up the can and said, "I'm starving. Does anybody else want some of this?"

Hank said no as he sat down at the table. Mae looked like she was going to barf and shook her head. Gary rinsed off a spoon in the sink, and put the spoon in the can of stew. Then he took the stew and his glass of water to the kitchen table and sat down next to Mae.

Mae said, "Aren't you going to heat that up before you eat it? Better yet, why don't you throw it away?" Mae wrinkled her nose. Gary had sat too close. She could smell the stale stew.

Gary shook his head as he chewed on the large spoonful of stew that had just reached his mouth. Mae said, "You know there's still some of that chicken that we cooked earlier in the fridge. Wouldn't you prefer that? That crap you're eating was never edible in the first place, and it's been sitting on the stove, unrefrigerated, for hours."

Gary had forgotten about the chicken, but after he swallowed he said, "I'm hungry. It tastes fine."

It didn't taste fine. The stew was cold and the grease had congealed, but Gary was already sitting down and he was exhausted. A trip to the fridge didn't seem worth it. He also didn't want to admit that the chicken would have been a much better option. Maybe he could stop eating the stew when Mae stopped paying attention.

Mae said, "Well don't exhale in this direction; that stuff stinks." Then she changed the topic. "I'm starting to wonder if the CME is ever going to happen. It was supposed to hit at midnight, then the arrival time was changed to three AM. Now it's almost three thirty. All the lights are still on, and nothing has happened. Maybe the whole thing was a scam."

Hank was physically, mentally, and emotionally exhausted. He wanted a drink – a real drink – so bad it hurt. The Moscato had helped, but it was now gone. Hank looked at Mae and said nothing. When he had come up from the basement, Hank had gone to the living room. He intended to sit down in his easy chair, and go to sleep. He had come back to the kitchen for a glass of water, and he was now wondering why he had stayed in the kitchen instead of going back to the living room. Mae had been slightly helpful during the basement projects, but she was now getting back to being her usual pain-in-the-ass self.

Gary glanced at Hank before responding to Mae. He could tell what Hank was thinking. "Mae you know that the exact timing is impossible to predict. We'll just have to wait and see what happens."

Mae looked at Gary and his can of stew as if he were a creature in a science experiment. Gary took another spoonful of the stew.

Gary wanted to talk about something other than the CME, and said the first thing that popped into his head, "Remember that time when Josie took off her pull-up and peed in the back yard. She's done really well on the potty training lately."

Gary thought, *Potty training, what a normal thing to do. Wouldn't it be wonderful if the CME didn't happen, or didn't cause widespread damage, and we could all get back to normal frustrating things like potty training? If civilization ends, won't potty training have to continue? How much more frustrating will potty training be without store-bought pull-ups?*

Gary wasn't craving alcohol, but like Hank, he wanted to go to sleep. He had been going non-stop since . . . since he had gotten the call from Blake at about 10:30 AM. That had been, Gary glanced at the kitchen clock, less than seventeen hours ago! Gary shook his head. He wanted to sleep, but his brain would not shut down. *What happens next? How does this end? I've been going for seventeen hours straight, and I still don't know whether any of the non-stop movement and preparations were necessary.* Gary's body was being held hostage by his busy mind. He wouldn't be able to go to sleep until he knew whether Blake's prediction of a worst case scenario had been accurate.

Mae said yes, she did remember Josie's diaper incident even though she hadn't been there. Gary had told her about it right after it happened. He'd even snapped a photo of Josie, from the waist up as she held her pull-up gleefully over her head. Every moment in a kid's life was now potential material for a Facebook update.

Mae said, "That was what, like three weeks ago? You said Josie's had only about half a dozen accidents since then."

Mae had looked at Gary as she talked. Gary took another dose of the stew. His stomach grumbled, but he didn't think Mae could hear it.

Hank had a headache and was not interested in potty-training stories, or any other conversation topic. While he was in the Army, Hank had been in this situation dozens of times before; it was called the "hurry up and wait" mode. Soldiers were expected to move at a hundred miles an hour, and then stop and do nothing. Then repeat the cycle again, and again, and again as they prepared for one real or imagined crisis after another. During the preparation phase, soldiers often didn't know whether anything would actually happen. Like a lot of soldiers, Hank had become completely desensitized to it. Going nonstop for hours or days only to stop or back up, seemed normal to Hank. It wasn't something worth worrying about, or talking about. The CME would happen or not happen, and Hank had no control over it.

As he got up from the table Hank said, "This CME thing could still happen. Keep your headlamps close to you even while you sleep."

Hank's headlamp was around his neck as he spoke. He didn't wait for a reply or an acknowledgment, as he walked into his clean, bleached living room. The smell of the chlorine was still strong and it even burned his eyes a little, but Hank had a solution for that. The hurry-up phase was over. It was now time to wait. Like most soldiers, Hank was an expert at the wait phase. Unbidden, the soldier's mantra ran through his mind, "*Don't stand when you can sit, and don't sit when you can lie down, because you don't know when your next rest will come.*" Hank sat down in his chair, and drank the last few swallows from his water glass. He dropped the empty glass on the floor and tilted back in the recliner. He closed his eyes and the bleach burn ended. Hank wanted to be sound asleep when the end came. Within minutes, his wish was granted and he slept.

3:31 PM

Gary and Mae discussed their own sleeping arrangements for a few minutes. The guest bedroom was relatively clean, but the bed was already occupied by the two girls. Mae thought she might be able to squeeze into the bed with the two girls, but what would Gary do? Sleep on the floor? Gary decided he would go to the garage and get a sleeping bag, and then find the cleanest six feet of floor space to spread the bag. He'd probably end up on the guest room floor next to the bed. Maybe he could put down a tarp or some plastic, before he put the bag down.

Gary stood up to get a sleeping bag, but he couldn't remember where the bags had ended up. Were they in the trailer or the roof top carrier? He looked toward Mae as he stood up. Thinking about Mae and sleeping arrangements, made Gary wish he could share a bed with his wife. Perhaps some intimate time with Mae would help his busy brain shut down so he could sleep. With a smile, Gary recalled the image of his wife disrobing on the courthouse stairs before she put on the leathers. The scene jarred to an unpleasant halt as he remembered the red lace thong. *How could I have forgotten about that damn thong for the last fifteen hours?*

Gary was convinced his wife had somehow received the thong as a gift. *Who, besides a lover would give her such a gift? Is she cheating on me? Was she about to divorce me when news of the CME arrived? Did the CME save my marriage as well as Hank's life? What do I do now? Should I just ask her straight up if she was having an affair? Is there any innocent explanation for wearing a thong that neither she nor I purchased?*

Gary couldn't suppress the troublesome questions. With no preamble, he asked flatly, "Where did that red lace thong come from?"

"What?"

Gary knew Mae had heard and understood the question. She didn't need to have the question repeated; she just wanted more time to collect her thoughts. Gary repeated the question, and added context.

"Where did that red lace thong come from? You know, the one I saw you wearing at the top of the courthouse steps?"

"Really, Gary? The world is about to end, I'm sitting in your brother's garbage dump, after playing cook, cleaner, and construction worker for the last several hours, and you want to talk about a thong? Do you know I broke a nail and got two splinters helping you with those stupid projects downstairs? Now you want my underwear to be the topic of the last conversation we have before the civilization ends? Really?!"

Mae paused, then added, "You are one crazy son of a bitch, Gary." Mae got up from the table and took a couple of steps toward the back door of the kitchen that led to the deck.

Gary had gone this far, and he hadn't gotten an answer. *I might as well press on.* "Mae, I know you didn't buy that thong, and I know I didn't buy it for you. So where did it come from?"

Gary had overstated his case. He didn't and couldn't *know* Mae hadn't purchased the thong because Gary never accompanied Mae when she shopped for clothes. But at home, Gary did most of the laundry and he had never seen the thong before. If Mae had purchased the thong, it must have been a very recent purchase. Mae paused for only the slightest moment before answering Gary's question. If he hadn't known his wife as well as he did, he wouldn't have known that she was about to lie to him. He also knew she wouldn't tell him a complete lie.

Mae looked Gary in the eye as she said, "You're right Gary. It was a gift, but it's not what you think. It was given to me at the office today, well yesterday actually. I wore it on a dare."

Mae paused, broke eye contact, and looked out the back window of the kitchen. Her answer to Gary had raised more questions, and Gary felt a surge of disdain. Perhaps the complete truth was really bad, or perhaps Mae was too tired to tell one of her really good lies. Gary looked at Mae in disgust. *So that's it? She's just going to turn away and not give me the full story?* Gary stood still for a moment as he tried to decide what to do. Should he pursue Mae and attempt to get the truth, or go find a place to lie down and try to get some sleep?

Mae was still looking out the window. She had turned away to get away from Gary and his questions, but she had also noticed that the night outside seemed unusually bright. Mae went the rest of the way to the back door and opened it to get a better look. She was stunned by what she saw. Every negative thought about her husband and his inquisition disappeared in an instant. If she had been looking for a distraction to change the conversation topic, she could not have found one more beautiful.

Loudly, Mae said, "Gary, come see this!"

As he covered the few steps to the back door, Gary said in a low tone, "Mae, I'm right here. Stop yelling or you might wake up the –" He got to the deck and abruptly stopped talking.

The aurora borealis was a dazzling display of white, red, and blue light that was sweeping down from the north and advancing across the sky. Soon it would be directly overhead. On the front edge of the advance, the light was mostly white and looked like wavy window curtains. To the far north, the light was much brighter and the intense red and blue colors danced and swirled like nothing Gary had ever seen.

After looking up for a while, Gary looked down. He could clearly see his shadow on the deck. He glanced around at the backyards of the other houses and could see everything about as clearly as he would at dusk on a cloudless evening. If Gary had been driving, he would not have needed headlights to see the road. Mae moved closer to Gary, but didn't hug him or touch him. The two of them spent a full minute looking here, there, and everywhere, while they took turns pointing to a particularly impressive portion of the expanding light show in the sky.

Gary finally said, "Hank needs to see this," and he walked back into the house.

Hank had woken up when Mae had yelled for Gary to go outside, but he hadn't opened his eyes or gotten out of his chair. He was aggravated that Mae had woken him, and he was now in the process of going back to sleep. Hank didn't hear any motion or voices from the guest bedroom. The girls apparently had no trouble sleeping through their parents' excitement, even though it didn't happen very often.

Gary stuck his head into the living room and said, "Hank, I know you're tired, but you're going to want to see this. I'm sure you've never seen a light show like this. In fact, I'm pretty sure nobody on Earth has seen a light show like this in more than a hundred years."

Gary didn't wait for Hank to respond, but instead went back out to the deck. The show was too good to miss. It took Hank two full minutes to catch up to Gary. When he got outside, Mae and Gary were both looking upward to the north. Hank looked up. The aurora borealis was spectacular, but Hank had a more urgent task. He had consumed a large glass of water just before he went to sleep in the living room. Hank walked to the far left corner of the deck and urinated off the end of it.

From his casual manner, it was clear to Gary that Hank was a committed conservationist. This wasn't the first time Hank had saved the two-and-a-half gallons of water that a toilet flush required. Mae snorted with disgust and turned away from Hank and her husband. Now she would never be able to recall the spectacular light show, without also recalling Hank's crude potty break. Hank zipped his pants and looked up again. For a long moment, all three of them looked wide-eyed at the sky and said nothing.

Gary thought he'd felt a whoosh, as the electrical pulse hit, but it was more his imagination than anything else. At 3:40 AM, the lights inside the house went off, then flashed on for a brief moment before going out for good. Gary heard a couple of car alarms going off in the distance. Two nearby electrical transformers exploded with showers of sparks and flame in a ground-level fireworks display.

Gary used his headlamp to go into the house, and light the propane lantern. He put it on a low setting to save fuel. He went to the guest room and used his headlamp to check on the girls. Even the explosions of the transformers hadn't woken them. As Gary went back to the deck to rejoin Mae and Hank, his stomach grumbled uncomfortably. Things were not going well down there.

All the man-made electrical lighting in Monroe, New York had gone out. For several minutes, the transformers burned, popped, and hissed, but they too eventually went dark and silent. The night got very quiet. Even the insects made no noise.

The nightmare was now reality. Life as they knew it had ended. Hank, Gary, and Mae took no joy in the fact that frenzied preparation had not been for naught. The lights had also gone out in New York City, the rest of the state, and most of the country. It was indeed, a worst-case scenario. Texas, and certain isolated portions of the nation's two main electrical grids had defied the President's "Lights on!" order. The isolated areas did not include any densely populated metropolitan areas. The vast majority of Americans no longer had electricity.

The CME's effects had been massive and the results were catastrophic. Transmissions from foreign ham radio operators, and a few state-side operators who had protected power supplies, reported that most of the US power grid and the United States itself, were toast. Very few Americans heard the reports. On the other side of the world, China and Russia were almost entirely unaffected.

The President's decision to leave the lights on to save the lives of a frail few, would contribute to the deaths of a far higher number of far healthier people. If the President wanted to increase the body count, he could not have made a more deadly decision while attempting to appear blameless. Shortly after the blast, the President stood alone at a podium in a fully electrified, well protected, non-disclosed location. He said the catastrophic damage was "An act of God." Less than five percent of the US population got the message.

The President also said he had done the best he could. He had compassion for those who might suffer, but America would rise to the challenge and endure. Then he left the podium and went back to the bunker's well-stocked, palatial living quarters, as many Americans began the brief journey to their death.

More than eighty percent of the approximate forty-five million electrical transformers in the United States had been destroyed. Even under the best possible post-calamity circumstances, it would take years to return the grid to its previous condition. The lengthy duration of the blackout would lead to the deaths of millions of people. The devastated area was huge, and there were too few replacement transformers available to repair the system. Functional repair trucks, with crews who were not preoccupied with trying to stay alive, would also be a problem.

The effects of the disaster were compounded by the fact that most of the electrical transformers in the US were manufactured overseas. With a service life of about thirty years, foreign manufacturers produced enough transformers to replace just four percent of the world's transformers per year. Suddenly, the US needed twenty times that amount. Foreign manufacturers said they would radically increase production. However, production was hampered by global supply-and-demand challenges. Within days of the catastrophe, geopolitical issues surfaced that led to the hoarding of the raw materials needed to produce the transformers. Production slowed even in those foreign-owned factories that had all the required resources and materials.

The world's new super powers soon gave voice to the new reality. If the US wanted transformers from foreign manufacturers, the cost would be far more than just the purchase price. Certain political, military, and territorial concessions would have to be made. As for the monetary cost of the transformers, the retail price would have to be paid in something other than the US Dollar. The US Federal Reserve debt-Note was no longer the world's reserve currency.

The traditional allies of the US were very slow to provide any sizable and useful assistance. They claimed to be busy with their preparation for a second super-CME which, according to some renowned British astronomers, might soon follow. The truth was the former allies did not want to offend the new masters of the globe, because their former protector, the US military, was no longer available.

The federal government publically estimated the US power grid would return to normal operation within six months. That government estimate proved to be wildly optimistic. But even if that feat could have been accomplished, it would have had little effect on the death toll. The majority of those who would die, wouldn't survive the next three months.

The United States had literally entered a new dark age. Two percent of the US population had the wealth and resources to flee the country and set up a residence in a country unaffected by the CME. Farmers who had the ability to produce their own food perpetually, without electricity from the grid, comprised about three percent of the US population. Preppers, who had stored up at least one year's supply of food, were an additional three percent of the US population. The other ninety two percent had only two survival options. Instantaneously become self-sufficient, a skill which usually took years to master, or take what they needed to survive from someone in the six percent who had it, but hadn't fled the country.

The problem for the "Have Nots" was the "Haves" had guns and would not give up what they had without a fight. More often than not, attempted acquisition efforts by the Have-Nots merely hastened their demise. At the start of the crisis, the government estimated sixty percent of the US population would still be alive twelve months after the dawn of the New Dark Age. That estimate also proved to be wildly optimistic.

The majority of the population learned the hard way the lesson that the preppers already knew. Big government did not have the ability to fix a serious crisis. When a crisis comes, be it a CME, a plague, or a world-wide financial collapse of fiat currencies, you can count only on you, and those around you who think like you. For many of the non-preppers, it was the last lesson of their suddenly abbreviated lives. By their inaction prior to the crisis, the unprepared had already made their "prepare or die" decision.

After ignoring reality long enough to enjoy the light show, the enormity of what had just happened settled into Gary like a heavy sickening weight. The CME was real. It had delivered enormous, widespread, catastrophic damage. All the doubts and second-guesses had been resolved. The ultimate questions had been answered, and all of the answers sucked. It was, as Blake said it would be, a worst-case scenario; a phrase Gary had heard hundreds of times. He'd even used it himself dozens of times, but never to mean what it actually meant. The CME was as bad as it could have been. It was the biggest CME in human history, and it had been aimed directly at the United States.

The CME was not technically an extinction level event, because a large percentage of human kind, on the other side of the world, was mostly unaffected. That technicality was little comfort to the tens or hundreds of millions in the western hemisphere who would die. The human race would not be extinct, but certain families, entire bloodlines, communities, cities, and states would cease to exist.

The sickening weight inside Gary had a name, and it was affecting his bodily functions. It was fear. Gary was more afraid than he had ever been before. He knew he was ill prepared, and if life was "fair" he would perish along with millions of others. Most of the CME's victims would not die quickly or painlessly. Death would be long, slow, and agonizing. Hunger would gnaw away at life bit-by-bit from the inside, while exposure to the elements – the oncoming winter with no electrical heat or light – would gnaw away on the outside.

In all likelihood, Gary would get to watch death's deliberate jaws methodically masticate his daughters' hopes, dreams, health, and sanity before their emaciated bodies exhaled for the last time. Within the next couple of weeks, the process would begin, and his darling girls would soon leave this world without mercy or a shred of dignity. Then what? Would Mae be next, or would he and Mae leave at about the same time; perhaps with the help of two merciful bullets? Was he capable of delivering such mercy to his wife or his daughters even one minute before their time? The uncontrollable fear increased Gary's pulse rate as adrenaline pounded through his body and made his legs tremble. Nauseating shame came with it.

Gary had failed in his most important role in life. How could a man call himself a father, when he couldn't feed or protect his kids? How could he even call himself a man? He had failed his daughters so completely that a .357 caliber head shot from Daddy might be their best possible future. Gary's autonomic fight-or-flight reaction arrived like a speeding freight train. He suddenly needed to urinate.

Out loud he said, "I've got to pee," as he walked toward the edge of the deck only a few feet in front of him. He knew his body's instinctual response to fear was going to empty his bladder before he could get to a toilet. Hank's earlier edge-of-the-deck maneuver was now a best-case scenario. If Mae or Hank had heard Gary or seen his stumbling movement toward the deck rail, they gave no sign or verbal response.

Hank was already turning around to go back inside the house when Gary announced his potty problem. Hank kept walking toward his easy chair. A short while ago, Gary had woken Hank from a sound sleep to see the aurora borealis. It was a nice show, but for Hank, sleep was far more precious. Contemplating the CME's deadly consequences had not scared the piss out of Hank. He was too exhausted to contemplate, and he had already taken a piss.

Unlike Gary, Hank had already seen death's deliberate jaws masticate the life out of other people. Almost all of them had been men. Some of them had been good men; his men. With its frequent appearance on the battlefield, Hank had developed a regular relationship with Death. After his recent trip to the edge of the abyss, just before Gary's arrival, Hank felt like he and Death were now on a first name basis. Well, Hank just didn't feel like talking right now.

Maybe he and Death would have another face-to-face conversation later today or perhaps tomorrow or next week, but Hank's next trip to the edge would not be his idea. He would have to be dragged or pushed. For Hank, life had suddenly gotten more interesting than the abyss. He settled into the easy chair and was soon fast asleep.

Like Gary, Mae was attempting to process the post-CME reality. Just before Gary started walking toward the deck rail, Mae had turned around and taken a few steps toward the kitchen. When she got there, she didn't know why she was walking or where she was going. She walked several more steps and was soon in the guest room. In the beam of her headlamp, she could see Jane and Josie sleeping peacefully. For the two girls, this night was just like the previous night except they were sleeping in a different location. They slept the oblivious sleep of blissfully ignorant children.

Mae collapsed to her knees by the side of the bed and cried. She tried to suppress the volume of her sobs. She was mostly unsuccessful. When Gary had first told Mae the CME was coming, Mae had gotten on the motorcycle and played along because she mostly believed a CME might really happen. She had, however, remained convinced the impact would be minimal, or like Hurricane Sandy, at least manageable. She had fully expected to return to work at the law firm the next day, or within a few days after that. She now believed the blackout would not be a short term thing. This was far, far beyond Sandy.

She now knew the CME was real and the devastation that she had steadfastly refused to think about would be overwhelming. Her perfect previous life was gone. Her career was gone, the law firm was gone, her expensive house, car, and clothes were – hell, all of New York City was gone! She would never make senior partner. Mae had the sinking feeling that even her trust fund would perish. The fund's investments were diversified among stocks, mutual funds, exchange-traded funds, and bonds. She had ignored the advice to diversify further and put some of her money into real estate, and bullion. Gold and silver bullion; not the paper gold and silver of the commodity exchange, but the physical metal that she could hold in her hand, or a safe-deposit box. Her millions of dollars were invested in paper. It was all paper or just digits, and she suspected it was all gone. She would never get that house in the Hamptons.

Mae began crying loudly and uncontrollably. She was convinced she had nothing left.

Out on the deck, Gary didn't quite get his zipper all the way open in time. He had intended to piss off the side of deck like his brother had, but it didn't happen that way. The piss arrived before he was ready. Some of it did go off the deck, but some went on it, and some of it never left his pants. Embarrassment took hold for a brief moment. Gary looked around. Hank and Mae were gone. He was alone. His bladder felt better but his stomach didn't. He swallowed hard to keep the partially-digested stew down.

The questions about whether the CME would occur, and whether it would cause a devastating blackout, were now settled. Gary forced himself to breath slowly as he attempted to suppress the penetrating fear, and think logically about what he should do next. With the information from Blake and Ralph, Gary understood the odds he and his family were now facing. Hank, Gary and Mae, were not preppers, or farmers, and they were not rich enough to flee the US. *What makes us so special? What's going to keep us from dying along with the majority of other Americans who did nothing to prepare?*

At this point, it seemed their only hope was somehow to link up with Grandpa. *Would Grandpa welcome five additional mouths to feed, four of whom were strangers? Would Grandpa have enough food even for himself, let alone five others? Was Grandpa even alive?*

Gary could feel the penetrating questions pushing logical thought from his brain as raw fear took over. He again fought the urge to vomit. He had to slow down. He couldn't afford to panic. He had to take control of himself. What was his new rule? *Do one thing at a time. Forget about Grandpa. Breathe in. Breathe out slowly. Forget about Grandpa's farm and how much food it might or might not have. What is the one thing that must be done now?*

The next "one thing" to do is to get out of the residential area. Get out of Monroe. There's no excess food in this community, and violent crime is about to skyrocket. Breathe in, and let it out slowly. If I cannot get my family out of Monroe, then nothing else will matter. That is the one thing that needs to be done now. Get out of this town, or starve to death. Breathe in, breathe out. If we get out of Monroe, we will of course head toward Grandpa's farm, but right now I just need to focus on getting on the road!

Gary took a long deep breath and let it out slowly as he tried to keep his mind on positive, productive thoughts. He was feeling a little better. *Focus on one thing. Don't panic! Focus on just one thing at a time. My family and I will survive because we have a plan. The plan is to get out of Monroe, and head toward Grandpa's. That's the one thing that must be done right now. Pack up whatever still needs to be packed, get everybody into the two vehicles, and leave now!*

Despite his efforts, Gary was again overwhelmed by reality. For a moment, he forgot to control his breathing. He got light headed as blood again flowed to his thighs and made his legs feel rubbery. His stomach gave a spasm and Gary began to believe he would not be able to hang on to the stew.

The panic seeped into him because he *knew* the lives of his daughters were in *his* hands – the soft, civilized, incapable hands of a college professor. A man who had not built or stocked a safe haven. A man who didn't know how to hunt, farm, kill, or keep from being killed. What he did or failed to do would determine whether his family lived or died. He was not up to the task. Gary started to cry. He leaned hard against the deck rail to keep from falling. His vision narrowed to the point where he could see only what was directly in front of him, and that was mostly darkness.

"How can anyone in my family make it out of this alive? How can I possibly succeed when so many others will fail? What special thing do I have that will get my family out of a residential area, and perhaps all the way to a rural safe haven like Grandpa's?

Then a ray of hope penetrated the darkness of Gary's downward spiraling thoughts. *I have Hank! Hank was a soldier! He knows how to do stuff! And he's got a four-wheel drive SUV! My family will survive because . . . because my dear brother Hank will get us out of Monroe and all the way to Grandpa's!*

Hope flared for a brief moment then disappeared like a snuffed out candle in a pitch black room. Under the crushing weight of another thought, Gary fell to his knees into a cooling puddle of his own piss.

How is my dear unemployed, bankrupt, hung over, overweight, unfit, suicidal, alcoholic brother going to get us to Grandpa's in vehicles that probably no longer run?

Crap. Maybe it was time to panic.

Gary puked.

****

Author's Note

Question #1: Is an eighteen-hour time span too short for a novel? No, not when the subject is a super CME. In the real world, you and I are probably not going to get an eighteen hour warning for a catastrophic CME, particularly if it travels to Earth in less than twenty-four hours. So the "short" time-line of the story is probably longer than any real-world scenario. What if instead of a CME, we get hit with a man-made EMP? We would almost certainly get *no* warning at all.

When I attended the US Army's Airborne (Paratrooper) School, one of the "Black Hat" instructors gave a class on how to deploy our reserve parachute if our main canopy failed to open. He said, "Pull the reserve-chute release handle, and throw the reserve chute in the direction that is opposite to the direction of your spin. If the reserve chute doesn't open, pull it back in and throw it out again. If it still doesn't open, shake it, and blow into it if you have to, but get the damn thing open!" A student asked how much time we would have to follow all those steps and get the reserve chute open. The Black Hat responded, "The rest of your life."

Everyone who ever made it to the third week of jump school can tell you the same story. The student's question was planted by the Black Hat, and the punch line is used in every class.

How much time do you have to prepare for a lengthy, life-threatening crisis? The rest of your life. With the world as it is today, some would say we have already been pushed out of the plane, and our main canopy has failed. At some point soon, high altitude nuclear EMP weapons could be used on a large scale, and they would be more devastating than a super CME. One nation could annihilate another nation's population without destroying any buildings, roads, airports or other non-electrical assets. On the ground, there would be little to no radioactive fallout. The attacker could then seize, and repopulate the affected area.

If we, as individuals and as a nation, get prepared for an EMP that doesn't happen, what's the downside? What if we don't prepare and it does happen?

Question #2: Was the ending of the story a cliff-hanger? No, and yes. The main characters in the story are completely unprepared. Most of us, who are completely unprepared for a life-threatening crisis, are going to be terrified and ineffective when the crisis hits. For the unprepared, the story you just read is complete. The crisis arrived and the unprepared (who weren't already suicidal) trembled, cried, pissed, and puked. *Of course, they are all going to die!* THE END.

But yes, among the unprepared there might be a very lucky few who somehow survive such a crisis. My biggest fans, and some critics, have interceded on behalf of the novel's unprepared characters. They don't want the story to end in Monroe. Yes, they are the ones who told me the story was a cliff hanger. I explained why it was not (see above), but they persisted. Yes, I had already drafted a plot line that could continue the story, but I wasn't anxious to turn it into a book because the first novel was so much work. Anyway, by popular demand, there will be a Book Two (if the Good Lord's willing, and an EMP doesn't hit us first). An excerpt follows.

Excerpt: *CREDIBLE WARNING*, Book Two

Even in the darkness, it was obvious to Hank that the man with the shotgun on the porch of Grandpa's house, wasn't Grandpa. Perhaps Grandpa had died, or sold his farm and moved to town. Hank's goal was to extricate himself from the situation, and leave the property without getting killed or wounded. If Mae, Gary, and the girls were also able to escape, that would be great. Saving all of them from an enemy, who already had his gun out and pointed toward Mae, seemed unlikely.

Hank blamed Mae for aggravating the gunman. For a brief moment, he thought about doing nothing to save her, but he was the only one who could possibly send a bullet in the gunman's direction. Gary and Mae were unarmed and could not save themselves. If Hank was fast and lucky, maybe he could at least keep the girls alive. The open SUV door partially concealed him from the man on the porch. Hank's pistol was on the floor of the SUV to the left of the driver's seat. He could reach it without taking a step. Hank knew he would have to shoot for an immediate kill, so the man would not live long enough to shoot back. If the man did get a shot off, it would hopefully hit Mae and not the girls.

****

45572229R00148

Made in the USA
Middletown, DE
08 July 2017